25/12/22   To Kate,

CW00543658

THE BLACK VEINS

DEAD MAGIC BOOK ONE

ASHIA MONET

Copyright © 2019 by Ashia Monet

First paperback edition July 2019

Cover typography by Spire Eaton

Book jacket and artistic elements by Mana U

ISBN 978-1-7332458-1-4 (paperback)

ISBN 978-1-7332458-0-7 (ebook)

www.ashiamonet.com

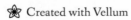 Created with Vellum

In loving memory of Mommom

*And to every LGBTQIA+ reader of color,
this one's for us.
This one's for you.*

CONTENT WARNINGS

- Discussion of deceased parents, siblings, and potential parental and familial death
- Description of mild bloodshed in violent scenes
- Mention of drugs and drug use, primarily marijuana
- Gun use
- Supernatural horror in the form of monsters, primarily found in Chapters 6, 12, and 25
- Car accident in Chapter 19
- Discussion of anxiety disorders and panic disorders primarily found in Chapters 22, 23, and 25
- Racial n-word slur, ending in -a, found in Chapter 21 (before you drag me, yes, I am Black)
- Mild anxiety attack in Chapter 25

Once upon a time, a young girl lost her family.

OVERTURE

THE MAGIC WAKES AT MIDNIGHT. IT ARRIVES IN THE FORM OF A song.

It isn't a remarkable tune. It carries only a piano's chirps, a violin's easy hum, and the subtle plucking of harp strings. It breezes through Greenland, Rome, London, Quebec, and everywhere in-between. It tangles through city streets, tumbles over bridges, and plunges to the depths of subway lines.

It is a song that knows no bounds and no country lines. It travels like the breeze: free.

Most of its notes fall on deaf ears. City dwellers pause in the middle of their midnight journeys, raising their heads as they catch a few notes. But the moment passes as quickly as it begins. The melody flies on.

Others recognize that they've heard a song. They are the ones who harbor secrets in their lives and in their veins. They also know better than to speak of the forbidden *m*-word that has brought the melody to their ears: *magic*.

These are the people who rise to search for the source of this tune. Curious souls wander both the streets and social media feeds, searching, quizzically, for an explanation.

No one finds one. Not in any corner of the world. The source is untraceable, even for the magicians who happen to be employed behind high-powered energy scanners (and take advantage of their equipment to search for suspicious power spikes). The song has come from everywhere and nowhere.

And while there lies a story in where the melody has come from, more interesting is the story of where it is going.

Blythe Fulton is asleep when the song slips through the crack in her window. Her fairy lights are turned off, but the song finds her in the darkness, tucked in her blankets. The notes dance through one ear and tumble out of the other.

Anxiety and agitation tangle in her dreams. The song is gone. But it has left something in its wake.

Consciousness returns to her. Blythe tries to open her eyes. Her lids don't move. She tries to push the blankets off, to roll onto her back. Her body stays rigidly still.

Something is very wrong.

Blythe's heart thunders in her chest. Could this be sleep paralysis? Maybe she just needs to wiggle her toes, like that blog post said, and her limbs will respond.

Above the quickening of her desperate breathing, there comes a voice. It isn't one she hears with her ears. The words hum in her ribs and speak in time with her heartbeat. The voice is not hers but it comes from inside her.

Get up, it says. *And go to the roof.*

An electric pulse wakes her nerves, shooting from her feet to her scalp. Her eyes open before she can even think about moving her lids.

Blythe opens her mouth and screams. Except her mouth doesn't open at all. Instead, her body slams upright. The blanket fly off of the bed as her legs swing to the floor.

Her body stands, but Blythe does not *want* to be standing. She fights to bring her weight to her knees, to collapse onto the carpet.

The only thing her legs do is walk toward the door.

She shuffles like a zombie beneath the dim hallway lights. The whole house is silent.

Her parents and sisters lie sleeping behind closed doors. None of them hear the window open or see her knees on the sill as she climbs into the cold night air.

Blythe has never gone to the roof, but her body moves as if this is familiar. The gutter groans as her arms grab hold of it.

Her feet slip free of the sill—and there is nothing beneath her but air. She screams, but her mouth stays shut. The sound travels nowhere.

Her body hoists her up, landing with a *thunk*. Blythe prays the sound is loud enough to wake her parents.

The voice vibrates against her ribcage. *Go to the edge.*

Blythe summons every force of her will to keep herself lying against the rough asphalt, to sink her skin into the roof. Her body raises effortlessly.

Blythe tries to move backward. Her body pays no mind.

The street is dark and silent and still. Every window in her neighbors' houses are black, curtains drawn against the night.

Blythe Fulton is about to step off a roof and no one will know.

Clouds roll in from the horizon. They are not the fluffy clouds of a summer afternoon but the thick grey masses of an impending storm. They bleed into one hulking entity that towers over the neighborhood, creeping across the stars and swallowing them whole.

For a moment, Blythe is foolish enough to think the clouds will pass her. Fear drips down her spine as realization sinks into her.

Those clouds are not natural and they are not coming toward her. They are coming *for* her.

Someone grips her arm from behind. She spins around so quickly that the world spins with her. It happens so fast, it feels as if the voice dissipates, as if everything has shifted back into its rightful place.

"What the hell are you doing up here?!" Her savior asks.

Blythe looks up—and nearly sobs when her body obeys and her head actually *moves*.

Her father stares down at her. While Jamal Fulton is a strong man, he cannot hide the fear plaguing his face as he studies his daughter.

Blythe's eyes burn with tears. "I..."

What is she even supposed to say? How is she supposed to explain?

"I don't know," she manages. "It wasn't me. It just...it wasn't me."

Jamal's expression morphs from worried to horrified. "Oh God."

He pulls her into a tight embrace, wrapping his arms around her like he could shield her from the terror she's already experienced. As if he isn't too late to protect her.

"You're safe now, sweetheart. You're safe," he whispers. "Let's get you back inside, okay?"

As Jamal guides her down the roof, the clouds retreat as well, shrinking into the horizon until they are gone.

———

Curled on the living room sofa, Blythe stares into the steaming mug of tea in her hands.

Magic is a secret.

It has existed since the first breath of life was drawn on Earth's surface. Despite its age, magic has never been a force with any particular agency. It is neither benevolent nor malevolent, because magic has no agenda at all. It bends itself completely and totally to the intent of its user.

And while magic is capable of immense good, it is also capable of immense destruction.

The Common world faces its own dangers but there are always limitations; bodies and weapons can only cause a finite amount of harm. But in the whispered world of magic, where families like the Fultons hide their abilities from Common eyes that should not see, limitations do not exist. The possibilities for pain and loss are infinite.

No matter how dangerous or twisted or vile, any action is possible —like controlling people into walking off rooftops.

There is no doubt in Blythe's mind that what happened to her was caused by magic. Probably a complex form that required massive amounts of energy, but magical all the same.

But why *her*? The victims of attacks like these are usual important politicians and powerful men with armies behind them. Not sixteen-year-old girls asleep in their bedrooms.

The subtle burn of tea spilling down her fingers makes Blythe realize that her hands are shaking. Again. Thoughts like these are only going to make her *more* anxious. She can't reason her way out of this. Not now. It's too soon.

She leans further into her mother's arms. Blythe has inherited Amber Fulton's long curls and golden-brown skin, but not her ability to remain calm in every situation.

Amber strokes Blythe's hair with the same smooth motion she's made since Blythe was a child. "You'll be alright," she says. "Everything's gonna be alright."

But the living room is ominous in its darkness, a living contradiction to her words. From the blank TV in front of them to the staircase off to the right, this home now feels stark and cold. Like a battlefield. Blythe may live here, but these walls can't protect her.

The stairs creak. Jamal is coming downstairs. He'd gone to check on Blythe's sisters. Unlike her, they are curled in their beds, exactly where they are supposed to be.

Jamal lets out a long, slow breath as he looks at the two of them. "I think we should call."

"Of course," Amber agrees, soft. "They've protected us all these years, I doubt anything will change now. They'll handle it."

Blythe's brow furrows. But Jamal heaves another sigh and leaves the room like that sentence made sense.

"Who's he calling?" Blythe asks.

"The Sages," Amber answers.

A weight settles onto Blythe. The Sages are the seven leaders of the magician government known as the Black Veins. If the Black Veins were a country, the Sages would function as its presidents. They are beacons of guidance, protection, and power. But if the Black Veins were a country, the Fultons would *not* be living in it.

"They're government leaders," Blythe says. "And you guys have their phone number?"

A sly smile comes to Amber's face. "Your parents are *connected*."

"Bullcrap. We're not even a part of their government."

Amber laughs at her own joke—or at Blythe's annoyed expression. "We *used* to be a part of their government. How do you think you became a Guardian? They wouldn't hand that title over to magicians who weren't affiliated with them."

Blythe has known she was a Guardian since she was a small child. But it has never mattered, not really. She knows that, as a baby, she was gifted immense magical abilities by the Sages themselves. But magicians don't gain control over their magic until puberty—and on that front, Blythe is a late bloomer. She can't do anything magical-related yet, so how is being a Guardian supposed to benefit her?

And maybe her parents *have* mentioned the whole "we used to be a part of the Black Veins" aspect of their lives, but that was *so* long ago, and the story was *so* boring. The Fultons aren't affiliated with any magician government now. Blythe has never bothered to remember any of that.

Suffice to say, tonight has given her a very persuasive reason to remember.

"...are the Sages still going to help?" she asks. "I mean, we left the government. Won't they like...not care?"

"You're still a Guardian, aren't you?"

"Last I checked."

"Then they'll be on the phone with Dad in the next two minutes. They *want* to protect you. Now, fix your face—" she taps the middle of Blythe's furrowed brow. "—and drink your tea."

Blythe cannot remember a time when she didn't know about magic, about the Black Veins, about the Sages or about her status as a Guardian. They are facts that are as clear to her as the sky being blue.

But knowing the sky is blue is different from understanding *why* it is blue.

"What are they even going to *do*?" Blythe asks. "The song's already come and gone, they can't fix anything."

"Baby," Amber interrupts. "We can talk about this at a better time. For now, let's just...let's just relax. Okay?"

It's ironic that a day before Amber and Jamal's anniversary, while preoccupied with thoughts of dinner and celebration, their oldest daughter almost falls to her death.

Blythe has never seen her mother afraid because Amber responds to every emergency with the same cool, collected grace. Blythe may have her dark curls, the soft curve of her lip and the shape of her eyes, but Blythe doesn't know what Amber would look like if she were afraid.

But maybe this unblinking stare in her dark eyes and this smiling nonchalance...maybe this is her fear.

Blythe can't argue. At least, not tonight. For her mother's sake.

"Okay," she says, and takes a gulp of tea.

Amber holds Blythe a little tighter. "I think this is a good excuse to keep you home for a few days," she says. "Me and Dad can handle the café."

"No," Blythe blurts. She can't spend tomorrow alone in this silent, empty house. Her mind will fill the quiet with that *melody*. "No, I'll...I'll work tomorrow. I can't stay here. I know Dad's gonna worry about me, but I don't want to stay here."

Amber nods. "I'll talk to Dad about it. He'll let you come if you want to."

Something creaks at the top of the staircase. Blythe's heart leaps into her throat.

Huddled on the top stair are two small forms, cloaked by darkness but growing more visible with every impatient twitch.

"Lily, Lena," Amber calls. "I see you up there."

Busted. Blythe's little sisters shuffle into the light: identical nine-year-olds with identically brown skin, curly ponytails, and pouting faces.

"We wanted to make sure Blythe was okay," Lily whispers.

"And what's *her* excuse?" Blythe eyes Lena, the more boisterous one who has never once cared about Blythe's wellbeing.

Lena rocks on the balls of her feet. "I just wanna know how to get on the roof." Typical.

"No one is getting on the roof," Amber says. "But I know two little ladies who are going back to bed."

The twins whine as Amber gets up and herds them back into their bedroom. Their voices fade into silence as they disappear upstairs.

A hush falls over the empty living room. Blythe clutches her mug a bit tighter. Snippets of Jamal's conversation drift from down the hall.

"A song?" he asks. "Blythe mentioned it. But none of us were awake to hear it. She—"

He pauses. Blythe can't imagine her dad speaking with the leaders of the Black Veins. Maybe he just got their assistant.

"That sounds fine," Jamal answers. "Well, we'll be...waiting for their decision. Thank you."

Jamal returns, ambling slow and rubbing the back of his neck. "Hey, Bubbles." It's her childhood nickname, coined after her favorite Powerpuff Girl. Jamal only calls her that when things are *really* rough. "This is something, isn't it?"

"Is that what the Sages said?" Blythe asks.

"Nah. I didn't even get them. I talked to one of their advisors, Sessa. She said that they're going to handle the situation and 'call back with more information'."

"Sounds like bullcrap."

"Exactly what I was thinking," Jamal huffs. "But it doesn't matter if they do or not. You'll be fine either way, y'hear? Nothing's gonna happen to you. Not while I'm here."

Blythe smiles—and it's the first time she's smiled all night. "Thanks, Dad."

He simply nods. He's never been prone to extended conversation. "I'm gonna let you sleep," he says. "You staying down here?"

Blythe can't go back to her room. Not now. "Yeah. I don't want to move."

"I'll stay with you," Jamal says. Before he leaves to fetch an army of pillows and blankets, he turns on the TV and tosses Blythe the remote.

Jamal must've been watching it last—he's the only one who watches the magician stations. There are certain channels that are only visible by enchanting your TV with a particular spell, and it took Jamal a whole weekend (and a whole power crystal) to properly spell their TV.

The Alastair French Show is on. Alastair himself is a charming man with iconic brassy hair and an iconically wide smile, but Blythe is iconically tired of seeing him. As if his nighttime talk show weren't enough, he has his own radio station too, flaunting his monopoly on the "magician news" market.

Tonight, Alastair's guest is a sharp-faced man in a slick grey suit. Blythe doesn't recognize him. But what he says makes her skin go cold.

"We think of the Trident Republic as a weak government but that is a genuinely dangerous underestimation," the man says. "If they wanted a fight, they could get one. All it would take..."

He holds up a skinny, pale finger. "Is one act. One random, hostile action could completely tip the scales. Word would travel to the Black Veins, the Sages would get a call and *boom*. The whole situation explodes. Next thing we know, there's a war on our hands. All because of one act and one phone call."

ONE

The Full Cup is more than the Fultons' coffee shop. It is Blythe's oasis.

Her parents had always dreamed of running a magic-based café but didn't get a chance until the family moved to Washington. That was when they found the perfect vacant building in the middle of a block that wasn't too busy or too slow, too noticeable or too tucked away. It was just right.

At the time, Blythe was thirteen, naive to the coffee world but not blind to the joy it brought both her family and every magician that walked through the café's doors. In short, she fell in love instantly, and has remained in love for every day since.

Outside, the Full Cup is a plain brick building with a hanging neon sign. Inside, it is a paradise: fairy lights drip from slanted rafters, folded napkins adorn vintage redwood tables, and sunlight pours from the windows.

During the school year, Blythe baristas as often as her schedule allows. Once summer vacation rolls around, the Full Cup transforms into Blythe's home away from home. She spends hours behind the counter, soaking up the scent of espresso and pouring latte after latte.

She is pouring steaming milk, watching the froth morph into art from the sway of her wrists, when her mind flashes with sharp memories. The view from the roof, her numb limbs, the hum of the melody in her ears.

Her hands tremble. She shuts her eyes, stilling herself. She is not on a roof. She isn't even in her house. She is at work, at the Full Cup, and she is okay. She is safe here.

Jamie, the only non-Fulton café employee, leans over Blythe's shoulder. "What *is* that?"

The floating shape in the espresso looks obvious. "A bunny," Blythe answers.

Jamie arches a thin eyebrow. "That's funny because it looks *exactly* like Cthulhu."

Blythe rolls her eyes. She's been doing latte art since she was thirteen-years-old—Mr. Bunny may look a little rough but he's not cosmically ugly. "He clearly has *ears*, Jamie."

"Not to the human eye."

Blythe scoffs, sliding the mug down the polished counter to the customer—where the recipient wrinkles her nose.

"Um," the customer begins. "...what is this picture on the top supposed to be?"

Blythe's eye twitches. "It's an abstract representation of the daily trauma my soul endures from living in this hell we call a modern-day society."

The customer stares at her. Blythe stares back.

"Or a bunny," Blythe relents.

The customer gives an indignant sniff. "I'll take the bunny," she says, and carries her coffee away.

Blythe makes a mental note not to be snide with the customers. Especially not today, when the café is already warm with tension. A variety of people sit at the tables, typing on laptops or gazing longingly past the windows, nibbling eclairs and sipping caramel lattes. But the Alastair French Show plays from both TVs, on either side of the space, sandwiching the space with piercing political worry.

Blythe's been tuning it out since she clocked in. There is no possible way for her to handle the world's problems along with her own.

Jamie leans against their register to watch Blythe wipe down her station. "Is bad latte art like, a weird magic thing?"

Their questions are usually a welcome distraction, a rope pulling Blythe back into the mundane. One month ago, Jamie was the new kid at school—they were also a magician who didn't know magic existed.

Jamie had exuded an aura, the same kind that resonates from every magician and every magical location, this slight *hum* of energy not dissimilar from the sparking static emitted from old electrical appliances.

Blythe had introduced herself and started a conversation about magician politics that absolutely blindsided poor Jamie.

By the end of this very awkward introduction, Blythe ended up offering Jamie a job at the Full Cup—and gave herself the job of teaching Jamie the basics of magic.

"Does it curse people?" Jamie asks. "Take away their magic? Damn them to hell?"

"Y'know," Blythe begins. "Sometimes bad latte art just means your barista is fucking out of it."

Jamie winces. "I was really hoping it'd be a curse."

Blythe smiles tightly, the best she can offer. She's not exactly in the best headspace to be a patient teacher and an awkward silence falls between them. Jamie seems to be out of questions.

"Are you doing okay?" Their gaze is unblinking on her. Jamie is, apparently, never out of questions.

"I'm fine." At this point, Blythe's answer is automatic. Talking about her emotions, showing her emotions, admitting she *has* emotions—that's not really her thing.

"Alright, but like..." Jamie plays with a tuff of their short, purple hair. "Your latte art is usually really good. That last one looked like *I* made it."

Blythe barks a laugh. Jamie absolutely beams. "Okay, I'm not sure if I should be happy that you laughed or offended that you agree," they chuckle. "But if there's anything I can like...do for you...just let me know. For realsies."

Despite their laughter, there is heaviness behind Jamie's voice. They're not kidding.

So Blythe smiles at them. And it's an actual smile this time. "How about you just do me the favor of never saying 'for realsies' again?"

Jamie shoots finger guns at her. "No promise-sies."

Blythe turns back to cleaning before Jamie notices the smile spreading on her face. Blythe usually keeps herself company these days—friendships start strong and fade into awkward glances and wondering when it's appropriate to unfollow on Instagram.

But Jamie is annoyingly likable—from their awkward, tall, lankiness to their charmingly harmless smile. And the two of them have too much in common.

While Jamie is nonbinary—agender, to be specific—they're into girls, and when Blythe told them she was bisexual, their response was a punctuated, "*Hell* yeah, broski", which was equally endearing and painfully corny.

The two of them are going to be best friends if Blythe isn't careful.

A group of girls walks in, their arms weighed down by shopping bags as they gossip adamantly. Customers like these are common at the Full Cup. When Blythe used to imagine a café for magicians, she assumed she'd be serving adventurers overflowing with stories, or magic scientists carrying mysteriously powerful artifacts. But the truth is, most modern magicians are just normal people with families to take care of, bills to pay, and a life to live in-between.

It is painfully mundane. But it is exactly what Blythe needs today.

Blythe makes their drinks with as much passion and flair as if the Sages themselves were standing before her. The orders pile in until Blythe is lost in a haze of lattes and iced coffees.

She barely notices when she passes a drink to one of their regulars. The woman cocks her head to the side, blonde hair falling in her eyes.

"Will you guys be closing?" she asks.

Her question makes Blythe freeze. All stores close eventually, but she's probably poking at something much more serious.

"What do you mean?" Blythe asks in her Customer Service Voice.

"A lot of magician-run stores are closing until things cool down. You know, because of all the stuff going on with the Black Veins and the Trident Republic."

Blythe swallows thickly. She just can't escape this situation, can she? Even at the Full Cup, it lingers over her, heavy and palpable and ruining everything.

"No," she manages to say. "Not to my knowledge."

Blythe hurries back to her station as if she could outrun the thoughts clouding her mind. But the anxiety sticks around, tensing her shoulders as she mixes drinks, delivers them to customers, and tries her damned hardest to force a smile. She doesn't stop, not once, until six o'clock arrives and the seats in the Full Cup are empty. Closing time.

Jamie claps their hands emphatically. "Time to clean!"

Blythe frowns. "You're excited to *clean*?"

"No, but you've been having a bad time, so I was trying to like..." they make awkward hand movements to replace the words they can't find. "Trying to make Blythe feel better", may be what they mean?

"Well said," Blythe teases through a smile. "Time to clean, indeed."

The sky fades into the red and purple gradient of twilight as they mop, sweep, and put away the mugs. Jamal, who has been isolated in the back for most of the day, makes an appearance to stack chairs.

The TVs fill the silence. "...the object that was found, reportedly an ancient stone, is currently in the Black Veins' hands. The Sages, however, are yet to make a statement."

Jamie's gaze snaps up from the broom in their hands. "Wait, what happened?"

Blythe clenches her teeth as she stares at the screens. "The Black Veins and the Trident Republic are...getting into some shit."

"Is it bad?" Jamie asks.

Jamal snorts. "It ain't new."

He's right. Magician governments function like kingdoms without borders. Every magician government has leaders, in the same way a kingdom has kings and queens.

And, just as the citizens of a kingdom are not required to remain in the kingdom forever, it is not mandatory for someone to stay allied to the government their parents raised them under. People can switch governments or leave their power entirely and become unaffiliated—as the Fultons did years ago.

But unlike kingdoms, magician governments care less about their physical land—which usually consists of scattered, hidden cities—and more about the size of their citizenship.

A magician government is only as powerful as the number of people who pledge allegiance to it.

Most of the western world—from the Americas to most of Europe, and including several Hispanic countries—are under the control of the first magician government ever established: the Black Veins.

Their very name is associated with castles of white marble, the Sages in fine silks and velvet robes, cities of scholars and scientists where magic is celebrated in the streets.

The Trident Republic, however, is three years younger than *Blythe*. An up-and-coming government of rebels, they are the lost, the young, and the hungry.

They only have one city, Electric City, located in no-mans-land in the middle of the desert. They have no business even speaking *ill* of the Black Veins—and yet here they are pushing their luck by trying to ignite a war.

Blythe has no proof that the Trident Republic is behind what happened to her last night. But since she is a Guardian, and under the Sages protection, she would not be surprised if they had organized it to get under the Sages' skin.

She would not be surprised if she were just a pawn in their game. And that knowledge makes her sick.

She must wear her emotions on her face because Jamal glances to her and goes to grab the remote.

Alastair French stops mid-sentence as the screen clicks off. "*The Trident Republic in Electric City—*"

"That's enough of that," Jamal says. "Let's get ready to go."

Blythe couldn't agree more. She takes out her phone to let her mom know they're on their way home, but she feels eyes on her skin. She glances up to find Jamie staring at her.

"...Hi," Blythe greets.

Jamie's obviously ready to go—they're wearing their oversized jean jacket and their backpack hangs off one shoulder—but they're just...watching her.

"Oh, sorry, I was just," Jamie hesitates, their cheeks going pink. "I was going to um...ask you something."

"Alright."

Jamie takes a deep breath. Oh boy. "Right. So. Um. I know today sucked for you, but I have an, uh, idea that could be fun—if you're down, of course. It's okay if you're not. But me and a friend are going to the shore tomorrow night. It's just us but my friend's cool. I mean, he's not a magician. Obviously. You guys are the only magicians I know. And, uh, it might rain so we probably won't go—okay, I'm rambling but I'm shutting up now, anyway, yeah, do you want to come?"

Blythe has to switch mental gears from "impending magician war" to "beach vacation".

"Oh," she says. "That sounds great. But it's my parents' anniversary and I always watch my sisters while they go out."

If Jamie is disappointed, they don't show it. "That's cool, I get it. When my moms got married a couple years ago it was like...a whole big thing."

"Well," Blythe eyes her father. "*My* parents never had to deal with courts telling them their love was illegal. They're just overly dramatic."

Jamal scoffs loudly enough for her to hear.

"Nothing wrong with celebrating love," Jamie shrugs. "But let me know if you...change your mind or something."

Blythe smiles politely because she definitely will *not* be changing her mind. But Jamie doesn't need to know that. She doesn't want to hurt their feelings.

Jamie starts out, but they've barely reached the door before Jamal's voice echoes around them. "Hey, Jamie. If it rains, how 'bout you drop on by? Blythe could use the company."

Blythe shoots her father a look before she can stop herself. And then she realizes Jamie has seen her.

Their face pales. "I wouldn't want to bother anybody. I-It's cool."

Blythe's face burns with embarrassment. She never meant to be mean to Jamie. "It's fine," she relents. "You can come."

Jamie hesitates. As if this is some sort of trap. "...Really?"

Blythe nods. "Really."

"Oh. *Oh.* Awesome. Cool," the smile they break into is bright enough to light up a whole street. "Yeah, okay, see you tomorrow maybe!"

The bells chime above the door as they leave.

Blythe locks eyes with her father. "*Why?*"

Her parents, of all people, should understand why she doesn't bother with people. They're the ones who moved the family from state to state, uprooting them so many times, Blythe spent every school year in a different region of the United States.

But Jamal's face is impassive. "You like Jamie," he says.

Liking Jamie isn't the point. Blythe pouts, keeping her gaze on him, letting the silence linger.

He sighs at her defiance, shutting his eyes as if she is being irrational. "You need to make some friends, Bubbles," he says. "I know that's hard for you, but if something goes wrong while your mother and I are gone, Jamie can help." He pauses. "You need *people*. Not just us, or your sisters. Your mother and I won't always be here."

Blythe doesn't want to talk about this. "I'm going to turn up the cloaker," she says, and hurries to the back before he can stop her.

It's not that Blythe *can't* make friends. She could, easily. There's just no point. It took her until seventh grade to realize how quickly friends became strangers once she moved away.

The Fultons have stayed in Washington since Blythe was thirteen, but there is no guarantee they will be here next year. Why would Blythe risk getting attached to someone who won't even remember her name next summer?

Friendships are fleeting. Her family is constant. Magician war be damned, Jamal said it himself—he'd protect her if anything happened again. So why is he asking *Jamie* to be around in case something goes wrong?

Blythe stomps down the stairs into the dim basement. The cloaker leans against the farthest brick wall, an egg-shaped generator that operates without cords or wires. Like all forms of magic, the only thing it requires is a power source. Without a power source, no magic can be done under any circumstances—and stronger magic requires a larger power source.

Thankfully, the cloaked requires a very low-energy, cheap power source that comes in the form of a crystal—power sources are often forms of crystals or rocks—that the Fultons replace yearly, after a short trek to a magician-run shop on the east end of town.

In exchange, the cloaker powers a constant illusion; while magicians see the café for what it is, Commons pass by an abandoned building. Blythe turns up the dial, strengthening the illusion, which is best for when the café is unattended.

She's barely made it back up the stairs before her phone vibrates. *We need to talk when you get home,* the text from her mother reads.

This day just keeps getting better.

The drive back home is silent. Blythe doesn't initiate conversation and Jamal only sighs, occasionally rubbing the back of his neck.

The Fultons' current house is one of the nicer places they've lived in. Lena is in the backyard, thundering soccer balls into her net. Blythe greets her, but she only gives an offhanded "hey" before refocusing on her aim. Sister of the year right there.

The TV plays for an empty audience in the living room, but Blythe can hear someone typing in the family office. She peeks in to find her mother at the desk, hair pulled into a bun behind a headscarf, working on her recipe blog.

Lily is sprawled on the rug, surrounded by her "arts and crafts", which are little more than colorful pieces of ripped paper. Today, Lily's project is a circle of rainbow confetti.

"Hey," Blythe greets. "Colorful."

"Thanks," Lily smiles down at her handiwork. "I was going for a diverse color palette."

"I wanna ask how you learned to talk like that but I'm afraid of the answer," Blythe replies.

Amber is already closing tabs on her laptop. "Hey baby, we can go talk in your room."

That means she doesn't want the twins overhearing—which isn't a good sign. But Blythe doesn't protest.

By the time she's gotten upstairs and changed into her sweats and a Sailor Moon t-shirt, her mother is already opening the door.

Amber leans against it as it shuts. Her gaze is heavy with an emotion Blythe can't place.

"The Sages called us back," Amber says.

Of course they did. Blythe tucks her feet further beneath her as if she could sink into her bed. "What did they say?"

Amber takes a long, slow breath. "Well. I spoke with their main advisor, Sessa. She basically said that the Sages haven't identified *who* tried to hurt you, but they are very...concerned. Because the same thing happened to two other Guardians."

Blythe's heart drops to her feet. She wasn't the only one. The Trident Republic are using *three* Guardians as pawns, manipulating their minds and their lives, just to get a response from the Sages.

Somewhere out in the world, two other people are as frazzled and terrified as Blythe. It makes her stomach ache.

"This situation is...a lot bigger than us," Amber continues. "We can't risk them controlling you again. Sessa told me about the precautions the Sages want to take, and I agree. It would only last for a few weeks—or a month or two, at the most. Just until they have the situation under control—"

"What will?" Blythe asks.

Amber doesn't answer. She makes her way to Blythe's side and sits, slowly, on the bed. "Baby..." she begins. "You're a good girl. And we're proud of you. You're mature, you're smart, you're responsible—"

Amber doesn't need to finish. There is only one situation where Amber would dance around the truth like this. There is only one outcome that would shatter Blythe.

"I'm leaving, aren't I?" Blythe asks.

Amber's eyes have gone glassy. The look she wore when she walked in is the same look she wears now: worry. "They're sending someone to pick you up on Saturday," she whispers.

And just like that, the day comes to a final, messy, tragic crescendo. Blythe is used to moving with her family—she's done that for years. But this?

"Me," Blythe repeats, her voice a whisper. "Alone."

"I know, I know," Amber takes Blythe's hands into her own, intertwining their fingers. "But you won't be by yourself. They're taking all of the Guardians to Frost Glade. The Sages didn't want to take any chances."

Amber and Blythe's fingers cross like they fit perfectly together. Blythe does not want to let her go.

"I don't want to move to some foreign city," Blythe snaps. "I live *here*. I just—I don't want to go into hiding."

"What do you think will happen if you don't?" Amber asks.

The truth clogs in Blythe's throat. She could be killed if she stays here.

"We can't protect you like the Sages can. And we're strong enough to admit that," Amber says. "When the Sages offered to make you a Guardian, we had to agree that the Sages would house you if we weren't able to protect you. Because we knew we were giving you a destiny that was so much *bigger* than us. And everything that's happening now? It is more than we can handle. So, we're letting the Sages take over for a bit."

Blythe bites her lip. Hard. It's the only thing that can hold back the tears.

Amber grips her hands tighter. "You'll just be going to Frost Glade. And it's a great city. We used to live there, y'know."

Blythe looks up at her. She is desperate for some positivity, some light. "You never told me that."

"That was back when we were a part of the Black Veins. You were about three, I think." Amber breaks into a smile, so similar to Blythe's own. "On holidays, we would take you out to see the lights. They had fireworks conjured straight from magicians' hands, bursting in the night sky. You loved them then. You might love them again."

Her voice is warm, filled happiness and love. Like these are cherished memories. "Why'd you leave?" Blythe asks. "Not just Frost Glade, but like...the Black Veins too."

Amber deflates a little, looking away. "It...became overwhelming. The world of magic is constantly in strife. There's always danger looming on the horizon; as soon as you solve one problem, another three appear. And being right there, in the capital city, allied to the largest, oldest magician government...it was too much. I mean, the year we left, some rich family got banished for a capital crime. And it barely made a one-minute segment on the news."

She pauses. "But, at the same time, there's nothing like the Black Veins. And there's nothing like Frost Glade. I mean, there are no roads because cars *fly* between buildings. The Sages' castle sits right at the city center. The whole south side is a beach, and when you're on the shore at night, you can hear the sounds of the city and feel the waves against your feet. It's like the whole city is breathing with you. It's unlike..."

Her voice trails off because Blythe's gaze has dropped. She is fighting back tears.

Frost Glade sounds amazing, it really does. She would rather see it with her family, where her mother can fall in love with that place again, than be trapped on its shores because the Trident Republic wants to kill her.

Amber pulls Blythe into her arms and Blythe squeezes her eyes to hold back the tears. "I know, I know," Amber whispers. "It's a lot. But you're strong, and you're *ours*. You can do this. You could do it in your sleep. You'll get there, you'll make good memories, and you'll be home before you know it. Then you'll show us all the photos you've taken and tell us about everything you did."

But that wasn't promised. Not really. No one knows how long war could last. Blythe could be stranded in that city for years.

And there is nothing, absolutely nothing, she can do to stop this.

Blythe doesn't run from her problems—she runs away from the things she cannot change. She runs from the truth that everything and everyone she loves is going to be snatched away.

"MOMMY!" Lily's voice echoes from the hallway. "I think I broke the hot glue gun!"

Blythe pulls away from her mother as Amber sighs, knitting her brow. "Lil, why are you using a hot glue gun?!" Amber calls.

She's already getting to her feet, pointing to Blythe as she heads out the door. "We'll talk more at dinner. I tried a new cake recipe for dessert, it's actually really popular in Frost—"

"I think I'm just gonna sleep," Blythe interrupts.

Amber's brows pinch. She gets worried when Blythe keeps things to herself like this. But Blythe can't help it.

"Okay baby," Amber says. "Just don't worry too much, alright? You'll be okay." She kisses Blythe on the forehead before she leaves, closing the door behind her.

Blythe stares at the smooth white plane of her ceiling. In a few days, she will be sleeping in a new bedroom, in a new city, surrounded by strangers.

Her eyes sting. Blythe bites her lip. Hard. She hates crying.

Her parents' voices drift in from the hall. "...said she's just going to sleep," Amber is saying. "She'll be alright, she just needs to process everything. You know how she is."

———

Blythe wakes in the middle of the night. On her desk is a plate of cake covered in saran wrap.

The gesture has her parents written all over it.

TWO

AMBER AND JAMAL'S ANNIVERSARY DINNER SHOULD BE A CAUSE for celebration, but Jamal refuses to leave the girls home alone. Blythe refuses to let him cancel the reservation.

"In two days, I'll be *gone*," Blythe explains. "And until then, I just...I just want everything to be normal. I don't even know when I'll see you guys again. I don't want to remember us being...sad and scared."

Usually, Blythe's parents take her opinions with a grain of salt. But now, with the knowledge that these may very well *be* her last days with them for a long, long time, Jamal can't refuse.

"But if you hear even the *slightest* noise," he says. "Call me."

Like most magicians, Amber and Jamal developed their magic during puberty, flaunted it as teenagers, and considered it mundane as they settled into comfortable adulthood. Magicians are more than capable of using magical items, but most stick to the specific, singular ability they inherit in their youth.

But Jamal has little use for his invisibility these days, and while Amber loves to tell stories of materializing force fields while raising clumsy toddlers, she does not use her magic often either.

Now, the Fultons are a family of curly-haired, brown-skinned creative souls (excluding Lena, who prefers spending her summer afternoons on a soccer field) with magic being only a small part of their identities. But that doesn't mean Amber and Jamal don't remember how to use their magic.

Blythe does not doubt that they would break out their magic out to protect her. Her family would do anything for her—and she'd do anything for them.

In the living room, once her parents have gone for the night, Blythe scrolls through her laptop. On the other end of the red leather couch, the twins are playing a very intense round of Mario Kart.

Their round eyes stare unblinking at the screen, tiny fingers death-gripping their controllers. Blythe tunes them out to focus on her research. See, she tried ignoring the Black Veins and the Trident Republic, hoping the situation would simply dissipate, but it did the exact opposite. It came right to her door, slammed it open, and is now dragging her out by her hair.

If a potential war is forcing her to leave her home, Blythe wants to know every single detail that *exists* about this situation. No one will be able to lie to her. The moment the coast is clear, no one will be able to tell her she can't go home, that she can't be with her family again. She will control her own destiny.

It feels like the only form of power she has left.

Luckily, the political tension has made headlines across multiple magician news outlets, making her search extremely easy. From what Blythe gathers, the conflict began two weeks ago.

The Trident Republic was laying foundation for a new high-rise hotel in their capital, Electric City. One of their machines hit something small, hard, and radiating with magical energy.

They sent the object to their head thaumologist—a scientist who specializes in studying magic and magical artifacts—and they realized that the stone was a power source. But not just any power source, like the tiny one used in the Full Cup's cloaker. No, this was a crystal

26

with enough energy to power *any* magical spell, regardless of how large...or how destructive.

In less than a day, the Black Veins army swept into Electric City and took it.

The Sages explained that the stone held "potentially dangerous amounts of magical energy" and was "unsafe to leave in public hands".

The Trident Republic took high offense. As far as they are concerned, the stone belonged to them, regardless of how dangerous it may be. But the Sages neither apologized nor returned the stone.

Now, the Trident Republic is *pissed*. And Blythe's is entire life is being uprooted because they're throwing a temper tantrum.

Blythe chews her nails, watching her sisters' karts fly through colorful race tracks. Couldn't the Sages just return the damn stone? But if it is as powerful as they say, maybe it's safer if they didn't. The Trident Republic is too new, too unpredictable. They wouldn't know how to properly protect the stone from getting into the wrong hands.

Or, perhaps, the Trident Republic may very well *be* those wrong hands.

"You cheated!" Lily screams. "You cheated *again*, that's the only reason why you won—"

"No I didn't, no I didn't!" Lena yells.

Blythe rolls her eyes as their argument pounds against her eardrums. Lena probably *did* cheat, but Blythe doesn't have the energy for this.

"Alright!" she yells. "It's my turn. Pass me a controller and prepare to lose."

Their race ends with Blythe in first, Lily in fifth, and Lena dead last.

Lena, pointedly, does not look at Blythe. "You can't play anymore," she pouts.

Blythe raises her chin and sniffs the air. "Hey. You smell that? Smells like...smells like a sore loser."

Lena's face skews. "I'm not a sore loser you're a sore winner! We let you play with us, you're not supposed to win!"

Lily kicks her feet. "Mom said you're going to live somewhere else," she blurts.

The three of them fall silent. The twins stare unblinking at Blythe, but she's not quite sure how to talk to them about this. They're too young to truly understand how much danger she's in. They probably think she's just abandoning them.

"Just for a little bit," Blythe says. "But I'll be back soon. I promise. I don't even *want* to leave."

"Are you gonna come back on the weekends?" Lena asks.

Blythe hesitates. "No. I don't think so."

Lily twists her mouth to the side. "Who's gonna bring us extra slices of cake?"

"I'll be back as soon as I can, I *swear*," A smile creeps onto Blythe's face. "But in the meantime...if you wait until Mom and Dad go to sleep, you can sneak downstairs by walking near the railing so the floorboards don't creak. Then just use paper plates and forks so you can throw away the evidence. *Boom*."

The twins' jaws drop simultaneously. Blythe winks. Her parents are definitely going to kill her for sharing this information, but it's worth it.

"So...can we have cake now?" Lena asks.

The answer should be no; the twins are *demons* when they're having a sugar rush. But this could be the last time Blythe hangs out with her sisters for a long, long while.

So she jumps to her feet. "Y'know what? Let's do it."

The twins cheer as Blythe races into the kitchen. Streetlights from the backyard bleed through the curtains and the whole room smells of vanilla extract and icing.

Blythe peeks out the window. Night has fallen, heavy and dark, drenching the world in shadow. Lena's soccer goal rests against the fence. And behind the fence is a man.

He faces their house, the brim of a hat concealing his face. When Blythe sees him, he lowers his head and walks away.

Fear clogs Blythe's throat. Who was that? *Who was that?*

She rushes to the back door. It opens up to the backyard but it's locked. Of course it is, they're a Black family and they always keep their doors locked. Blythe just needed to make sure.

Blythe returns to the window. There is no trace of a man. It feels like seeing a spider in your bedroom; the real terror hits when you lose sight of it.

The doorbell rings.

"I'll get it!" The sound of Lena's voice makes Blythe's blood run cold.

"Lena, sit *down!*" she yells.

Blythe rushes into the living room. The twins sit, frozen and confused on the couch. Blythe never yells at them like that. Ever.

The cheery video game music plays through the living room as Blythe stares down the front door. If only she could see past its metal frame, out onto the porch.

The doorbell rings again.

Blythe walks slowly, carefully. She has no weapons and—what chills her most—no specific magic ability of her own. Not yet. But she will fight to the death before she lets this man get anywhere near her little sisters.

The knob is ice cold against her palm as she twists it. The hinges squeal as the door eases open.

There, on the porch, is Jamie Monvarian. "I spent a really long time trying to think of a cool one-liner for when you opened the door, but nothing good came," they say.

Shock and relief hit Blythe like a crashing wave. "Jamie! What the *fuck?!* What are you doing?"

Jamie's brows shoot up. They're dressed in ripped skinny jeans and a sleeveless Nirvana tee as if they've just come to hang out—oh.

"Well, you said I could come by if it rained and uh," they point upwards. "It's rainin'."

"I did, I'm sorry. I just...forgot," Blythe sighs, running a hand through her curls. In the messy tangle of everything she's had to deal with, Jamie's visit got a little lost. "I know I said it was cool, but now's not a good—"

"Whoa!" Lena yells. "Blythe has *friends*?"

Blythe throws the door open, smiling at Jamie. "This just in! You can now stay for as long as it takes to convince my sisters—and possibly my entire family—that I *am* capable of making friends when I feel like it!"

Jamie chuckles as they step in, a raspy sound that is actually quite pleasant. "Cool, I love social experiments."

Blythe looks behind them, out into the street. The figure she saw in the backyard was definitely *not* Jamie. But there is no one around, not from what she can see. Still, she locks the door when she closes it.

The twins stare Jamie down, fascinated by this tall, purple haired person Blythe has brought before them.

"You work at the café," Lena observes.

"I do," Jamie agrees.

"Does your hair grow out of your head like that?" Lily asks.

"No," Jamie answers. "It grows out of a little bottle I buy from Hot Topic for ten bucks."

"Hey!" Lena suddenly screams, breaking out of the trance Jamie put her in. "Where's our cake?"

Oops. "Oh shit, sorry," Blythe apologizes. "Jamie, do you want cake? My mom made it, it's like...buttercream and tapioca or something? It's good."

"I'd never turn down free cake, count me in."

There's no way Blythe will be able to keep an eye out for the man while entertaining Jamie *and* the twins. She might be able to make it work if she lets the twins play Mario Kart while she takes Jamie upstairs. Her bedroom has a view of the backyard *and* enough stuff to keep Jamie occupied.

Everything will be fine.

Blythe gets the plates from the cabinet as Jamie leans over the sink to wash their hands—except water explodes out of the faucet the moment they turn it on.

Jamie shouts, stumbling back. The water returns to a meager drip.

"That could *not* have gone worse," Jamie grumbles. "Like, that was the worst-case scenario."

Blythe bites back a smile. Water has reacted oddly to Jamie ever since Blythe met them. Magic can be an elusive creature that requires practice and studying to fully tame, and Jamie's magic is still out of their control.

"Last week you flooded the whole sink at the café," Blythe says, handing them a towel. "So, technically, you're getting better."

"That's all I aim for. Not good—just better," Jamie teases.

As they dry themselves, Blythe checks out the window. The backyard is empty.

"Is something wrong?" Jamie asks.

"Hmm?" Blythe feigns an innocent rhythm in her voice. Could she tell Jamie the truth? Sure. But why scare them unnecessarily? "No, no way. I'm just gonna give the twins their cake and we can eat upstairs."

Blythe tells the twins not to answer the door if someone rings, but they're too invested in their cake to care about doorbells anymore.

So Blythe leads Jamie upstairs, opens the door to her bedroom, and watches Jamie's jaw drop. "Whoa," they gasp.

"Good whoa or bad whoa?" Blythe asks.

"*Aesthetic* whoa."

Blythe's chest warms with pride. She makes a lot of art, but her bedroom is one of her best projects yet. From its baby blue walls adorned with fairy lights and floating bookshelves, to her desk lined with Pop Funkos and anime figurines. It is her corner of the world, a mini-museum of Blythe Fulton—especially her camera collection stacked beside her closet.

But Blythe's magnum opus is where Jamie travels first: her wall of photos, strung up on silver wire, surrounded by twinkling lights. Jamie's slim fingers graze the pictures as they drink it all in.

"You're a photographer?" they whisper the word like it is sacred.

Blythe bounces over to their side. "Yep! Amateur but...yeah."

"Amateur?" Jamie scoffs. "Don't knock yourself."

Blythe stares at the photos anew, as if to see them through Jamie's eyes. Some are selfies: sixth-grade-Blythe with permed straight hair and pink braces; her at Comic-Con as Sailor Moon; her holding a bi-flag with her parents during last year's Pride parade.

Others are photos of old friends she's fallen out of contact with, neighbors who used to babysit her, teachers who inspired her.

They're more than photos. They are memories of places and people she has left behind.

Blythe's never shown this wall to anyone who didn't live with her. But when she catches the awe in Jamie's expression, she has a feeling she's picked a good person to open up to.

These photos mean the world to her. She never imagined anyone else could see value in them.

"They're beautiful," Jamie says.

"...thanks," she says, because she's too dumbfounded to think of anything more.

Jamie doesn't even realize. They point to a Polaroid of a constellation. "What's up with these guys?" they ask. "You have a bunch of pictures of stars, but most of them are of these lil' round boys."

Blythe has been drawn to the moon and the stars ever since she was young, but there that is one part of the night sky that calls to her the loudest.

"That's Calyvorra's Crown," she says. "It's my favorite constellation. And it comes with a really good story."

Jamie smiles down at her. "I love a good story."

"Well, Calyvorra was the last king of the Black Veins. She's the one who gave her political, reigning power over to the Sages and ended the rule of the monarchy. People say that on the night she died, her body was carried into the sky on tendrils of moonlight, where she became that constellation. And she's been watching over magicians ever since.

"It's a ring of seven stars, impossible to spot if even *one* of those stars is missing. But if they're aligned and shining in perfect harmony, you can glimpse it. A perfect crown above the horizon. A halo in the sky."

Jamie's mouth has formed a small *o* of shock. "Holy shit," they breathe.

Blythe nods. She's told that story to the twins many, many times, and the two of them always have a similar reaction. But it never gets old. "Yeah," Blythe says. "It's pretty cool."

Thinking of the twins reminds her of the man—the one who could very well still be outside the house.

She makes her way to the window as casually as she can, pushing aside the curtains. The backyard is still empty.

Jamie wanders her room, drinking in everything they see. "Actually, while we're talking about magic, I was thinking about something earlier," they say. "What's *your* magic? I've never seen you use it."

Blythe hesitates. "Yeah, uh...I...I don't really have my magic yet."

A normal magician would turn up their nose at such a thing, but Jamie just frowns a bit. "Don't people normally come into their magic around puberty?"

Blythe inhales slow. "I'm a late bloomer."

"Eh, I'm sure it'll happen eventually. Is that why you're so secretive?"

Blythe barks a laugh. "You think I'm secretive because I can't use magic yet?"

Jamie's face flushes. "I mean, ok, when you say it, it sounds stupid. I just meant like, y'know, you...don't talk about personal stuff. Which is fine, I totally get that. But I just..." They sigh. "Okay, I'm rambling again. I guess what I'm just trying to ask is...if you're doing okay."

Oh. The words are surprisingly sweet. Blythe feels guilty for thinking something like that—Jamie has never been anything but kind to her. But Blythe can't say she's been entirely kind back.

"I'm sorry," she apologizes. "I'm...really glad you care enough to make sure that I'm okay. I've just been...dealing with a lot lately."

An explanation would probably be the best way to fix this. Plus, Jamie deserves it after putting up with Blythe's nonsense for so long.

"Remember that day I was super distracted?" she asks.

When Jamie nods, Blythe describes the situation as best she can: the roof, the Trident Republic, everything. Throughout all of it, Jamie's expression grows increasingly concerned. Their eyes worry over Blythe's face.

"What the hell?" they whisper. "Are you okay?"

Nobody has asked Blythe that yet. She realizes, slowly, that she does not have an answer. "I don't know," she admits.

Jamie takes a tentative step forward but they stop. As if they want to offer Blythe sympathy, but they don't quite know how to offer a shoulder to someone who has pushed them away so many times.

Blythe has done this to herself, she supposes.

"So now you're...moving to some secret magic city," they say instead.

"Basically."

"How long will you be gone?"

"I don't know," she admits. "The Sages said until everything is 'safe'. But that's not a time frame. All I know is that me and all the other Guardians are going to be living in Frost Glade for the foreseeable future."

Blythe has had multiple conversations like this with people she considered friends. This is the part where people realize Blythe won't be a part of their life. This is the part where people begin to lose interest in her.

Because Blythe is good at making friends—she's confident,

outgoing, and pretty cute—but keeping them is a game she never learned how to play.

"Oh," Jamie says. "Well, I don't know if you want to hear this, and I know we just met a month ago but..." their voice trails off. "...You've done a lot for me."

Words escape her. But Jamie isn't finished. "Before my moms adopted me, my family sucked. They pulled a *lot* of shit. Like, I'm almost positive they knew about magic and just refused to tell me.

"But Kit and Laura, they're *great*. They listen, they respect my pronouns, they take me seriously...the only problem is that they're Common. So, everything I learn about being a magician, everything I learn about myself? I can't share that with them."

Their crystal blue eyes don't stray from Blythe. "You and your family are the first people I can really talk to. You guys get along so well and love each other so much it's almost cliché. But I...I feel so lucky to be included in that love and that acceptance.

"When I came into class, you could've ignored me. You didn't have to make friends with me, or give me a job, or introduce me to your family. So, I guess, I'm just saying all that to say...I wish you didn't have to leave, but I understand why you do. And I'll miss you."

Blythe takes them in, this pleasant stranger she has adopted into her life. Jamie is so sweet. So, so, sweet. Sweeter than Blythe deserves, even.

Maybe, if Blythe had more time, and maybe, if Blythe were better at keeping people around, the two of them could really have something.

But Blythe has no time. And she doesn't know how to open up to people either.

So all she says is, "I'll miss you, too."

Jamie nods, their gaze falling on anything that isn't Blythe's face. Blythe could say more. She *should* say more. Not just to be grateful, but also to tell Jamie that there is another reason why she gave herself the job of introducing them to magic.

That reason is called "the Erasers". The Erasers are not violent people and they do not make threats. They do not harass or even speak.

They watch.

Magicians would only see them through the corners of their eyes. The Erasers are silent sentries, invisible to Commons. But they are there, and they see you even when you do not see them. They are waiting for you to break their rules.

If you speak about magic to a Common, if you show them an enchanted item, if you give them even the *slightest* idea of magic, the Erasers will come. And they will take you.

Erasers don't drag you into a truck and drive away. One minute you're there, the next, you are gone. No one remembers you, anything you've made, or anything you've done.

You've been erased.

They are the reason no Common would ever believe magic exists. They are the boogeymen of magician culture. And if Blythe hadn't seen them herself, she would never believe they were real.

The Erasers are also the reason her family has moved so often. Blythe has memories of playing in parks, or playgrounds, and glimpsing the Erasers from afar. Her parents would snatch her up from the slides or the swings, racing back home to pack their bags, and driving as far as they could.

They traveled from home to home, just to keep the Erasers off their trail. It was only once they reached Washington that the Erasers disappeared.

No more men in suits watching from afar. No more nights spent hurriedly packing suitcases.

Blythe never found out *why* the Erasers followed her family. But it is a disheartening story that Jamie does not need to hear.

Blythe peeks behind the curtain again out of habit. At the end of their driveway, near the opening to the street, stands a figure in a brimmed hat.

The man has returned.

Blythe's heart thunders in her ears. He looks like he's holding something to his ear.

"What's up?" Jamie asks.

Blythe's mouth feels dry. After everything Jamie just confessed to her, she owes them this.

"There's a man outside," she says. "It's my second time seeing him tonight. He was in the backyard earlier."

Jamie is at her side in an instant. They push aside the curtains and lean into the glass.

"I don't know who he is," Blythe stammers. "Or if I should even do anything."

Jamie studies him. It's like a plan is forming in their mind. "Let's go scare 'im," they say.

Blythe's jaw drops. "What?! Jamie—" But it's too late. Jamie is already running out of her room, footsteps clunking down the stairs.

"Jamie!" Blythe yells, darting after them. "This is the whitest idea you've ever *had*!"

She slides into the kitchen as Jamie throws open the back door, their form disappearing into the darkness of the backyard.

Blythe can barely see them hop onto the fence in one fluid motion, leaning forward to see past the edge of the Fultons' property.

The lawn gives under Blythe's sneakers as she joins them, bracing her feet against the lowest wooden panel to hoisting herself up on the fence.

The man still lingers in the distance. His face is obscured, but his gaze feels like slime on Blythe's skin. He is watching her.

Something bronze glints on his wrist. The air shifts and hums with an energy Blythe recognizes—it's the energy of magic.

The air morphs into a frenzied wind that is anything but natural. It blows against the man, his form dissipating into tiny pieces, carried away, out of sight by the air itself, until there is no man at all, only a fading summer breeze. And then there is nothing at all.

"Ha!" Jamie yells. "We got him!"

"We literally just looked at him," Blythe grumbles.

Jamie is already plopping back down onto the ground. "He's still gone."

But Blythe doesn't understand why he was here in the first place. Or what he wanted. But he could return, just like the Trident Republic could return to her mind, along with that melody. Her stomach curls at the thought.

Two forms are huddled in the doorway, outlined by the yellow kitchen lights.

"Who the hell was that?" Lena shouts.

Blythe's jaw drops. "What the fuck?! Watch your language!"

She has to coax the twins back inside with lies, crafting a story about Jamie thinking they saw someone outside.

When her parents return, Blythe will tell them the truth. But besides locking their doors and making sure the house is secure, there is not much the Fultons can do.

Now, Blythe is almost glad she's leaving. The Trident Republic can put her life in danger without harming her family too. And maybe that's all that matters.

Jamie and Blythe settle in the kitchen while the twins wreck havoc in the living room, the disturbance making them shout louder and run faster.

Jamie pulls up a YouTube video about elusive teen heartthrob Joshua Hoffman, a celebrity who rarely appears in any pictures or real-life events.

Blythe *loves* conspiracies theories. Especially ones about this kid. "He's like a celebrity cryptid," she says.

Jamie snorts. "I never thought I'd hear the words 'celebrity cryptid' in my lifetime but fate had other plans, I guess."

Blythe can't help but chuckle. Something about the sensation of laughter in her chest makes her relax into her seat.

Something is waiting for her out there, past the safe bubble of her family, the Full Cup, her home. She doesn't know what, but she can feel it. She can't escape the reality of it, just as she can't escape the Trident Republic or Frost Glade.

The Blythe Fulton who returns to this house will not be the Blythe Fulton who left it.

But for now, her parents are having a romantic evening, her sisters are screaming in the living room, and she is watching conspiracy theories beside someone she could almost consider a friend.

For now, Blythe is okay.

THREE

THE FULL CUP IS UNDERSTANDABLY EMPTY. NO ONE GOES OUT for coffee when rain is pouring from the sky.

It is a dull, stormy Friday, and the winds grow stronger with each passing hour. Blythe's parents are taking inventory in the back, like they do every Friday.

Lily and Lena are finally on summer vacation, which means it's their job to clean the tables and chairs. Instead, they're shoulder-to-shoulder at a table, smiling and poking at Lena's tablet.

The TV is an easy hum in the stillness. *"No new developments from Electric City or the Trident Republic. The Sages have remained silent..."*

Jamie is getting more bored with every minute. They insist they can juggle, and when Blythe only cocks a suspicious eyebrow, they prove it by keeping five apples in the air for about three seconds before they all bounce to the floor. The twins applaud anyway.

"You know you have to pay for those now, right?" Blythe asks.

Jamie sighs. "Yeah, I didn't think this through."

"It's okay," Blythe laughs. "We can just conveniently forget to take stock."

The wind howls as they clean up the apples. Blythe pays it no mind until something *groans*, a sickening, echoing sound, just outside the window.

She looks up just as a force crashes to the ground, hard enough to shake through Blythe's sneakers.

Lily jumps with a scream, spooking Lena, whose head whips to the window behind her. Jamal and Amber's footsteps approach from the back room.

Blythe rushes over to the window, peering out of the glass. The pouring rain blankets the street in grey. The wind is so fierce, it pushes the trees almost parallel to the ground, ripping their branches off.

It's no wonder that the Full Cup's neon sign has fallen into the road and blinked into death.

"Holy shit!" Blythe yells. That sign was on a sturdy metal pole; it would take a storm from hell to bring it down.

Lena peeks under Blythe's arm. "Dad," she gasps. "The sign fell down!"

Jamal curses under his breath as he joins them, leaning into the glass. "How the hell are we gonna get that fixed...?"

"Insurance?" Blythe asks.

The lights flicker, blanketing the café in black before resurrecting again. The TVs stutter with static, their screens blinking in and out.

"The Trident Republic in Electric City—Electric City—Trident Republic—Electric City—"

Jamie surveys the room. Their face has gone pale white. "Oh, that's...bad."

Before Blythe can agree, a new silence falls. Blythe is so used to the noise that it takes her a moment to realize that the generator has died.

The electricity shuts off. With only the faint light echoing from the windows, the Full Cup is a different place, distorted by silence and the sickening light of the storm.

"Mommy!" Lily wails. The dark has always spooked her.

"You're such a baby," Lena huffs.

"You're alright, Lily," Amber says. Her shoes click against the floorboards as she joins them at the window. "God, it must be terrible out there. We should call it a night. Nobody's coming out in this weather, anyway."

"Oughta wait until the storm passes," Jamal mutters. "Jamie, grab a few candles from storage. I'll see what I can do with that generator."

"I'll help," Amber says. "Blythe, stay with the girls."

The three of them head into the back while the twins lean against Blythe. Lily is trembling, so Blythe turns on her phone's flashlight. White light bounces across the tabletops.

"See?" Blythe says. "Light."

"That's because you have a Zadis," Lily mutters. "They have superior technology on all levels. Our phones are stupid."

Blythe can't disagree. Zadis is *the* technology corporation—from phones, to tablets, to laptops, if you want to buy modern technology, you'd better buy Zadis.

"Dad said you can get Zadis phones when you're twelve," she reminds them.

"But our phones suck *now*," Lena says. "We can only download four games." Her ponytail has somehow slipped to the side of her head.

"I didn't even have a phone when I was nine," Blythe says, taking off Lena's hair tie. "Actually, no, I had like, a flip phone."

Lily's eyes light up. "It did flips?"

"Oh my Christ," Blythe sighs. This must be what getting old feels like.

The wind shrieks outside again. Except, this time, the windows... rattle. Even behind them, the frame trembles—as if resisting an unseen force. The glass door of the entrance struggles the most.

A crack appears, racing across the glass.

"Get down, *get down!*" Blythe yells. She drops to the floor, pulling the twins down with her.

Every single window in the café bursts. Rain and glass hit the floor tile in a flood of freezing water and tiny shards.

The wind enters, cold and cutting. Wooden chairs screech as they skid across the floor. Paper cups and napkins are sucked into the air, cycling around the café in a tornado.

Lily is on Blythe's left, Lena on her right. Their screams are piercing, their bodies curled up. Blythe locks her arms around them.

"It's okay!" she yells. "It's just the wind!"

The sound of a boot crunching on glass lets her know that she isn't entirely correct.

The café door is only an open metal frame with a sea of tiny, sharp pieces strewn in front of it. A man steps through the frame.

He is dry from head to toe. On his wrists are bulky cuffs carved from bronze. They glint in the light of the storm, but there is another bronze item shimmering on him: a trident pin on his blazer.

Blythe recognizes him instantly: his height, the breadth of his shoulders, the confident way he stands, it's all too familiar. He's the man who stood outside of her house.

The air pushes at Blythe's back like it has formed physical hands of wind and rain. The twins fall silent, their identical brown eyes wide on the intruder. Blythe grips them closer.

The man's hat covers his face in shadow as he turns to them. His voice lilts with an Australian accent. "Isn't that just the cutest."

The wild coils around Blythe with the strength of a cyclone— forcing her arms off the twins. Their bodies rise off the ground, guided through the air even as they flail their limbs.

Blythe's heart drops. The winds are carrying her sisters to that man.

"BLYTHE!" Lena screams. Lily shrieks her lungs raw.

The air is like sandpaper in Blythe's chest. "Lena, I got you!" she screams. "It's okay!"

She reaches until her shoulders ache. Their fingers brush, but it isn't enough. Blythe throws herself forward and—

"Let's not get ahead of ourselves, eh?" the man says. "Nobody's going anywhere I don't want 'em to."

Wind thuds into Blythe's chest. She flies backward and her spine slams into the unforgiving ground.

She tries to inhale. Her lungs can't draw air. Her hands fly to her throat. *Breathe. Breathe. Breathe.* She tries to inhale, opens her mouth, gasping.

"Amber, Jamal," the man says. "I visited your house yesterday, but it seemed you weren't home, so I had to postpone. I can't see Jamal but I know you're there, mate."

Something heavy and solid *thumps* against the back wall.

"Found you," says the man.

The invisibility drips from Jamal's body, revealing his form slumped against the wall. The back of his head is darkened. Blood.

His eyes spear into the man like a pair of knives. "Put them down you son of a—" His mouth freezes, open wide. He is choking on air.

Weightless, he is lifted off the ground, floating over the tables, towards the man.

The intruder sucks his teeth. "Don't be rude and don't waste my time. Do I look like I want to be here?"

A dome materializes around Blythe's body, transparent besides a slightly blue sheen. Blythe inhales and air finally fills her lungs.

She coughs, clutching at her chest, catching her shirt in her fists. The wind still runs wild through the café, but for Blythe, the world has gone still. Nothing can touch her.

She has seen this dome before, in her childhood memories. It's a force field.

Amber Fulton stands behind the counter inside a field of her own. Her expression is granite hard.

"Why are you here?" It is not a question, but a demand.

"MOM!" Blythe yells. The word springs out of her. She doesn't know why. She wants her mother.

The man has not moved a muscle. He remains close to the

doorway, with Lily, Lena, and Blythe's father hovering in mid-air around him.

"I have orders," he huffs. "And, I mean—" he jerks a thumb toward Blythe. "—you can probably guess."

The words cut into Blythe. This attack—the pain her family is feeling, the tears wetting Lily's cheeks, Jamal clawing at his throat—it is happening because of her.

"Your orders mean nothing here," Amber growls. "*Leave.*"

A thin smile spreads across the man's face. "Funny," he says. "I said the same thing to a bunch of soldiers a couple of days ago."

He lifts his hands. His wrist cuffs glow as the air around him twists into sharp, agitated wisps—as if he has made bullets out of thin air.

They shoot toward Amber, rocketing into her force field and popping it like a bubble.

Blythe screams, her voice echoing off the walls. The force field around her own body dissipates into nothing. Tears burn and blur in her eyes. She can barely see the wind pluck her mother up.

Anxiety and instinct thunder inside her ribs. She doesn't have magic. She can't fight. This man is taking her family. What is she supposed to do? *What is she supposed to do?*

From the counter comes a rising wave of water. It crashes into the man, throwing him again a table. He's barely opened his eyes before another wave slams him into the ground.

It is as if the cafe has been turned into a wave pool. The chairs are buoyed as the water settles, pooling against the floorboards.

Behind the counter, Jamie's jaw is clenched as tightly as every other muscle in their body. Their palm is angled beneath the sink's faucet. "GET! THE FUCK! *OUT!*"

Water bursts from their hand, growing into a surge that crests against the ceiling. But when it meets the man, plowing into him, his body is as still as a statue.

He pushes to his feet, clothes heavy and dripping wet. "C'mon kid," he grunts. "Don't be annoyin'."

His heavy bronze cuffs burst with light. Blythe inhales sharp.

"Jamie, *move!*" she screams, but the wind moves faster than her words.

Its bullets hit Jamie square in the torso. They are the same forces that pierced through Amber's force field—but Jamie remains standing.

Blythe doesn't understand what's happening until the blood appears, blooming against Jamie's t-shirt, tiny holes opening from every place the wind has touched them.

Blythe shrieks their name. Jamie grips the counter, eyes wide, unfocused and unseeing. They stumble, mouth agape, before their body gives out. They collapse behind the counter.

"I woulda let you go home free if you woulda minded your business," the man says.

Blythe is on her feet before she can think. The wind twists around her legs, spinning until her balance is thrown.

She hits the ground with tears stinging her eyes. She screams, making incomprehensible noises, struggling to her feet.

She has to do something. She's a Guardian—she's a fucking *Guardian,* goddamn it, she's supposed to be able to bring this whole *building* crashing down if she wants it to.

She balls her hands into fists and shuts her eyes, summoning all of her will, her energy, her power.

But her magic does not come to her. Nothing happens.

Lily and Lena choke on their tears. Amber and Jamal hang in the air on either side of the man, her father's movements growing slower and slower. Her mother is unconscious.

Black bubbles form around them, like four cages of spilled ink, until they are erased from sight, leaving only hovering black spheres.

"Put them down!" The words claw out of Blythe's throat. *"Put them down!"*

The man faces her. For the first time, light falls across his features. But he is not something grotesque, shocking, or monstrous.

He is white and brown eyed with a strong brow and a chin covered in dark stubble. He's just a man.

"I know how it feels to have your whole life overturned," he says. "Trust me...you'll get over it."

A blinding flash of light sears Blythe's eyes. She winces, shutting them as dancing colors echo against her eyelids.

But the wind has died. The café is still.

The electricity has returned, bringing back the lights along with the chattering TV. The café is empty. The man—and her family—are gone.

Napkins and glass cover every inch of the floor. The tables are scattered, the chairs overturned. The counter is a mess.

Blythe gasps. "Jamie," she pushes to her feet. "*Jamie!*"

Behind the counter, Jamie is on the ground. "Jamie...Jamie, please..." she whispers.

Their body is still, long limbs splayed out at awkward angles. Blythe drops to her knees. Her tears drip, salty, into her mouth.

She presses her head against their chest. A heartbeat taps against her cheek. Their chest rises, ragged and pained, yes, but they are breathing. They're breathing.

They need to get a hospital.

The Fultons are no longer part of the Black Veins—or any magician government. They are free from their rules and their wars. They are also free from their protection.

The Sages hold claim over Blythe and Blythe alone, only because the title of *Guardian* has been branded upon her.

There are no magician officials to help her family. To help Jamie.

Blythe runs for her phone, fallen near the windowsill (with the flashlight still on), and dials nine-one-one.

Outside, the fallen neon sign bursts alight. It faces the window, echoing the words THE FULL CUP. Blythe is covered in Jamie's blood. It is on her hands, on her shirt, against her face. And her family is gone. Stolen. Choked and terrified and stolen.

When the paramedics arrive, they will be Common. They will

see not a café, only an abandoned building. They will not see the perfect lights, the fallen neon sign, the glass, the chairs, the menus.

They will not know there were once four other people here.

Approaching police sirens sing to her. She does not know how long she's been sitting in the middle of the café, covered in blood, surrounded by glass, drowning in neon light.

The Alistair French show echoes on the TVs. Only parts make their way to Blythe, the other words mangled and lost in static.

"In Electric City...Electric City...the Trident Republic...in Electric City."

FOUR

MEN ALWAYS THINK THEY'RE RIGHT.

She can read the paramedics' eyes. They think they understand this whole scene: two teenagers were being dumb in an abandoned building and one got hurt.

She isn't going to correct them.

They take Jamie into an ambulance on a rickety stretcher. The two police officers have few words for her, besides asking for Jamie's moms' numbers and telling her it'd be best if she went home.

She nods when they ask if she has transportation. She's not going to put herself—a Black girl with a missing family—in the back of a police car.

She goes to the train station, alone, in the dark. She gets to her house, unlocks the door, and steps into a familiar space made unfamiliar.

The people who inhabit this house include two nine-year-olds, a father who never stops working, and a mother who never stops creating. This space is supposed to be an oasis of life and energy.

Now there is only darkness; there is no movement, no sound. The house has become a hollow corpse.

The silence pins her feet to the floorboards. She can't move, can't speak, can't stop the tears from burning down the length of her face.

Their lives shouldn't be like this. The twins should be enjoying their first days of summer vacation. Her dad should be watching the news and grumbling under his breath. Her mom should be searching for new recipes in her office.

It shouldn't be *this*, her standing alone in a home she no longer recognizes, her mind too scrambled and her chest too tight to think of what to do next.

She was supposed to be scared and hunted by the Trident Republic. Not her sisters or her mom or her dad.

She lingers until she runs out of tears to cry. Her body is weak and her head is light. She needs to lie down.

She moves up the creaking stairs to the bathroom, where the shower bathes her in warmth. She turns up the cold water, higher and higher until her skin turns to ice. Ribbons of blood swim down her body and into the drain.

She can't get the images out of her head. Jamie collapsed on the café floor. Her mother crumbling to the ground. The twins outstretching their arms to her.

The worst image of all is how she stood there. Doing nothing. A powerless, useless girl without magic.

Her room is as untouched as it was when she left it this morning. Her pajamas are where they always are. Her bed is as warm as it always is.

She hides under her blankets, pulling her knees to her chest. And she sobs.

Tears have long since left her. But her body shakes and heaves as sounds choke her. She buries her face into her pillow and screams.

There is no way to judge how long she stays there, veiled from the world beneath her blankets. But when it is over, she is empty and hollow and exhausted.

Her head is heavy. She squeezes her eyes shut. At some point, unconsciousness claims her.

When she wakes, the sun has risen.

Golden light leaves nothing untouched; the blue stationery stacked on her wall shelves, her favorite denim jacket folded over her desk chair. Her wall of photos glow; every single one of her best memories smiles down at her.

She stares at the ceiling as if her thoughts are written across it.

Her family left the Black Veins to escape the violence of the Uncommon world. But magician governments found them anyway and brought their war raining down on them.

She could lie here and lament this until the end of time, but sadness will not save her. Her family is gone. Staying in this room will not bring them back. Crying won't conjure them out of thin air to console her.

She can't stay in this house.

She spent most of her life running from the Erasers. Her parents taught her how to pack up her things and leave a place as fast as possible. They taught her how to navigate the roads, how to check into hotels, how to watch her back. She learned how to travel fast and hard and unseen.

Her childhood has prepared her for situations that look *very* similar to this.

She started to hate the Erasers as she grew older. She would slam her clothes into her suitcases, burning with resentment. She hated the drive away from a town she'd fallen in love with. She's always hated running. She has always wanted to defend what was hers.

Because Blythe Fulton is not a girl who hides. She is a girl with white fire in her veins. She is a girl who fights.

The Trident Republic wants to take casualties in their stupid war? Fine.

Blythe will muster everything inside of her—all of her cunning and determination and pain and anger—and she will go to their city, stare them down, and take her family back.

———

The Full Cup is closed.

The cloaker runs on high, twenty-four hours a day. Commons see an abandoned building. Magicians see a destroyed café with a handwritten *"BE BACK SOON! :)"* sign that looks like it was crafted by a sixteen-year-old. Because it was.

Blythe tapes cardboard around the shattered window frames to keep looters out. It's the best she can do, especially since she has more important things to focus on.

Legs folded on her kitchen counter, and armed with a triple espresso latte, Blythe scourges the internet for the location of Electric City.

She finds it in the Nevada desert, and though she doesn't have the exact coordinates, she *does* have a mapped route to the general location saved on her phone.

Blythe sleeps in her parents' bedroom, surrounded by the life they left on pause: her mother's brush on the corner of the dresser, her father's shoes by the closet door.

It feels like they could walk in at any moment, but Blythe is still alone when she wakes. So, she presses on.

She Googles "road trip supplies" and amasses a list of materials. Using her father's credit card and all of her cash, Blythe buys bags full of items: containers for food, first aid kids, bug and pepper spray, a sleeping bag, and more.

She drops the bags in the foyer and heads for the garage. Blythe doesn't have a license, but her father's been teaching her how to drive since she was fourteen. He had to—he never knew if the Erasers would show up when Blythe was alone with the twins. They always had to be prepared to run.

Their main car is still parked outside the café, but it isn't suited for extensive driving. For long trips, the Fultons have their second car.

Blythe throws up the garage door to reveal Jamal's old, musty minivan. He hates driving it because he thinks it's ugly, so they only use it for emergencies or big trips. Ironically, this situation qualifies as both.

It's a pastel yellow Volkswagen, a bloated round van that screams hippie 60's road trip.

Blythe exhales. "Yeah," she says to herself. "That's ugly as shit."

The inside is surprisingly nice; the rows of beige leather seats are spotless, with every wood surface on the armrests and the walls shined to gleaming perfection.

There's enough space for Blythe to load up her supplies...right beside the Fourth of July firecrackers that linger from the last time the Fultons drove this thing.

And then, finally, everything is done. Blythe is ready.

Anxiety itches up her spine. Maybe she should take another day. Just to rest and think things over. She's a sixteen-year-old magician whose powers haven't bloomed yet, and she's traveling—alone—into a war zone.

But if she doesn't leave now, her fear will grow until it is too large for her to leave the house.

She just needs to bring one more thing.

Back in her room, in the top drawer of her desk, among the loose ribbons and washi tape, is a small photo album.

Blythe thumbs it open, finding a page covered in sparkling snowmen stickers.

Last Christmas, Amber wanted a family photo with everyone in silly, festive sweaters. Blythe is on the left, her curls a shorter version of the huge mane that now halos her head.

She beams at the camera, making bunny ears behind her dad's smiling face. The twins show off their missing teeth on either side of Amber, who is the embodiment of elegance.

They are a family with caramel brown skin, dark curls, and smiles. They are normal. They are happy. They are perfect.

Blythe takes the photo and tucks it, carefully, in the front pocket of her backpack. Now it's time to go.

Blythe's first stop is the hospital.

She is directed to a room at the end of a hall, lit by grey, post-storm sunlight. Blythe knocks on the doorway as she creeps in.

Blythe's never met Jamie's mothers in person, but she has heard enough about them to tell who is who.

Both of them are white. Laura lingers by the window: tall with pin straight, white-blonde hair, looking every part of the FBI agent that she is.

By Jamie's bedside is Kit, a redheaded artist with a checkered blouse and a pattern of freckles across her cheeks.

The two of them lock eyes with Blythe, but only Kit smiles. "Hello," she says. "Are you Blythe?"

"Yeah," Blythe agrees, doing her best to sound polite. "I'm sorry to drop by unannounced. I just wanted to...see how Jamie was doing."

Blythe has texted Jamie with updates on her life, but she's more invested in the updates Jamie gives to *her*. Last Blythe heard, they'd had surgery for internal bleeding. They said everything went well, but anxiety still twists Blythe's stomach.

Jamie lies beneath a thin sheet of blankets, cheek against an overstuffed pillow. Their purple hair has gone limp and stringy. Their face is pale.

The moment they catch sight of Blythe, they break into their charming smile. Suddenly, everything feels okay.

Kit twists in her seat, eyes sparkling as she drinks Blythe in. "Oh no, don't worry about it, don't apologize, you're *completely* welcome! Jamie's told us a lot about you; I *love* your hair, it's just like Jamie described, so big!"

Blythe's smile twitches. She didn't know this visit would include a white woman commenting on her curl pattern like it's an exotic animal—and not, you know, attached to her very normal, human head —but here she is.

Kit is oblivious, excitedly waving her over. "Pull up a chair, take a seat, we don't bite!"

"I'd love to but sadly I can't stay," Blythe says. "I have to leave for a trip today with..." The words clog in her throat. "With my family. I just wanted to say goodbye."

Jamie's eyebrows arch. They may be in a hospital bed, but they're still Jamie, and they're still quick.

"Where to?" Asks Kit. "I heard—"

"Mom," Jamie interrupts. "Can we have a minute? Please."

Kit looks taken aback. Over by the window, Laura stands up straight.

"We'll go grab something from the vending machines," she says.

Laura locks eyes with Kit with a pointed head tilt, and Kit gives Blythe one last smile before she slips out of the room.

Laura pauses in front of Blythe. She towers over Blythe in her heels, the lapels of her black blazer ironed sharp enough to cut flesh.

"I always meant to thank you for getting Jamie a job," Laura says. "Unfortunately, we never got the chance to talk."

"Oh, we needed the help and Jamie was a great fit. It was no problem, really." Blythe sounds almost like Kit now. Rambling.

There is something depthless about the intensity of Laura's eyes. "You're not in any trouble, are you?" she asks.

Of course she would question Blythe. Jamie probably hasn't explained much. Laura and Kit are confused, terrified for their child and what secrets they could be hiding to protect their new job and their new friend.

And here is Blythe, the girl who dragged them into this whole situation and nearly got them killed.

Laura and Kit deserve the truth. But they can't have it—not now, not ever. Because the truth is magic, and to reveal that would be to endanger the entire Monvarian family.

Here is a concerned mother trying to protect her child, and Blythe has to look her dead in the eyes and lie, because Laura is Common, and Blythe isn't allowed to tell her a damn thing.

"We just had an accident at the café during the storm," The lie squeezes thick out of Blythe's throat. "I'm so sorry about this."

Laura lets out a long, slow breath of defeat. Her voice is tight. "Well, I'm glad everyone's safe now. Say hi to your parents for me. And don't hesitate to come visit."

So many emotions swirl in Blythe's chest—pain from the mention of her family, gratitude from the invitation, guilt from every word she's spoken during this conversation—but all that comes out is, "Thank you."

Amber was right when she said the world of magic was endlessly heartbreaking.

As Laura leaves, Jamie's gaze locks on Blythe. "I told them you were a bisexual photographer and now they're obsessed with you."

Blythe exhales, letting the tension leave her body in a swift breath. "I can tell. Besides the whole 'wow, you're Black, that's so interesting' thing, they seem...nice."

Color rises in Jamie's cheeks for the first time. "I-I'll talk to them about that."

Blythe shakes her head as if to shake the situation away. She takes Kit's seat at Jamie's side, and up close she can see how bright Jamie's eyes are, even though their body slouches into the mattress.

"How're you feeling?" Blythe asks.

"Better. The surgery went well," Their hand drifts to their stomach. "I've got some pretty badass scars. I'm thinking I'll tell people I was bitten by a shark. Y'know, something deadly, lots of teeth."

Blythe barks a laugh. "Also something that'll make you seem like a badass for escaping?"

Jamie beams. "You know I love a good story."

They press their palms into the blankets to sit up, but shivers run up their arms.

Blythe reaches forward. "Do you need—"

Jamie interrupts her. "Nope, let me keep my dignity, I'm fine."

They manage to sit up on their own, with a tiny grunt of effort. "So... what's the plan?"

"Get to Electric City, scope the place out, see what I can find, and leave with my family."

She says the words with a stern determination, but Jamie's gaze wavers on her and settles, finally, over her shoulder. "You got important stuff in that backpack?"

Blythe slides it off her shoulder and plops it on the bed so Jamie can rifle through it. "I've got more in the van. This is just survival supplies," She explains. "Y'know, in case I get stranded somewhere."

Jamie slowly pulls out a shampoo bottle. "...These are hair products."

Blythe doesn't blink. "If my curls fail, I fail."

"You're getting better at one-liners."

"I learn from the best."

Jamie gives a satisfied chuckle as they close the bag, letting Blythe hike it back onto her shoulders, but the uncertainty in their gaze hasn't faded.

"I actually *do* have important stuff in the car," Blythe promises. "I swear."

"I know. You know what you're doing," Jamie says, but their face has gone hard and serious. "I would never say that you didn't. I just..."

Their long fingers pick at a stray thread in the knitted blanket resting heavy across their legs. "While I've been here I've just...had a lot to think about. About you, and the war, and everything going on out there, and I...I came up with an idea. But I don't know if you'll like it."

"Tell me anyway."

Jamie doesn't, not immediately. They watch the careful movements of their fingers as if the courage to speak lies within the yarn of the blanket.

When they do speak, their words are soft. "I think you should find the other Guardians and get their help."

Out of all the things Blythe expected Jamie to say, that was certainly last on the list. Blythe doesn't even *know* the Guardians. Why would she waste time trying to find them?

And why would they help her, how would she convince them? The whole idea is illogical, requires too much time, too many resources, and is just generally impossible.

But Blythe can't say that. Not to Jamie's face. Not after Jamie worked up the courage to even say those words. The whole reason they're in this hospital is because they were selfless enough to try and save Blythe and her family. Blythe can't be *that* ungrateful.

"I...I don't think that would help, Jamie," she says. "But I'll—"

Jamie sits up straighter. "No, listen." Their jaw is set. "I know you don't believe me, but I'm pretty sure they could help you."

"Jamie—"

They speak over her, the sharp gaze of their unblinking blue eyes spearing into hers. "You're going to this city *by yourself*, in the middle of a magician war, to fight a guy who kicked our asses and put me in *here*. I don't want you to get hurt. You're gonna need someone to watch your back. And it can't be me, so it needs to be somebody."

They freeze as if their words are as much of a surprise to themselves as they are to Blythe.

So that's what this is about. It has nothing to do with the Guardians, not really. They just want Blythe to be safe.

"I just...I just want you to consider it? Okay?" they ask. "I wanna know that someone's looking out for you."

"Okay," Blythe relents. "I'll think about it. I promise."

And she will. For Jamie, this wonderful person who has risked their life for her and her family, who has been there for her even when she kept pushing them away. This person she definitely does not deserve.

Jamie reaches out and takes Blythe's hand into theirs; their palms are soft, but their grip is strong.

"I don't want to scare you," they say. "You're gonna find them either way. I just want you to be safe while you do it."

But Blythe must be wearing her anxiety on her face because Jamie leans toward her.

"Hey," they say. "Look at me. You got mind controlled into walking to the edge of your roof and you survived. A man broke into your café and attacked your whole family and you survived. Hell, you spent your whole life on the road, constantly moving, never staying anywhere long enough to call it home, and you still survived."

They squeeze Blythe's hand as if they could transfer their own will straight into her veins. "You come from an amazing family, Blythe. They're strong. And so are you. They believe in you, and they know you haven't given up on them, and they believe, with every fiber of their heart and being, that you're coming to save them. You're going get in that van and you're going to drive. Drive until you find your family again. Drive until you that find fucker from the Trident Republic and give. Him. Hell." Jamie's eyes blaze. "Drive until you light Electric City the *fuck* up."

FIVE

BLYTHE OPENS THE GPS ON HER PHONE, PROPS IT ON THE dashboard, and revs the car engine. Washington to Nevada shouldn't be a long journey.

She avoids highways because something about the nonstop adrenaline gives her heart attacks. But she has no problem challenging common speed limits while hour-long playlists blast musical numbers. The wind is playing through her hair and her hands are drumming against the steering wheel.

She stops only when the growling in her stomach becomes unbearable. Even then, she grabs lunch from a fast foot joint, eating in the parking lot with her feet crossed on the dashboard.

She is humming along to the radio as she races out of town and enters the depths of the forest. These roads aren't unfamiliar; her family would to drive this way to go camping. But the GPS takes Blythe on a slightly different route, one surrounded by twisted trees against a horribly grey sky.

The farther she drives, the more she lowers the volume on the radio. The air is getting colder and her legs are starting to cramp. The

GPS wavers as night falls; the blue dot that represents her wobbles all over the map.

Her headlights beam white cones of light onto the dirt road, as if they are the only light left in the world. Blythe's supposed to continue straight for the next half mile, which would be fine if the tires weren't catching.

"Please don't get stuck," Blythe whispers. "Please don't get stuck, please don't get stuck, please don't—"

The van lurches and splashes into a patch of mud. The tires whirl. But they don't push forward.

Blythe groans, letting her forehead drop against the wheel. She's fucking stuck.

Her sneakers slosh in the mud when she jumps out, squatting down to find the tires downing in mud. The van is too heavy to push. She'll have to get on her hands and knees to clear the sludge out.

"Unbelievable," Blythe mutters.

She kneels, her weight sinking into a pool of freezing dirt. The muck is cold and wet in her hands as she claws through it. She did *not* imagine her first day going like this.

She's mostly done digging when the hum of an approaching motorcycle reaches her. No, not one motorcycle. Several. And, somehow, they sound as if they are coming from the forest itself.

Blythe curses under her breath. These bikers could be harmless, but what kind of harmless bikers ride through the woods?

She brushes the mud from her clothes, scrambling back into the van to shut off her headlights. Hopefully, they won't notice her.

In the rearview mirror, Blythe notices light echoing through the trees. The buzzing hive of engines grows into a thundering mass of growls—and a hoarde of motorcycles explode onto the dirt path.

"Shit!" One of the riders screams. "There's mud everywhere!"

"Don't be a baby, Twin," says a man. "It ain't gonna kill ya."

They're a group of eight men in black jackets on black motorcycles with black boots and black jeans. They can't be older than twenty, but the youngest looks to be the aforementioned "Twin": a skinny white boy with blonde hair slicked up straight.

"I have a name," Twin snaps.

"Yeah, well, I can't tell you apart well enough to care," says an ambiguously tan young man with shaggy, honey brown hair. "So you're both Twin."

"Eh, Rocco, what about the shards?" another man asks.

"Shit man, I don't fucking know," the ambiguously tan one, Rocco, seems to be the leader. The others watch him as if his words have enough weight to sway their lives. But, despite the squint of his eyes and the hard set of his jaw, he can't be much older than twenty.

"Whiteclaw's gonna kill us," Twin laments.

"Not if Whiteclaw doesn't know," Rocco counters.

"But we weren't supposed to fucking drop it!" Twin yells. "Evangeline's gonna kill us if we deliver it to her like this! They explicitly said they're *fucked* without this thing and we dropped it like a hackey-sack—"

"Hey! Shut the fuck up!" Rocco barks. "What are you doing, providing exposition!? Do we look like we're performing for a live studio audience or some shit? We were all there, we know what happened!"

Blythe chews the inside of her lip. Whoever Evangeline and Whiteclaw are, they're probably dangerous people to screw over. And if this gang just messed up, the last thing they'll want is a random teenage girl *knowing* they messed up.

Maybe if she stays very, *very* quiet, they will (somehow) fail to notice the huge yellow van stuck (less than a mile) down the road.

"Now just lay 'em out flat," Rocco barks. "If we put it back together it should work fine. Just make sure we got all the pieces, 'cuz if we miss one, the whole thing's fucking shot."

He snatches a drawstring bag from his back and turns it upside down, dumping a pile of bronze shards onto the street. And then he picks one up.

The moment his fingers touch the shard, a sharp ringing hits

Blythe's head like a bullet. The nails-on-a-chalkboard shriek scratches through her brain.

Blythe holds her ears, curling herself forward, gritting her teeth to keep back a scream. It is like her brain is glitching—the ringing continues, incessant, never-ending.

Beneath it all lie the faint noises of a familiar melody.

Suddenly, it stops. In the rearview mirror, Rocco has flung the shard back onto the road.

He says something, but Blythe can't hear it above the sound of her own gasps for breath. "Holy shit," she whispers. "*Holy shit.*"

She knows that song. She *remembers* it. It's the one that played before she took an unwanted trip up—and almost off—her roof.

And that feeling of something being in her head, controlling her, that's familiar too. Except, this time, it felt broken. Shattered. Like the pieces lying in the dirt.

Those shards could be the remnants of the magical item used to controlled her.

If Blythe is right, then these bikers aren't random thugs. They're very threatening thugs who probably work for the *Trident Republic.*

Her mind whirls with ideas. Rocco said that the item wouldn't work if it were missing a piece. Which means...if Blythe can steal even one shard...the Trident Republic won't be able to control her.

Blythe steels her nerves. "Okay, Blythe," she whispers to herself. "Time to be brave."

She rifles through her supplies: food, road flares, clothes...and, underneath the seats, an old box of Fourth of July fireworks.

Bingo.

Armed with a handful of cherry bombs, a lighter, and her burgundy beanie, Blythe slips out of the van.

The bikers are still talking, their voices filling the night, drowning out the sounds of Blythe slipping into the trees. She needs to place the fireworks far from her truck, but close to the bikers.

She walks until their voices are too loud and too close. Off to her right is a log, unassuming and almost hidden in the underbrush. The perfect target.

Blythe gets on her knees, peering into its hollow center. It's just big enough to fit the fireworks inside.

She lights the cherry bombs and hurries through the trees as they begin to hiss. Sticks and dry grass crunch beneath her feet as the bombs pop and spark.

Rocco's voice slices through the trees. "What the fuck?"

Blythe checks over her shoulder. Between the darkness and foliage are the bikers' faces; they stare, quizzically, into the forest.

"Sounds like a bomb or something," says one.

"Sounds like fireworks," says Twin.

"Don't be an idiot," Rocco snaps.

"You know," Twin begins. "I feel very unappreciated as a member of this group."

"God, you *are* an idiot," Rocco says. "You gonna sit here and spout more bullshit or are you dumbasses gonna go see what it was?"

Four of them move into the trees, but three linger around Rocco.

"What if it's that vigilante kid?" a lingerer asks.

"Why would she be here!? She never leaves Philly," Rocco growls. "Stop stalling and *go*."

Blythe ducks behind the closest tree. The rough bark scratches the back of her denim jacket. She wrings the beanie in her fists as the bikers ease into the forest.

One by one, their boots crunch against the underbrush. All except for Rocco.

Blythe curses low. She planned on all of them going into the forest. How is she supposed to distract the *leader*?

"Holy shit, it's on fire!" someone shouts.

Oh shit. Blythe hadn't considered how flammable a dry log would be. Smokey the Bear is probably shaking his head somewhere.

But Rocco sucks his teeth, moving toward the trees. "*Put it out, genius!*"

There's only a bit of distance between Rocco's turned back and the pile of shards. It is, at the most, a few feet. It isn't much. But it's as good a shot as Blythe is going to get.

Blythe runs on the tips of her sneakers—her steps land soft and silent. She slips the beanie around her hand. Maybe, if her skin doesn't touch the shard, she won't incapacitate herself.

The closer Blythe comes to Rocco, the more she sees of him. He's taller than she thought—much taller than her—with a black snake tattoo choking around his neck. And, most importantly, he isn't paying attention to the shards.

They are piled on the ground, gleaming in the dim evening light. They range between large and small, and between thin and wide, all jagged edges and smooth, bronze surfaces.

Blythe can't be picky. She snatches the one on the top and bolts so fast, her hair whips behind her.

"HEY!" Rocco's voice hits her back like a knife. Shit.

Her legs pump harder. Back to the truck. She just has to get back to the truck.

Something arcs through the air with a *whoosh* and then—heat. Burning on her right forearm.

Her jacket is on fire.

Blythe gasps. She slaps the beanie against the flames. Her skin singes beneath the denim.

"Who the fuck are you, you piece of shit?!" Rocco screams. "Twin! Get her!"

But Blythe doesn't hear movement.

"Why are you still standin' there?!" Rocco screams.

"You call us the same name," says one of them. "How are we supposed to know which one you're talking to?"

"*BOTH OF YOU!*" Rocco bellows.

The footsteps start just as Blythe reaches the van. But the twins are fast.

Blythe dives into the driver's seat, slamming the door behind her. She gasps for breath as she revs the ignition.

The tires spin in place.

"Fuck, fuck, *fuck*," she curses. In the rearview mirror, the twins' forms grow larger as they run closer.

Behind them is Rocco. His gait is a slow, ambling stalk. The sharp white lights of the motorcycles draw hard, sharp shadows along his face. Towering flames pulse from his balled fists, licking up his arms.

If Blythe couldn't fight a magician who controlled air, one who controls fire will kill her.

Blythe presses the gas pedal to the floor. "Come on!" she screams as the tires wail. "Please! Come *on!*"

The tires rip free. The van jerks forward with a screech.

Trees blur past as Blythe grips the wheel, her heart in her throat. She's not in control; the van spins to the right.

She crosses hand over hand, pulling the wheel all the way to the left. The old metal creaks and groans as it rights itself.

The twins grow smaller in the mirror. Behind them, Rocco arcs his arm like he's throwing a baseball. A fireball shoots over the twins' heads, pivoting toward the van.

Blythe shrieks, spinning the wheel. The van swerves and the flames explode against the roof. In the backseat, the embers echo down the windows, orange flickers that extinguish into nothing.

The fire hasn't caught. Probably because the van is metal. And the bikers can't stop her from driving away. The van is under her control again.

She's free.

Blythe laughs, shoving a middle finger out of the window. Success has never tasted so good.

Until one of the twins pulls something from his hip and aims it at Blythe. "Oh fuck," she gasps.

The gun fires with a *bang*. Blythe braces herself; a tire could go flat, a bullet could shoot through the truck. But nothing happens. He missed.

Three more rounds go off. With every sound, Blythe's heart skips a beat. But none of them land.

The twins and Rocco shrink into dots in the distance as the other bikers flood back onto the path. At the fork in the road, Blythe banks a hard, quick left.

Blythe's blood has turned to frost. The bikers don't follow her, but her unease does.

She constantly checks her rearview mirror, even miles later. Maybe that was a mistake. She shouldn't have stolen that shard. What if they *do* follow her? Was this more trouble than it was worth?

Her whole body shakes. She can't tell if it's from fear or exhaustion. Probably both. Fully Awake Blythe would've never done what she just did.

She needs to stop for the night. Her forearm is killing her; she definitely has a burn.

This is only her first day on the road. How is she supposed to get to Nevada like this? She got lucky because those guys were idiots, but what happens when she runs into people who aren't?

Electric City is the *capital* of the Trident Republic. There is no telling what the universe has in store for her there.

Blythe tightens her grip on the wheel. She can't think like that. She can't view this as impossible. Because if it is impossible, then there is no hope for her family.

The forest spits her out onto a main road. She drives, weary, until she spots a run-down, retro motel sign reading *Mercury Motel* in old, blocky neon letters.

The van sputters as she pulls into the parking lot and finally, *finally,* turns the engine off.

*

You can always tell when you're nearing a magician location from the way the air crackles. Your hair stands on end as you travel through an alleyway, or goosebumps rise on your skin as you past a dark doorway.

The energy, that static, means that magic is near. Stumbling into a magical town in a Common city is just a matter of making the wrong turn down the wrong road, following a path for too long, heading into a shop just as the clock strikes midnight.

There are other cities hiding right on top of the ones Commons have come to know.

That very energy assures Blythe that this motel is run by magicians—or, at the very least, is accepting of them. She'll be safe here.

Blythe slouches against her seat with a long exhale. Her beanie rests in the passenger seat. Carefully, she peels it open.

This is the first time she can actually inspect the shard. It is curved inward, concave and bronze, with more of a luster than a shine. It's about the size of a large cell phone, and if it were a piece of jewelry, it would be quite beautiful.

It could be a shard from anywhere. But it's invaluable, and Blythe would be an idiot to disrespect it. This shard—and all the others like it—could have her screaming, helpless on the ground, anywhere and at any time.

Blythe inspects her boxes of food and decides to empty out the Fruit Rollup box. She buries her beanie at the bottom, stacking the silver containers on top.

There. Foolproof plan.

She switches her burnt denim jacket for her pastel blue bomber, stuffs her wallet in her pocket, and heads inside.

The old white woman behind the desk has a nametag reading "Candice".

"Ya got ID?" she asks.

And Blythe freezes. This isn't some swanky, decked-out hotel with diamonds dripping from the ceiling. It smells like mold and cigarettes. Everything is dark. The only other people in the (cramped) lobby are a woman and a teenage girl. This place is supposed to bend the rules.

"...excuse me?" Blythe asks.

"ID," Candice repeats. "Ya gotta be eighteen to book a room."

Blythe is silent—the silence of a sixteen-year-old without ID.

The other woman, the one waiting with the teenage girl, glances at Blythe. She seems too polished for a place like this—Middle

Eastern and rather young, with dark hair falling across her shoulders in waves. Her eyeliner is perfect but her nail polish is chipped.

The teenage girl is even more high class, eyes glued to her Zadis phone. She's about Blythe's height and age, East Asian, and slim with elegant black hair brushed to glossy perfection. Her pastel pink flats match her skirt, and Blythe is sure she saw her white tube top online for three hundred dollars.

Blythe tries not to stare. Now is not the best time to be dazzled by pretty girls.

"You need a room?" asks the older woman. Her voice is a scratchy, nonchalant drawl.

"Yeah," Blythe answers.

The woman looks her up and down. "You're Blythe Fulton, aren't you?" The teenage girl looks up from her phone. Her eyes are a deep brown.

Blythe has never seen these people before. Or at least, she doesn't think so—she's lived so many places that faces tend to blur. But with everything that's happened in the past three days, the answer is probably not that simple.

"How do you know my name?" Blythe asks.

The woman stands up straighter, smirking at the girl. "C'mon," she goads. "Tell me my luck isn't amazing. C'mon, do it."

The girl furrows her brow.

The woman sucks her teeth. "You're no fun."

"Hey, excuse me?!" Blythe snaps. "Who are you?"

But the woman doesn't answer. "We were actually on our way to your house," she says instead. "What the hell happened to you? You look like hell. Worse than hell, actually. You look like you just mud wrestled Satan."

Blythe studies the woman for a second time: she doesn't seem to have any weapons. Her attire reads more "average person" than "threat"—she's even in six-inch heels. Nothing is adding up, but Blythe isn't about to act confused.

69

"Let's try this again," Blythe says. "Who are you and how do you know who *I* am?"

The woman sighs, as if a serious explanation is an inconvenience. "You heard a voice in your head, right?" she asks. "Lost control of your body, took a trip up a roof, whatever? Your parents made a phone call and good ol' Sessa told them everything would be taken care of?"

Oh.

Shit.

"Well, surprise," the woman smirks. "My name is Katia Darkholme. I'm a Lead Imperial Advisor for the Sages and I'm getting paid to haul *you* to Frost Glade."

SIX

At first, Blythe only stares at Katia in shocked silence. She completely forgot about going to Frost Glade. After her family disappeared, the only things that mattered were the things that would bring them back.

To abandon her plan and disappear into Frost Glade would mean abandoning her father, her mother, her sisters. But it's doubtful that Katia will understand.

"I don't mess with magician governments," Blythe says, like that's an excuse.

Katia snorts. "Like that's an excuse."

Well, it was worth a shot.

Blythe keeps talking—maybe eventually she'll hit a point that actually makes sense. "I'm not going to Frost Glade either. I can take care of myself. Just tell the Sages I don't need their protection or whatever. I'm good."

Katia arches an eyebrow. "Took care of yourself pretty well when you almost walked off a roof, didn't you?"

Blythe swallows down all comments about the bronze shard sitting in her van, about how she's already ensured that the Trident

71

Republic won't control her again. Katia doesn't need to know her business.

"Can I go to the room?" A voice interrupts.

The teenage girl looks up from her Zadis. She's beautiful without her phone hiding her face: perfect Instagram brows and dewy makeup. Her voice sways with an English accent. "It's late and I'm exhausted."

Katia regards her for a moment before she turns to Blythe. "How about we take this somewhere more comfortable?" she suggests. "You can room with us."

"I don't *know* you," Blythe snaps.

Katia sighs—a sound too light to be real. "Fine," she relents, but Blythe watches her through narrowed eyes.

Katia's voice is too calm as she turns to Candice. "Can you set her up with a room? It's for Black Veins business. I'll cover it."

Behind the counter, Candice wrinkles her nose but shuffles around in some drawers and presents Blythe with a key. "Out by tomorrow morning," she grunts.

"Thanks," Blythe mutters. She just wants to get to her room and be done with this whole situation.

But Katia's voice perks up again. "So, if you're not going with us, where are you taking that God-awful car to?"

Blythe doesn't *have* to tell her, but maybe Katia will leave her alone if she does.

"Electric City," Blythe says. "...And it's not God awful. It's moderately awful."

Katia draws back a bit. "Electric City's been desecrated, what are you going there for?"

"To get my family back."

"The Trident Republic *took your family*? And told you to go to Electric City to find them?"

"Yes. Wait, well, no—the Trident Republic took them, but I had to figure out the Electric City part myself."

"How?"

Blythe can't say she got a good feeling when she heard the TV say it. "It's the capital of the Trident Republic and they're the ones who kidnapped them."

"They're not..." Katia pinches the bridge of her nose with a sigh, as if Blythe is an idiot and *Katia's* not the one who is misunderstanding. "There's no proof that they're in Electric City. But they honestly just took your family?"

Well, Blythe was wrong. Explaining herself has obviously been no help at all. "Yeah," she says, turning for the door. "And thanks for the room, but—"

"Okay wait," Katia interrupts. "Let's pretend that you, a teenage girl, manage to make it all the way to Electric City, on your own, without getting robbed, mugged, or worse. This is already a fantastical situation, but let's keep going."

Blythe grits her teeth.

"You get there. Every building is falling apart, the streets are filled with debris, and the whole place is a danger zone. Now, let's pretend you aren't killed by a falling steel pipe or a sinkhole. You're probably running out of food and money, and you're wandering in a foreign city you've never even *seen* before.

"But let's say, somehow, you find the building with your family inside. That's great! Except the outside is guarded to the ninth with traps and magic shields. Now let's pretend that you somehow get past these with the power of determination or whatever the fuck.

"As soon as you reach the front door, a militia sniper has you through the skull. Because the Trident Republic is trying to start a war and they knew someone would come for these people. They just didn't think that 'someone' would be a little girl in a sassy Forever 21 bomber jacket.

"But besides all that," Katia flashes a bright smile. "Sure. Heading to Electric City? Great plan."

Blythe glares at the woman as if she could burn the grin off of her face. She has to ball her fists at her sides to keep herself from shaking.

The teenage girl doesn't even glance at them as she heads out, and Katia follows—but she pauses in the doorway, looking over her shoulder at Blythe.

"We're in room 302, down from yours," Katia says. "Pop in when you're ready."

It takes all of Blythe's resolve not to curse the cockiness right out of that woman. But once she's gone and Blythe has snatched her keys from the desk, reality starts to sink in.

Katia is right. Blythe hasn't considered what Electric City could have in store for her. It's a city that has been attacked by the Black Veins army—it's not *Disneyland*. Her whole mission could be a disaster. She could end up dead.

A staircase leads up from the parking lot and straight to the door of her motel room. It's a ridiculously cramped space, but Blythe can't be picky.

She showers the mud from her skin and scrubs it out of her clothes. But her mind spins the whole time.

If Katia's right, Blythe can't make it through Electric City on her own. But she can't just leave for Frost Glade. Her family is waiting for her. She has to find them. She *has* to.

The bed doesn't give under Blythe's weight; it feels like concrete. But her body aches, her heart thumps against her ribs, and she is too weary to care.

Drowsiness fogs her mind, drifting into unconsciousness...

Blythe snaps awake. She never locked the van. And the shard is still in there.

She snatches the van keys from the nightstand and heads to the top of the staircase. Thankfully, her van is in the same parking spot, untouched.

At the end of the street, where two dark roads intersect, is a figure just outside the reaches of the orange streetlights. A blue-eyed man in a suit.

Blythe can feel the heat of his gaze. He is watching the motel. He is watching her.

Goosebumps prickle along Blythe's skin. She has not seen that man since she was thirteen years old. She didn't think she'd ever see him again.

The Erasers are here. They found her.

Blythe locks the van. She hurries back to her room, locking that door too. She goes to the only window in the room and shuts the curtains. It's all for nothing. Locked doors and closed windows won't stop the Erasers. Nothing can stop the Erasers.

Blythe sits on the concrete mattress. But nothing happens. The night is silent and still.

Why have they appeared again after *three years*? Why now? Blythe hasn't broken any rules. She's kept magic a secret, done everything the Erasers could ever want her to do. Is it about Jamie's moms? But she lied, she didn't tell the truth.

Cold chills race up her arms. Her head feels light. Blythe could go to Katia—it's her job to protect Blythe, after all. But Blythe refuses to walk in there, tail tucked between her legs, like the powerless child Katia sees her as.

Blythe left home to find her family. She won't give up just because she's *scared*. She can't. What she needs to do is sleep, wake up energized and refreshed, and hit the road again.

Blythe slips back into bed.

It takes her a while to fall asleep.

———

"Get up."

Blythe rapidly blinks her eyes open. The golden light from the streetlamps sneaks in-between the curtains, outlining Katia's form in the darkness.

She stands over Blythe, arms akimbo, stoic. "Get up and get under the bed," she whispers.

Blythe has to press her hands into the mattress to keep from rocketing out of bed. "What the hell?! How did you get in here?"

Katia wrinkles her nose. "Can you not ask questions?!" she hisses. "Get. Under. The Bed."

Of course Katia would just waltz in here and bark orders. Of *course*. "Fuck. *You*," Blythe growls. "And if you don't get out of here, I'm calling the front desk."

"What? I'm an Imperial Advisor for the Sages of the Black Veins, what the hell is *Candice* gonna do?"

"Send you to jail for breaking and entering!"

Katia looks like she's about to pop a vein. "I'm the one paying for the room!"

Across the room, the wallpaper beside the bathroom door ripples. As if something is coming through the wall. The thought of seeing the Erasers in her motel room chills Blythe. But it isn't them at all.

The humanoid form floats like a weightless ghost. Its skin is alabaster white, from its oversized head to the shoulders that end in rounded, uneven stumps.

The only features on its white plain of a face are two red, bulbous eyes, bulging from their sockets.

Blythe doesn't ask what they are. She doesn't wait for Katia's instructions. She does something her father calls African American Survival Instinct—she runs.

Katia shouts after her as she rushes out the door and the stairs. Blythe isn't amazingly fast on her feet, but she can get some distance on them, and once she reaches the van—

Blythe realizes, too late, that her foot has caught between two stairs.

She plummets down, stairs piercing into her body as momentum carries her forward. Her hip hits the concrete, and finally, she is still.

This is definitely not good.

A humming grows behind her. It is an inhuman sound, like rattling bones. She's barely caught her breath before a red searchlight lands on her, bathing the world in crimson.

She can feel that thing behind her. Coming closer.

A second light hits her. The humming grows louder. There's more than one.

Blythe pushes herself to her feet—a hot, stinging pain shoots up her leg. She winces; a slice down her calf drips blood onto her ankle. Perfect. Amazing.

The creature hovers down the staircase, two identical beings flanking it on either side. They have no legs; from their hips are the scaled black bodies of snakes, slithering down each stair.

Their eyes shine like beacons, six beams of piercing red light straight onto Blythe.

Blythe shifts her weight onto her good leg and limps to her van. The red lights stalk her, and all she sees is red, red, red.

She tries to open the door. It won't give. It's locked. She locked it before she went to sleep. And the keys are in the motel room. "Mother of *fuck*," she whispers.

One of the creatures shrieks. It is a high, pained sound. Blythe whirls around.

The things have gone still at the bottom of the staircase. Jutting through the middle one's chest is the pointed end of a knife.

Black blood leaks from the wound like tar, creeping down the creature's white skin, catching no light as it falls. The creature has gone still, its mouth frozen in a soundless wail.

And its eyes melt. Blythe gags as they drip red down the creature's chin, swirling into its blood.

A second knife spears through the one on the left—and another through the one on the right. They are three bleeding statues, mouths wide, eyes crying.

The middle creature collapses like a ragdoll. And there, standing on the balcony, is Katia.

Katia's eyes are steeled. "I said: *Hide. Under. The bed.*"

Blythe can barely catch her breath. "How was I supposed to know you meant 'hide under the bed because there are monsters' and not 'hide under the bed because I'm a weirdo pedo or something'?!"

Katia looks at Blythe like she's gone insane. "Do I look like a pedophile?!"

"Pedophiles can be anybody! We learn that shit in first grade!"

"Hey!" A gravelly voice booms.

Leaning over the third floor balcony is Candice, a shotgun aimed in her hands. "You bring trouble?!"

Katia doesn't even blink. "It's over, Candice. It's been taken care of."

Candice sucks her teeth as she lowers her weapon. "Too bad for me," she huffs. "I wanted to shoot."

Something wet brushes Blythe's feet. She didn't put on shoes before she ran out, and now the creature's red and black liquids are running like a river down the asphalt and pooling across her toes.

She clamps a hand over her mouth, holding back the sounds (and vomit) threatening to rise from her throat. Tonight has been a night that no amount of rest could ever help her recover from.

Katia watches her from above, arms crossed, hip jutted out. Blythe catches her eye. But Blythe doesn't have a sarcastic retort for her. Not this time.

"Can I..." Blythe's voice trails off before she can speak the words. "Sleep in the room with you guys?"

And Katia smirks.

———

Katia's room is only slightly larger than Blythe's own, but Blythe is still peeved about it. Two queen sized beds are squished inside, with a whole nightstand between them (why couldn't Blythe get a nightstand?).

The teenage girl sleeps in the bed closest to the door, sheets pulled up to her shoulders with a pink, silk mask hiding her eyes. If Katia's job is to bring the Guardians to Frost Glade, then this girl is either her assistant or another Guardian.

Blythe has never met another Guardian before. In all honesty, she hasn't even *thought* about them—what they looked like, what their lives were like. And now one of them is, potentially, in the same room as her.

"Did she just sleep through all that?" Blythe asks.

"Thankfully," Katia huffs. "You'll have to take the floor. Not a good idea to share a bed with her—she bites."

Blythe recoils. "Like, for real?"

"No, but she will bitch and yap until your ears bleed," Katia says. She turns on the bedside lamp and the room turns yellow. "And I actually like my ears so please, for God's sake, don't wake her up."

Knowing Katia, this is definitely an exaggeration.

Draped over the edge of the free bed is a black cloak. Katia's hands seem to disappear into its folds as she reaches into its pocket, pulling out a spool of bandage, a salve, and a small vial of what looks like alcohol.

"Give me your leg," Katia orders.

Katia dresses the wound with skilled, careful hands. She eyes the burn on Blythe's arm. "I know the wraiths didn't do that, so where'd that come from?"

Blythe hesitates. "A small...altercation. I handled it."

"Of course."

Blythe stops herself from rolling her eyes.

"Do you know what those things were?" Katia speaks again.

"No," Blythe doesn't feel bad about her answer. It's impossible to know everything about magic; people attend magician colleges to major in thaumology, the study of magic, and certified thaumologists spend *years* perfecting their practice. It's incredibly extensive—and Blythe is no thaumologist.

"They're a species of Calling creature," Katia explains, carefully dabbing the dried blood from Blythe's skin. "Calling is a difficult spell that requires a lot of energy, but it allows you to summon a few creatures of an otherworldly species to follow your commands."

Blythe wrinkles her nose. "So like...summoning demons?"

"Almost, but less hell-ish. There are hundreds of species of

Calling creatures; thaumologists think they come from an alternate dimension, something like that, but it has nothing to do with...forces of good and evil. They're just creatures. It's the intent of the magician that shapes what they're capable of."

She winds the bandage across Blythe's leg, pulling tight. "What you saw tonight were Wraiths," Katia continues. "They're like walking cameras. Whoever summons them can choose to look through their eyes, seeing everything they do—or they can have them report back and replay everything they've seen like a projector."

Blythe grits her teeth. The list of people who could have sent them after her is too extensive. The Trident Republic? Those motorcycle bikers? The Erasers?

"And," Katia continues. "I sent them."

"What?" Blythe blurts. Anger boils hot in her chest. "What the hell is wrong with you?!"

She tries to snatch her arm back but Katia holds her in place, her grip tight and her gaze unflinching.

"You weren't in danger," Katia says. "Wraiths can't hurt people, they just watch and cry when you kill 'em. Wanna know *why* I did that?"

"Because you're an asshole," Blythe spits.

Katia ignores her. "Because the Trident Republic specializes in Learned Magic—including Calling. Which means Electric City is crawling with Calling creatures ten times worse than the ones you just *ran* from. Let that sink in."

Blythe holds Katia's gaze but says nothing. Because she has no defense. Katia is right.

If the Trident Republic plays dirty, they probably use all kinds of magic to protect their capital...including Lovecraftian creatures that could crush Blythe without a thought about her existence. If she charges headfirst into this city, she will not make it out alive.

"You didn't even run away correctly," Katia adds.

Blythe grumbles. "Now you're just shitting on me."

"You fell down the stairs."

"*Okay,* alright, Jesus Christ! I get it, you get it, we all get it."

Blythe remains silent as Katia secures her bandage. But Katia's bedside manner sucks, because she nearly shoves Blythe's leg off of her as she stands.

"So," Katia sighs contently. "Can I expect you to join us in the morning?"

As much as Blythe was to storm out and return to her own motel room, rejecting Katia wouldn't be wise. Going to Electric City, with the lack her lack of knowledge and lack of magic, is a ridiculous plan.

Blythe's best bet is to stick with Katia and learn what she can—then escape when the time is right.

"Momentarily," Blythe mumbles. "Where are you headed after this?"

"Montana."

Blythe sighs. They're going northwest and she needs to go south.

"You could just join us for breakfast," Katia says. "We'll talk about what we can do for your family, see if we can figure something out."

It certainly sounds better than Montana. And Blythe isn't going to pass up free food. "Okay, fine," she relents. "We'll get breakfast."

Katia tosses Blythe a pillow and blanket from her own bed. Blythe makes a space on the carpet, and it isn't much, but when the lights are turned off and the world feels still, she tosses and turns for a few hours until she manages to finally drift into sleep—

"Rise and shine, Rugrats!" Katia yells. "We've got places to be and not a lot of time to get there!"

Blythe groans, squinting against the light. Outside the window, the sky blooms golden. "What time is it?" she asks.

Katia hovers in the bathroom doorway, dressed in a pair of skinny jeans and a white blouse, outlined in sickening electric light. "Six thirty!"

"Jesus Christ..." Blythe rubs her eyes. Her brain doesn't wake up until noon.

Katia's voice is piercing. "Gooooooood morning, Cordelia!"

Over on the second bed, the teenage girl is slowly sitting up. Her eye mask rests on her forehead, revealing shadowy brown eyes cutting Katia a sharp glare. Without makeup, her face is a bit plainer, but just as stunning.

"Don't," she growls.

But Katia ignores her. She's watching her reflection pull her hair into a topknot.

"Oh right, you guys haven't been introduced," Katia says. "Blythe Fulton, meet bratty Barbie supreme, Cordelia Deleon."

Blythe smiles sleepily and waves—but Cordelia misses it because she's still glaring at Katia. "That joke wasn't funny the first three times you said it," she snaps.

"Wasn't a joke," Katia chuckles to herself. "You guys can be friends or ignore each other, I don't give a shit. Either way, we're out of here in fifteen minutes."

"Fifteen minutes...?" Blythe repeats. It's gonna take her fifteen minutes to sit up, let alone be ready to go.

"Blythe, we'll take your throwup van to the diner," Katia continues. "Go get your stuff and we'll meet you in the parking lot. God, I need a haircut."

Blythe wrinkles her nose. "Why don't you guys have your own car? And if you want to use my van you can't call it a *throwup*—"

"Your fifteen minutes are dwindling!" Katia shuts the bathroom door as if to shut Blythe up.

Blythe and Cordelia are left to early morning silence. Cordelia slips out of bed on graceful feet, picking up a pastel pink, name brand backpack.

Blythe feels like she should say something. "So...are you a Guardian? Or do you work for Katia?"

Cordelia turns to Blythe with the same splintering glare she gave Katia. "You think I'd willingly employ myself under *that* woman?"

Rough start. "Sorry, I just...figured I'd ask."

Instead of replying, Cordelia rifles through her things, pulling out a pair of round Gucci sunglasses and an off-the shoulder mini dress.

82

Blythe tries again. "Did you...go up to your roof too?"

"Of course," Cordelia answers without looking at her. "After a bit of fighting, I got free. Didn't you?"

Blythe absolutely did not. The only thing that saved her was her father. But Cordelia stopped the melody through sheer willpower?

Blythe almost doesn't want to admit the truth. "...no."

Cordelia's perfect eyebrows raise. She fishes out her Zadis phone and drops the bag to the carpet. "Well," she says, already more invested in her notifications. "I suppose that's the difference between you and I."

The words are sharp—almost too haughty and cutting to be real. But they were indeed real, Blythe heard them, and Cordelia is no longer acknowledging Blythe's existence, so Blythe sees no reason to continue this conversation.

Blythe spends her remaining fifteen minutes throwing on a fresh set of clothes and returning her room key to Candice. Cordelia and Katia are already waiting outside her van when she enters the parking lot; Cordelia's gaze is still glued to her phone, while Katia watches Blythe approach with folded arms.

Blythe tries to climb into the driver's seat. Someone grabs her collar and drags her back.

"Wh—what the fuck?!" she sputters as Katia climbs in. "Who said you were driving?"

Katia arches an eyebrow. "Do you know where we're going?"

It's s filmy excuse to get Blythe away from the wheel, but Blythe can't do anything besides groan the whole walk to the passenger seat.

Judging from how she tears out of the parking lot and shoots down the street, Katia is a reckless driver.

Blythe can't say she's any better, so she starts looking through her backpack to make sure everything is in place. But her photo of her family, the one from Christmas, is gone.

Blythe didn't move it. She hasn't even touched it since she left yesterday morning. So where is it? How could it just disappear?

The van is moving faster now. And faster. And *faster*. Blythe's gaze shoots to the speedometer. They're pushing ninety MPH.

"Katia—?" she begins.

"Shush!" Katia orders.

Up ahead, racing closer, is a fork in the road. But Katia isn't following its split to the left *or* to the right. She keeps the wheel locked straight ahead—they're heading toward the forest of towering trees between the road.

Blythe's heart leaps into her throat. "I hope this is some crazy magic shit because I really don't want to die!"

"Don't worry!" Katia hollers.

The speedometer needle climbs higher. The forest rushes toward them. Blythe screams as they burst into a mass of branches.

Twigs and foliage smack the windshield. The tires bounce and roll straight onto a patch of bright green grass—

Bright green grass? The grass in the local forests is the dullest shade of green imaginable. Blythe frowns, taking in the world around them.

A world of trees and dewy grass surrounds them, stretching on infinitely, to the horizon. Tree trunks the width of cars spread their moss-covered roots like spiderwebs across the ground.

A rainbow's array of plants sparkle in the white sunlight, as if they are sculpted from diamonds. There is no mud, no cloudy skies and no drooping trees.

The air is sweet and the ground is soft beneath the tires. Everything hums with the same ethereal electricity that accompanies magic.

Katia smirks. "It's totally some crazy magic shit."

The grass parts like water beneath the van as it cruises. "What *is* this?" Blythe asks.

For some reason, this makes Katia wrinkle her nose. "What? Have you never even *heard* of the Tempore?"

Blythe has to think about how to say "no" without sounding like a whole dumbass. "...No," she manages.

The van shrieks to a halt. Blythe didn't think it was that serious, but Katia throws open the door and jumps out.

"Alright, class is in session," Katia announces. "Follow me for a sec. Cordelia, you can come if you want."

Cordelia is scrolling through her phone in the backset, legs crossed. "Absolutely not."

Blythe hops out of the van and follows Katia's black cloak through the trees. She doesn't lead Blythe far, just through a few hanging branches and past a shimmering glade.

Katia stops before a chasm that yawns wide at their feet. The abyss extends so far below that its bottom is just a line of undefinable darkness.

"Whoa," Blythe breathes.

Katia pulls a water bottle from the folds of her cloak. "Want a swig?"

Blythe chugs most of it—she hasn't had anything to drink since last night—and hands it back.

She expects Katia to comment on it, but Katia just tosses the bottle into the chasm, watching blankly as it bounces off the walls, spewing water like a fountain.

Blythe doesn't know what she's supposed to learn from that. "Nice aim," she comments.

Katia is unperturbed. "Thanks."

A sound like crinkling paper thunders in the sky, the air heats, and something drops from above. Blythe jumps with a gasp.

Lying in the grass is the water bottle, completely filled with the cap screwed on tight.

"This place is called the Tempore," Katia says. "It's a forest that folds time and space. Usually it makes sense, but there are a few spots like this chasm where both time and space are...flawed. Best to stay away from them. Oh, and don't drink that water. Thaumologists have yet to discern what these flawed areas do to the things they absorb."

Blythe gapes. This is a time traveling forest, a place that doesn't adhere to the laws of reality.

"You make a *really* stupid face whenever something blows your mind," Katia points out.

Katia starts back toward the van without even waiting for Blythe to follow. Typical.

"Anyway," Katia continues. "The Tempore is a natural landmass that existed long before magician governments did, but it belongs to the Black Veins now. It connects every forest and grove in the world, regardless of size. As long as a location has trees, the Tempore has access. You could walk from California to New York City in minutes as long as you know how to navigate correctly. Lucky for us, I know a lot about traveling the Tempore."

Blythe hears her, sure, but what Blythe's really thinking about is how she could use the Tempore to travel straight to Nevada. No more side streets and pit stops. She could be there within minutes.

"How did you learn about navigating in here?" Blythe asks.

"Studied it for a few years in college," Katia answers.

Jesus. A few years. In *college.* Blythe can't even think that far ahead into her future.

But it raises some interesting information about Katia. "Are you a thaumologist?" Blythe asks next. If Katia studied the Tempore in college, she probably went to a magician college. And most people who attend magician colleges end up as thaumologists.

"Me? Fuck no. I'd die if I had to sit inside for that long. Do I look like a nerdy scientist?" Katia jumps back into the van and slams the door, ending Blythe's interrogation.

Well, it was useful while it lasted.

Blythe keeps thinking about the Tempore even as she buckles up. One thought makes her freeze. If the Tempore is mainly used to cross long distances in a short period of time...why the hell are they in it?

"Wait, where are we going?" Blythe asks.

Katia smirks her cutting, haughty smirk. "We're going to a diner..." She whips around, her smile humongous. "*In Montana!*"

Her entire body shakes with laughter, sudden and strong. "Aaah, I kidnapped you," Katia chuckles. "Wow, I am so good at this."

"What?!" Blythe shrieks.

"Did you really...did you really think I was going to let you just... just *decide* if you wanted to go with us or not?!" Katia can barely speak through her cackles. "Oh my god this is so great, because you can't even leave! We're in the Tempore! You don't even know how to get out! I got you *and* your ugly car! Oh MAN!"

Blythe can only stare at this woman, this stranger who has conned Blythe into coming along with her, stolen her van, and lied to her face.

Blythe thought...what? That Katia would actually give her a choice? How naive could Blythe be? She's an idiot for ever trusting her.

Blythe's family is waiting for her and she's too dumb to even leave the state successfully.

Her eyes burn with tears. Katia's laughter fades as Blythe slouches into her seat, staring hard out of the window to keep from breaking down.

"Aw, come on, don't cry," Katia sucks her teeth. "Crying kids make everything awkward."

Blythe holds up her hand to shield her face. She hates crying in front of people. "I'm not crying," she lies. The only sound in the van is Blythe trying to even her breathing before she *really* starts sobbing.

"Listen," Katia begins. She sounds...solemn. "Do I look like I want to waste my time wrangling a bunch of random ass teenagers to escort them to Frost Glade? Do you think *I* don't have something I'd rather be doing? The Trident Republic is trying to goad us into war and the Sages have me, one of their best advisors, on babysitting duty.

"I don't care *what* you do. I care about my paycheck. And for me to get said paycheck, I need you to come with me. Last night, I called the Sages and told them about your family. By now, they probably have a whole team of people out searching for them. They'll find them. But until that happens, the Sages have declared your safety— and the safety of the other four Guardians—priority. So here we all fucking are."

The engine starts with a growl. Katia's gaze doesn't waver from the road. She is here to do a job, and, judging by the set of her shoulders, nothing will get her to abandon it.

Blythe clenches her jaw. She can't even escape; Katia has her van, which means she has all of her supplies—*and* the shard.

Blythe doesn't know how to leave the Tempore. The layout of the trees would twist and turn her around. Knowing her luck, Blythe would probably fall into one of those damn chasms and get tossed out of the sky.

There is no way for her to fight, no way for her to escape.

Blythe is stuck.

SEVEN

WHATEVER MAGIC BROKE CORDELIA OUT OF HER MIND CONTROL must also keep her from being tossed around by ridiculous driving.

She sits pretty in the backseat, even though Katia drives like she means to hit every uneven patch of ground in the forest. Blythe has to fight to keep her butt in her seat as the van charges between skyscraper-like trees.

An explosion in the distance steals Blythe's attention. Cordelia's too, apparently.

"What was that?" she asks, face pressed against the glass.

"Probably the Trident Republic trying to pull something," Katia says. "I wouldn't trust anything you hear. The Trident Republic has Fae on their side and the Fae are the fucking *worst*. You can never tell what's real with them."

The van hums as it picks up speed. Blythe narrows her eyes—if Katia truly isn't worried, why is she rushing?

"The Trident Republic have men inside the Tempore?" Cordelia asks.

"Maybe," Katia says.

"But the Tempore is Black Veins property, correct?"

"Yes."

"So, isn't this...an invasion?"

Katia makes a face. "Cordelia, did you miss the part where the Trident Republic is trying to start a war right now?"

Cordelia grimaces and sinks back against the seats. Blythe's turn.

"The Black Veins and the Trident Republic aren't already in a war?" Blythe asks.

"The Sages haven't declared anything yet. The Trident Republic has been trying some shit, but the Black Veins is just squashing it down. Its defense, not retaliation. The Sages would only start a war if the Trident Republic proved to be a real threat. At the moment, they don't have a strong government or military force. There's not much they can actually do."

"They almost got rid of three Guardians," Cordelia scoffs.

Katia clenches the steering wheel with tight fists. "That was fighting dirty," she snaps. "Cheating and strength are *not* the same thing."

But Cordelia is unperturbed. She sits, chin in hand, as easily as if she were at a Sunday morning picnic. "If the Trident Republic isn't a threat, why are the Sages sending all seven Guardians to the equivalent of a war bunker? We should be allowed to stay home—especially the other four who weren't even mind controlled. This all seems very presumptuous—"

"Are you done?" Katia interrupts. "Because your cliché accent makes everything you say sound three times bitchier."

Cordelia doesn't even blink. "Good."

Holy shit. Cordelia's *dangerous* whenever she actually looks up from her phone.

Blythe looks back and forth between her and Katia. "Katia, you just got *owned*."

"Real mature," Katia snorts.

Cordelia leans forward, her hair swinging over her shoulder. "And earlier you said 'the other four'. But, including *this* one and I, there's seven Guardians in total."

"My name's Blythe, I...told you that..." Blythe's voice trails off as she realizes Cordelia is not looking at her and definitely does not care.

She almost forgot Cordelia's as rude as she is clever.

"Usually if something happens to one of you, it affects all of you," Katia says. "You're all Guardians, which means you're pretty much all on the same level. But...the last Guardian isn't a factor in all this."

Cordelia rolls her eyes. "This makes absolutely no logical sense."

Suddenly she leans back into her seat, snatches up her phone, and exits the conversation.

"Hey, it might help if you even knew what being a Guardian *meant*," Katia snaps. She quickly glances to Blythe. "She didn't know anything about magic when I picked her up a couple days ago. I've been explaining—"

Cordelia's head snaps up. "Are you honestly telling my business to the whole world while I'm sat right here?"

Cordelia didn't even know magic existed? She still managed to break free of the thing that plagued Blythe for days after it happened? And she can analyze the inconsistencies of this situation, inconsistencies that Blythe didn't even think of?

Who *is* this girl?

Katia ignores her, smirking now that she's finally grappled the upper-hand. "Just listen up, buttercup," she says. "You too Blythe, if you don't know already."

Her explanation feels more like a ploy to get Cordelia to shut up than to actually educate them, but Blythe isn't going to look a gift horse in the mouth.

She came with Katia to learn, and now that Blythe's lost the opportunity to escape, she may as well pick up what she can.

"So. Magic, any form or type or shade of it, is just using energy to manipulate one or more of the seven Elements: Nature, Animals, Time, Death, the Body, the Mind, and Ether."

As a child first discovering the existence of magic, Blythe started listing the places in the world where she could see the Elements in action. By now she has seen them all in various forms.

The Element of the Nature: quiet rain cried from the clouds, a bursting volcano, the chill of a breeze carried over a field of wheat.

The Element of Animals: a newborn bird's first chirp, the hum of a thousand bees, the snapping teeth of a hungry wolf.

The Element of Time: history books heavy with memories of the past, a moment you wish you could remain in forever, alternate timelines reaching into worlds beyond.

The Element of the Body; a healing wound, a gentle kiss against the skin, every breath brought into your lungs.

The Element of the Mind: imagining worlds you have never seen, the joy of thinking of a clever joke, remembering the face of an old friend.

The Element of Death: the closing chapter of a life once lived, making space for life to begin yet again, the final, eternal rest.

And, finally, the Element of Ether: moonlight, black holes, the energy of light and the power of your determination, the stars that make up the universe yonder and the universe inside each of us. Life itself.

"Every magician is born with a single ability that forms during puberty, and this ability—their magic—allows them to manipulate one or more of the Elements. For example, someone could communicate with fish, which scholars would define as a manipulation of the Elements of Animals and the Mind. If someone can see visions of the future through the stars, scholars would call that a manipulation of Ether and Time.

"This singular ability is called Inherited Magic, because you're born with it. All forms of magic require an energy source and Inherited Magic uses the energy of magicians' own souls, but this rarely has any ill effects on the magician."

Okay, Katia *definitely* went to a magician college and studied magic for a few years. No magician without a degree talks about magic like that—

Blythe almost flies forward as the van shrieks to a halt.

"Oh fucking finally," Katia blurts. "We're here."

The forest around them doesn't seem to be any different from the forest they've spent the last half hour traveling in, except for the fallen tree blocking the road.

Katia hops out as if it's no big deal.

"Wh—are we just going to leave the van here?!" Blythe calls after her.

"For now!" Katia replies.

This can't be safe. Blythe takes the keys, just in case, and locks the doors after she and Cordelia are out. It's still *her* van, and she'll be damned if anything happens to her baby.

"What about my magic lesson?" Fake enthusiasm drips from Cordelia's voice.

Katia waves a dismissive hand. "Read a textbook."

She hops over the fallen tree with the grace of an athlete; Cordelia wrinkles her nose and walks around the edge.

Blythe grunts as she crawls over the trunk. "God, I hate nature," she murmurs.

She looks up and almost takes back her words. Seven trees line their trail, trunks as huge as houses and roots snaking across the ground for miles.

They've grown far past the canopy of the other trees; if they have branches, the human eye will never glimpse them.

There seems to be no forest beyond their presence; darkness clogs the space between their trunks. Blythe looks over her shoulder at the fallen tree, but it isn't a tree at all, just one of many gigantic roots.

Wherever Katia has taken them, it definitely holds *some* significance.

Katia's headed for the darkness between their trunks, but the closer she gets, the larger they seem. "C'mon! Remember what I said about time not being on our side? First time I wasn't being sarcastic!"

The ground quakes, shuddering through the tree branches. Katia freezes. Blythe holds her breath. Cordelia stops mid-step. But the forest is silent.

A mountainous feathered form throws itself between Katia and the girls. It lands with a force that makes Blythe stumble backward.

Cordelia screams as it moves, too large to see all of it at once. A pair of sharp talons flash against the grass. A wing splays, filling Blythe's vision with slippery feathers the color of an oil spill.

A sharp, yellow beak opens above. Sunlight shimmers against something in its mouth as it *caws*, a noise that shakes Blythe's bones.

"Cords, Blythe, stay where you are!" Katia screams.

Metal glints in the air before a knife stabs into the creature's wing. It screeches, folding inward.

Two knives plunge into its core; Katia rolls across the ground to their right, identical knives clenched in her fists.

The beast swipes a wing at her. Katia leaps aside, black cloak swishes. She tosses another knife with a shout, and the creature stumbles back.

Its feathers are melting; drops of black goo drink onto the forest floor in thick, bulbous globs.

But Katia edges backward, a dangerous serenity in her eyes. Then Blythe realizes: she's luring it away.

With a powerful bat of its wings, the creature surges forward for her. But it leaves the path to the trees wide open.

"Run for the trees!" Katia screams. "Go through, I'll meet you there!"

Blythe sprints. The monster seems to grow larger the closer she comes, its hunched form the size of a building, a skyscraper, a mountain.

Blythe has no weapons or magic. If it turns around, she's fucked.

She pushes her legs to move faster. "Go through the trees, go through the trees," she chants to herself. "Don't think about what's going to happen, just go through the trees."

She bursts into the darkness. And the entire world goes black and silent.

She is alone. There is no Katia, no Cordelia, no giant monster. A tingling warmth covers her skin. The air smells...clean.

Gravity has not left her, and she pushes forward into nothingness, sneakers hitting a spongy ground that gives easily under her weight.

"God, please don't let me be dead," she whispers.

She doesn't know how the Tempore works—or what happens when you leave it. Was that monster normal? Or should she be scared?

There's so much she doesn't know.

Light pierces her vision. Blythe winces, shielding her face as the darkness slips away like water—and in its place is a sky, peachy with sunrise.

She is standing on a hill, staring down into a town of humble brick buildings. The sun peeks around a mountain range on the horizon, spreading an orange haze across the rooftops. She's definitely not in the Tempore anymore.

Cordelia bursts from the trees, gasping for breath, stumbling over her own feet.

"Oh my god..." she mutters. She covers her face, hair tumbling across her shoulders.

"You okay?" Blythe asks. Cordelia's annoying, but she looks two seconds away from falling apart. Blythe's not *heartless*.

Cordelia peeks between her fingers. Her gaze is cutting. "Don't patronize me."

Blythe scoffs. "You're an asshole, I get it. But you're laying it on damn thick don't you—"

"Do you truly believe this is me being an asshole?" Cordelia interrupts. Her face is still flushed red from running and she's yet to catch her breath. "I could point out every flaw and insecurity I've observed over the past few hours. I could explain the fourteen courses of action you could have taken that actually would have helped you, but you were too dumb to realize. I could ruin you. Frankly, *ignoring* you is the kindest thing I've done thus far. If anything, you should be thanking me. You do not know me, Blythe Fulton. I could very easily

95

be an asshole." Her perfect brows furrow hard. "Don't give me a reason to."

Cordelia Deleon is not the first mean girl Blythe has ever encountered. She will not be the last.

Blythe knows exactly how to react in situations like these, and her fist is already balling tight when Katia appears.

Her cloak is a ragged shadow behind her. The creature's head sticks out from the trees, massive enough to swallow a human whole.

It opens its beak to caw, but Katia lets out a scream of her own—and sinks her knife into its feathery neck.

The creature's beady eyes bulge. Its feathers go slick and formless, dropping as oily goo onto the grass. The eyeballs sink and roll out of their sockets as the neck loses form.

The creature is melting.

Katia's knife drops into a pile of lumpy blackness, along with something much lighter.

Katia sighs, fishing her weapon out. "Damn Trident Republic and their fucking Calling creatures...I only have two knives left..."

As the goo settles, it slips farther away from something suspiciously rectangular at its center.

"Wait," Blythe calls. "Something else came out of that...thing."

"What?! That's all you have to say?!" Cordelia screams. "We were just attacked by some...some spawn of hell and all you say is 'there was something else'?! What is *wrong* with you?!"

"I was two seconds away from punching you in the face, so I suggest you shut your mouth because I *know* your posh English ass can't fight," Blythe snaps.

"*Hey!*" Katia snaps. "Both of you shut up. I don't like either of you and I don't feel like dealing with drama."

She plucks the object out of the goo; it looks like paper. Or rather, a photograph.

Katia's face goes blank as she inspects it. "Oh. This is nothing. I'll throw it out when we get to town. Anyway—"

But Blythe is missing a photo. The only one she took from her bedroom, the one of her family.

Blythe is moving without thinking, walking toward Katia. "Katia, what is that—"

Katia moves it behind her cloak. "Nothing, kid. We have to get down there and find the next Guardian and we don't have all day."

But Blythe can see it poking out behind Katia's leg. It *is* Blythe's photograph.

Except all of her family's faces have been crossed out with black marker, leaving only Blythe's smile.

Spots appear in Blythe's vision. Her hands tremble. This is not a part of the Trident Republic's war. That monster wasn't sent to do anything. It was only meant to deliver her this picture.

The Trident Republic is toying with her.

Blythe's eyes snap to Katia. "Who runs the Trident Republic."

Katia's expression is a blank canvas. "That's irrelevant right now."

"Irrelevant!?" Blythe yells. "My family's been *kidnapped*! If anyone has the right to know, it's me! Nobody else gets to say whether or not I know who's making my life hell!"

Katia's jaw clenches. "If I go shouting names at you, you'll be making a hit list. Just trust that the Sages are taking care of things. You don't *need* to know."

"I want to know," says an English voice.

Cordelia's shoulders are squared, her jaw clenched. "What?" she scoffs. "I know less about what's going on than either of you. Blythe's not the only one who's suffering. I had to leave my home—my entire country—and come to a place that's being ransacked by a secret magical war." Her face hardens. "I may as well know *why*."

Blythe hates it, but she has a point. Cordelia hasn't had it as rough as Blythe, but these past few days can't have been easy for her.

Katia is a statue. Unmoving, expressionless. Then she rolls her eyes. "Don't tell anyone I told you this. Some of it's strictly classified.

"The Trident Republic gets its name from its three tiers of government leaders. Rue Whiteclaw is the third tier—he's in charge of army and defense, I think they call him a general. I talked to a friend from the Black Veins Imperial Army and he's pretty sure Whiteclaw is the man who took off with Blythe's family."

"Whiteclaw?" Blythe repeats. The name is clunky on her tongue.

Katia nods. "Was he a big, Dorito-shaped guy who looked and sounded like Hugh Jackman as Indiana Jones?"

Blythe would have gone with "Australian McCree". "That was him," she agrees.

"We figured," Katia agrees. "But Whiteclaw is a follower incapable of original thought. The real mastermind is Walden Oliver. He's the first tier, the president and founder of the Trident Republic. We're pretty sure he's the one behind the mind control and the roof incident. He just prefers to send Whiteclaw out to do his dirty work. That's why the Black Veins Imperial Army is out searching for Walden Oliver as we speak."

Walden Oliver. Rue Whiteclaw. Being able to put names to all this feels like a weight lifting from Blythe's shoulders. Names make people feel less like imposable figures and more like normal humans she could stand a chance against.

"But what could Walden Oliver gain from terrorizing me?" Blythe asks. Then she remembers Cordelia is there. "Well, all of us Guardians," Blythe amends. Cordelia rolls her eyes.

"That's what we don't know," Katia continues. "We think Walden wanted to use the Guardians to get the Sages to declare war, but then he kidnapped your families and left you behind. So the motive doesn't completely make sense."

She pauses. When she speaks again, her voice is soft. "The Black Veins has been in wars before but they've always been with the Medallion. Never with the Trident Republic. And Walden...he's a troublemaker, and he's dangerous, but he isn't stupid. And he's never done anything like this. He usually just pretends to be some rebel leader, a freedom fighter and a 'voice for the people' but not a...not a murderer. He's gone to jail before but never for anything like this, and a punishment for a crime like this could mean banishment to the islands...so something's not right. I just don't know what."

Blythe doesn't understand—she doesn't know what the islands are or Walden Oliver's history.

But it doesn't seem like Katia's words are for their ears.

Cordelia scoffs. "You talk like you actually know him."

The words snap Katia out of her thoughts. Her face goes hard. "Anyway," she says. "That's enough classified information for one day. We gotta move."

Blythe recoils. Katia hasn't addressed Cordelia's statement at all. And yes, ignoring Cordelia is Katia's main hobby, but something about that felt...different. Blythe doesn't like the cold chills it sends up her spine.

If Katia knows Walden Oliver, then she knows the Trident Republic. And that makes her far more than just being a protector that's supposed to lock Blythe away in Frost Glade. That makes her potentially dangerous.

Katia starts down the hill, black cloak echoing behind her. She doesn't even glance over her shoulder to see if Blythe and Cordelia are following.

But they are. Of course they are.

———

The town seems to be a quiet, peaceful suburbia. The breeze is crisp and cool, even for summertime. Pine trees grow between red brick buildings crawling with vines and the asphalt roads are only large enough for two lanes. Occasionally, the silence is broken by the hum of a passing car. All of the shops look to be Ma-and-Pop, family owned businesses.

Every person Blythe sees—walking on the sidewalks, or in the cars, or in the shops—is white. Blythe hopes this place isn't so old fashioned that it's outfitted with good old-fashioned overt racism because she, Cordelia and Katia are three women of color who are obviously *not* from here.

"Where are we right now?" Cordelia asks. Exactly what Blythe is thinking.

"Broughton, Montana," Katia says. "A small magician town hidden by the mountains and home of a little boy named..." She tucks a hand into her cloak and retrieves a paper scribbled with words and numbers—names and addresses.

"Daniel Quinton," she finishes. "Speaking of the Quintons, they're a bit...different."

"You're saying 'different' like a thinly veiled insult," Blythe says.

The way Katia rolls her eyes must mean she meant it as such. "They used to be scientists—thaumologists and astrophysicists. Then they left Alabama for Broughton, built a house on top of a hill in the middle of a forest, and never left. From what I hear, neither of them work anymore. They communicate with the Black Veins in handwritten letters only, and the roof incident was the first time they called us on the phone in *years*. So yeah, they're...*different*."

Blythe twists her mouth to the side. She isn't one to judge—living in a forest away from civilization sounds great. But it could easily turn into accidental solitary confinement.

"We're meeting them at a diner because I refuse to hike all the way up to their weird ass house," Katia snorts. "Plus, we'll be able to get some food."

They arrive at a quaint hole-in-the-wall at the end of a road. Walking through its door feels like stepping into a time capsule; from its red cushioned booths lining the windows to the checkerboard tile, the atmosphere screams 1950's wholesomeness.

Katia slides into a booth across from Blythe and Cordelia. The English girl's nose has been wrinkled since they got here, but Katia pays her disgust little mind. Blythe just isn't a fan of how the tabletop is only *barely* clean.

The sound and smell of sizzling bacon has Blythe's stomach

growling. The sun creeps up the sky, echoing golden rays off of the salt dispenser and condiment bottles.

The waitress swings by to pass them sticky, lamented menus before she disappears to give them time to pursue their options.

Blythe's looking over the bacon selections—they smell *really* good —when Katia takes a deep breath.

"Let's get back to that magic lesson," she says.

Cordelia looks up from her Zadis. "Because you don't want to talk about the Trident Republic any longer?"

"Because you need to *learn*."

Cordelia snorts. "You told me to read a textbook."

Katia shrugs out of her cloak as she speaks. "I changed my mind. I need to help the younger generation, and as a Millennial, there's little I can do besides pass on knowledge, so let's get to leaning!

"Remember what I said about the Elements? In the Black Veins, there's a Sage for every Element. A Sage of Nature, a Sage of Time, and so on. The Sages are immortal—they've ruled the Black Veins since the fall of the Roman Empire. They live in Frost Glade, handle all government affairs, and protect the cores of the seven Elements.

"Now, the cores are seven orbs which, if destroyed, would obliterate the magic of the Element they contain. So, say the orb for the Element of Nature was destroyed. Magicians wouldn't be able to make tornadoes, or hurricanes or earthquakes—but they also wouldn't be able to grow fruits and vegetables instantly, or stop avalanches from burying small towns.

"These cores are, as you can imagine, *filled* with magical energy. The Sages were even bestowed with magic from them back in the ancient times when they first became Sages—which is one of the reasons they're so powerful. Fifteen years ago, one of the Sages became power hungry. After years of planning in secret, he attacked the other Sages and nearly destroyed Frost Glade in his attempt to absorb the power of the seven cores.

"It was a gruesome battle. Frost Glade...it looked like hell. Fire flooded the hills, buildings collapsed onto families running to evacuate. The beach waves swallowed the boardwalk and took screaming people out to sea. The streets were filled with blood and screams and, above it all, the Sages were battling."

Goosebumps prickle along Blythe's arms. A shadow has passed over Katia's face.

"I was there. I was about your age at the time," she whispers. "And that night was...indescribable. I thought the stars would fall out of the sky. It felt like we were all going to die."

She takes a long, deep breath. "But, obviously, some of us survived. But the Sage who went evil wasn't as lucky—the other six Sages managed to stop him, but it...cost him his life.

"After that, the Sages decided that the cores were too overpowered to be left in their raw state. So, after consulting with thaumologists, the chose seven annoying, crying babies and gifted them with *huge* amounts of magic from the cores, in the same way that a drop of the cores' magic had been given to the Sages themselves. They called these whiny brats Guardians, because it is through them that the cores are less powerful, and therefore less appealing to greedy, evil magicians."

Katia's dull gaze drifts between Blythe and Cordelia. "And here you are today, the Guardian of the Mind and the Guardian of Ether. Both being annoying and ruining *my* life."

Something clicks for Blythe. Cordelia is the Guardian of the *Mind.* That's why she broke free of the mind control—it's literally her Element.

It had nothing to do with Cordelia being inherently better like she implied. She just had an advantage. Of course she broke free.

Cordelia casually turns away from Blythe, glancing out of the window as if she knows Blythe has caught on. What a dirty little liar.

"But," Katia continues. "Having large amounts of magical energy means that your Inherited Magic manifests...differently. Unlike the rest of us who have *one* ability, you seven can completely control every aspect of your given Element. Your only limitation is that you can't control another Element. Besides that?" Katia smacks the table for emphasis. "You could do *anything*.

"Remember what I said about the Element of Nature going wild and causing tornadoes, earthquakes, hurricanes, all that?" Katia asks. "The Guardian of Nature could cause that with a snap of his finger."

Bells tinkle as the diner door eases open. A white family of three shuffles in; their old-fashioned clothes are plain, and their hair and skin are dull, as if they've been run through the wash too many times.

There is a tall, wiry man, a small woman with hair that is not quite red or blonde, and then there is a boy who looks no older than fourteen.

He is short and round-faced with blonde curls and a flushed face. His lip trembles and he clutches a small, leather-bound book to his chest.

The third Guardian has arrived.

The woman notices them first. She waves and hastily guides the boy and man toward the booth.

Katia plasters a pleasant smile on her face. "Hi, you must be the Quintons."

The man's expression does a balancing act between pensive and annoyed.

"Yes," he clears his throat. "My name is Silas. This is my wife, Carol, and our son, Daniel."

The boy, Daniel, stares at Blythe and Cordelia like they each have two heads. He shows no sign of speaking. Blythe smiles, but it doesn't seem to make anything better.

"I believe we've met before, Miss..." Carol's voice trails off.

"Katia Darkholme," she answers. "And we have. I've been working for the Sages for sixteen years. I used to babysit for the Guardians when they were younger."

That's news to Blythe. Blythe's life has been in Katia's hands more than once and Blythe's somehow still breathing.

"I don't remember that," Blythe blurts.

Katia turns her fake smile to her, which is somehow much more threatening than her usual glare. "You were three. And there were seven of you. And one of me."

Carol's mouth opens, closes, and finally come the words: "Miss Darkholme, I...trust that you are a responsible woman, otherwise the Sages would not have chosen you for this job, but...I must ask this of you personally." Her voice trembles as much as her hands. She takes a breath. "I can't begin to describe to you what it that night was like for us...the absolute fear we felt... Please...please keep my son safe. I just—"

"I'm sure Miss Darkholme is more aware of the dangers than we are," Silas interrupts. "She's adequately prepared for them."

Carol sends Silas a withering look.

"But in any case," he hurriedly adds. "You must promise us that no harm will come to him."

When Blythe looks back at Katia, she is surprised to find that her expression has lost all of its fake joy. What is left is the solemn seriousness of the woman Blythe glimpsed when she started to cry in the van.

"Daniel will be safe," Katia promises. "You have my word."

Carol and Silas's heads bob in approval, but Daniel looks more terrified than before.

Blythe almost pities them. They're not like her family: the Quintons are reserved, passive. They are not built to survive danger.

Silas clears his throat again. "Well, son," he says to Daniel. "It's time for us to go. Stay safe and be sure to write. Come, Carol."

Daniel stares after his parents, but his father walks to the door without a second glance. Carol hugs her son, a few seconds too long.

"*Carol,*" Silas calls.

Carol lets Daniel go, fixing his curls and his argyle sweater. "You'll be fine, sweetheart, I promise," she whispers. "We love you." She smiles at the three of them. "Goodbye, Katia. Goodbye, girls. It's been nice meeting you."

They leave like startled birds, the bells chiming as the door shuts behind them. Daniel lingers beside the table, clutching his small book.

"Here, have a seat," Katia scoots toward the window to make space. "We were just about to order some food, you can use my menu."

Daniel sits gingerly, placing the book on his lap. "N-No thank you," he whispers. "I-I-I'm not hungry."

Cordelia watches him like he's the human equivalent of a used tissue. Daniel meets her eye and instantly snaps his gaze down to the table, cheeks heating.

"Your eyes are quite red," Cordelia says.

Actually, it looks as if he's been crying the whole way here.

"He probably has allergies," Blythe lies. "Mind your business."

"Allergies, y-y-yes," Daniel mutters. "I...umm...allergies."

When the waitress arrives, Blythe and Katia are the only ones who order. Cordelia pretends the woman isn't there and Daniel mutters, "Ah...I'll just...water..." to the table.

For a few moments, the four of them sit in awkward, heavy silence. That's until Daniel's face skews and he sneezes—except a small burst of flames explode from his mouth, shooting red and orange embers that extinguish into smoke.

Blythe and Cordelia gasp, almost in unison. Daniel's face turns red.

"I-I'm sorry!" he blurts. "T-That just started happening, I-I-I don't know why, I'm sorry, r-really, I-I-I..." He covers his mouth, eyes brimming with tears.

Katia frowns at him. "Gesundheit."

Daniel just sneezed fire. Fire...and he's a Guardian. "You're the Guardian of Nature?!" Blythe whispers.

The Element of thunder and earthquakes, of oceans and mountains and tornadoes. The Guardian who can cause worldwide panic with a snap of his fingers.

Daniel stares at her, brow pinched, hand still clasped to his mouth. He nods slowly.

Well, shit.

Katia leans forward, resting her arms on the table. "So, Daniel, tell us about yourself," she prods.

Daniel drinks his water, eyes huge. He is silent.

"Well, you sound like you have a sparkling personality," Katia says. "Glad you're here."

Daniel stares at his shaking hands.

"I hate to interrupt this heated conversation but I have to use the bathroom," Katia says. "This is the only potty break we're gonna get for a while, so it's now or never, kids. Our next stop is California."

"I'll be fine," Cordelia says.

"I think all of my internal organs dissolved as soon as I saw that monster in the Tempore," Blythe says.

Daniel stares at Katia.

"Just me then," she says. "Don't go anywhere, because I *will* be a total mom and drag all of you into the bathroom with me if I have to." She eyes them as she leaves, heels clicking against the tile as she goes.

With Cordelia being Cordelia and Daniel staring at a nonexistent spot on the table, Blythe doesn't have many options for conversation.

"I-I'm fourteen," Daniel suddenly whispers.

"Oh, that's cool!" Blythe says. The last thing she wants is for him to feel like he can't talk to them. "I'm sixteen, and Cordelia is...uh..."

Cordelia's on her phone again. "Minding her business."

Blythe smiles at Daniel. "Probably also sixteen."

"Fifteen," Cordelia corrects.

Their food arrives; Katia's omelet and Blythe's bacon and waffles. Daniel's eyes droop sadly as he watches the plates sail right past him.

Blythe offers to share. He thanks her so quietly she almost doesn't hear it and, gingerly, digs into a waffle.

Cordelia sighs. "Finally," she mutters, dropping her phone on the table.

Blocks of small words like her screen, but the words "*Classified: Trident Republic*" jump out.

Cordelia snatches her phone up, turning up her lip at Blythe. "I'm sorry, did *you* just spend three hours hacking through Trident Republic servers using only a single Zadis phone?"

"You're a *hacker*?" Blythe's jaw almost drops. "Jesus, if you weren't so terrible we'd probably be able to accomplish a ton of stuff. We're literally in the same situation—"

Cordelia barks a laugh. "Oh, we are *not* in the same situation. I want nothing to do with all of this magic, Sages, Trident Republic nonsense. My family is safe at home as we speak, and the second all this is over, I get to go home. There will be no gallivanting across God's green earth for *my* relatives. As soon as I stop the Trident Republic—which I will—I'm taking the first jet home, where I will take a nice, big, long nap."

Blythe clenches her teeth. The only thing keeping her from attacking Cordelia is the weight of Daniel's terrified gaze.

"Don't get haughty," she snaps. "There is *nothing* you know that I can't get out of Katia."

Cordelia's lashes don't even flutter. "You're an idiot if you think she's actually going to tell us everything."

EIGHT

THEY EAT WITHOUT SPEAKING, BARELY ACKNOWLEDGING THE presence of anyone else at the table.

Cordelia's nails tap against her phone and Katia's knife clinks against the plate as she cuts into her omelet. Blythe hopes to find some company with Daniel, but he stares at an invisible spot on the table, pressing his lips into a fine, worried line.

Friendship sure is great.

When their plates are clear, Katia pays the bill and only tells them where they're going when they're already walking in the opposite direction of the Tempore.

"It's called Gilded," she says, and does not elaborate.

Gilded, it turns out, is a small shop bearing the full name "The Gilded Wardrobe". *Thrifted Goods,* reads the subtitle on the sign sticking in the withered lawn.

It is a weathered, single floor building with no windows. It is also completely unimpressive.

"I hate to sound like Cordelia, but...we're going thrift shopping? Now?" Blythe asks.

Cordelia doesn't even grace her with a glare, and Katia shoves the door open without bothering to hold it open behind her.

Blythe snatches hold of it. How chivalrous.

"Hey!" Shouts someone inside. "Don't leave the door open, you'll let in a draft!"

"It's at least seventy degrees," Cordelia grumbles.

"A draft of hot air," the voice amends.

The items in the Gilded Wardrobe are crowded together and slightly askew, making the space feel more like someone's neatly organized attic than an actual store.

Rows of clothes form messy racks in the center of the room, while bookcases line the walls, displaying cups, vases, silverware and other knick-knacks.

At the front of the room is a glass display case, where pieces of fine jewelry glitter inside.

The cash register rests atop it, and behind that register, on a stool, is a young man. Judging from his head of shaggy dark hair, the comically large glasses on his nose, and his very tired expression, he's probably a college student.

He's watching Katia as she looks through the bookshelves. "I remember you," he says. "How's that cape holding up?"

"It's been great but, for the record," She sends him a look over her shoulder. "It's a cloak. I don't wear capes."

"Okay, Dracula," says the boy.

Blythe is walking before she realizes it, following a line of items, each more interesting than the last. A miniature glass airplane hangs from the ceiling and refracts light onto a silver globe, spinning atop a table covered in abstract art. Blythe has to say, she doesn't hate this place.

A row of Matryoshka dolls sit on the edge of the table, smiling cheekily. They are round and porcelain, each more dainty than the last, but they emit...an energy. A magical energy.

Blythe steps back. She looks around the shop again. It's like a blindfold has been stripped from her senses.

Her skin prickles with chills. The Gilded Wardrobe appears the same, but every item, every nook and cranny, even the very walls, *everything* hums with magic.

"...what *is* all this?" Blythe asks.

The boy's tired eyes lock on her. "This is called a store. You can buy things here, with money. Money can be exchanged for goods and services."

Great, another smartass. "Hilarious," Blythe quips. "I meant is it all..." She lets her voice trail off to imply the word. The *m* word.

A small smile curls on the boy's face. "Nobody's gonna arrest you for saying 'magical' in here, it's safe. And yes, we sell people's donated magical items. Speaking of—" the boy looks past her. "—is that a grimoire?"

Blythe glances over her shoulder—and is shocked to see that the boy is speaking to Daniel.

Daniel jumps. He presses the small book to his chest. "Y-Yes. I-It's mine."

"Fascinating," says the Register Boy. "Where'd you find it? Those things are usually *ancient*."

But Daniel's face twists and his shoulders set tight. Blythe's never seen him upset before—she didn't know he *could* get upset.

"*I* made it," he snaps.

"*What?*" Blythe blurts.

A stillness falls over the room. Even at the back, Katia looks at Daniel with new eyes.

The Register Boy raises an inquisitive eyebrow. "Why'd you make a grimoire?"

Daniel's gaze drops to his feet. He does not speak.

"And what, pray tell, is a grimoire?" Cordelia asks. She's still by the doorway, as if her ears are deaf to the Gilded Wardrobe's siren song.

"It's a book of Learned Magic rituals and information. A spell book," Katia speaks while her gaze burns through Daniel.

The people who make grimoires are experts with a deep,

unparalleled understanding of magic. They are scholars and thaumologists who have studied their craft for *years*. And yet Daniel is here with one of his own making.

"What's it for?" Blythe asks.

Color blooms from the tip of Daniel's hairline to the bottom of his neck. Still, he does not speak.

"Well, this magic shop is unaffiliated to any government and any magician rules, so we don't judge here," The boy leans over the counter, extending his palm. "Mind if I take a look?"

Daniel clutches his little leather book so hard, his knuckles turn white. His eyes have gone wide, but his jaw is set firm. Translation: *absolutely not*.

The boy sighs, plopping back onto his stool. "Oh-kay then, nevermind."

And just like that, the conversation is over.

Blythe isn't sure what to feel. Learned Magic isn't inherently *evil*, it's just another form of magic. In fact, the cloaker used to conceal the Full Cup Café was Learned Magic.

But if Daniel isn't doing anything wrong, why is he being so secretive? He could just be nervous. Or maybe there's something more at hand.

Either way, he isn't going to speak about it now, so Blythe moves on. She drifts over to the clothes, looking through enchanted prom dresses from the eighties and business blazers with unknown origins.

Katia heads to the register carrying a pile of throwing knives, setting them before the Register Boy.

He studies them for a moment, then taps the edge of his glasses. The coppery metal flicks out rows upon rows of lens, descending in scale, like a Victorian watchmaker's glasses.

"More throwing knives?" he plucks one up. "These are still in mint condition. Do I have to give you the whole spiel or—"

"No, I know," Katia interrupts.

Blythe's not sure how Katia's been here before. If she was in Broughton earlier, why not pick up Daniel?

It makes Blythe grind her teeth. Too many things about Katia Darkholme are confusing. Too many things don't add up.

She parts through a line of hanging blouses and spots a hockey stick lying on the carpet. It's blue—Blythe's favorite color—with white stripes shooting up its side.

Blythe's never played hockey in her life, but for some reason she likes the energy rising from this thing. She kneels to wraps a hand around its handle; the material chills her skin, like it hasn't been touched in years.

She likes it.

"Um, excuse me?" she calls. Katia and Register Boy stare at her as she holds the hockey stick up. "What's this?"

The lines of lenses make Register Boy's eyes bug-like and huge as he squints.

"Oh," he says. "It's an enchanted hockey stick. It's been there for a while though, I don't really remember what it does."

He ducks behind the glass case and pops back up with a Zadis tablet. After scrolling a bit, he says, "It's an average hockey stick, but, when swung backward, the stick charges and builds up energy. When struck against an object or—oh my god, this is really ominous— living creature, it exerts that energy into a blast of force. The impact of their force depends on the magical ability and intent of the wielder." He pauses. "And when the tip is held out it fires beams of light like laser beams."

Blythe knows a joke when she hears one. "Funny."

"No, I'm serious," the boy insists. "That's what the description says. Sounds like a powerful item. It's enchanted using Learned Magic, obviously, and the Element of Ether."

Ah. Maybe *that's* why Blythe likes it. Ether is, after all, her Element.

Katia smirks at Blythe as if she's realized this too. "Unsurprising," she says. "Too bad I never said you could buy anything."

"Aw, what?" Blythe whines. "*You're* getting something."

Katia cocks an eyebrow. "Yeah but it's not a weapon."

"They're *throwing knives!*"

Katia is clearly messing with her. "And they cut a mean steak. You don't know what I'm using them for."

"I watched you kill a monster with them! Your jokes suck!"

A loud groan echoes through the shop. "Can you just let her get the hockey stick so we can leave?" Cordelia huffs.

Katia gives Blythe a once over. Blythe tightens her grip on the hockey stick. If Register Boy was telling the truth, she could use this thing to defend herself. She wouldn't have to worry about being powerless ever again.

And if Katia doesn't buy it, Blythe'll just have to find her way back here once she finally manages to—

"Fine, I'll buy it," Katia relents.

"You may need something to hold that in," Register Boy says, and disappears behind the display case.

He returns with some sort of leather sling that reminds Blythe of a fantasy scabbard; except instead of a rounded end, there are two openings.

Huh. "That's...weirdly convenient," Blythe says. "...thanks."

"Anybody else wanna get some weird shit?" Katia asks. "It's Christmas and I'm Reluctant Santa Claus."

Daniel holds up a bouquet of withered, odd looking flowers. Katia's nose wrinkles. "Eew. You really want that?"

Daniel bobs his head.

"Why?" Katia spits.

"I need it," Daniel whispers.

Katia recoils. "Holy *shit,* I thought you were mute. Alright, fine, go ahead." She turns to the only other Guardian. "What about you?"

Cordelia's arms are folded, hip poked out. "I'd rather die."

"I *wish* you were mute," Katia mutters.

Katia pays for their items and they leave the shop with her throwing knives hidden in her cloak, Blythe's hockey stick slung across her back, and Daniel's flowers in a plastic thank-you-for-shopping bag.

Blythe waves goodbye to Register Boy as they go.

"Come again," he says. "Or don't. It's fine either way, honestly."

———

Despite time ticking into the afternoon, Broughton is no more alive than it was that morning. The only difference is that Blythe no longer fears what could be following them, or following *her*.

The hockey stick is awkward to carry, but the warm, magical energy emanating from it is comforting. Blythe *dares* someone to come fuck with her.

Naturally, Katia leads their group. She hasn't mentioned where she's taking them, but they seem to be returning to the Tempore. Cordelia struts close behind her, her face skewed into an almost permanent scowl.

Daniel, meanwhile, hides his small body behind Blythe, more shuffling his feet than walking. Something about him reminds Blythe of her sisters, how they waddle awkwardly around unfamiliar places. The memory of them is as endearing as it is painful.

"So..." Blythe looks over her shoulder. Daniel's shoulders are nearly hunched into his ears. "Are you excited to go to Frost Glade?"

If Daniel looked terrified before, he looks like he's about to burst into tears now.

Blythe tries to stay cheery. "Is that a no?"

Daniel shakes his head frantically, his curls flying around his face. "I-I-I think someone's following us."

The only person of interest is yards behind them: a man in a black suit. He is still and staring at them.

Behind him, a black truck turns onto the street and creeps toward them. It doesn't fit here in Broughton, with its massive size and boxy, modern cut.

Blythe forces herself to breathe. Men wear suits all the time. Maybe that man just lives here.

But deep, deep down, the truth burns in her stomach. She knows the Erasers when she sees them.

"What's going on?" Katia asks.

She's gone still, her cloak like a shadow along her body. Cordelia studies Blythe, watching her trembling hands, the gape of her mouth.

Calm down, Blythe tells herself, steadying her nerves. "Nothing."

Katia sneers. "No, not 'nothing'. If something's going on, you need to tell me."

Blythe hesitates. Daniel picks at the hem of his sweater. She can see his pleading expression in the corner of her gaze.

"I think..." her voice trails off. "I think we're being followed."

The truck is halfway to them now. Katia's eyes flicker to it. She does not look shocked, confused, or angry. Her face simply goes blank.

"Just keep up," she says.

Her pace is brisk—not quick enough to be a run, too hasty to be a walk. Blythe grabs Daniel by the arm and drags him to her side as they approach an intersection.

The four of them are dead center in the road when the ground shakes. The sound of approaching tires hits Blythe's ears.

The black truck drives straight toward her.

Katia flicks her wrist. A blast of wind shoots past her, bursting into the truck's hood.

The wheels squeal and swerve as the truck sways into a lamppost, metal crunching like paper. Smoke rises from the crushed hood. But no one emerges.

The man at the end of the street still lingers. Except another, identical man has joined him, standing across the road, watching, unblinking.

Blythe spots another face farther behind them, almost unseen, behind a shop window.

They are all around, from the alleys to the shops. Hidden, unseen. The figures in black suits. The Erasers.

They have followed Blythe before, and they have watched her. But they've never sent a truck after her.

She's never seen so many of them before. She gets the cold, creeping feeling that their faces may be the last thing she'll *ever* see.

A gust of air soars around Blythe. For a moment, fear shoots through her—has that man returned? The one who broke into the café?

She can hear the screams of her mother, her father, the twins. Her heart races, thumping against her ribs, and she cannot catch her breath—

But there is only Katia, shoulders set square as the wind dances through her cloak. Her expression is impassive.

The winds are under *her* control. Whatever her magic is, it must allow her to control the air.

Her gaze catches on the faces of the Erasers, shifting easily from one to the next. "Okay kids," she whispers. "Who remembers how to get back to the Tempore?"

Cordelia speaks up. "I do." Blythe hopes to God she isn't lying. If they don't do something, they're *all* getting Erased.

"Good," Katia says. "I'll meet you there."

"W-W-We have to go alone?!" Daniel stammers.

Katia scans the suited figures in the distance. "There's some business that needs handling here. Just start walking and stay calm."

Cordelia hurries across the street, her back turned to the flood of Erasers in the distance. Blythe hurries after her, pulling Daniel in her wake.

If they move quickly enough, if they do no provoke them, they just might reach the Tempore in one piece. Maybe.

But something strange happens. A voice enters Blythe's mind that is not her own; but it is not unfamiliar.

I know you're frightened, Cordelia speaks in the same fluid manner as Blythe's own thoughts. *But I can hear these people's thoughts, and I can hear where they are. I can keep us from running into them, but you have to stay quiet and you must follow me.*

116

Cordelia does not stop walking, her fists balled tight at her sides.

Blythe thoughts flow instantly, without filter. *You're in my head? How? Could you always read minds? Have you been reading my mind this entire time?*

The frustrated shake of Cordelia's head is Blythe's only proof that it actually *is* Cordelia in her mind.

Why would I care about what you think?! Her voice returns. *Focus on what I've said!*

You're absolutely insufferable when you're being bossy but do your thing, I guess, Blythe thinks, and she audibly hears Cordelia scoff.

Daniel, who is usually quite pink, looks white as snow. "W-W-What's happening?!"

Blythe glances over her shoulder. At the end of the street stand two suited men. Watching.

"Just keep up with us, Dan," Blythe whispers.

Streets blur as they rush down them, too similar to discern. But the suited figures no longer appear in the distance.

With each step Blythe takes, they seem to edge forward. Each white face appears closer than the last. And their numbers are growing.

Blythe has run from the Erasers like this before, racing on foot with her parents. It wasn't effective. If they keep up this pace, they will be ambushed.

New plan, Blythe thinks, hoping Cordelia can hear her. *Get behind me.*

"What?!" Cordelia asks.

Blythe doesn't wait to explain. She darts to the center of the street, feet set square on either side of the yellow dividing line.

There is no guarantee that her plan will work. But she can't wait to see what will happen if the Erasers corner them.

Plus, she's itching for an excuse to use this thing.

"Get behind me, Daniel!" she screams. His curls bounce as he runs behind her.

Cordelia has gone shock still with indignant confusion. A suited figure appears in the storefront behind her.

"*Cordelia!*" Blythe screams.

Cordelia's fists ball and her nose wrinkles. Muttering under her breath, she hurries into the street.

Before Blythe is an empty street plagued with ghosts of people that are not people, men that are not men.

She takes in a long, deep breath and draws the hockey stick from her back.

"Alright," Blythe mutters. "Let's see what you can do."

The stick's weight shifts in her hands as she raises it above her head. It hums with energy; tension builds as it floods with magic, filling until the power leaks into her palms, drips down her arms, into her shoulders.

God, Blythe has always wanted to get back at the Erasers.

Blythe arms the stick through the air and slams it into the asphalt. An explosion ripples through the ground, cracking the street in thousands of crumbling pieces.

Buildings shake. Chunks of brick drop onto the sidewalk. Trees shutter as fissures race up their trunks.

Blythe has brought an earthquake to Broughton.

As quickly as it starts, it is over. The street is still.

Blythe searches for the men's faces; she checks the alleys, the trees, the ends of the streets, the windows. There are no figures. The Erasers are gone.

A booming laugh bursts from her. She has never, not once in her entire life, made the Erasers *run* from her. And here she stands today.

If only her parents could see her now. Her father would sweep her into his arms, her mother would scream with pride and joy.

If only. If only.

Her eyes sting from just the thought of them, but she quickly blinks them away. She checks over her shoulder to keep herself from crying.

Cordelia and Daniel are unharmed—but they are also splayed out on the ground. Daniel's eyes are open as wide as his mouth.

Cordelia gives Blythe a withering glare. (She's kind of cute when she's angry. Or maybe that's just the surge of magic talking.)

"Sorry," Blythe smiles. "Still gotta get the hang of it."

"You're *mad*," Cordelia growls.

Blythe outstretches a hand to help her up anyway. "And *you* were leading us back to the Tempore, so let's hurry up before those guys realize I don't actually know what I'm doing."

Cordelia makes a face, standing up on her own. Daniel rises too, neatly brushing pebbles of asphalt from his khakis.

Blythe wants to point out that she saved Cordelia's life; there was an Eraser right behind her, literally inches away from snatching her out of reality.

But if Cordelia can hear thoughts, then she must already know this. And if she can read thoughts, then she must already know that Blythe does not hate her, and all she wants is to find her family again. Which means that, whatever angry demon lives inside Cordelia, it's a creature she manifested on her own—one that has absolutely nothing to do with anyone else.

Cordelia leads them back to the hill outside of the Tempore without a hitch. Blythe dramatically collapses onto the grass, staring up at the string of clouds drifting through the baby blue sky.

The hockey stick makes her feel like she's lying on an iron rail, so it isn't the most comfortable position, but still. She fought the Erasers. And *got away*.

She's been waiting her whole life to do that.

A figure with an echoing cloak floats into her line of sight. "You know, when I saw those people, I expected someone actually threatening," Katia says.

Blythe immediately flashes back to that night in the Full Cup, the way the air escaped her lungs, how it threw her to the ground.

Katia lands on easy, gentle feet. "They were gone in a matter of minutes," she says. "Left as soon as I put up a fight. I was afraid someone had sent them—"

"Someone like the Trident Republic?" Blythe interrupts.

She doesn't know why she said it. Maybe because she is suspicious and high off of momentary power. Maybe because she's tired of Katia.

Katia grimaces. She's getting tired of hearing that phrase from Blythe's mouth.

"Speaking of," Blythe continues. She pushes to her feet. "You know an awful lot about this situation."

"What?" Katia asks.

Blythe could leave this alone. Claim it's nothing and shut up. But something builds in her chest—pride, suspicion, hurt, or a mix of all three—and forces the words out.

"From the Trident Republic, to Walden Oliver and Rue Whiteclaw. And while we're at it..." Blythe narrows her eyes. "*I* never knew you could control the wind."

For a moment, Katia only stares at her. Then she draws herself up. She starts toward Blythe, eyes steeled like a bull charging forward.

Blythe forces herself to stay put, to stare Katia down, even though the woman towers over her in her seven-inch-heels.

"Listen, *little girl*," Katia spits. "I had nothing to do with what happened to your family. You think because I use Inherited Magic to control the weather, it means I helped kidnap your family?"

Silence falls. It occurs to Blythe, as she stares into the dark fire that is Katia's eyes, that she may have made a mistake.

"I haven't told you anything because you don't *need* to know anything. You're a sixteen-year-old girl who is dumb enough to try and get herself killed running off to Electric City. You don't deserve information. I'm not here to coddle you and make you feel better. I'm not your mom. I'm not your babysitter. And I don't give a single *shit* about your feelings. The only thing I'm here to do is get you to Frost Glade and I am not getting paid enough to patiently deal with your bullshit. The next time you come for me, I will have you *blown* into that city in a goddamn hurricane. So shut the fuck up and take a fucking seat."

Cordelia stares unblinkingly at Blythe. Daniel keeps his head down.

Without another word, Katia slips into the trees.

NINE

Winter has slipped into the Tempore. The cold sears straight through Blythe's clothes. The grass is buried beneath smooth, untouched snow. Sheets of ice coat the logs and newly barren trees. The air smells of frost and snowflakes fall in flurries, grabbing hold of every surface they touch.

"I-I-It's June," Daniel stammers. "Why...why is it snowing in June?"

Katia pulls her cloak tighter across her shoulders; it moves over her like a shadow. "Because something's not right. The Tempore is magic and it may not have consistent weather, but it never changes seasons like this."

The difference is palpable. It's like the energy in the air has changed; it has quieted and become something...worrying.

The sky is a blanket of black. There is no sound besides their feet crunching the snow. This place is no longer the serene forest it was when they left.

"I think someone's messing with the Tempore," Katia says.

Daniel lets out a tiny, scared shriek.

Katia glowers at him. "Are you dying?" she asks.

Of course, he doesn't answer.

Katia grumbles as she keeps walking. The Guardians follow, and Blythe tucks her hands under her arms to hold back shivers.

"So, we were right earlier," Comes Cordelia's voice behind Blythe. "The Trident Republic *is* in the Tempore."

"Most likely," Katia mumbles. Her mind seems to be elsewhere. "Flexing their strength by taking one of our biggest assets. Trying to piss the Sages off enough to make them declare war."

"I knew stopping for breakfast was a mistake," Cordelia's face is flushed pink, her lips set tight in annoyance. "You all ignore me because you don't like what I'm saying, but I'm the only one who seems to understand the gravity of this situation—I'm *right*. We need to stop—"

Katia's cape echoes as she spins around. "Speak again. I dare you."

Cordelia stares her down, but does not dare.

They finish their walk in silence. Nobody wants to talk under Katia's dictatorship. If something doesn't change before they get to Frost Glade, this is going to be the worst journey of Blythe's life.

The snow is fluffy and fresh enough for Katia to simply wipe it off the windshield before getting the keys from Blythe and starting up the engine.

Blythe takes the passenger seat, as per usual, leaving Daniel and Cordelia in the backseat. They've barely been driving for ten minutes, plowing effortlessly through the snow, before Katia's phone rings.

Katia sandwiches it between her shoulder and her ear. "What is it, Val?"

A male voice responds. "Hello to you as well, my dear. We've received a worrying report on the Tempore. I'd suggest your steer clear for the foreseeable future."

"Too late, we're already in it," Katia mumbles. "I'm looking for the nearest exit as we speak. Are the Sages going to issue a statement?"

"The media beat them to it. People are panicking."

Katia fumbles with the radio, scanning through stations until she hits a magician frequency. "*—This is Alastair French here to report that everything's going to—excuse my French—shit. The Tempore seems to be under enemy control and is deemed unsafe for civilian travel—*"

Katia curses under her breath.

"But I've an ulterior motive for calling," the voice continues. "And I want to apologize sincerely for what I'm about to ask of you."

Katia rolls her eyes. "Spit it out, Prince Charming."

The voice, Val, hesitates. "I need you to aid us in the search."

"What do you need to know?"

"Nothing. We need you *here*."

Blythe ears perk up. She keeps herself from looking too alert, focusing her attention on the passing branches weighed down by snow.

If Katia takes this Val person up on his offer, she'll probably have to leave the Guardians unattended, at least momentarily.

That'd give Blythe a clear way out without *any* hassle.

She has a weapon now and she can probably figure out how to use the Tempore. If she could survive the Erasers, surely she could survive Electric City.

Not to mention, if she could convince them, Cordelia and Daniel may even join her. She won't even be alone.

She could really do this.

"What?" Katia blurts. "Val, I have to get the Guardians in under a day. As of right now, I've only gotten three and—"

Her gaze flickers to Blythe before she whispers something too low for Blythe to catch. Maybe it's about her family. But it could honestly be about anything. Katia isn't the most trustworthy person in the world.

"I'm sorry to hear that," Val replies. "But no one knows him as well as you do. My men are running out of options. It's as if he's disappeared into thin air."

"I wouldn't put that past him."

Desperation bleeds through Val's voice. "Katia, please."

Katia's grip on the wheel tightens. Whoever Val is searching for seems to have a very emotional impact on Katia, if the heavy look in her eyes is any indication.

"Try his old apartment in Virginia," she says. "If you don't find him, you'll probably find some clues. Worse case scenario, you'll have to visit the Fae Lands. But I seriously have to go, Val, I can't...I can't help you. I'm sorry."

It is the first time Blythe has heard Katia apologize.

"Don't worry, we'll make it work," Val says. "Go on with your journey. Good luck to you, my dear."

Katia sets her phone into the empty cupholder. No one asks who she spoke to, or what that conversation was about.

If Blythe had to guess, she would assume that Val is looking for someone in the Trident Republic—which only strengthens Blythe's assumption that Katia has ties to them.

Katia Darkholme cannot be trusted.

They arrive at the line of seven trees again, the space between their trunks just as dark as Blythe remember. Even though snow falls around them, nothing moves or shifts in their darkness.

When the van plunges into the shadows, the world is extinguished until sunlight reappears, and suddenly they are driving out of a patch of trees and onto a road. It seems that the seven trees represent an exit; their darkness is a multi-purpose exit back into the real world.

Katia is entirely unphased. "We'll have to get to San Diego, California using nothing but highways. Which is about as annoying as you can imagine."

And it is. The drive lasts hours; Blythe watches the sun shift places in the sky as the hours drip past, until her body grows cramped and tired and Daniel gets carsick in the backseat.

They stop for meals cooked with too much oil and wrapped in

crinkly foil. Their bathroom breaks take place in abandoned rest stops with worrying odors.

The sky melts from day to night. When stars take over the sky, Katia drives the van toward a tall, spiraling white building.

It looks like a magician's hotel, especially judging from the lights that shine down from balconies, into the parking lot. But the air is calm and still, as if there is no magic to be found.

"Is this a magicians' hotel?" Cordelia asks. Blythe wouldn't be surprised if Cordelia stole the question right out of Blythe's own head.

"No," Katia says. "Just a boujee one."

Blythe wishes she could rest. Honesty, nothing sounds better than burying herself under a pile of cool, crisp blankets and finally shutting her eyes.

But within a few hours, Katia will be asleep and the van will be in the parking lot. This is the perfect opportunity to escape.

If Blythe's going to leave, it needs to be now.

The words *"THE THORNE"* hang in bold, golden letters above the revolving glass doors. Blythe whistles low as they step into an expansive golden foyer with shiny tile and white sofas.

As if the four sparkling chandeliers weren't extravagant enough, a fountain spews arcs of water in front of a glass elevator.

"Finally, we're staying somewhere *normal*," Cordelia snorts.

The Guardians head for the comfortable seating and complimentary chocolates while Katia approaches the front desk.

"Is Willow working tonight?" Blythe hears her ask.

"No, not tonight," replies the man. "Can I help you with anything?"

Katia sighs. "Two rooms'll be fine."

Blythe wonders who this Willow person is, but the conversation becomes a simple exchange of identification and payment.

Cordelia and Daniel are pretending everyone else doesn't exist, so Blythe slouches and takes out her phone. Her first task is to text Jamie to let them know she's alright and still alive.

She's watching Instagram stories when Katia walks up to them, keycards and two brown paper bags in hand. "Daniel, you're with me. Cords and Blythe, you're in the room across the hall."

The glass elevator smoothly escorts them to their floor, where Katia and Daniel disappear into their room, leaving Blythe and Cordelia to their own devices.

The hotel has gone above and beyond with their amenities. They have two beds with white sheets and overstuffed pillows that are practically calling Blythe's name, plus a huge flat screen and a view of the city that is absolutely sublime.

But Blythe has a mission.

Cordelia sits on the edge of the closest bed, already unlacing her wedge sandals. Blythe, however, lingers near the door.

"I'm leaving tonight," she announces.

Cordelia doesn't even look up from her feet. "I figured," she replies. "Well, goodbye."

Exactly what Blythe thought she'd say.

Blythe could just leave. Rough it through Electric City with just her hockey stick and, maybe, Daniel. But Cordelia is a competent hacker and a *mind reader*.

The advantages of having someone like that on Blythe's side are too many to count. Leaving her behind would be foolish.

So Blythe sighs, leaning against the door. If she wants Cordelia to come, she's going to have to speak her language.

"Listen. I know it seems like I was being annoying for no reason with the whole 'wind magic' thing, but I really don't think Katia is trustworthy. *Or safe.*"

Cordelia doesn't look at her. But she doesn't speak either.

"The man who called her asked for help finding someone. She told him he may have to go into the Fae Lands. And who did she say was allied with the Fae? The Trident Republic. She *also* mentioned having a friend in the Black Veins Imperial Army, the same army who is currently searching for Walden Oliver. And who did you ask her about, when she refused to answer your question? Walden Oliver.

And finally, let's be real," Blythe pauses for effect. "Do you really think the Sages would send *one* person to get all six Guardians?"

Boom. Blythe resists the urge to mime a mic drop.

Cordelia's hair falls along her back as she raises her head, eying her. "I'm a mind reader, Blythe," she says. "You just want to find your family."

"Yeah, and?" Blythe retorts. "You want to stop the Trident Republic so you can go back home. You think Katia's going to let you do that?"

Cordelia glares at her.

"Do what you want," Blythe says. "But I'm going to do what'll work in my favor."

Cordelia sits up straight. Blythe isn't sure what to expect from her—Cordelia Deleon isn't always the most predictable person. Especially since Blythe's never been able to prove her wrong before.

Cordelia stands, goes into the bathroom in the back of the room, and shuts the door.

Well, maybe that conversation went about as well as it could have. At least Blythe tried.

She sinks into the mountain of pillows on the second bed, scrolling through Instagram until Cordelia leaves the bathroom, which doesn't happen until a whole thirty minutes later.

Cordelia doesn't speak to Blythe, only raises her chin a bit higher as Blythe passes her. Whatever. Blythe cares more about this amazing shower she's about to take.

Under the warm water, Blythe tends to her curls and her skin. Her leg is healing quickly and the burn is coming along as well. She doesn't have time to indulge in her usual routines, but at least she can make herself look presentable.

Blythe expects to see Cordelia fast asleep when she emerges, silk sleep mask covering her face and hair braided.

Instead, Cordelia sits on the edge of her bed, fully dressed and applying gloss to her lips through a handheld mirror.

"Well," she says to her reflection. "Let's go."

"You're coming?" Blythe is too stunned to think of a better response.

Cordelia rolls her eyes. "I know you aren't *that* dense, Blythe. We haven't got all night."

"Actually, we kinda do—y'know what, nevermind, I'm not gonna press my luck."

Blythe has to toss her things into her backpack to be ready by the time Cordelia is heading into the hallway. You'd think this was *her* mission by the way she's strutting around. But maybe she's just more confident in her abilities than Blythe.

Blythe lowers her voice as she closes the door behind them. "How long have you been reading minds?" She asks. "Like, before you knew about magic?"

"No. It started happening after the roof incident. I assume that exposure to magic made it—" Cordelia catches herself and makes a face. "This has nothing to do with anything."

"Just trying to make conversation," Blythe shrugs. "Can you do that mind thing and tell Daniel to come out?"

Cordelia turns up her lip. "And make him scream out of surprise because he's never experienced that before?"

"Alright, fair," Blythe relents. "Do we have his phone number?"

Cordelia tosses her head back with a dramatic eye-roll. "Why are we bothering with him? He's a liability."

"I am *not* leaving him. Plus, Katia has the keys to the van. We need to get in there."

A pause descends between them, Blythe unyielding, Cordelia narrowing her eyes and, seemingly, weighing her options.

"Fine," Cordelia finally says. "I'll do it."

But instead of using magic, she whips out her phone. Blythe does wait patiently—at first. The minutes tick by.

"Um," Blythe says. "If he's not answering, we could just—"

"I wasn't texting him," Cordelia interrupts.

There's no time to ask what she *was* doing, because the keycard slot turns green.

"Holy shit," Blythe whispers. "Did you just hack through a locked door? Is that a thing? That can't be a thing."

Cordelia only presses a finger to her lips as she eases the door open.

The room is dark, but not too dark for Blythe to make out Katia sleeping in the far bed. Daniel is curled under the blankets near the door, staring at the wall.

He sits up as they enter. Thank God he's quiet; Blythe doesn't have to worry about him waking Katia.

Blythe points Cordelia toward Katia. She doesn't have to explain: Cordelia already knows to go find the keys.

Blythe, meanwhile, kneels beside Daniel. "We need to leave," she whispers. "I'll explain in the car."

Daniel studies her face; his eyes are wide with fear but his brow is wrinkled with confusion.

"You can stay if you want," Blythe continues. "But me and Cordelia are going to try and get to Electric City. It'll be dangerous, and it'll take a while, so you don't have to come if you don't want to. I just wanted to give you the option."

Daniel looks down. Cordelia's in the doorway now, raising the keys in her hand. *Hurry up,* her stretched eyes say.

Daniel seems to be debating, fingers digging into the bed as his brow wrinkles.

Katia shifts. The mattress groans under her weight.

"Okay, time to go, speak now or forever hold your peace," Blythe rushes.

Daniel's jaw clenches. He tosses the sheets off of himself and points over Blythe's shoulder.

A leather bag slouches against the mattress: his stuff. Blythe grabs it in time to see Daniel reach under his pillow and take his grimoire.

"You sleep with that thing?" Blythe asks. "Isn't that uncomfortable?"

Cordelia storms out of the doorway.

"We'll chat in the car," Blythe says, and runs after her.

They are three teenagers with stuffed backpacks rushing into the parking lot, but the hotel staff pays them little attention besides a few suspicious glances.

Blythe has never been happier to unlock the van and curl her fingers around its steering wheel. She smiles so hard it almost hurts. She's back, baby.

The tires sing as Blythe rips out of the lot, leaving the Thorn to shrink smaller and smaller in her rearview mirror.

Cordelia's rolls down the window, closing her eyes against the wind that bursts inside to greet them. A laugh grows and bubbles out of Blythe.

They did it. They're gone.

"You okay back there, Daniell?" Blythe asks.

He seems bothered by something. "I'm outside in my pajamas," he observes.

Blythe grins at him. "I have a feeling that's gonna be one of the least weird things that happens to us."

Cordelia brushes a few stray strands of hair from her face. "So, what's the plan? Are we stopping somewhere or going straight to the city?"

Blythe considers this. They don't *need* to stop anywhere. But... there are a couple places they *could* stop at.

Katia was right about one thing—Blythe will never survive in Electric City on her own. Yes, she has Daniel and Cordelia, but imagine if she had more.

It'll take more than two people to help her brave Electric City— Blythe's going to need a team.

"First," Blythe says. "We're going to California."

Cordelia cocks an eyebrow. "California? What for?"

"Because," Blythe begins. "We're gonna find the other Guardians."

Cordelia rolls her eyes, so Blythe starts explaining before she can

131

interrupt. "Katia was shady, but I don't think she was lying when she said Electric City was dangerous. We're gonna need help if we don't want to die there. The other four Guardians are our best bet. Er, three Guardians. Whatever, we'll get whoever we can get."

Cordelia groans, pressing two pastel pink nails against her temple as if to pry Blythe's thoughts out of her head.

"Let me just make something *abundantly* clear," she snaps. "I am not coming along to feed your ego. My goal is to get the Trident Republic off my back so I can live my normal, non-magical, Common life. Don't assume I'll be giving up my own resources to help you. I'm not *with* you."

Blythe scoffs. The longer she's around this girl, the less all of her talk matters. "Whatever, Cordelia."

Silence falls, leaving the hum of the engine as the only sound between them.

"*I'm* with Blythe," Daniel whispers.

Blythe smiles. "Thank you, Daniel."

TEN

THEY TRAVEL UNDER MOONLIGHT AND STREETLIGHTS, PAUSING only at red lights and speeding forward the second they turn green.

Cordelia sits with her legs crossed prettily, chin on her palm. With her flawless flushed skin and pastel pink dress, Blythe could snap a picture of her and place it on the cover of a magazine.

"Your entire plan relies on the assumption that the other Guardians have something to offer," Cordelia says.

And, of course, they've barely been on the road for twenty minutes and she's already complaining.

"One of them is the Guardian of Death," Blythe says. "They should be able to do *something*."

Cordelia tilts her head. "You want to kill people?"

"Well, maybe they could like, stand near us and be scary so no one bothers us."

"They're the Guardian of Death, it's not like they have a stun setting," Cordelia spits. "Looking for these Guardians will waste time. We have a lead on Katia, but since we can't use the Tempore—"

"Oh," Blythe interrupts. "We're still using the Tempore."

Daniel's gone pale in the back. "B-But the Trident Republic stole it!"

"The Trident Republic steals lots of things, including my family and peace of mind, but you don't see that stopping me," Blythe says. "We'll never make it anywhere if we don't use it. If something attacks us, we'll just...hide."

"But we could get lost," Daniel protests, as if being lost is one of the worst fates to befall man.

"Oh, that reminds me," Cordelia says. "Daniel, hand me the cloak back there."

Blythe can barely get her words out. "The wh—*you stole Katia's cloak?!*"

Sure enough, Daniel passes Katia's black echoing cloak into Cordelia's hands.

"It was on the chair beside the keys," Cordelia explains coolly. "I figured she may have some clues in here. Now, how does this—"

Her words cut off with a scream. She's absolutely fine, besides the fact that her hand has disappeared into the cloak, the darkness reaching up to her pale wrist.

"Whoa," Blythe breathes. "That's cool."

"My hand is in there!" Cordelia yells.

"Better yours than mine."

That snaps Cordelia back to her senses. She rolls her eyes, collecting herself before she plunges both hands into the cloak.

A horn honks, bringing Blythe's attention back to the road. If she keeps glancing at what Cordelia's doing, the only place they'll end up is inside a wrapped around a pole.

"There are some loose dollars here," Cordelia says. Items clink together as she sifts through them. "And...a compass?"

"It has to be magical somehow," Blythe says.

"Whatever. Um...more cash. Christ, there's so many things."

Apparently, Katia's rolling in dough. Maybe she won't mind if they borrow some of it. After all, this is, technically, an emergency.

Blythe glances into the rearview mirror. "Hey Daniel, what's your phone number?"

"I-I don't own a phone," Daniel stammers.

"Well, shit," Blythe exclaims. "Why not?"

"I-I never needed one."

Of course. If he never left his house and his family communicated via handwritten letters, what use would a cell phone be?

"Well, you'll need one now," Blythe says. "We can stop and get you one. Looks like we've got cash to spare."

Cordelia tries to argue about rationing it, but Blythe points out that they'll need to contact Daniel if the three of them ever get separated.

Cordelia's voice echoes in her mind. *I don't think we should be spending money on someone that's expendable.*

Blythe almost balks aloud. *I can't believe you just came into* my *head and said that to me. We're getting him a damn phone; he's not expendable, he's a* person.

Cordelia side eyes her. *An expendable person.*

"We'd have to pay for phone service as well," Cordelia adds aloud.

"There are apps for that," Blythe snaps.

"What are apps?" Daniel asks.

Admittedly, Daniel Quinton is a piece of work—but he is *not* expendable.

Blythe explains the concept as best she can, but modern technology is such a puzzle to Daniel that she doubts any of it makes sense to him.

They soon come to an intersection bustling with activity. On the other side lies a forest of trees, branches bent like heavy arms toward the trampled grass.

Blythe takes in a steadying breath. "God I hope this works."

If they don't get into the Tempore, they'll certainly get into an accident.

Cordelia sits up bolt right. "Blythe, we can't drive straight through an intersection! Are you crazy?!"

"Little bit!" Blythe yells, and slams the gas.

Blythe summons all of her will and magic as the needle climbs. Her grip tightens on the wheel.

Take us to the Tempore, take us to the Tempore, she thinks.

A horn honks on their left. Daniel screams as the van crashes through the trees.

The tires bounce, catapulting them into a forest of shadows and snow.

Blythe smirks at Cordelia. "You were saying?"

Cordelia is glaring at her. "I hope your driver's license gets revoked."

"Joke's on you," Blythe smirks. "I don't have one."

"T-That was a really obvious use of magic, w-w-we're not supposed to do things like that!" Daniel shouts.

"We'll be fine," Blythe says, but only because she doesn't want thoughts of the Erasers to linger in her mind. She may have scared them off before, but there's no guarantee she'll be able to do it again.

In the haunting emptiness of the Tempore, they are free to drive as quickly as they'd like, as long as the windshield wipers are on a high enough setting to slap away the snow.

Cordelia raises the compass in the moonlight; it is golden and white-faced, engraved with swirling textures and a sparking wand.

"Do you happen to know how to get to California from here?" Cordelia asks.

The compass wand twitches.

Blythe narrows her eyes. "Say that again."

"What? No."

Jesus. Blythe reaches over and snatches the compass. "California! *California!*" she shouts. The wand wiggles. "Uh...San Diego, California!" It twitches west, then snaps back into place.

Realization dawns in Cordelia's eyes. "Didn't Katia have a..."

She snatches a whole laundry list of things out of the cloak: water bottles, a hair clip, fistfuls of change.

Finally, she reaches a slip of paper and unfolds it. "25 Maple Drive, 91932!"

"25 MAPLE DRIVE SAN DIEGO CALIFORNIA 91932!" Blythe shrieks.

The wand spins to the east: and there it stays.

"Holy shit, I did it!" Blythe shouts

Cordelia looks like she's about to burst a blood vessel. "*You* did it!?"

"I-I feel like it was more of a group effort," Daniel stammers.

Blythe laughs, because either way, with this compass, their journey is set. They don't need to study the ins and outs of the Tempore for years before they can use it. They have a cheat code.

They drive with the windows up to keep out the cold. Cordelia puts on the heat, draws her knees up to her chest, and gets on her phone.

"What are you doing?" Blythe asks.

Cordelia doesn't look up. "Handling *my* business."

Blythe sighs. "Okay, even *you* have to admit this is stupid. We're both going to Electric City, we could help each other."

But Cordelia does not speak. She is holding her secrets tight in her perfectly manicured hands.

The line of seven trees appears in their path not long after three A.M. It is too late to appear on anyone's doorstep, let alone to even be awake, so the three of them agree to spend the rest of the night just outside of the darkness. If something tries to attack, Blythe can stomp on the gas and have them out of the Tempore in no time.

"Have you got any blankets in here?" Cordelia asks.

"Are you going to show me what you're doing?" Blythe asks, which makes Cordelia sneer and turn her back on Blythe, making herself comfortable without blankets.

Blythe glances to Daniel in the back. "I could give you a blanket. Consider it a consolation prize for not being an asshole."

Daniel brushes the curls from his face. "Oh, n-no thank you," he stammers. "I-I-I don't sleep. I haven't slept in four days."

"Christ!" Blythe gasps. "Why not?"

"I—" Daniel swallows hard. "The song could come back."

Sometimes Blythe forgets that she is not the only one who heard the song that night. The roof incident is not only her trauma. And it's selfish to think so.

She should tell Daniel about the shard—it might be reassuring to know that the Trident Republic can no longer control them.

But perhaps it's safer to keep that information to herself for now. There's still no telling what kind of trouble that shard will get her into. What if Daniel gets in trouble just for knowing where it is?

"I'm sorry, Daniel," Blythe says. "But I...have a feeling it won't be coming back soon."

If Daniel senses anything off about what she's said, he doesn't mention it.

"There's food in the cooler if you get hungry," Blythe adds. "Wake me up if you need anything."

"Thanks," Daniel says.

Blythe shifts to her side, facing the ice crawling up her window. Sleep is just beginning to overtake her when Daniel's voice reaches her ears.

"Blythe?"

"Hmm?"

The world is silent and still around them. Daniel's voice is as soft as a breeze. "Thanks for not leaving me."

In the rearview mirror, Daniel's eyes are set on her. He has the expression of someone who fears being seen as expendable.

"Of course," Blythe says. "I'm glad you're here, Daniel."

She falls asleep not long after, entering a world of fitful dreams.

The Full Cup explodes.

She's driving down a road and it's too dark to see.

Someone is screaming. Screaming. Screaming.

Blythe jolts awake as soon as she realizes she is hearing her own screams.

Cordelia is still asleep, her head against the window and her hand over her eyes. Snow has piled on the window and Blythe's skin shivers with cold. She checks the heat, but it's on.

The backseat door is open.

A couple yards away, Daniel is kneeling in the snow. Blythe checks her phone: seven thirty in the morning. It's a good enough time to wake, especially since they are in no position to waste time.

Blythe opens her door and, shuddering from the numbing snow leaking into her sneakers, wanders over to Daniel.

His grimoire lies open on his lap. Blythe's not sure what she expected the book to contain, but the pages are cramped with notes in handwriting too small and fine for Blythe to read. There are complex sketches and diagrams, one of which Daniel is currently creating with a fountain pen.

Daniel jumps, looking wide-eyed over his shoulder.

"Sorry," Blythe apologizes. "It's just me."

Daniel's breath escapes in a cloud. "I-It's alright. Hello."

He does not return to his work. Instead, he stares in front of him, as if he meant to write alone.

But Blythe's nosy, so she lingers anyway. "What are you doing?" she asks.

"Recording notes."

"On what?" Blythe asks. Maybe a better question would be "*for* what".

The sketch on the cream page is strikingly similar to the plant in front of Daniel. They look like blueberries, if blueberries grew in the hearts of silver-petaled flowers. Daniel's sketch is less like art and more like a scientific dissection.

"These flowers here," he answers. "They thrive in the cold and their bulbs form edible berries. The petals and stem are edible as well, but most of the nutrients is found in the..." He stops. "Sorry. Y-You probably don't want to hear about that."

"No, no, it's cool," Blythe says. "I mean, I love talking about space and the stars, y'know, all that NASA type stuff but most people...do not. And I don't want to bore them. So, I feel you."

Daniel moves his fingertip along the petal's edges. The flower grows toward his palm, the stalk stretching higher and the leaves reaching toward him.

"You can make plants grow," Blythe whispers.

"Just small ones," Daniel says. "I-I'm not very good yet."

As she watches the flower patch shake off its snow and glow in the moonlight, Blythe realizes that these are the moments she imagines when she thinks of magic. Perhaps Daniel *is* a junior thaumologist.

"It's still cool," Blythe insists. "What're you looking at these flowers for, though? Just for fun?"

Daniel is quiet. Blythe wonders if he'll even reply. "No," he finally says. "I...need them."

"For what?"

Daniel has gone silent again. He folds his hands in his lap, staring at the flowers as if they could give him advice on whether or not he should speak.

"I'm..." he begins. His gaze trembles along the ground. "I'm making something."

"What is it?"

Daniel's blonde lashes brush his cheeks. He closes his book, tucks it under his arm. His face is beet red. "I-I'd rather not say."

"That's fair," Blythe relents. She can't push him to say any more —not without feeling incredibly guilty, at least. The last thing she wants is to make him uncomfortable.

Daniel faces her head on, squinting against the falling snow. "The people who attacked us took your family, didn't they?"

Now it is Blythe's turn to swallow. But this interrogation is only fair.

"Yeah," she agrees.

"Do you miss them?"

"Every second."

Daniel hesitates. It is almost as if he does not want to speak. "What happens if we can't save them?"

The question weighs hard on Blythe's chest. Those words have lingered in the back of her mind since she left her house.

"I'd rather not say," she says.

———

They wake Cordelia, but she insists on changing her clothes and redoing her makeup.

(Blythe's never seen Cordelia wearing anything other than pastels, and she has perfected the natural glow of "no makeup" makeup. Blythe would never say this out loud, but it's very cute).

Meanwhile, Blythe runs through their supplies; thanks to the money Cordelia stole from Katia, they're in pretty good standing.

When everyone is ready, they buckle up and drive straight into the darkness behind the trees.

And, just like that, they have entered California.

The van stops in a park. Gone are the piles of snow and numbing cold. The land is flat enough for Blythe to see for *miles*.

The breeze carries the scent of the sea, palm trees sway beneath a crystal blue sky, cement paths twist through green grass, seagulls caw and car horns sing.

It's all such a contrast to Broughton; that town had small streets and small shops, while San Diego sports towering buildings, long highways and tangling streets.

And, of course, on their right, the beach holds hands with the ocean.

"I love it, we're staying forever," Blythe blurts.

Daniel frowns. "T-This Guardian lives in a park?"

"No," Cordelia grumbles. "Katia said the Tempore accesses groups of trees. It'd be safe to assume that this park is as close as it could bring us. I'm just worried we'll get in trouble for driving in here—"

Blythe slams the gas and they rip forward, shooting through the park and bursting out onto the street to a flurry of panicked honking.

"*Nyoom,*" Blythe teases, grinning.

"Every time you get in a good mood, you nearly *kill us!*" Cordelia screams.

Blythe laughs; it's hard not to, with the sunlight bathing warm on her skin and hot, shirtless guys skateboarding down the sidewalk.

"Calm down, we're in California, we'll be *fine,*" she says.

Daniel takes one look out of the window and instantly pales. "I-I've never..." he stammers. "Those buildings are huge..."

"Welcome to the city, Daniel," Blythe says.

Daniel shakes his head, curls bouncing. "I-I want to be un-welcomed."

"Oh, that reminds me, you still need a phone," Blythe says. "We can stop at a Zadis store on our way to this kid's house. What's their name?"

"Antonio Torres," Cordelia answers. "And Zadis phones are far too expensive."

"Fine, Mom, we'll get him an Android," Blythe says. "Sorry we had to do this to you, Daniel."

Using the GPS on Cordelia's Zadis, they navigate to an air-conditioned mall where they're most likely to find an Android store.

Cordelia immediately departs to buy clothes. "You don't *need* clothes," Blythe says.

"By splitting with Katia, we've doubled the length of this trip to a duration I did not accommodate for while packing," Cordelia retorts. "So yes, I *do* need clothes."

She flips her hair and walks off, while Blythe calls, "You just want to be able to say you shopped in California!"

"Sorry, Blythe, I can't hear you!"

"You're ten feet away and my voice is a public disturbance!"

Cordelia just keeps going.

Daniel and Blythe manage to purchase a phone without her, and as they head out, Blythe asks Daniel if he knows how to use it.

Daniel is mesmerized by the piece of technology in his hand. "Not at all."

Blythe runs him through the basics and adds in herself as one of the contacts.

"Do you remember your parents' numbers?" She asks.

"W-We had phone landline at our house...could we try that?"

"Sure!"

Daniel punches in the number. He actually looks excited.

"I hope someone answers," he says as he raises it to his ear. Moments later, his expression fades. "Oh..."

"No one answered?" Blythe asks.

Daniel studies the dark screen. "N-No," he stammers.

Blythe tries to tell him he can try again later, but he has gone back to his usual resigned silence.

Cordelia waits in the van. She has amassed three shopping bags, a pair of Black shades, and a Starbucks iced tea.

"It's eight in the morning," she says from the passenger seat. "Tea will put me in a better mood."

"What do you mean 'better'? All your moods suck," Blythe snorts as she climbs in. "Here, add your number into Daniel's phone. Oh, and mine, so I can make a group chat."

Cordelia arches an eyebrow behind her shades. "Blythe, how desperate are you to have friends?"

"Fine, don't add your number. Then, if you get kidnapped, I won't even have to bother trying to find you."

Cordelia sighs, but she does it. The first notification appears instantly.

BLYTHE FULTON *has named the group chat* GUARDIANS

And then Blythe's phone buzzes.

CORDELIA DELEON has named the group chat NEUTRAL
GC NAME

"You've just put the identities of three Guardians in one place and *named it Guardians*," Cordelia snaps. She has a point. But still.

"'Neutral GC name' isn't less suspicious," Blythe retorts.

Her phone buzzes again.

DANIEL QUINTON: Hello.

Behind them, Daniel gasps. "Oh my, it works." His earlier pensive attitude has been replaced with wonder as he leans into the front seat to see Blythe's phone. "And you can both see it?"

Blythe is about to explain when she gets the sensation that her body is no longer hers.

Her muscles seize. Her foot hits the gas and the van flies toward a palm tree.

The hood slams into it. *Hard.* Blythe rips forward. Her forehead bounces off the wheel and throws her back against her seat.

Her thoughts are a broken record of *oh God oh God oh God.*

This couldn't have happened. It *couldn't have.* She has the shard —the Trident Republic can't control them without the shard.

If anyone outside noticed them, they haven't come to help. The radio plays as if nothing is wrong. The airbags haven't even deployed.

Cordelia's tea has sloshed over the dashboard. "What was that?!" she shrieks. "Did you just—"

"No," Blythe says. "It wasn't me! But that was...that was different! It was different this time."

The force felt as if it were controlling her limbs like a puppet on a string. It was not the all-encompassing, internal warfare the Trident Republic brought upon her.

Sobs echo from the backseat. Daniel has curled forward, his face in his hands.

"Daniel?" Blythe calls. She can't stop shaking. "Daniel, it's okay, we're alright."

He looks up at her with eyes rimmed red. "No, we're not! We're not okay, *I'm* not okay! It was different, I know it was different!"

"We've all been through this before," Cordelia growls. "We all know the Trident Republic is trying to kill us. That's not new."

There is no way Blythe and Daniel are both wrong. It *had* to have been new. Blythe looks toward the trunk.

"What are you doing?" Cordelia asks as Blythe crawls over the seats. She searches through the bags and boxes of snacks until she spots the Fruit Rollup box.

She dumps it out on the van's floor. The last thing to plop out is—relief washes over Blythe—her beanie.

"Please tell me there's something other than Fruit Rollups in there," Cordelia says.

"It's a shard," Blythe answers.

She explains the situation as best she can; how she stole the shard from the men before meeting Katia, how the Trident Republic can't mind control them without it.

"Which means that control must have been something different," She finishes.

Daniel is still pale white. He doesn't keep eye contact with Blythe.

Cordelia snorts. "And when were you going to tell us this?" she snaps.

"If I didn't have to? Never," Blythe retorts. "I shouldn't *have* this. I'm pretty sure the guys I took it from are going to pull a lot of shit to get it back. The less people who know about this, the better. But you see what I mean, right? The Trident Republic has no way of controlling us. Not anymore. It had to have been different."

An idea clicks in her head. "Wait, you're the Guardian of the Mind though, right?" Blythe asks. "You could do something about this, can't you? You broke out of the mind control before. Maybe you could…"

Cordelia is gaping at her. It is not the shock of someone who is having an epiphany, but the shock of someone who has just been ridiculously offended.

"Are you *mad*?" she yells. "I don't know where this is coming from, o-or how to block it! I don't know a thing about anything, this is—!"

Cordelia stops. She takes in a deep breath before she speaks again, lower. "I don't understand magic, I don't care to understand magic, and I'm certainly not going to put myself in danger because of some…off *chance* that I could do something."

There must be some misunderstanding, because there is no way Cordelia is blatantly refusing to do anything to help them. "What… what are you talking about?" Blythe asks.

"Hacking is easy," Cordelia says. "I can make myself untraceable while I work. The worst-case scenario is that I get doxxed, which I have heavily protected myself against. Whatever it is *you* want me to do? I have no way to protect myself. Stopping the Trident Republic through hacking could simply reveal my identity. What you're asking me to do could kill me. I've weighed my options and I'm content with doing things my way."

Blythe is speechless. "Are you…" Her thoughts are going so fast, she can't even articulate them.

At least, not without coming for Cordelia's entire life. But maybe that's what this girl needs.

"Daniel, plug your ears," Blythe orders. Daniel's hands tremble as he clamps them over his ears.

Blythe summons all of her hatred for this selfish, spoiled girl, into her eyes. "You would rather let someone freely enter your mind— someone who could make us drive into a building, or make you stop breathing, or make you plunge a knife through your own chest—but not only your mind, the minds of you and six other innocent people, than to put forth the singular effort to try and save not only your life, but *literally six other people's*?! Is that what you're telling me?"

Cordelia is still shockingly pale, but her eyebrows shoot up. "Did I stutter?"

Her words ring and fade in the air.

"Do you remember one of the first things you ever said to me? I believed you, but you were wrong," Blythe hisses. "Because this? *This* is the real difference between you and me."

ELEVEN

THE ONLY SOUND IN THE VAN IS THE HUM OF THE AIR conditioner.

The bumper is scraped and the hood is dented. Blythe shifted the part in her hair so her curls fall over the developing bruise on her forehead. Cordelia cleaned the spilled tea before it grew sticky in the heat.

Physically, they have recovered. Mentally, they are fucked, and it is not nice.

Cordelia controls the radio whenever she's not on her phone. Daniel stares out the window, squinting at the city—or maybe at the thoughts in his head.

No one tries to interact with each other. How do you bounce back from the conversation they just had? What do you say?

They ignore each other for the entire drive.

———

Antonio Torres lives on a small beach, spotty with palm trees. Blythe thought the drive through San Diego was picturesque but the Torres property is like a scene from a California vacation ad: smooth sand, twinkling ocean, white house with a verandah high atop stilts.

Cordelia huffs. "This looks my family's vacation house."

It seems they express their stress in different ways: Blythe pretends she doesn't have it, Daniel cries, and Cordelia makes everyone around her feel like pieces of shit.

"Can you at least *try* not to sound like an elitist asshole?" Blythe snaps.

Cordelia isn't even phased. "My mum's an artist, my dad's a musician, and my older sister is a poet. None of them are very successful, but when my grandfather died he left us the estate and a large sum of money. I'm not lying, simply speaking from experience."

"A hacker in a family of artists," Blythe says. "Finding the black sheep in your family is way too easy."

Cordelia smiles sweetly. "At least I know where I can find my family."

Her hair tosses like a black curtain as she sashays toward the Torres' house.

The beach suits her almost too perfectly, with her model's figure and grace. Blythe hates her, but she has to admit, this scene would make a nice shot.

"I hope we meet someone twenty times richer than her so she'll feel upstaged," Blythe grumbles.

Daniel is making a face too, but his is directed toward the horizon.

"I've never seen the ocean before," he whispers.

It's a positive, pleasant distraction from Cordelia's nastiness. Blythe follows his gaze. "Pretty, isn't it?" She asks. "I used to live in Florida and we'd visit the beach all the time. But seeing it never gets old. Ironically, I never learned how to swim but..."

Daniel stares unblinking, unmoving, at the water.

"You alright?" Blythe asks.

"It's..." Daniel's mouth forms a small *o*. "It's communicating with me."

Blythe recoils—but Daniel is the Guardian of Nature. Of course he'd have a connection with the sea.

"Well, it doesn't usually do that," she says. "What's it saying?"

A frown pinches Daniel's face. "It's stopped."

The ocean seems unchanged to Blythe. Whatever it's said to Daniel, it doesn't seem to care whether or not he understood. The waves push and pull, as unbothered as ever.

Daniel shakes his head. "Nevermind," he says. "Um, could I... could I talk to you?"

"About the ocean?"

"No, about...well, about—"

"HEY!" someone shouts.

From the other end of the beach comes a form, approaching at high speed. A boy runs with his arms waving in the air, as if to get their attention, but everyone is already watching him.

Cordelia drifts back to them. Blythe's not surprised; Cordelia doesn't feel bad for what she said, she just doesn't want to be the first person to greet this overeager stranger.

The boy grins when he reaches them; he has a dimple poking in his cheek, and the kind of smile that makes you feel like the most important personal alive.

"Hey hey, I'm Antonio!" he shouts. "Did the Sages send you guys? Someone called us about that a couple days ago and I've been waiting ever since."

He is the beach personified. From his skin, golden from the sun, to his fluffy blonde hair that reminds Blythe of a Studio Ghibli character. He's pulled the front into a topknot, but the rest is long enough to hide his ears and brush his jaw.

"Uh," Blythe stammers. First of all, Antonio's smile is blindingly brilliant. Second of all, Blythe isn't totally sure of how to answer him.

The Sages didn't send *them*, not really, and they are not here to bring this boy to Frost Glade. But it's a little soon to drop the "my family's been kidnapped" bomb.

Blythe puts on a smile and prays for the best when she says,

"Mostly!"

"Awesomeeeeee," Antonio replies. "Gimme names, don't be shy!"

"Oh, um, I-I'm Blythe, this is Daniel and Corde—"

"Cordelia," the girl interrupts. "Who can introduce herself."

Her annoyance goes completely unnoticed by Antonio, who smile remains as bright as ever. "Blythe, Daniel, and Cordelia," he lists. "Got it. I'm good with names, I won't forget. You guys are Guardians too, right? I've never met any other Guardians before, this is gonna be *so* cool! Wait, how long have you guys known each other—"

"*ANTONIO!*" Someone screams from inside the house. Daniel nearly jumps out of his skin, poor thing.

Antonio lets out a puff of air. "That's my mom, hold on. MA! ESTOY AQUI!"

A woman saunters onto the verandah, orange maxi dress fluttering in the sea breeze. Her hair is pulled back, and her eyes are as dark as Antonio's and as sharp as her jawline.

She leans against the railing, taking in her new guests. "Oh, hello," she says. "I didn't know you all were here. Breakfast's inside, come in and help yourselves."

"We'll be there in a bit," Antonio answers. "I'm just gonna show them my board and then—"

His mom cuts him off. "Antonio. Focus."

Antonio sighs dramatically. "Alright, alright," he relents.

He turns his bright smile back to them as his mother disappears inside. "Sorry about that. I did make breakfast though, so you guys can come in and eat!"

Antonio makes life feel two-times faster than it ought to. Before Blythe can fully process what's happening, something new captures her attention.

White feathers poke out from Antonio's shoulders. They point skyward as two bones form, the feathers multiplying on top of them, layering, until they extend into a pair of huge, angelic wings, unfolding from Antonio's back.

Wings.

Blythe stammers, "Wh....wait a minute."

Cordelia blurts, "What the hell?"

Daniel screams. No words. Just raw power.

"Hm? Oh yeah, I can grow wings!" Antonio says.

He has *wings*. Two seconds ago, they were invisible—no, two seconds ago, they did not exist. Blythe has heard of magicians who can materialize new limbs, but she's never seen someone do it right in front of her.

Antonio's wings flap, sending the sand around his bare feet into a frenzy. His muscles tense and he is gone, a trail of sand in his wake.

Fifteen feet above their heads, Antonio glides on air, moving as if flying is as fluid and natural as breathing.

"You have *wings!*" Blythe repeats.

Above their heads, Antonio's smile widens. "Heck yeah, I'm the Guardian of Animals, bro!"

Cordelia and Daniel are already halfway to the porch by the time Blythe even *thinks* about walking. She has to keep her jaw from dropping as she hurries after them.

"They're seagull wings!" The moment Antonio lands on the porch, the wings sink effortlessly into his skin, leaving not a trace behind. "Don't tell my mom I did that though," he says when they catch up to him. "She panics when I fly."

Antonio holds the door open for them, and they're instantly greeted by his mother shouting, "Antonio, I don't want to be sweeping up sand later!"

"Oh, don't forget to wipe your feet." Antonio, however, walks straight into the kitchen. He's tracking sand.

The Torres' home consists of one flat layout; the living room and kitchen are blended into one breezy, open space. It's amazingly clean besides a few items—a denim jacket across the couch, worn sandals near the kitchen doorway, white feathers below a window—that look like Antonio's.

A Puerto Rican flag hangs in the living room, and on the walls hang a huge assortment of pictures: Antonio with his huge smile and blonde hair, growing up with his family members, but a few of just Antonio and his mom.

The Alastair French show plays on the TV; his mom sits forward on the living room couch, eyes glued to it.

"E-Excuse me, Antonio?" Daniel's walking slower than usual. "Y-You don't have a dog, do you?"

"I used to have three!" Antonio chirps from the kitchen. "And a few cats, couple turtles, some birds—oh, and a ferret!" His eyes sparkle with excitement. "His name was Bill. He liked to hide in the rugs. Oh, and I had a snake and some mice, but not at the same time. What was the question?"

"Dogs," Blythe reminds.

"Oh! No, not anymore, why?"

Daniel doesn't elaborate.

Cordelia does it for him. "He's terrified of dogs. Among multiple other things."

"I-I've just never...seen them before..." Daniel's defense is whispered, and of course, Cordelia ignores it.

"Don't be scared, bro, it's all good! No pets here, just breakfast!" Antonio promises. "I made it before I went surfing, so it might be a little cold, but we can pop it in the microwave."

Blythe's stomach is growling, but she's not sure if she trusts Antonio's cooking. He seems a little too...easily distracted to do well in the kitchen.

"Thanks," she begins. "But we're not—"

Antonio picks up a tray and whips off the lid. This time, Blythe *can't* stop her jaw from going slack.

This boy with Studio Ghibli hair has made Studio Ghibli food.

"Nutella crepe cones filled with fresh berries and whipped cream, and bite sized omelet cups topped with basil on the side," Antonio describes. "Half the cups have ham squares and the others have extra red peppers, just in case you're not into meat."

A light snow of powdered sugar adorns perfectly golden crepes, the Nutella melted into a thick, chocolate stream. The omelet cups are folded like small flowers, the eggs blooming with a warm yellow hue.

"I'll take a plate," Cordelia blurts.

"M-Me too," Daniel stammers.

"Holy crap, you made this?!" Blythe screams. "With your own two hands?!"

Antonio laughs. "Well, I had bowls and spoons and stuff but yeah, I made it! I love cooking! And I...kinda ate most of it earlier. But here's what's left!"

The Guardian thank him and grab their plates while he leaves to gather his things from his room. They eat at the table in the center of the kitchen, quietly stuffing their mouths, each forkful tasting too good to be true.

A sigh comes from the living room before the TV clicks off. Antonio's mother joins them with a small smile; her eyes look tired, but up close, she seems rather young, maybe only a little older than Katia.

"How's it?" she asks.

"*Delicious*," Blythe answers.

"Good. That boy knows his way around a kitchen," She chuckles a bit. "I haven't seen you all since you were babies, so you'll have to tell me your names again."

Ms. Torres speaks like she knew them before. But, then again, the process of becoming a Guardian was not *forced* on their families. Each set of parents had to agree, sign official paperwork, and meet certain criteria.

There were probably multiple meetings involving all seven families in the same room, maybe with the kids off playing while the adults talked practicalities.

The other Guardians' families may have met Blythe when she was too small to remember.

"I'm Blythe," she says. "This is Daniel and that's Cordelia."

Miraculously, Cordelia doesn't interrupt. Maybe because they're in front of an adult.

Ms. Torres studies Blythe. "You're the Fultons' girl, I remember you. Did your family ever move out of Frost Glade?"

Blythe hesitates. She can feel Cordelia's gaze burning on her. *Don't mess this up.* She cannot break down and tell this woman her family has been kidnapped and she's actually here to convince her son to help her find them. She can't.

"Yeah, when I was...really young," she forces the words out and shoves a slice of crepe into her mouth to keep from continuing.

"Ah, I see," Ms. Torres nods. "Maybe that's for the best, considering how people are about Ether."

Blythe starts at that. She swallows quickly. "What's wrong with Ether?"

A shrug. Whatever Ms. Torres is about to say, it doesn't particularly offend her. "Nothing at all. But since the Sage of Ether is the one who turned, people tend to be...simpleminded."

Katia never mentioned which Sage became obsessed with power. She never said it was the Sage of Ether who killed hundreds in Frost Glade.

Blythe's stomach twists. This doesn't mean she is destined to become evil—of course it doesn't—but the same Element that once ran through his veins now runs through hers.

And that is chilling.

"Your house is lovely," Cordelia says, and the conversation moves on without Blythe.

It is for the best. Blythe is having trouble doing anything besides staring at her food. Her thoughts are a thick fog.

Maybe it is for the best that she can't use her own magic. She is the Guardian of the Element that drove a man to insanity.

"Where's Katia?" Ms. Torres suddenly asks.

Daniel coughs.

Cordelia doesn't even flinch. "She's not with us right now," she says.

"So, you're unsupervised," Ms. Torres' brow furrows further.

"For the moment. We had to travel separately, but we're meeting back up with her at the next Guardian's house."

Cordelia's lies come out confident and smooth. But Ms. Torres only makes a vague "mhm" noise, saying nothing more.

Cordelia's voice enters Blythe's mind instantly. *She doesn't believe us.*

Ms. Torres rests her chin in her hand. Her gaze carries the weight of someone who has seen too much to be easily fooled—a suspicious wall that Antonio does not seem to share.

"And you're the three who heard the...voices, correct?" she asks.

Blythe nods. "Yeah. Did Antonio not...?"

Sofia doesn't even blink. "No."

That explains his excitement. Not even the most optimistic person would be able to brush off an experience like that.

Antonio returns with a backpack, wearing flip flops as if he isn't about to leave the beach.

"How's the food?" he asks.

Cordelia turns her fake hospitable act on him. "Perfect. You're an excellent cook."

"Aw, thanks, that's so sweet!" he says. "Whenever you guys are ready, we can..."

His gaze drifts over Blythe's shoulder. And, for the first time since they arrived, Antonio's smile disappears.

The largest window in the Torres house has a picturesque view of the beach—except a mass of clouds are rolling over the sun, taking all light along with them.

The kitchen falls into a grey despair as the waves crash against the sand, fitfully pulling back and forth.

It's happening far too quickly to be natural.

Blythe's skin perks with the hum of magical energy in the air. The palm trees bend against the wind. They move just like the trees outside of the Full Cup.

"Miss Sofia," Blythe begins. "I think we should leave, like...now."

Antonio's gaze snaps to his mother. "What's happening?"

Ms. Torres' jaw clenches. "I don't like any of this— Katia not being here, the voices you three supposedly heard, the war. I don't want to send my son out into this." She pauses. "But keeping him here would be no better."

Her chair clatters back as she stands. "Come on," she says. "I'll walk you out." She eyes them sternly. "*No* panicking."

Antonio seems to be doing just that, his attention divided between their faces and the storm brewing outside. "But like, this... this isn't a big thing, right?"

"No," Ms. Torres agrees. "Not if I can help it."

The house seems to sway on its stilts as Ms. Torres leads them to the door. Blythe thinks it's her imagination until a vase crashes to the tile and shatters.

"Ma..." Antonio mumbles.

She turns to him, holding his face in her hands and speaking words in Spanish that are beyond Blythe's one year of studying it in school.

Whatever she says, it is serious, and Antonio nods, repeating it back to her. She smiles, pats his cheek, and opens the door.

Wind bursts into the house, strong enough to make everyone but Sofia stumble on their feet. The air curls through Blythe's clothes, tossing her hair into a frenzy.

The stairs shift and groan beneath their weight. The beach has completely changed; the friendly ocean now froths and vomits foam. All of the colors are gone, replaced with a sickening grey that spans from the sky to the sand.

Ms. Torres is unfazed—like the eye of the storm, she only presses forward.

Sand cuts against Blythe's exposed skin. She has to squint against it. The only way she knows where she is going is by following Ms. Torres' calm movements.

When Ms. Torres stops, Blythe realizes they are standing in the beach grass that marks the end of the Torres' property.

"Go on, hurry," Ms. Torres ushers them ahead, giving Antonio a gentle push.

He whirls around to hug her, and she holds him tight before pushing him off again, rushing him to go.

"I'll call!" Antonio yells. "And bring you back something cool!"

Daniel and Cordelia follow him through the grass without a second glance; Daniel folds his arms tight across his body while Cordelia's hair flies wild in the wind.

There is something familiar about the way the air blows against them. Blythe has felt its sharp, cold hands on her skin before.

She is the only one who looks back at the beach.

A man hovers above the raging ocean waters; a hat rests on his head and bronze cuffs glow on his wrists. The general of the Trident Republic. The executioner of Walden Oliver's war. Whiteclaw.

Rage tears through Blythe's chest, choking her throat. She can't go after him. He is above the ocean and she can't swim. And she left her hockey stick in the van because this is the the last place she expected to see Whiteclaw.

Pain sinks Blythe's stomach as she realizes that she is, yet again, powerless.

But Ms. Torres has not gone anywhere. With her back to Blythe, she watches Whiteclaw's approach with squared shoulders. Like a warrior prepared for battle.

Blythe is not the only one affected by the Trident Republic. She is not the only one hurting.

Blythe has never met Cordelia's family, but she imagines they are worried about her safety. And the Quintons were clearly terrified, but they fought back in their own way, coming out of hiding to make sure Daniel was safe.

And here is Ms. Torres, fists balled as she stares down the storm.

So Blythe runs to join the others. She may be powerless now, but this upcoming battle is not hers to fight.

When the time comes for Blythe to face Whiteclaw, to remind him of what he did to her family—to *her*—she will not be helpless.

She will be ready.

TWELVE

ANTONIO HAS GONE QUIET.

He slouches into the backseat of the van, head against the window, playing with the rope bracelet around his wrist.

"So..." he begins. "Are there...always people popping up like that?"

Blythe speaks as gently as possible. "Basically," she says, and Antonio studies her face, willing her to say something a bit more optimistic. "I mean, to be fair, they're not always people. Sometimes they're monsters."

Antonio blinks. "Oh," he says. "Variety."

That probably wasn't what he wanted to hear. "Sorry," Blythe apologizes.

She wishes she could do more for him; not only did he have to leave home, he had to watch a storm shift into something terrible and ruined.

Antonio's quiet. Then he musters a perfect, sunny smile. "It's okay," he says. "I'll just get used to it."

Blythe wants to tell him the truth: about how they left Katia, about where they're really going, about the *actual* plan. But he has enough to work through as it is.

Somehow, within a matter of minutes, Antonio slips back into his normal personality. He shares the radio with Cordelia, which means bubbly chart toppers have joined Cordelia's selection of slow, dreamy indie pop. He alternates between toying with whatever he can get his hands on and leaning his head out of every hole in the van.

He's halfway out of the window when he turns to Daniel. "Do you play video games?"

Previously, the van was plagued with unbreakable silences—but that will never happen again, not as long as Antonio Torres is here.

The good thing about him is that he never stops talking. The bad thing about him, however, is that *he never stops talking*.

Daniel regards this energetic stranger warily. "W-What are video games?"

Antonio considers this. "...Where are you from?"

"Montana."

"Montana must be weird," Antonio muses. "What did you do all day?"

"Read. A-And plant."

"Oh, cool!" He pulls himself back into the van, and Blythe takes that opportunity to roll his window all the way up. "What kind of plants? Did you ever grow your own food?"

"Oh, a-all the time," Daniel nods. "My mom has a huge vegetable garden in our backyard. It's very pleasant, especially to pick things from whenever we want to make something. Plants grow really easily around me, so I'd spend most of my afternoons there, just reading."

"That sounds so peaceful. Did you like it?"

"Immensely. But not as much as the rest of the forest. I...I knew every tree and bush on our land, and I never strayed far but it was still beautiful."

Blythe has never heard words pour of Daniel like this before. He's talking like a normal human being.

She has to hand it to Antonio, the boy knows how to make anyone talk to him.

"But our house was interesting as well. Some days I would stay in our library all evening and read the nonfiction, and sometimes I would have to help Father in his study," Daniel continues. "Oh! And I get to drink all types of tea in the morning, and help my mom bake pies. It's lovely."

"I wanna move to your house," Antonio laughs. "I've always wanted to grow my own food but eh, cons of living on a beach. It's good for surfing though, and I do surf a lot."

"Surfing has always seemed unsafe to me."

"It is! Especially since I just started and I'm not good at it yet! I almost drowned once!"

Daniel checks out of the conversation after that. The concept of doing something dangerous for fun seems lost on him.

Antonio turns his attention to the front seats. "So, where are we headed?"

"Right now I'm just trying to find a good way into the Tempore," Blythe says. "Do you know what that is?"

"Yeah, of course!" Antonio says. "My uncle uses it to get to work in the morning. But isn't it closed now?"

"Nothing's closed if you're brave enough," Blythe says and Antonio shouts, "Hahaha, heck yeah dude!"

Cordelia looks up from her phone. She picked it up to add Antonio to their group chat and never put it down.

But, apparently, she's sensed a moment of weakness. "I'm beginning to think growing up with magic stunts your logical development," she grumbles.

"Wait, were you not?" Antonio asks. "Where are you from?"

"I'm from London but my family—" Cordelia catches herself. "*Ugh*, whatever, it hardly matters."

"I-I knew about magic, I just didn't know I was a Guardian," Daniel joins in. "My parents told me everything really slowly because they thought I-I'd cry when I heard I'd be leaving home..."

"Did you cry?" Cordelia asks.

Daniel hesitates. "...Yes."

"Dude, you never left your house?!" Antonio yells.

Daniel's face has gone red. "W-We had no reason to leave...F-Father says we m-moved to the house when I was five, b-but I don't remember living anywhere but there."

"Wait, y'know what, I was actually thinking about that," Antonio begins. "Like, dude, can you imagine if like, the apocalypse happened and you had to make your entire life revolve *inside* your house because there's nowhere to be except your house?"

Cordelia and Daniel stare at him in confusion. Even Blythe's brow is furrowed.

"I'm not even talking about like for a few days or something, I mean for like, forever," he continues. "Like, what if aliens attacked and destroyed the world? Would I have to like board up the windows and stuff? And only eat like, canned foods? I couldn't live off canned foods! They're basically all vegetables. Okay, there's like, canned ravioli and stuff but you have to cook that, you can't eat it cold. You ever think about that?"

Blythe is speechless. "Uh, not really—"

"Oh, wait, I *did* eat cold ravioli once. It was weird. My mom got mad at me for eating straight out of the can, but I was like, six. I forget out how I got it open," He frowns. "I think I used my teeth. Which is pretty weird when I think about it, actually." Antonio takes a breath. "What were you guys like as kids?"

"Might wanna put a pin in that one, Antonio," Blythe says. "We're heading into the Tempore."

At this point, entering the Tempore has become a routine—find trees, drive into them, reappear into...a scene that looks completely different from what Blythe remembers.

The Tempore is in the middle of autumn. The trees are bare and their fallen leaves coat the forest floor in a patchwork of red, orange, and gold.

The sky is still a blanket of darkness. Someone—possibly a

traveler who hasn't stopped used the Tempore—has hung lit torches from the trees. The light makes it easier to see, but doesn't help the Tempore's creepy atmosphere.

"Whoa," Antonio gasps. Whoa indeed.

"...Do we have time to care about this?" Blythe asks.

Cordelia is already flattening out Katia's paper of addresses. "No."

Their next destination is Philadelphia, Pennsylvania, home of a girl named Storm Crane.

They've barely begun their drive before a scream pierces through the car like a bullet. At least, that's what it sounds like. It may be an animal. Or something else entirely.

Blythe eases up on the gas. The van goes still enough to be part of the forest.

"What was that?" Antonio asks.

Cordelia is already tucking her phone into her purse as if she needs to be prepared to run. "We're in the Tempore so it was probably a bloody monster," she grumbles.

"Oh, monsters already?" Antonio asks. "That was quick."

Blythe tunes them out. She has to think. Whiteclaw may have seen them leaving Antonio's house. If Sofia couldn't fend him off, this could be an attempt to find them.

Or maybe it's none of that at all. Maybe the Trident Republic is causing trouble that's completely unrelated to them.

In the rearview mirror, Blythe sees it. It moves at the tops of the trees and looks like a gust of darkness shooting through the air. Right for them.

"Hide," Blythe can't speak quickly enough. "In the back away from the windows, on the ground—go *now!*"

Daniel goes pale as he rushes to the trunk. Antonio stares outside.

"Shouldn't we fight it?" he speaks as simply as if he's asking if they should stop for gas. "I mean, we're all Guardians right? We could totally fight that thing."

"We need to figure out what it *is* first," Blythe responds.

Antonio relents, moving to join Daniel. The rear windshield is wide, but it's high. If they sit on the truck bed, they could go undetected.

It's a big "could". If the creature sees them first, it gets a head start on its attack. And Blythe doesn't even know what this creature is capable of.

Blythe slides against the left wall of the trunk, shoulder to shoulder with Daniel. Cordelia and Antonio have squeezed in on the right, Cordelia's head right beneath the glass.

They are silent. Blythe's hands have started to tremble, and she tucks them against her stomach. Her mouth is dry. But nothing is happening.

"Are you sure it—" Cordelia starts.

A caw cuts her off, identical to the one they heard before, except this time, the sound is only feet from their window.

Cordelia clamps her mouth shut. Antonio pulls his legs against his chest as he straightens to see through the window.

A streak of billowy black fabric shoots toward the driver's seat.

A sound chokes out of Daniel's throat. Blythe covers his mouth. The back rows of leather sets are tall enough to obscure them from the thing's view—but they don't block Blythe's view of the monster.

It is not a shadow; it is a cloaked, humanoid figure. Its black hood covers most of its features, except for a forked tongue that licks between yellow fangs. Its exposed skin is yellow and wrinkled, black veins pulsing beneath its surface.

The creature screams, a shriek that shakes Blythe's eardrums and rings through her head. She swears the entire van vibrates.

The creature settles in front of the windshield. Its black cloak takes up every inch of the glass, curling and echoing in a nonexistent wind.

Blythe's hockey stick lies under the backseat, a good three feet away from her right hand. She can grab it and *maybe* fight this thing. As long as there's only one.

But it doesn't attack them. It shoots up in a blur.

"...is it gone?" Antonio whispers. Blythe shushes him.

Daniel pries her hand from his mouth. "That was a Krubim," he whispers.

"You know what they are?" Blythe blurts.

Of course he does. This is the boy that made his own grimoire. He probably knows more about magic than all of them combined.

Daniel bobs his head. "They're a species of Calling creature. They're blind, so perhaps if we don't make noise, it'll flee."

Cordelia peers out of the back window. The creature appears behind the glass with an echoing caw.

The thing dives forward. Blythe reaches for her hockey stick, but she doesn't get a chance to grab it.

Cordelia screams and the creature grasps its head, spine arching, cloak shaking. It collapses beneath their view.

Cordelia's eyes are huge. Blythe can't stop watching her. "What did you *do*?" she whispers.

Cordelia shakes her head. "I...I don't know. I don't *know*. I had this ringing in my head and it just..." she points a shaky finger forward. "It travelled to that thing."

"Whoa," Antonio breathes.

Cordelia is the Guardian of the Mind, sure, but there are so many ways to incapacitate a person—or, apparently, a Calling creature—using the Element of the Mind. Did she shut down that thing's mental processing? Did she put it in a coma?!

Regardless, that creature's down. And it doesn't seem like it'll be getting up anytime soon.

A cacophony of shrieks echoes in the distance, identical to the ones before, but much larger in number.

"Oh no," Daniel breathes, because outside the rear windshield is a swarm of black cloaks soaring straight for them.

"There's *never* only one..." Blythe mutters. "Guys, lay flat and don't make a—"

"Cordelia could just do that thing again!" Antonio interrupts.

"Cordelia doesn't know *how* to do that thing again!" Cordelia screams.

"Get down!" Blythe orders.

She can hear their cloaks fluttering on either side of the van. Like a swarm of birds, or one hundred waves crashing at once.

Blythe pulls herself into a ball, pressing her forehead against the cold metal floor. The creatures' deafening shrieks pierce the air like an ocean of startled birds.

One of their bodies hits the passenger door; the force wobbles through the van. Another slam has Blythe's side up in the air.

Her body slides forward and she slams her hands against the floor to keep still. Daniel yells as the car rights itself; another slam and it happens again, on Cordelia's side.

Those things are going to turn the van over.

As quickly as it starts, it's over. Blythe can hear the creatures above them, a mass of cawing monsters, swarming like vultures above their prey.

Blythe is silent and still. They all are. Antonio stares at the ceiling as if he can see through it. Cordelia's jaw is clentched. Daniel gasps for breath.

The cawing fades. Through the windows, Blythe watches them soar back into the forest, returning the same way they came.

At this point, Blythe should get back behind the wheel and drive them to Philadelphia. *Should.* But if those things were Calling creatures, someone had to summon them—and there's a chance those Krubim are returning to the magician that did so.

It could be Whiteclaw. It'd make sense; he could have entered the Tempore and saw them. Blythe's heart races. She has her hockey stick now. She could actually do this. She could fight him.

This is probably the dumbest idea she's had in her life, but she's desperate enough to do it.

"We should follow them," she blurts.

Cordelia's head snaps up. "Where do you get these ideas from?! Do you want to die?"

166

Blythe tunes her out. The tail end of the Krubim swarm is about to fly over their heads. It's now or never.

"Fine," she says, standing. "You all stay here, I have to go."

"*Blythe!*" Cordelia calls, but Blythe is already crawling over the seats. She can't waste time trying to convince them. If they're too scared, that's their problem. She's not missing this opportunity.

She bursts out of the van, leaves splashing under her sneakers. The Krubim are a living gust of wind against the sky. They travel in a wobbly, curving line, like a giant snake slithering through the trees, the tail end lagging slightly behind.

"Blythe, wait!" Antonio shouts. Blythe ignores him. And she runs.

Grass crunches beneath her. Her breath escapes in loud puffs. She is moving faster than she ever has before. Despite all her noise, the Krubim never look down at her. They shoot forward, ever forward.

I am going to find Whiteclaw, Blythe thinks. *I will save my family. And he will regret what he did to us.*

The front of the Krubim's line drops toward the ground like a black waterfall. They are flying toward someone, but it isn't Whiteclaw. It's a woman.

Her back is turned, palm raised above her head. The Krubim disintegrate into her hand, their figures morphing into black liquid and swirls of darkness that her skin ingests. Black veins snake up her wrists, like ink flowing beneath her caramel skin.

Blythe slows to a stop. She has never seen Learned Magic used like this. Making drinks in the Full Cup was one thing, but this? This is the aspect of Learned Magic that made people wary.

And this woman—with her beige mini dress with long, billowing sleeves and her lax, high bun—she isn't supposed to be here. Blythe came for Whiteclaw. If he isn't here, why should Blythe bother?

Blythe checks the ground for twigs before she leaves. What if she breaks one and calls the woman's attention? That always happens in movies. But there are no twigs to be found, so Blythe starts back.

Her foot catches on a rock.

On her way to the ground, Blythe ponders what a cruel mistress fate is.

The moment she hits the grass, she instantly looks back at the woman—who is staring right at Blythe.

Something about the curve of the woman's face is familiar. Her expression hardens and her eyes turn black with magic. She lowers her skyward hand to point a single finger straight at Blythe.

A wave of Krubim explode from her fingertip in a mass of snapping teeth and echoing black cloaks. *Yeah,* Blythe thinks. *I really goofed this one up.*

The creatures hit Blythe like a living wall. Claws tear her skin. Dark cloaks and wrinkled yellow faces swarm her vision.

Every inhale brings the stench of decay into her lungs. She tries to kick or move her arms but their spindly bodies pin her body to the dirt.

The ground rumbles against her back. Something explodes from the ground beside her. It is as thick as a table, shooting up and taking a whole slew of Krubim out with it. And near her legs emerges another, and a third by her arms.

They are vines.

Like something out of a fairy tale, they rise, large enough to crush cars in their grip, snatching the Krubim from her body.

These things have come from nowhere. Blythe is the Guardian of Ether—and Ether has nothing to do with vines.

Blythe tilts her head back. Behind her stands Antonio, Cordelia, and Daniel—Antonio's wings have sprouted from his back and Cordelia stares the woman down.

But Daniel's expression is the only one of pure shock. "I-I-I didn't know I could do that," he stammers.

Cordelia's voice is like steel. "I killed one of your pets. I can show you what it felt like, if you'd like."

The young woman laughs. "Look at you trying to be *scary*. Shut up. I'd have you tangled in thousands of monster limbs before you could even *consider* it," she spits. "*I was told I'd never have to interact with any of you. You're lucky I don't mind surprises.*"

Blythe wiggles through the vines and rises to her feet, facing this coy stranger. The two most striking things about her are the bronze, trident pin glinting on her shirt and the long, discolored figure pulling dark across the left side of her face.

The woman catches Blythe's stare. "Like the scar? It's new. If you want one all you have to do is ask the Black Veins Imperial Army to invade your city unprovoked."

Blythe hopes this woman isn't expecting sympathy from her. Who cares if she was in Electric City during the attack? Blythe was in the café, but that didn't stop Whiteclaw from breaking in and kidnapping her family right in front of her.

"You have two choices," Cordelia snaps. "Leave willingly or leave by force."

"Don't be pushy," the woman huffs. "Your friend ran here like she couldn't wait to meet me. We should at least chat."

Her eyes slip, like water, over to Blythe. They have lost their magical glow, but they remain dark and cutting. "How did you like my gift, Ether? I stole that cute picture out of your backpack while you were asleep. Added my own spin, of course."

Blythe's vision goes red with rage. She snatches out her hockey stick before she can think. The Trident Republic must think this is a game.

If they believe she's going to give up—go collapse somewhere and *cry*—then they are damn fools.

"Oh please, don't waste your time," the woman continues. "You don't have much of it. If the Black Veins decides this is a war, they'll attack us. And you wouldn't want them to accidently harm our hostages in the process."

The other Guardians have gone silent behind Blythe. But the woman's lying. She's just trying to provoke Blythe.

"The Sages wouldn't do that," Blythe snaps. But she can't stop her mind from wondering—what if they did?

The woman sets her hands on her hips, her giant sleeves echoing. "You trust your Sages so much?" she smirks. "War is war and time is ticking, so give me what you stole and we'll both head our separate ways."

"Bullshit," Blythe growls. She winds the hockey stick back—it vibrates with magic. "You're the one with something of mine."

Something about Cordelia captures the woman's attention.

"Oh, see," the woman says. "*She* knows what I'm talking about."

Cordelia's eyes have gone wide—but she quickly neutralizes her expression. "We lost it when we threw stuff out of the van," she says. "It's back in Montana somewhere. Go find it if you want it so badly."

The woman *tsks*. "Nobody likes a liar."

An amalgamation of Krubim shoot up from the ground. It is a looming blob of limbs and bodies fused into one form—a form that wraps around Cordelia and forces her into the air.

Antonio's wings splay wide and he flies toward the woman. Cawing Krubim burst from thin air, shooting at him like bullets.

He weaves through them, effortless, until one grabs him by the arm, pulling him to the ground.

"I *really* did not sign up for this," the woman groans. "Give me the shard and I'll free your friend."

Blythe surges forward, her hockey stick glowing fluorescent white. "Give me my family, you piece of shit!" she screams.

The woman catches sight of her. Krubim leap from her hand at the same time Blythe swings.

The hockey stick hits a Krubim with an explosive burst of energy. The whole forest trembles from the ripples of force.

It throws the woman off her feet, her body slapping into a tree and collapsing onto the leaves.

The energy has blown the Krubim amalgamation into dripping pieces of oily sludge—sludge that now surrounds Cordelia's form on the ground. She screams, but not out of pain. The goo just looks really, *really* gross.

The sound of shifting leaves alerts Blythe to the woman sitting up.

"God," she growls. "You're all a pain in the ass aren't y—"

A surge of tree roots reach through the ground, coiling around her limbs. She frowns, trying to lift herself to her feet, but the earth does not let her go.

The roots coil tight along her arms, snaking up her torso to twist across her mouth, tying her every limb to the forest floor.

Daniel stands with his hands outstretched, face gone pink with the effort.

"Hell yeah, Daniel!" Blythe yells.

Something *whooshes* past her—it's Antonio, back in the air, snatching up Cordelia so quickly, it looks like she's disappeared. Blythe grabs Daniel by the wrist and darts after them. Despite all of his earthly magic, Daniel does not run very fast, and Blythe is mostly dragging him.

Cordelia screams in Antonio's arms. "I DON'T REMEMBER ASKING YOU TO *SNATCH ME OFF THE GROUND!*"

"Sorry dude, we gotta move!" he yells.

Honestly, Blythe considers this a lucky break. The encounter could have been worse; one of them could have been injured, or the woman could have sent some new monstrosity after them.

The ground shakes. "Blythe, she's sending something after us!" Daniel yells.

"I had to fucking jinx it," Blythe groans.

It's much bigger than Krubim; the trees tremble from its footfalls. A bird-like caw shoots over Blythe's shoulder, along with the sound of massive, flapping feathers.

Blythe curses aloud. It's probably that giant bird from earlier; another one of the species Katia killed.

"Daniel, we gotta run faster!" Blythe yells.

But Daniel does the opposite—he stops.

"This is not the time to be frozen with fear—"

He interrupts Blythe."Nightshade!"

Daniel rips free, running toward the trees, and Blythe yells for him as she races after him. He kneels over a patch of flowers and berries in the grass.

"I need this!" he insists. He rips up a handful of them. "I-I need to—"

There is a shuddering *boom* that shakes through Blythe's body. Movement to the left catches Blythe's eye. A falling tree is racing toward them.

Daniel screams. Blythe pushes him ahead, running fast enough to kick up dirt in her wake.

The tree snaps through the canopy of branches as they race out of the way, hitting the ground just as Antonio lands on top of the van.

He yanks open the passenger door and tosses Cordelia in—and of course she shrieks the whole way.

Antonio's expression is desperate. "Guys, hurry!"

"Can't you drive?!?" Blythe screams. He could at least get behind the wheel!

"I'm fourteen!"

"*What?* How are you almost as tall as me?!"

The creature caws behind them. Blythe can feel the air ripple from its movements. It's getting too close for comfort.

Another tree collides with the ground as she and Daniel reach the van. "

Who has the compass?!" Blythe yells.

"I do!" Cordelia answers.

"Put in Storm Crane's address!" Blythe leaps into the driver's seat, slamming the door behind her. She reaches for the ignition and hits thin air. "Keys, keys!"

"I found 'em!" Antonio throws them to her.

She shoves them in. The engine roars to life. "Where to?!"

Cordelia stares at the compass in her hands. "I don't know, it's not giving a direction!"

"*Cordelia!*"

"Its coming!" Daniel shrieks.

A massive body of oily feathers fills the sideview, as large as a building, stomping toward them. They *cannot* fight that thing.

"East!" Cordelia shrieks. "*East!*"

Blythe floors it. The van rips forward. Judging from the mirror, the bird is close, but not close enough to—

The back end of the van swerves as something slams into it.

Blythe yanks the wheel, setting the van straight as the creature shrieks and pitches forward again.

Objects in view may be closer than that appear, the sideview mirror reads. Goddamn it.

"Stay east!" Cordelia screams.

The ground crunches as they break through a patch of branches and trees. Blythe doesn't let off the gas. The creature's footfalls are hard enough to bounce their tires off the ground.

"Daniel, can you keep it off us?!" Blythe yells.

"N-N-Not while it's moving!" Daniel screams.

Blythe grips the wheel harder. The van feels like it wants to fly out of control.

"Go left a bit!" Cordelia yells.

Blythe turns and the line of seven trees swing into view. The van screeches as it moves. It's leaning *way* too far right.

"No, no, no, c'mon," Blythe mutters. "Antonio, shift over to Daniel's side!"

Antonio launches over the seat. The van balances just as the creature slams a sharp claw behind them with a sound loud enough to vibrate through Blythe's seat.

"That is *not* how momentum works—" Cordelia is interrupted.

"I got it!" Daniel yells.

The ground rips and shreds. The trees' huge roots, the ones as massive as buildings, yank free from their ancient slumber and catch the bird in their grasp.

Blythe laughs. "Fuck yeah, Daniel!"

The van screeches forward. They're going one hundred miles per hour and the needle is still climbing. If Blythe messes up even a bit, the van will swing out of her control.

Blythe doesn't let up. The seven trees grow larger as the creature's caws grow louder.

The world falls silent as they rush into darkness.

Blythe hits the breaks as light breaks through the windows. They burst back into the world, skidding and squealing on asphalt.

Cordelia is thrown forward. "Brake, *brake!*" she shrieks.

The car skids, screams, grinds...and comes to a halt.

They're in a parking lot, but judging from the old buildings, new corporate towers, and Ben Franklin statue atop a far building, it's Philadelphia.

Blythe can't catch her breath. She checks on the others; Cordelia seems to be in shock, Daniel looks nauseous and Antonio—Antonio is *beaming*.

"That was SO cool!" he exclaims.

Blythe laughs a bit. She can't help it. Was it crazy? Of course. But it feels more like they deserve a sticker that says *Baby Guardians Survive Their First Baby Fight*.

Of course Cordelia has to ruin it. "*No*, what is wrong with you?!"

Antonio pouts. "I just meant in general. Didn't have to be anytime soon," He brightens again, nearly bouncing out of his seat. "Cords, you were so cool with that lady, and Blythe with her hockey stick! Man!"

Blythe gives him a dramatic wink. Cordelia scoffs, pretending to not care as she rolls her eyes, but her cheeks flush pink.

"An all-girl's school for rich brats teaches you how to be intimidating," she says.

Antonio's not done yet, and his attention turns to Daniel. "And those vines were amazing! You did such a good job!"

Daniel shoves the door open and throws up.

"Aww, dude," Antonio sighs.

"You gonna be okay?" Blythe asks.

With his head still ducked, Daniel gives a thumbs up.

Blythe wants to ask exactly *why* he needed those berries so damn bad, but she has a feeling he won't explain in front of Antonio and Cordelia. Plus, he *just* saved their asses. It'll have to wait, at least for a bit.

Cordelia whirls to Blythe. "And *you!*" she hisses. "What do you call that, how you just ran off!"

Blythe opens her mouth to explain—and realizes, really, she... doesn't have a good reason. "I don't know," she admits. "I'm sorry."

"You have a plan to get your family," Cordelia retorts. "Don't stray from it and put us *all* in danger."

"Your family?" Antonio asks. "What happened to your family?" He frowns as Daniel dry heaves. "And do we have anything for him?"

One of those questions is a lot easier to answer than the other, so Blythe takes the easy route. She'll have to explain things to Antonio eventually, but now is not the time. "There's some water in the trunk —and some snacks."

"Ohhhh, you shouldn't have told me about the snacks," Antonio says, reaching a hand over the seats.

Blythe has so much to think about: Daniel and those berries, updating Antonio on everything...and what the woman said about the Black Veins attacking the Trident Republic and, indirectly, putting her family in danger.

She hopes they'll be driving for a while because she needs time to process.

"We have to get rid of that shard," Cordelia blurts.

"That shard is the only thing keeping them from brainwashing us," Blythe replies.

"What do you call what happened in the parking lot? Sometimes you just get the itch to run cars into trees?"

"Maybe! I do whatever the hell I want!" Blythe snaps. "But that couldn't have been them. It felt nothing like what happened on the roof."

"Then who? Who else wants to control us into killing ourselves?"

"I don't know. And if you care so much, Miss Guardian of the Mind, go ahead and do something to stop it."

"I already told you why I'm not doing that. But since you don't want to listen to anyone who isn't yourself, *I'll* figure something out for the damn shard."

"Yeah, you go on ahead," Blythe huffs. "While you're at it, get the directions to Storm Crane's house."

THIRTEEN

CORDELIA IS IN A MOOD. SHE SITS SIDEWAYS, HER BACK TO Blythe. But there are too many thoughts crowding Blythe's mind for her to care.

They're stuck in traffic, which gives Blythe a moment to think and take in the city. In-between Philadelphia's anachronistic old buildings and modern towers is a bustling crowd of businessmen in crisp blazers, young trendsetters, tourists, dog-walkers. It's like New York City Lite. *Super* lite.

Blythe sits with her legs against the wheel—they haven't moved in a while and probably won't be moving anytime soon.

That woman said her family could be killed as causalities of a second Black Veins attack. Blythe's stomach ties in knots. What if Blythe is wrong? What if her family isn't in Electric City, but some other Trident Republic territory? What if that territory gets leveled before she figures it out?

Blythe turns on the Alastair French show, but even he doesn't have any news. The other Guardians don't even notice. They're too busy chatting.

"I wish I would have brought Uno or something," Antonio

whines. He's resorted to flicking his flip-flop on and off for entertainment. "I didn't even bring my Switch, this *sucks*..."

Daniel actually looks up from his grimoire just to frown at him. "I don't understand half the things you say."

"You're speaking for both of us," Cordelia agrees.

Antonio takes that as a cue to lean toward her seat. "*You* have to know what video games are."

"I do," she says without looking at him. "But the only game I am even remotely interested in is Mario Kart."

"Dude! Maybe when we get to Frost Glade, we can find a Switch and play a round—"

"How are you okay with this?!" Blythe blurts.

She hadn't meant to say that out loud. Anger and anxiety had raged too strongly in her chest, forcing sharp words out from even the slightest annoyance.

"Sorry," Blythe sighs. "I'm just...nevermind."

But Antonio doesn't seem to mind. "It's okay. I figured it'd be nice if we all hung out together, y'know? We're all Guardians and—"

"No, not that," Blythe interrupts. She may as well be honest. "I mean the monsters, the Trident Republic, the 'leaving home to save your life' thing—all of that. How are you so...how are you so happy?!"

Antonio's expression remains as peacefully bright as the sunshine around them. "Because I can't change what happened to me, but I *can* change how I respond to it."

Blythe never expected to hear something so insightful from Antonio Torres. There is no sin in finding the light in darkness. And right now, Blythe is worried. She is tired. She is hungry and her body yearns for a good bed to sleep on.

She wants to find happiness again, even just for a moment.

"Anyway," Antonio continues. "I kill it as Peach."

"No way," Blythe says. "I'm literally a Peach main."

"Oh, in your dreams, Blythe," Cordelia scoffs.

Blythe points to her. "I have two little sisters and have mastered the art of clicking a character before anyone else can get to it. *Try me.*"

"Who is Peach?" Daniel asks.

The conversation shifts to explain Mario Kart and Nintendo lore to Daniel. By the time they park in front of Storm Crane's house, Daniel has decided he'd race as Mario (much to everyone's disappointment).

Their destination turns out to be a townhouse smashed in the middle of its block. The yard is neatly trimmed, contrasting with the rusty metal gate. Blythe leads the way up the cracked cement stairs to ring the doorbell.

They wait. And they wait. And they wait even longer.

"My god, does anyone live here?" Cordelia mutters.

A lock finally clicks and the door swings wide. A Black boy stands there, probably in his early twenties, with a neatly trimmed fade and thick eyebrows.

"Oh," he says. "You them kids."

Blythe puts on her most polite smile. "Yeah, hi, we're here for Storm Crane, is she home?"

The boy sighs. For a moment, Blythe fears he's annoyed at them. Then she realizes the wrinkle in his brow is caused by the mention of Storm. "Nah, she ain't here. I told her not to be running off but...hold on, I'll call her."

The Guardians stand there, awkwardly, as the boy casually pulls out his phone and dials a number. Over his shoulder lies the interior of the Crane's house; a white sofa rests in front of a huge TV, contrasted by the vintage wooden coffee table and homey carpeting.

The ringing of the boy's phone stops, but the only person that answers is the voicemail. The boy curses and hangs up.

"The one day she decides not to waste her life in bed," he mutters. "Look, I got class in fifteen minutes, but you can check the basketball court down the street. If she ain't there, you can swing back here and wait. Mi casa es tu casa, or however the hell you say it."

"You're right," Antonio replies.

Honestly, Storm's absence isn't the largest inconvenience. It'll give them a chance to take things easy for a bit—and for Blythe to snoop around her house before she meets her, maybe get a handle on what kind of person she is.

"Oh, but we have a dog," the boy adds. "He's a pitbull, but he's chill with new people."

Daniel goes pale. Right—he's terrified of dogs. There goes Blythe's chance to be nosy.

"We'll, uh, stay out here, but thanks," she says.

"Aw, I want to meet the puppy," Antonio complains.

"He ain't a puppy," says the boy.

"All dogs are puppies at heart," replies Antonio.

"...Anyway, I can give you her number, but her phone's prolly dead. I'm really sorry about this."

"It's alright, we'll find her," Blythe says. Cordelia scoffs. She hates any inconvenience, no matter how slight.

The Guardians drive to the basketball court and find a whole bunch of boys in Nike shorts and fresh sneakers, but no Storm. One guy tells them he hasn't seen her all day, which isn't the best sign.

They return to her house, but when they ring the bell this time, there is no answer at all. Blythe calls Storm's phone, but the ringing drones in her ear endlessly.

Antonio plops down on the stairs beside Daniel. Judging from how much Antonio's fidgeting, boredom is taking over.

"So, like, when you stayed in your house, did you ever wanna like... leave?" He asks.

Daniel squints from the sun. "N-Not really. There's too much... stuff out here."

"Whatdoya mean 'stuff'? You know the world's not out to get you, right?"

"You're not the world," Daniel retorts. "You don't know *what* it wants from me."

Antonio twists his mouth to the side. "So, you've never had a cheesesteak hoagie before?"

Daniel shakes his head. Antonio's hand shoots into the air. "Can I make a suggestion?" Blythe raises her eyebrows at him. "Let's go to the city and try some cheesesteak hoagies! I'll pay for everyone—I've never had them and neither has Daniel, and maybe when we come back, Storm'll be home!"

"No," says Cordelia.

Antonio ignores her; his eyes are on Blythe. Blythe's not sure when she started single-handedly calling the shots, but that's apparently where they're at.

It's past lunch, and she's hungry. And Storm obviously isn't showing up.

"Onward to the food," she says.

It doesn't take Antonio long to find good food. Fifteen minutes later, the four of them are splitting two Philly cheesesteaks on a city bench.

A diverse mix of city goers pass by them: families, students, wannabe artists, friends of every ethnicity, aesthetic and style. The Guardians blend in perfectly here—no one even looks their way.

If Blythe let herself, she could almost pretend they were just a group of friends enjoying their summer. She has to admit, she doesn't *hate* the Guardians' company.

Daniel takes a huge bite of his hoagie—and his face contorts as if he's swallowed a lemon. Antonio bursts into laughter as he spits it out.

"Dude, your face," Antonio chuckles. "Are you okay?"

"It's disgusting! And spicy!" Daniel whines. "This is nothing like my sandwiches from home..."

"Can I have your half, then? These are amazing."

Daniel nearly shoves it at him, nose wrinkled in disgust.

"Judging from your bland personality, I can imagine what your food tastes like," Cordelia mutters.

Daniel stares at Cordelia. "Did you just insult my mother's cooking?"

"Oh my God," Cordelia says. "Are you a momma's boy too?"

Daniel's face burns beat red. "S-Shut up." The words tumble awkwardly off his tongue, as if it isn't a phrase he's used to saying. He must've learned it from them.

More specifically: Cordelia.

Blythe beams. "Get WRECKED, Cordelia!"

"He's such a momma's boy that the only time he grows a spine is to defend her," Cordelia retorts.

"I-I always have a spine," Daniel mutters. "That's how anatomy works."

"WORLDSTAAAAAAAAR!" Blythe screams as Antonio hoots, "Ooooooo!"

Cordelia pointedly closes the foil over her tofu burger (she refused to "ingest the sloppiness that is one of those unhealthy monstrosities", as she put it).

"We should head back now," she says, as if gracing Daniel with a response is beneath her.

She has a point though, so they toss out their trash and hop back into the van. Antonio points out a very cute bakery, insisting that no meal is complete without dessert, and so they buy two boxes of cookies, and hit the road again.

But Blythe gasps as they pass the Philadelphia Museum of Art, with its echoing fountain atop the iconic sprawling staircase. She's passed up a lot of photo opportunities; she needs to take this one.

Cordelia groans as Blythe flicks the turn signal. "We were attacked by monsters less than an hour ago and for some reason you all want to..." her voice trails off. "Fine. Go. Take pictures. But don't expect me to join you."

"Yeah dude, I gotta call outta this one too," Antonio says. "Pictures are boring."

"Fine," Blythe dramatically turns her nose up. "I guess us cultured folk will go have a nice fifteen-minute photoshoot."

She leaves them parked in the car and hurries with Daniel to the museum stairs. "So, Dan," Blythe begins as she raises the camera to her face. "How're you making out?"

He watches every person that passes them, but not with interest or disgust. Just...confusion. A studying, slightly fearful gaze that searches for something he can't quite see.

"I don't quite know. I...thought leaving home would be different, and it's not *good* but..." his voice trails off. "I want to say I'm okay. But I don't know if I am or not."

"You're doing great, though," Blythe says. "You're battling monsters and—"

"I may be good at it, but that doesn't mean I *like* it," Daniel interrupts. "And Cordelia's mean, and I don't understand Antonio... besides my parents, y-you're the only people I know. And I feel like I...I've missed so many things. And I can't quite get them, even though I want to."

Blythe lowers her camera. She doesn't give advice often, but this is Daniel: a sweet, quiet boy who cannot understand this new world he's been dropped into. He deserves advice. And Blythe wants to help him.

"I know how you feel," she begins. "When I was younger, I was a really weird, energetic kid. I mean like, I talked *all* the time. Nonstop. And most of it didn't make *any* sense to anyone who wasn't me or my parents. So obviously, all of the other kids thought I was too weird to deal with and they left me alone. One night I was crying to my dad about not having any friends, and he told me to try listening. Going up to someone, asking their name and what they liked to do, and taking it from there. I tried it and I...made my first friend. And from then on I just started making friends by investing myself in other people.

She takes a low breath. "Friendship is an art, like gardening or photography. It's something you can get better at with practice. And not everyone does it the same way—some people like to keep some distance from their friends, other people want to talk every day. But once you learn how, you find other people who value the same things you do and make friends in a similar way. You've got your whole life ahead of you. And you've got all the time in the world to figure it out. So don't worry if you don't get it now. It'll happen." She pauses. "But for the record...I don't understand Antonio either."

Daniel smiles a bit, a wry curve of his mouth that doesn't show any teeth. "Thanks," he says. "That...that does make me feel better."

She smiles, giving him an encouraging pat on the arm as she focuses on her shots again, adjusting the exposure to catch the light *just* right on the stairs and pillars.

"There was...there was something else I wanted to tell you," Daniel says. "I-I tried to mention it back at Antonio's house."

"Oh yeah, I remember. What's up?"

His tone turns serious, as if to hide the way his voice shakes. "Promise not to laugh."

"I wouldn't do that," Blythe says.

Daniel stares off at the museum like he can't look at her. The sun seems too bright against his pale skin, catching in the curls of his hair. "There's a spirit trying to kill me," he whispers.

Blythe's blood runs cold. It takes her a moment to fully process the words. Because this is Daniel—the boy who stayed in his house for most of his life. Something is attempting to *murder* him?

"...What?" she asks. "Are you...are you serious? Are you *sure*?"

Daniel nods. His gaze is locked—unblinking and earnest—with hers. "I-It's been following me my entire life. It's always...there. I-I've never seen it, but I know it's...affecting things. It uses whatever's around to attack me. Weird things will just...happen."

Blythe frowns. "Weird things like what?" she asks. And then the memory strikes her—the feeling she got in the parking lot, when her body became a puppet on a string. "...Weird things like cars crashing?"

"Like accidents," he agrees. "T-Things that don't make sense. So I avoid a lot of things. O-Or at least I try to."

Holy shit. Blythe knew it, she *knew it*. What happened in the car was *not* the Trident Republic at all then—it was Daniel, or rather, the thing that hovers *around* Daniel.

Blythe can barely get her questions out fast enough. "Is that why your family moved to the hills?"

"No. We moved because my parents were afraid something bad would happen to me because I was a Guardian."

That was it? From what Blythe understood, all of the Guardians families had agreed to let them become Guardians. Why would the Quintons have signed Daniel up for this if they were so afraid?

But she doesn't want to ask such prying questions—and Daniel probably doesn't even have the answers.

"My parents don't believe me," he fiddles with his sweater. "T-They're scientists. Astrophysicists and thaumologists. They don't believe anything without...without concrete data. But I can't see it or feel it with any of my senses, I just *know* it's there. I just...I just wanted to tell you because I think...I think it might make things harder for us. *I* might make things harder for us."

Blythe doesn't know what to say.

"B-But it's not like I've been doing nothing!" Daniel insists. "I've been trying to create a cure for years!"

"That's what's in your grimoire," Blythe says.

Daniel nods. "I've researched every Learned Magic spell for banishment of spiritual entities that I could find. But every spell I've ever tried, all the ingredients I've used..." his voice trails off. "None of them have ever worked. But I-I have one left. It's the only one I haven't tried, because a lot of the ingredients don't grow near my house."

"You've been picking them up as we went along," Blythe realizes. "Like the nightshade just now. And the berries in the snow."

Daniel nods again. "I only need one more ingredient—silver-root. It's used in a lot of...recreational drugs. But...but if you just want..." his voice trails off. "If you just want to be rid of me, I-I understand. If it's too troublesome—"

"Daniel!" Blythe interrupts. "Don't even say that. I want you to be here. If there's some weird evil spirit demon thingy trying to kill you, we're gonna help you get rid of it, not throw you out on the street. You are not a bother." She places a hand on his arm. "Like I said, nobody gets left behind."

Daniel smiles. It's a soft one, and it makes his face go warm.

"Thank you," he's quiet for a moment. "You're my first friend."

Oh.

The words catch Blythe by surprise. But maybe the Guardians *are* her friends—not permanently, of course.

They agreed to join her on the trek to Electric City, didn't they? The least she could do is consider them Temporary Buddies. Sans Cordelia, of course.

"First of many!" Blythe forces a huge smile on her face.

Daniel lets her take the rest of her shots in peaceful silence, happily rocking back and forth on his Oxfords.

———

It's dark when they see the Cranes' house for the third time. They ring the bell, to no avail, and wait on the porch until Daniel complains about being hot.

They try the basketball court again, but the place is deserted besides the floodlights beating down on the baskets.

Blythe sighs. The thought of driving for even another *minute* makes her want to collapse. She, Cordelia, and Daniel have travelled nonstop since early morning.

"I think we should take a break," she says. "Y'know, find somewhere to sleep or something. Just for the night. We can try again tomorrow."

"We can't take a break," Cordelia snaps. "If anything, this afternoon counted as a break. Besides Storm, we only have one more Guardian to find before—"

"I know how many Guardians are left," Blythe interrupts. "I also know that I'm tired. No, not tired. Exhausted. Mentally, physically, *metaphysically*. And when I'm tired, I'm irritable, and you guys do not want an irritable Guardian of Ether."

Antonio's eyebrows shoot up. "Okay, time to find a place to sleep. Like, ASAP."

Cordelia's gaze doesn't stray from Blythe. "First of all," she begins —oh God, it's another one of her monologues. "No one is afraid of you, Blythe Fulton. Second of all, last I checked, we were a group and all had equal say as to what we did and did not do. You're not the only one whose opinions matter."

"Cordelia, I think—"

"Shut up, Daniel," Cordelia interrupts. "We're walking it through until we find Storm."

"But you just said..." Daniel's voice trails off. He frowns. "W-Well, I want to go to sleep!"

"You don't know *what* you want," Cordelia spits.

"I know I don't want to listen to you!" Daniel yells.

Their eyes spear through each other. Antonio pops his head in-between them. "Let's try this," he suggests. "Since Daniel and Blythe want to sleep, and I'm pretty tired too, we'll stop for the night and go looking for Storm first thing tomorrow. How's that sound?"

Cordelia stares at him, then scoffs. She isn't looking for a compromise. She's looking for power over the group. She's looking to *win*.

But this isn't that type of situation, and it never has been, so she has no choice but to relent.

The air stings with the aftermath of a disagreement that is not quite over. Even Antonio can't break the silence that falls as they search for a hotel.

Blythe worries that they won't be able to book a room since they're under eighteen. Cordelia, however, snatches up her phone.

"*I'll* get us a room," she says. They are the last words she speaks for the rest of the night.

———

Their hotel room comes with two full beds and—the part Blythe is most excited for—a bathroom with a fully working shower.

Cordelia resigns herself to one of the beds, back to the others to shut out the world. Blythe didn't have time for her attitude earlier and she certainly doesn't have time for it now.

Blythe inspects her wounds in the shower. With each passing day, her body takes more of a beating. At this rate, by the time they reach Electric City, she'll be missing a limb.

Being in the shower always causes her mind to wander. Memories of the day morph into memories of her family. Her mother, her father, Lily, Lena.

She spent today relaxing. But what if that was a mistake? What if, tomorrow morning, she wakes up to news that Electric City has been attacked again, and that there is no hope this time?

She doesn't know what else to do. She's trying her best, pushing herself as far as she can.

But what if her best isn't enough?

She doesn't want to be the girl who cries in a bathroom alone. She doesn't want to be the girl who cries at all. But once she's changed into her pajamas—ones that remind her of home—she can't take it anymore.

She rushes out of the bathroom, through the dark room where the Guardians lay sleeping, and straight into the night. She sits on the stairs, brings her knees to her chest, and cries.

The first few teardrops only pave the way for more. She is trying to make all the right decisions, to be strong, to keep the Guardians together when she can barely keep *herself* together.

But there is a murderous spirit lingering near their group and a woman who summons monsters and terrorizes Blythe with photos implying the death of her family.

No amount of strength can carry all of this.

Something clicks behind her. The door is easing open. She can't let anyone see her like this. She absolutely *can't*.

Blythe rushes to wipe away her tears, but they are only replaced by more, and quieting her sobs results in hiccups.

Someone sits down beside her. They smell like the ocean.

"I don't know why you're crying," Antonio whispers. "But I don't think I need to."

Blythe can't look at him. She hates when people see her cry. "I'm sorry, Antonio," she whispers. "I just...I'm sorry..."

"Hey, hey, don't be sorry," he says. "You should never be sorry for crying. I cry. All of the other Guardians cry. Everyone cries. Especially when monsters are trying to kill them." He places a warm hand on top of hers and squeezes tight. "It just sucks to cry by yourself."

Blythe takes in a shaky breath. "There's so much we didn't tell you, and I'm sorry," she chokes out. "I was going to but we never had the time—Whiteclaw was at your house and then we were in the Tempore and I should have told you today but I just—"

"It's okay, it's okay. I'm not mad. Look!"

He's taken his topknot out, and with the front of his hair brushing his cheeks, he looks much younger. He smiles, his pure, perfect smile, and there's that dimple.

"See?" he says. "S'all good. You guys had a lot on your plate, I get it."

Blythe wipes her eyes. Well, there's no time like the present. "My family got kidnapped by the Trident Republic. A guy named Whiteclaw destroyed my family's café, took them and...and attacked my friend. It happened right in front of me. But I couldn't even do anything. I was too weak to even do anything."

Antonio's brow pinches, but he lets her continue. "I want to get them back. But it's not even a want, I...I *need* to," Blythe takes in an uneven breath. "But I'm so scared. I don't know what to do. I thought I needed to take a break today, but what if that was wrong? The plan was to get the Guardians' help, but I never even asked you if you would help. I don't know what I'm doing at all. And that—that lady in the Tempore says my family could be killed and I wouldn't even be able to do anything about it?! And we can't find Storm and I just..." she hides her face in her hands as the tears bubble up again. "I don't know what to do..."

Antonio wraps his arms around her and holds her tight. She hadn't meant to say so much, to dump her problems on him like this.

He stays with her as she cries, until she has gone still and the only sounds she makes are raspy breaths.

"I'm really close to my mom," Antonio says. "All of my family, really. We sleep over at each other's houses, my cousins go to school with me, and sometimes we even share birthday parties."

"But..." his voice trails off. "If someone kidnapped them, especially my mom, I don't know what I'd do. I'd probably just...run to my grandma's house and cry. Or beg for someone to help me. But look at you. I mean, so what if you took a day to recharge? You're *out here*. You're crossing the country, getting all of us together so you can make it to Electric City and find your family."

He pulls her back, holding her at arm's length, making her look straight into her eyes. "You're more capable than you think you are. And you *can* do this. And if you can't, well, you're getting us for a reason. I guess all I'm saying is...you're doing everything that you can. And it'll be enough. You're enough. And where you fall flat, we'll pick you up again. Okay?"

Blythe's eyes are burning with tears again, but for a different reason this time: gratitude. "Thanks, Antonio," she whispers. "Really."

He beams. "No problem. And, by the way, I *will* help you get to Electric City."

Blythe laughs, wiping her eyes. Antonio said he had a seagull's wings, but Blythe is certain this boy is simply a walking angel.

"Whenever I'm sad, my mom makes me something to eat, like cookies and coffee," Antonio continues. "But we don't have any food right now. And I ate all the cookies from earlier."

Blythe sniffles. "It's the thought that counts, right?"

"Thoughts don't taste as good as cookies."

Blythe chuckles. Antonio asks if she'll come back in to sleep, but she thinks the night air will be good for her, at least for a bit longer.

When the door clicks shut behind Antonio, Blythe is left with a night sky full of stars and a head full of memories that don't hurt as much.

She is going to make it to Electric City—and she has people who will keep her safe, who will help her, who won't let her fail. And that knowledge sits warm and soft in her chest.

After a while, her phone buzzes. It's Jamie.

Everything still ok?

Even back home, there is someone looking out for her. Blythe truly is a very, very lucky girl.

She tries to text back, but the screen goes black. A red battery sign flashes at her.

Blythe sighs. Back inside, Daniel and Antonio are on their bed; Antonio has fallen back to sleep in remarkable time. Daniel faces the wall again, wide awake.

"Hey Cords," Blythe begins. "Can I borrow your charger..."

Blythe's voice trails off. The bed is empty.

Cordelia is gone.

FOURTEEN

"Daniel?"

"Huh?"

"Where's Cordelia?"

Daniel rolls over, slightly concerned. "I-I thought she was out with you."

Blythe curses under her breath. Of *course* Cordelia would do this. God only knows what she decided to leave for. Monsters and the Trident Republic be damned—the only thing that girl cares about is being right and making a point.

If Blythe waits for Cordelia to return, she may be waiting for the rest of her life. There are too many people out for Guardian blood.

"Daniel, can you call her?" Blythe asks.

He sits up and takes his phone from the nightstand. "How do I do that?" he asks the screen.

Blythe does it for him, but the phone rings with no answer. "I'm gonna go look for her," Blythe decides.

"S-Should we all come?" Daniel stammers.

They could help, but if this is just a false alarm, there's no use in getting everyone up and out of bed.

"I'll make sure she's not just throwing a hissy fit or something," Blythe says. "Can I take your phone with me? Mine's is dead."

"Of course. I wasn't using it."

Blythe puts her clothes on over her pajamas and throws her hockey stick on her back. "If I need you I'll call Ant," she says as she leaves.

Daniel's face is flushed. "O-Okay. B-Be safe."

Outside, the only light comes from streetlights and the occasional passing car.

The silence is what gets to Blythe the most; she is completely alone as she travels these dark streets.

Blythe tries calling Cordelia again with no luck. Cordelia could've just stormed off in bratty huff—but something terrible could have happened.

How is Blythe supposed to find a girl who has either gotten in trouble or simply doesn't want to be found?

Blythe's not too keen on walking around alone at night. She doesn't know this city at all—but neither does Cordelia. And Cordelia is definitely smart enough to know that.

Would she really run off for no reason?

Daniel's phone vibrates. Blythe is hopeful—at first. It's a text from Cordelia: no words—just a location.

Blythe stares at the red pin on the pastel map. This is either Cordelia being petty, or reason for Blythe to be very, very worried.

Blythe follows the GPS down street after street. There's a corner store here, a gas station there, a mini deserted plaza of no name stores.

The closer she gets, the colder her blood runs. The streets are becoming darker and quieter. The world seems dead.

You've arrived at your destination, the GPS reads. Blythe's breath hitches. The place in front of her is a decrepit auto repair garage, locked and barred with a "sorry, we're closed!" sign hanging from the doorknob. Light echoes through the smeared windows.

Nothing about this place screams safe. It looks like a serial killer's den. And Cordelia is *in* there.

Blythe refuses to call Daniel and Antonio. For what? To put all four of them in danger? And Blythe's not completely defenseless, something she remembers whenever she has to shift the hockey stick's weight on her back.

Blythe creeps up to the window. The door lies to her left, but it's shut and seems to be sealed with putty. Whatever is smeared across the glass, oil or thick grime, obscures her vision.

She makes out a group of men inside, wearing all-black. That's the dress code of the Erasers—but these people aren't in suits.

The door slams open. Light explodes into the night. Beefy fingers snatch Blythe's collar and yank her backward.

"Eh, Rocco!" the person shouts. "Here's another one!"

The attacker drags her inside like a lifeless sack; her body slips over the floor too quickly for her to stop. She reaches for chairs and passing countertops, tries to dig her heels downward to stop the momentum, but the grip on her shirt is like a vice.

Everything happens too quickly. Her body trembles as the attacker drops her against cement. A new pair of hands wrestle her hockey stick off of her body. She's lost her only weapon.

Something slams into her back, pinning her flat. Someone's boot is on her back. The dark filth in cold floor crushes her cheek. It reeks of motor oil.

"Well shit," says a familiar voice. "Look who it is."

The boot eases up just a bit, enough for Blythe to lift her head and scan the room. There are at least twelve guys encircling her at a distance, men with shaved heads, tattoo sleeves, full beards, cold eyes.

They sit atop dusty cars or lean against the walls. Two are posted at both doorways Blythe can spot. Some of them have guns holstered at their hips.

Cold recognition shivers through Blythe. These are the people she stole the shard from. The biker gang from Washington.

And they're all looking at her.

To the right, sitting on a metal table coated with black grease, is Cordelia. Her hands are held behind her back.

Blythe tries to echo her thoughts as loudly as possible, not breaking her gaze on the other girl.

Are you okay?! She asks. *Are you okay?*

There is no response but the unchanging, pleading expression widening Cordelia's eyes. She can't hear Blythe.

It probably has something to do with the metal chain around her neck—specifically, the stone hanging from it, glowing with a magical pulse.

Beside Cordelia is a familiar face indeed—Rocco, the leader of the group, black boots crossed, one hand in the pocket of his black jeans and the other holding Cordelia's phone.

He looks down at Blythe. "Didn't know we'd end up luring *you* here," he says. "But I ain't gonna complain."

His boots crunch against the concrete as he ambles toward her. Blythe resists the urge to shut her eyes as he kneels, bringing his dark gaze inches from her face. "Thought you were clever, hmm? With your damn *Home Alone* sparklers and shit."

He drags her to her feet with a grip like iron. "The Trident Republic can track their shard, you dumb bitch," he spits. "We were gonna find you eventually. It was only a matter of time before you fucked up."

Keeping her expression blank becomes a balancing act Blythe doesn't quite succeed in. That must be how woman in the Tempore found them—all she had to do was follow the location of the shard straight to them.

"Do you know who we are?" Rocco asks.

"No," Blythe snaps. She steels her breathing, swallowing her fear. "And I really couldn't care less."

Rocco twists her arm behind her back. There's a weird, sickening noise. It comes from Blythe's own shoulder. Pain shoots down her arm, searing and sharp.

She cries out through clenched teeth—the pain reverberates through every organ in her body. She has never broken a bone, not once in her whole life. The tears threatening to run down her face are thick and hot.

The look in Rocco's unblinking eyes is scarily impassive. "I wouldn't be so confident if I were you. Especially since your friend already gave us what we want."

An unseen hand passes Rocco a heavy beanie. *Blythe's* beanie. She presses her lips together to keep from begging him not to touch it, *pleading*, even as he reaches inside—

It feels like her mind tears in half, straight down the middle. Through the endless white noise blaring in her mind and the sound of her own screams comes Rocco's throaty voice. "The fuck?"

The other bikers suddenly come alive. "Wait...who are these kids?"

"Oh shit, Rocco, the last people they used that shard on were the—"

"We're not supposed to messin' with the Guardians..."

"Shut up!" Rocco shouts. "They ain't Guardians. They're a bunch of annoying ass kids. And we're gonna treat 'em like it."

The words come right beside her ear, sharp and hard. "You're gonna remember who the fuck we are because we're the last faces you'll ever *see*."

Disembodied noises in her mind leave no room for thought. There is only the endless, vast expanse of broken sound and distorted broken fragments, and, somewhere beneath it, the creeping fear that she will exist in this agony forever.

Until, suddenly, it stops. Blythe's mind falls silent. Her senses reopen to the world, but it takes her a moment to return to the present—to remember where she is, who she is. She blinks her eyes open to find the garage in chaos.

Rocco has risen to his feet, shouting. "What the fuck is that?!"

A different voice. "Shit. It's that girl on that bike."

Rocco grunts. "You gotta be shittin' me. Hawk, Skip, grab the Asian chick and the shard!"

He snatches Blythe to her feet. Her legs wobble, her arm burns, something warm trickles down onto her lip.

She barely hears his words. "You're gonna come with us, because we ain't done yet—"

An orange blur slams him into the ground.

"She's in here!" someone screams.

Blythe backs away, but the blur is already gone. The men are in a frenzy: black leather jackets shoot past Blythe's vision as they run, like a scattering wolf pack.

Through the chaos of bodies and movement, two Black Jackets usher Cordelia through an open doorway and into the night.

Blythe can't let them get far.

Gunfire bursts in the air. Blythe doesn't think—instinct takes over and she ducks behind a nearby car. The Black Jackets fire at the orange blur—their bullets sail right past it.

It darts around the room with precision and intelligence. Every man it passes collapses like he's been struck. They drop like flies, one instantly after the other, too fast for Blythe to fully see, until the garage is silent and littered with bodies. But not a single drop of blood has spilled.

The blur stops. And it is no longer a blur, but a girl.

An orange Harlequin mask covers her face. She's Black, pear shaped and athletically muscular. Her dark hair is parted into twin braids down her back, and her scuffed rollerblades should make her extremely tall, but she looks to be Blythe's height.

Blythe holds her breath as the girl reaches down to take the beanie from Rocco's limp hand.

"That's mine," Blythe blurts.

The girl seems to study her for a moment. She peeks into the beanie, pauses for a second, and tosses it to Blythe with disinterest.

Blythe can feel the girl's gaze as she awkwardly maneuvers her good arm to tuck it into her pocket.

"You hurt?" asks the girl.

"M-My arm," Blythe stammers.

Blythe doesn't see the girl move, but suddenly, she is at Blythe's side, assessing the state of her injury. The girl's eyes are a light, pretty amber brown.

"It's just dislocated," she says. "This is gonna hurt like a bitch."

"What's—" The girl shoves Blythe's shoulder into place with a pop that feels more like an explosion in her muscles.

"MOTHER OF *CHRIST*!" Blythe screams.

The girl is already rising to her feet. "We gotta go. C'mon. Get up."

"Can you give me a minute?!" Blythe winces. "My arm is freaking—"

"Do you wanna save your friend, yes or no?" the girl barks.

She is all speed and efficiency. She's also a really shitty superhero. Technically, yes, she is correct, but would it kill her to be a little nicer?

As Blythe stumbles to her feet, the girl skates out of the open doorway with the grace and speed of someone who is very used to moving on wheels.

But Blythe can't follow, not just yet. She hurries around the garage until she finds her hockey stick on the ground beside a car.

Now she's ready to raise hell.

Blythe jogs outside as she fits the strap over her chest. The girl sits atop a thin, lean motorcycle, her rollerblades replaces with a pair of black Nike's.

Her eyes glow with magic—but they make Blythe pause. When a magician's eyes glow from using powerful magic, both of their eyes blaze with color. But only the girl's left eye pulses orange.

"Get on," orders the girl. "Quick."

Something's not right about this girl's magic, but Blythe's not in a position to be choosy. Cordelia is getting farther away with every passing second.

Blythe hops on behind her. Pain rings up Blythe's arm, but she holds tight to the girl's waist anyway.

With a rev of the engine, they shoot down the street like a blasting rocket. Blythe's never been on a motorcycle, and everything from the balance of the ride to the wind slapping her face is novel. Houses shoot past them—they're moving so *fast*.

The whole situation is going too fast. Blythe is on a bike with a complete stranger. Getting Cordelia back depends on this girl's ability to take on the Black Jackets—and her willingness to even *help* Blythe.

"Who *are* you?" Blythe asks.

"Don't worry about it," the girl answers.

Blythe tries again. "Are you a superhero? Because that'd be really—"

"No," the girl interrupts.

Well, that makes her mask extremely confusing.

The girl makes a hard right onto a long street lined with lights. Up ahead, three Black Jackets ride on three separate motorcycles, but only the one farthest ahead has Cordelia's long black hair fluttering after it.

The girl revs the engine. "Don't let go!" she shouts.

Blythe screams as they burst forward with newfound speed. "WHY WOULD I DO THAT?!"

Their bike falls in-between two Black Jackets. Gunfire echoes; it is too loud and too close. Blythe does not have time to scream because their bike abruptly drops in speed.

They fall behind as the gunfire continues, the two Jackets shooting each other in their unstoppable line of bullets.

The bike to their left wobbles and crashes into the sidewalk. The bike to their right hangs on, but as they make a wide left onto another side street, it skids to the ground.

"Holy shit," Blythe breathes. This girl knows what she's doing.

The sound of a growling bike resonates over Blythe's shoulder. A Black Jacket approaches from behind, his motorcycle quickly gaining speed and closing the space between them. The girl is facing forward. She probably can't handle this guy—but Blythe can.

Blythe grabs her hockey stick and raises it above her head. The Black Jacket's eyes are hard on her, his mouth a thin line.

The magic sings to her, power warming down her skin. Blythe slams it down, dragging it across the asphalt.

The street opens up, splitting into two halves, like rippling waves after a passing surfboard. The entire block shakes.

Blythe looks up as the Black Jacket spirals to the ground, collapsing in a heap.

"Damn, girl!" comes the girl's voice. "Keep that shit up!"

Up ahead are a patch of trees near the edge of a sidewalk. Blythe almost curses aloud when she sees the last remaining Black Jacket, the one carrying Cordelia, racing toward it.

"Not the Tempore," Blythe whispers.

But of course, the bike shoots right into the trees and disappears.

Before Blythe can think, the girl slams the gas and has them moving at the speed of light, emerging into a world of black sky and uneven ground.

They are hot on the Black Jacket's trail, watching its headlights bounce off of the trees.

Their wheels bounce over the terrain and the girl grips the handles hard to hold the bike steady.

"Can you drive a motorcycle?" The girl asks.

"No!" Blythe shouts. This girl is *not* about to abandon her on this bike.

"Then you gon learn today," says the girl. She *is* about to abandon Blythe on this bike.

An orange blur shoots up ahead. The seat in front of Blythe is empty. "Fuck!" Blythe yells, scrambling toward the controls.

The bike is tilting. Blythe grips the handles, holding it upright. There's a small, cylinder of a pedal beside her ankle. Blythe shoves her foot into it and prays that it's the brakes.

The bike shrieks, the back tires spin, and it comes to a halt.

Blythe waits for her heart to stop racing. That girl just left her to drive a motorcycle on her own.

Blythe has been waffling back and forth on her opinion of this girl for the past five minutes and now she has definitely decided: this girl is the worst superhero. *Ever.*

Blythe looks up just in time to catch the scene playing out in front of her. And it is, indeed, a scene.

The bike has stopped. Its headlight illuminates the face of the Black Jacket who once drove it but is now collapsed on a bed of leaves.

It's one of the twins— the girl stands over him, fists balled at her side. He aims the sharp end of a switchblade up at her, but his hand is shaking.

Twin's eyes are wild beneath his furrowed brow. "Make one move and I'll—"

Blythe blinks and his hand is empty. The girl has the switchblade at her side.

"Tell me where you were taking her," she demands.

Twin only tenses his muscles and spits. The girl leans in, bringing the sharp end of his own knife to press against his throat.

"Again," she growls. "Where the fuck were you taking her?"

This is going too far. "Wait—" Blythe starts, but Twin speaks over her.

"I don't fucking know everything, I'm not *Rocco*, I just listen to what he tells me, and he listens to what Walden Oliver tells *him*," His face goes pale as the words tumble out of him. "We're not high on the food chain, man, we just do some of the dirty work. It's nothing deep. We were delivering the amplifier when we broke it and that girl back there stole a piece. We got Tahira to help us track 'em down but they got away from her, so we had to step in. Rocco swore these were just some kids, but I knew they weren't, I knew we shouldn't've messed with 'em. That's all I know and it's all I'm telling you."

"No, it's not," the girl snaps. "Madame Deveraux. Where is she?"

"Not a damn clue. I've never heard that name before in my life."

The girl considers this, her amber eyes taking him in for a silent moment. Then she kicks him in the head so hard, his body drops, limp, into the leaves.

"*Oh my God!*" Blythe cries.

Who *is* this girl, this masked vigilante walking the line between criminal and savior—and should Blythe be scared of her?

If Blythe's shock has phased the girl at all, she doesn't show it. Her voice is nonchalant and smooth when she speaks. "I wasn't actually gonna cut him. I'on like hurting people *too* bad. I just needed him to be honest—all his gang does is lie."

The girl closes the switchblade and drops it in her pocket. She looks at Blythe, but she's speaking to Cordelia too.

"Come with me," she says. "Let's talk."

———

The girl brings them to a junkyard overflowing with valleys of useless trash. In its center is a circular alcove adorned with a fire pit and faded furniture arranged like a makeshift apartment.

The girl uses this place as a hideout, judging from how easily she lights the flames and drops onto an armchair like it's her living room.

Blythe and Cordelia share a sofa opposite her. Blythe expects Cordelia to leave a cushion's space between them, but the girl sits shoulder-to-shoulder with her.

Cordelia stares at the rising embers, her face holding an expression Blythe has never really seen on her.

"I didn't think you'd actually come for me," Cordelia says.

It's an odd statement, but Blythe's reply is instinctive. "Of course I did. What made you think I wouldn't?"

Red firelight makes the shadows on Cordelia's face pitch black. "Because I was a bitch," she says. "And if the roles were reversed I... don't think I would have been brave enough to come for you."

Her honesty feels like a rock in Blythe's chest. Blythe knows, of course, there are people in the world who won't return the kindness she gives. She just never thought they'd openly admit it.

Cordelia's hands are trembling. At least she doesn't seem proud of this.

"That was both touching and terrible, but it doesn't explain how you ended up here," says the girl.

She has her rollerblades on again, and they hang off one armrest while her body slouches against the other. The weight of the girl's gaze shatters any chance for Blythe and Cordelia to have a private conversation.

"I went to get rid of the shard," Cordelia answers. She speaks into the fire like she can't look at them. "Those men approached me and said they would help. I should have been suspicious when they already knew about the shard, but I...went with them. You know the rest of the story."

"Do you normally trust anybody that pulls up to you?" the girl snorts.

Blythe expects Cordelia to wrinkle her nose. She would never endure such a snide comment. But she doesn't even blink.

"I used to," she says. "I won't. Anymore."

Her voice is too broken. Too defeated. Blythe's stomach churns. She leans forward, asking, low, "Did they hurt you?"

"No. When they took the shard they just...took my pride with it. And we only got one of those things back."

Her words make the shard feel heavy in Blythe's pocket. Saying "serves you right" would be rude. Saying anything else would be a lie. So, Blythe says nothing at all.

Cordelia looks to the girl. "Who were they?"

The girl tosses the switchblade into the air and catches it. "The Angelus," she answers. "They're a magician gang who runs errands for the Trident Republic. They usually sell drugs and claim turf, but I'm guessing Walden Oliver makes use of them 'cause they know how to go untraced. Apparently, *you* messed them up. They'll probably keep coming back until they get what they want."

The firelight glints off the knife in the girl's grip. "Where's the shard?" she asks.

The force of her tone makes Blythe sit up straighter. "I have it," she says.

"Let me see," the girl demands without blinking, as if she is used to being obeyed.

Blythe doesn't move.

Yes, this girl could snatch it out of Blythe's pocket before Blythe could move an inch, but once she got her hockey stick Blythe could blow her into next fucking year.

"I'd rather not," Blythe says.

The mask hides most of the girl's expression, but Blythe can feel her distrust rise. Through the smoke of the flames, her amber eyes narrow at them.

"Alright," she says. "Who are you two? And why you got that in the first place?"

"You first," Blythe challenges.

A scoff. "I never made up a name for myself. The news calls me Napoleon."

Blythe instantly recoils. "That's the worst superhero name I've ever *heard*."

"I think it's 'cause of the mask."

"How does your mask relate to a *French conqueror*?"

"No, like the ice cream jawns. With the three colors."

"That's *Neapolitan*," Cordelia mutters.

The Masked Hero seems to be considering this. "Well, shit."

"That is absolutely ridiculous," Blythe huffs. "Don't you know you gotta take this stuff seriously? This is what happens when you *don't* name yourself. You get stuck with something dumb, like *Napoleon*. You could have been anything. Instead you got that."

"I keep telling you I'm not some fucking superhero," Napoleon snaps. "I don't do this because I like it, I do it 'cause it's dangerous if people know my identity."

That's a practical reason, but frankly, Blythe prefers her idea that this girl is a superhero.

"You still coulda tried for a better name than *Napoleon*," Blythe murmurs.

Cordelia sits up bolt right. In her eyes is a spark of her usual gusto —but that energy is directed right at the girl.

"We've been looking for you all day!" she blurts. "I wouldn't have known who you were if I hadn't read your mind, where have you *been*!?"

The girl seems just as confused as Blythe feels. Then realization blooms on her face.

"Oh shit," the girl says. "You them kids."

She slides off her mask, revealing a face strikingly similar to the boy the Guardians met at the Crane's house, full eyebrows and all.

"Storm Crane," says the girl. "Guardian of Time."

FIFTEEN

"But I'm not coming with y'all," Storm adds.

Blythe's not sure who holds more shock on their face: Cordelia or herself.

"What?" Blythe blurts.

"Why not?" Cordelia asks.

Storm shrugs one shoulder like moving the other is too much effort. "The Sages want everyone to run to Frost Glade because *three* of y'all got sent up to a roof but ain't shit happen to me. So I'm not going."

Cordelia wrinkles her nose at Storm's logic. "Just because something didn't hurt you in the past doesn't mean it can't hurt you in the future." Blythe couldn't have said it better herself.

"I can hold my own," Storm says, unconvinced. "I got shit to do around here anyway. I can't run off."

"Shit like Madame Deveraux?" Blythe asks.

Storm goes rigid. Her eyes cut into Blythe with suspicion. "How do you know that name?"

"I heard you say it earlier."

Storm visibly deflates, turning back to her stolen switchblade as if Blythe has lost all importance to her. But

Blythe isn't finished. "Why are you looking for her?"

"Reasons that are my business."

"And you...do that by chasing down the Angelus?"

"Them and other magician gangs and shady folk. Anyone could know something. But I run into the Angelus a lot."

Well, there's Blythe's angle. "Coming with us could give you a better chance of finding her, wherever she is. We're traveling a ton. It'll give you an opportunity to search through more places than just Philadelphia. We need to find one last Guardian and then we're headed to Electric City."

"I thought y'all were going to Frost Glade," Storm wrinkles her nose. "Now I'm really not coming. I ain't going straight into a war zone."

Blythe curses under her breath. Okay, that backfired.

Storm swings her legs around and stands with alarming speed, snuffing out the fire and starting toward the bright street lights.

"Wait!" Blythe calls. "Hear me out, I—"

"Naaaaaaaaaah," Storm says, body swaying on her skates. "I'm bad at listening. Get home safe."

Blythe jumps to her feet. "Forget about the Sages," she blurts. "*I* need you to come."

Storm rolls to a stop. Her shadow stretches along the empty space between her turned back and Blythe. It is the slightest pause, but it is all Blythe needs.

Storm took on the Angelus single-handed without breaking a sweat—she is, without a doubt, an invaluable asset. But if Blythe doesn't explain this correctly, if Blythe does not convince her, it is all for nothing, because Storm will *not* hesitate to leave.

The Guardians couldn't even find her today; Storm can make sure they'll never find her again.

Blythe takes a deep breath. "The Trident Republic kidnapped my family right in front of me, and I'm going to Electric City to get them back. If I go there alone, I'll probably die. So, I've been gathering the other Guardians to help me, because without them, I don't have a chance. And if I don't have a chance...neither does my family. So if you're not going to come to save yourself, consider coming to save my family. I need all the help I can get."

Storm has not blinked once throughout Blythe's speech. She does not move even now, and her stillness gives Blythe hope.

"Sounds rough," Storm says. "Hope you find someone."

This girl is unbelievable.

"You must really think I'm a superhero," Storm continues. "I do what I do for *me*. I don't do favors."

"But you did tonight," Blythe argues. Her blood is boiling—for every excuse Storm raises, Blythe has about three points to discredit her. Eventually she has to run out of ways to say no. "You didn't have to save me and Cordelia, but you did. You still stuck around even when it was obvious we didn't know anything."

Storm shakes her head as she turns away. "Alright, whatever, but this conversation is done. I'm not coming. There's only one thing I want and I know you can't give it to me."

"But the Angelus can, right?" The words tumble out of Blythe. "You said it yourself, they're going to keep coming after us as long as we have this shard. They'll fall right into your lap if you're with us, which has to be better than searching for them every night." Blythe pauses. "At least, that's what I assume you're doing. I don't actually know. I'm just following genre rules with the whole superhero, vigilante thing—"

Storm skates up to her in an orange blur. Even in rollerblades, she is still a bit shorter, but she is stout and unmovable, with eyes that are absolutely fierce.

"If I come," she says. "You're gonna make me help with your damn family, aren't you?"

"Probably," Blythe agrees. "No. Definitely. I'm *definitely* going to do that."

Storm thinks for a moment. "Here's the deal. I tag along with you.

If we get to Electric City and find your family? Gucci, I'm gone. But if we find the Angelus first? And I get what *I* need? I'm still gone, family or no. Y'hear?"

By this logic, they could lose Storm tomorrow, if they wake up to find the Angelus outside of their hotel room. Or she could help them leave Electric City with Blythe's family in tow.

It's a risky deal, but Blythe's probably not getting a better offer out of her.

So, Blythe nods. "Sounds good enough to me."

Something about those words makes Storm turn up her lip. "You from the suburbs or somethin'?"

"I moved around a lot but, yeah, I'm from Washington."

"You sound like it," Storm grumbles. "Please tell me the rest of y'all ain't weird or nothing."

———

"...and it was the sunflower fairies all along! So, they gave me the magic toothbrush, and as soon as I got through the Twizzler forest to fight the giant Pikachu, I woke up!"

Blythe's only halfway through the door and this scene is already wild. Daniel and Antonio sit cross-legged on their bed, Daniel wide-eyed and hypnotized by Antonio's elaborate storytelling.

"Kids, we're home!" Blythe shouts.

Antonio breaks into a smile, one that only intensifies when he sees Cordelia.

"Cordelia!" he yells. "Where'd you..." His voice trails off as Storm enters behind her. "Oh, who's this?"

Blythe dramatically gestures to her. "Storm Crane!" she announces. "Storm, meet Antonio and Daniel."

Storm jerks her chin in acknowledgement and Antonio's right back to smiling. "Dude, we were looking for you all day! Nice to finally meet you! Were you rollerskating? I love your blades."

Storm takes in this eager, personable chatterbox, and leans away as if his happiness is contagious. "...no."

"Do you just...wear them all day?"

"Basically."

"*Ohhhh*, that's cool! I'd worry about rolling away if I did that."

"Good thing I'm me and not you."

Antonio is an unstoppable force. Storm is an immovable object. They eye each other in an awkward, silent dance, neither quite sure of the other.

Storm breaks first, arching an eyebrow at Daniel. "You okay?" she asks. "You look scared as shit."

Daniel has on the same nervous expression he wore back when Blythe first met him at the diner. Meeting strangers elicits his fight or flight response.

"That's his default expression," Cordelia mutters.

She's back over at her bed, braiding her hair with slow, careful fingers, as she does every night.

Daniel shrinks his body into a small ball behind Antonio as he stammers an apology. "S-Sorry..."

"No, it's all good," Storm insists. "My fault. I was just asking."

But Antonio can neither be stopped nor ignored. "Daniel couldn't sleep so I was just telling him about some of the weirdest dreams I've—what is it, what's wrong?"

Daniel is discreetly trying to shush him, his gaze locked on Storm, as if the last thing he wants is this stranger knowing is that he has trouble sleeping.

Antonio is, as Antonio often is, oblivious. "Why're you making that noise? Anyway, I was telling Daniel about my Pokémon dreams because I've had a *ton* of those—"

Daniel melts into a blushing puddle.

"Hey, don't you wanna hear about what happened to us?" Blythe interjects. "We almost died!"

Antonio is like a very excitable puppy—the loudest, most exciting thing is guaranteed to keep his attention.

Antonio turns to her, aghast. "Oh no, what happened?! Are you guys alright?"

Hook, line, and sinker.

Blythe tells the boys the short version of their adventure, including their trek back to the Crane's house to gather Storm's things (and let her leave a note for her brother and father, because the entire house was empty and dark when they entered, despite it being well past midnight).

Blythe leaves out the bit about her agreement with Storm. It's not exactly something she's proud of, and it's a truth she'd rather keep hidden.

Storm leans against the wall to slip off her rollerblades. "Where's the lady?" she asks.

"What lady?" Antonio asks.

"Um," Storm thinks, searching for a name. "...Katia?"

"Oh!" Antonio blurts. He opens his mouth to explain, but no words come out.

Blythe realizes it at the same time he does—Antonio doesn't know. Because Blythe hasn't told him a damn thing.

Guilt chills up her spine. She raps her fingers against her knee. This situation would be better if she weren't standing in front of the entire room.

"We...decided to split ways for a bit," Blythe explains. "So now it's just us."

Antonio nods in understanding. Storm doesn't.

"That's weird," she says. "'Cause earlier today, Mikey said she called dad and asked where the hell y'all were 'cause y'all just ran."

The entire room goes hush.

"...was I not supposed to say that?" Storm asks.

Blythe can *feel* Antonio watching her. "Okay, alright, uhh...here's the situation...we decided to split from Katia," she stammers. "But she wasn't in on the decision."

Antonio's head tilts with confusion. God, Blythe is so bad at this.

"We suspected she may have been working with the Trident Republic," Cordelia interjects.

"Yeah," Blythe agrees. "So we kinda just...bolted."

"And stole her things," Cordelia adds.

Blythe glares at her. "No, *you* stole her things, don't lump us in with your crime."

Antonio shakes his head. "Wait...wait," he says. "So we're like...runaways?"

"No 'like'," Cordelia says. "Are. We *are* runaways."

Antonio's gaze pierces into Blythe and Blythe alone. "You ran?" he asks. "Why didn't you tell me earlier?"

Because I'm unprepared, Blythe wants to say. *Because I don't know what I'm doing.* But she bites down the words. Nobody wants to hear that from the person they're following, even if it is the truth.

"Antonio, I'm sorry," she says instead. "I meant to, I honestly did, but like I said when I was talking to you outside, there was just so much going on..."

"Is there anything else I don't know?" Antonio asks.

"No—or, wait, at least, I don't think so—"

Antonio's eyes bulge. "You're not even *sure?*"

"For the record, I'on even care," Storm says. "Y'all breaking out into *Captain America: Civil War* over here, I just wanted to know what happened."

The room's awkward aura is stifling. For a moment that feels like a lifetime, no one speaks. They barely breathe.

"That was a good movie," Blythe mutters. "Civil War."

"You know what?" Antonio blurts. "It's fine. You're under a lot of pressure and it's overwhelming, I get it. I'm already over it. I just...I wish you would have told me about *everything* I was getting involved with."

"I know, I'm sorry," Blythe insists. "It was a mistake but I'll make sure to tell you about *everything* from here on out, I swear."

Antonio speaks without facing her. "Yeah," he says. "I get it."

He's already tuned her out.

The moment does not linger; Antonio lies back and pulls a mound of blankets over his body, effectively ending the conversation.

None of the other Guardians want to live in the remaining silence—Cordelia carries her pajamas into the privacy of the bathroom to change, while Daniel crawls back into bed beside Antonio.

Blythe doesn't blame them for running.

"Storm," Blythe doesn't dare raise her voice about a whisper. "Do you want to take a bed? I could sleep on the floor?"

Storm just shakes her head. "Toss me a pillow, I'll live."

Storm sleeps with her back to them, facing the wall. The position of someone who is not here to make friends.

Tonight has been, in almost every sense of the word, a disaster.

But as Blythe settles down to sleep, lulled by the gentle sounds of Cordelia's breathing beside her, Blythe tries to focus on the big picture.

Storm's alliance with them makes tomorrow a very big day: they'll wake with the sun, pile into the van, and set off to find the very last Guardian. Maybe, if luck is by their side, Blythe will be in Electric City tomorrow night.

In a little over twenty-four hours, she could have her family again. She wants that hope to drown all of her worries about the other Guardians. Her family is what matters, after all.

But it is still difficult for her to fall asleep. The Guardians—Cordelia and Antonio and Storm and Daniel—still occupy a sliver of her mind.

———

Antonio is up with the sun.

Blythe wakes to find him sitting on his bed, completely dressed, golden hair pulled back from his face, frowning at the phone in his hands.

Lined on the dresser are silver wrapped breakfast sandwiches and containers of tea and coffee. Even when he's pissed at them, Antonio is still unbelievably kind.

"You brought breakfast," Blythe says.

"Mmhmm," he says to his phone.

The silence only makes the guilt heavier in Blythe's chest, but she doesn't bother him again. The last thing she wants is to make things worse.

A few I-called-the-shower-first arguments later, the four of them stand in front of the van, finishing the last of their breakfast, ready for another day on the road.

"Well Storm," Blythe begins. "Welcome to the...uh...t-the car we use to get around."

Blythe looks to Cordelia, Antonio and Daniel. "Guys, why haven't we named this thing?"

"Because we hate it," Daniel says.

Blythe nods in agreement. "Yeah it is ugly."

But when Blythe jumps inside and turns the key in the ignition, the van only clicks at her.

"What...?" she mutters, giving it another twist. Nothing.

This is the part where Cordelia is supposed to complain, but she stares outside in silence. Blythe isn't sure if she should feel grateful or worried.

"That thing's shot," Storm says.

"You know about cars?" Blythe asks.

"No, but I know that don't sound too good."

Blythe sighs. Of course the van only breaks down when they have to get the *last* Guardian. It's lived through racing from monsters in the Tempore and driving for hours on end, but sitting outside of a motel kills it.

"I knew the second I called it ugly, I'd broken some unspoken bond," Blythe mutters. "Storm, do you know a mechanic around here? Preferably not the place from last night."

"Why would I take you back there?" Storm wrinkles her nose. "I can probably find a place."

Everyone descends into early morning silence as Storm scrolls through her phone. Daniel takes the lull as an opportunity to peer over Antonio's shoulder.

"Is that a video game?" He asks.

"No," Antonio answers. "It's a mobile game, which is like a video game, but for boring people and people who are bored."

"Y'on't know what a video game is?" Storm asks.

"I was raised on a very large hill in Montana," Daniel answers.

"Goddamn," Storm says. "The hell they got going on up there?"

"N-Not much," Daniel admits.

Storm barks a sudden, loud laugh, a sound that is filled with pure joy. Daniel jumps, but a small, proud smile appears on his bright red face.

Blythe doesn't realize she's smiling too until she catches her reflection in the rearview mirror. Also, her hair is slipping out of the high bun she threw it in this morning.

She watches her reflection stuff the loose curls back into place. But something else catches her attention. And every positive emotion in her body vanishes.

Across the street is a convenience store, its windows crowded with ads. Standing in front of those ads, checking something on her phone, is a woman. Blythe almost doesn't recognize her without her cloak.

"Oh shit," Blythe whispers.

Storm lifts her head. "What's up?"

"Katia's across the street and we're fucked if she sees us," Blythe says.

They can't drive off—the van won't even start. The remaining option breaks Blythe's heart. They have to leave the van behind.

She really shouldn't have called it ugly.

"Grab everything important, put it in a bag, and let's go!" Blythe shouts. "We're leaving the van here!"

"You sure you want to just leave the van?" Storm asks.

"Of course I don't want to leave my van! But we don't really have a choice!"

They scramble, snatching everything that is too important to abandon.

Daniel has frozen, watching the mad dash ensuing around him. "W-What am I supposed to take?!"

Storm grabs his leather bag from his hand. "I got it."

"Don't forget the snacks!" Blythe shrieks.

In the rearview mirror, Katia has locked eyes on them. Blythe *watches* the recognition dawn on her face.

Her shoulders square as she crosses the street, sunlight illuminating the hard line of her drawn brows. The Guardians are out of time.

"Fuck, she's coming!" Blythe announces.

"Leave everything and go!" Storm's hand is already on the door.

"No, no, no, wait!" Blythe shouts. "We'll run until we lose her, but we need to stay together, so we get out on the count of three!"

The Guardians' eyes are steeled on her. Through the back windshield is Katia's approaching form, halfway across the street.

They have to run and they have to run *now*.

"One. Two. Three—"

The doors fly open. They bolt like a group of frightened mice hauling awkwardly heavy bags.

"BLYTHE FULTON!" Katia's voice chases them like a siren. "You have got to be fucking kidding me—where are you going!?"

They cut through the motel's alleyway, following Storm through week old trash bags and suspicious puddles.

Antonio beams over his shoulder, waving a hand in the air. "Hi Katia, bye Katia!"

"Keep going, keep going!" Blythe screams.

"Where are we supposed to go?!" Daniel asks.

"Don't worry about it, just keep up!" Storm shouts.

She is smooth and fast on her rollerblades, making a wide, elegant curve onto a new street.

Blythe does her best to keep up. Storm doesn't slow down. There is a huge gap between her and the other Guardians, one that doesn't disappear even as they travel further and further, Storm leading them in front of shops, across patches of grass, between buildings—

Until, suddenly, everything freezes. Or, no. The Guardians are still running, growing smaller as they escape farther and farther ahead.

Blythe freezes.

Not on her own accord, of course. People have a habit of taking over her body these days.

Wait, Blythe wants to call out to the others, but her mouth does not obey.

It is not like the Trident Republic's song and it is not like Daniel's spirit in the San Diego parking lot. The goosebumps rising up her arms are caused by something entirely different. Something...otherworldly.

Her body turns around and faces a figure that was not present before. It is a blue-eyed man in a suit, one who does not quite look like a human man. The blue-eyed Eraser.

Blythe's body is not too numb to keep her from feeling pure terror.

"Last chance," says the man.

He disappears. Gone, as if Blythe has imagined him.

She is released into the world with her heart thumping and her hands flying to her head as if to make sure it is still there.

But she is still alive. She has not been erased. She can't make sense of what the *hell* just happened, but the very thought of it makes her want to hide in the nearest, darkest corner.

So she runs.

When she reunites with the Guardian, they shower her in questions about where she's been.

"Sorry, I just..." Her voice trails off. If she speaks about what happened, it will become too real.

"I lost you guys for a second," she lies.

"Did you see Katia?" Daniel asks, peering over her shoulder.

"No," Blythe answers. "I'm pretty sure we lost her, thanks to Storm."

"How did she even find us...?" Daniel wonders.

"She knows where all the Guardians live, right?" Storm asks. "Only a matter of time before she caught up. Can't be that hard to track down a bright yellow Volkswagen."

"Yeah, well, we won't have to worry about that anymore," Blythe sighs. "Now we've got a whole new set of problems, including: stranded, van-less, minimal supplies, and no way to get to the last Guardian."

And Blythe may or may not be erased in the next few days. She can't even think of a plan. It is so spectacularly terrible, Blythe could almost laugh.

"All I need is a public computer and I can book bus tickets," Cordelia says.

All attention turns to her. Blythe's pretty sure those are the first words Cordelia's spoken all morning.

"You coulda said that back when we realized the van wasn't gonna drive," Storm points out.

"I know," Cordelia murmurs. "I'm sorry."

Her words hang in the air. Since when does Cordelia know how to say those words?

"Apology accepted," Antonio says. "At least you're helping."

"Yes," Cordelia says, flat. "At least I'm helping." Well, there's some of her usual vitriol. "And before you try to paint the situation to look like I never help, I hope you realize it's been a while since anyone's gotten into our heads, Trident Republic or otherwise."

She's right. Besides what happened in California, and besides Blythe's own personal demons, no one has been in their heads. At all.

"You..." Blythe can barely get her words out. "You actually did what you said you *wouldn't* do?"

Cordelia tucks her hair behind her ear. "I've been practicing my magic these past few nights. I figured out how to shield our minds based on how Katia's mind felt when I tried to read it. It's not foolproof, but it should keep us generally safe. And if Daniel is willing to help me, I could potentially figure out a way to make it stronger. I don't have much knowledge about Learned Magic but...he does."

Daniel mouth has formed a perfectly dazed *o*. Blythe can't blame him; this is a whole new Cordelia Deleon.

Suddenly his face scrunches. "I'm not helping you, you're mean to me."

Cordelia grits her teeth. "I'm trying to be *better*."

"Try harder," Daniel spits.

"Look," Storm begins. "As much as I love watching you rip English Regina George a new one, this sounds like the kind of thing that'll end up helping you out in the long run. You should give it a shot."

Daniel regards Cordelia for a moment. "...fine."

Cordelia lets out a short huff. "Right then. Glad that we got that settled," she says. "Now, someone find me a computer."

———

Storm takes them to a public library, where Cordelia gets behind a computer screen and works her magic.

Blythe wanders the stacks with Daniel, letting him point out some of his favorite classics and non-fiction, until Cordelia tells them to come back by snapping her fingers very loudly.

"If she's always this rude, she's gonna make me kick her ass," Storm grumbles.

"Ay, no ass kicking allowed in the library!" Antonio declares as Blythe sighs.

"Can we leave the ass kicking to the monsters, please?" she asks.

Storm recoils. "Y'all got *monsters* coming after y'all?"

"I-I've learned that it's best to be ready for anything," Daniel whispers.

Cordelia spins around in her chair like a movie villain, legs crossed and fingers steepled. "Here's the situation," she begins.

Apparently, their destination—Lavender Heights, Quebec—is too small to have proper bus stops, so Cordelia has booked them tickets to the nearest major city and figures they'll take an Uber the rest of the way.

Their Greyhound to Canada isn't the most luxurious place in the world, but Blythe doesn't care, as long as she doesn't have to drive.

She nearly melts into her seat, letting every muscle in her body go lax. As she closes her eyes, Blythe realizes that this may be the last time she travels with the other Guardians.

When she thinks about her family, she feels like she's spent a lifetime missing them. But when she thinks about the Guardians... there's still so much to learn about them.

What is Cordelia's life like in London? She mentioned everyone in her family being an artist—how did they raise someone as STEM-oriented as her?

Or even Daniel. What was it like to grow up knowing some force beyond your control wanted you dead? How did he construct his grimoire?

What foods were Antonio's favorites to cook, how did he know he wanted to learn to surf? And Storm—there's a whole *myriad* of things Blythe wants to know about Storm.

Antonio remains quiet for most of the drive. Blythe checks on him, but he waves her off.

"I'm fine," he says, playing on his phone, curled up in his seat.

If Antonio's not leading a conversation, one won't start, so Blythe is left alone with her thoughts—and her thoughts can't stay away from things that make her want to anxiety-hurl.

Things like the Erasers. Chills raise up Blythe's spine from the memory of the blue-eyed man. She's never been that close to one of them before.

Last chance, the man had said. Her last chance for what? What did the Erasers want from her?

When the bus makes a rest stop, Blythe pops into a convince store to buy snacks. While looking through the chips aisle, she hears the sound of wedges against the floorboards and is not surprised to find Cordelia coming up to her.

"So," Cordelia begins. "I...didn't know that happened with the Erasers."

"I didn't tell you to read my mind," Blythe retorts. She's not *actually* annoyed. Cordelia just needs to know she can't invade people's privacy like that.

Cordelia purses her lips. "I know. I'm sorry. I just got bored on the bus and starting...poking about. But honestly, I've never even heard of these Erasers before. I didn't realize they were such a threat. And I'm sorry they've been...terrorizing you."

"Stop apologizing, it's not like you."

Cordelia tosses her hair back. "I do what I want," she says, but it almost sounds...playful this time. "Honestly, though, you've never spoken about them before."

"I almost did, back when we saw them in Broughton," Blythe says. "They've just...always been around. And I've always avoided them. My whole life. Even after everything they did to me and my family, we always just...ran."

Blythe scoffs at an ironic thought. "Y'know," she begins. "It's funny how I'm ready to cut my way through Electric City and face the Trident Republic. But the Erasers have been terrorizing my family for years and I refuse to acknowledge their existence. Because even though I scared them off in Broughton...I'm still scared of them."

Cordelia actually looks sympathetic. Not as if she can relate to the feeling, no, but like Blythe's sadness has a real effect on her.

"I should have paid more attention," Cordelia says. "I should have...done a lot of things differently."

A comfortable silence falls between them, as if Cordelia is content to stand here at Blythe's side, spending time in her presence.

Cordelia frowns up at Blythe. "Do you know what I find odd?"

"What?" Blythe humors her.

"I...haven't been entirely truthful myself. My family used to live very comfortably. You know, in terms of finances. But business has been dwindling since my grandfather died, and we were fine for a while but now...my parents keep a tight leash on things. After I brought our tickets, I was waiting for a call from my mum. She's diligent with checking the family transactions and would never miss something like that. But I haven't heard a word."

The Deleons, a family with only a sliver of their former wealth and glory, not noticing their youngest daughter purchasing upwards of three hundred dollars' worth of bus tickets? Something's definitely not right there.

"Yo," Comes Storm's voice. She bites into a Snickers' bar as she joins them. "Bus is boardin'. Antonio's already on but Daniel needs to look for a plant or something and he doesn't want to go by himself, so I'mma wait outside for him."

Daniel peeks out from behind her. He must be looking for silver-root—he said something about it being the last thing he needed.

Blythe can't help but notice that, if Storm were to take her rollerblades off, she'd probably be Daniel's exact height.

"Oh, okay. Thanks," Blythe says.

"I can't believe she can stand *Daniel*," Cordelia mutters as they leave.

"There's nothing wrong with Daniel," Blythe rolls her eyes.

But Cordelia has a point. Storm talks to the rest of them, but not in the casual way she chats with Daniel. Blythe never would've guessed the two of them would get along so well.

Blythe learns quite a bit about Storm as they travel. Not from what she says, but from what she does.

She is a silent protector, making sure the group stays together and keeping watch at night while the rest of them sleep (excluding Daniel, who never sleeps. And it's starting to show under his eyes).

One night, when Antonio and Cordelia are sleeping and Daniel has made one of his numerous bathroom runs, Blythe and Storm are the only ones awake.

Sleep hasn't come easily to Blythe, so she sits beside Storm, a pair of earbuds shared between them.

Their music tastes overlap slightly; they agree on SZA and Kendrick Lamar, but Blythe sits through Meek Mill in the same way that Storm tolerates Ariana Grande.

Blythe is watching the stars when Storm pauses a song. "I'm gonna call my brother," she says.

But her brother doesn't pick up, so she leaves him a snarky voicemail that makes Blythe smile.

"Are you guys close?" Blythe asks.

"Yeah," Storm says. "We've been through a lot."

This is the most Storm has ever talked about herself. "Does he have anything to do with this whole...Madame De-whatever thing?" Blythe asks.

There's a fondness on Storm's face as she laughs. "Girl, we ain't all like you," she says. "Not all of our families are mixed up in our shit." She pauses. "But what you're doing, heading out to Electric City to save them...it's dope. I like that."

They are only a few words, but they carry a large meaning. Storm isn't just congratulating what Blythe is doing—she's congratulating who Blythe *is*. The qualities that have brought her here in the first place.

Blythe smiles. "I like *you*, for what it's worth."

"I'm straight."

"I meant as a friend. You're not even my type."

"Now I'm insulted."

"Straight girls always are," Blythe teases.

Storm lets loose a full-belly cackle that is full and unapologetic and iconic. Blythe has a feeling that's just her normal laugh.

Storm falls asleep soon after, lashes against her cheeks and leaning on the rain-streaked window, leaving Blythe alone with *Dreams and Nightmares* playing in her ear.

SIXTEEN

IT IS THE LAST TIME THE GUARDIANS WILL TRAVEL IN SEARCH of another member of their ranks, and their entrance into Lavender Heights is appropriately ceremonious.

Or, at least, Blythe likes to think so. Because Quebec City appears as any other modern city—except more beige and French—but the world turns grey the closer their Uber comes to their destination.

They are piled in the back of a large truck, watching the outside world grow increasingly deserted as the summer air turns colder.

From what Blythe understands, Lavender Heights is not a magician town, which means that it is populated by Commons who have little awareness of the supernatural world just beyond their reach. Unexplainable phenomena will not go unnoticed—the Guardians will have to be very, very careful.

Their driver brings them to a cobblestone street, quirking his eyebrow as if he cannot believe anyone would willingly travel here. Blythe still tells him to have a good day as they step out.

Lavender Heights itself could be the setting of a classic Tim

Burton film: cracked pavements, barely populated thin streets, an overabundance of grey.

The way the fog erases the tops of the stone buildings is iconic, but it's the fields that take Blythe's breath away.

Right in the entrance of the town is a vast expanse of purple flowers, stretching as far as Blythe can see. It's a whole ocean of them. There is only one problem.

"They're all dead," Daniel breathes. "W-Why are they are all dead?"

He—their scholar of magic and Guardian of Nature—kneels at the edge of the field, pale and frowning. "I...I've never seen anything like this."

"To be fair," Cordelia mutters. "You haven't seen much."

Daniel is oblivious. He dips his hand into the dirt, lifts it in his palm. "This soil...it's completely lost its nutrients. Like someone has sucked all life from it. But these flowers have still bloomed, so it must've happened quickly, o-or recently, but I...I-I don't know what could do that..."

When Daniel turns around, his eyes are wide on Blythe. "W-We should go."

It is a bit ominous, being welcomed to the town by an army of dead flowers. But Blythe isn't one to worry about omens.

"Right," she agrees. "We need to keep walking."

"I-I meant leave this town and never return but o-okay."

The flowers are a reoccurring motif; lining the streets are shops with purple-themed items, displaying freshly bloomed bouquets. It seems the flowers are—or, considering their current state, were—their main tourist attraction.

Needless to say, all of the stores seem to be struggling.

Blythe fishes out Katia's paper of addresses. She doesn't want to spend *too* much time in Lavender Height's gloom and fog.

But beside the Guardian's name, where her home address should be, Katia has written "????".

Blythe freezes. "God hates me."

Cordelia barely has time to ask what the problem is before Blythe shoves the paper in their faces. "I do not feel like going through another day of Find the Guardian," she grumbles.

Storm is chewing on a Twizzler. She shrugs.

Cordelia narrows her eyes as if to read some unwritten line beside the other addresses. "This is so odd," she mutters. "If Katia got this list from the Sages, does that mean even they don't know where this Guardian is? And what did Katia plan to do here, just happen upon her somewhere in town? Is it really that small?"

Storm hums, looking around. "Let's find out."

A perfectly average man is walking down the sidewalk, staring at his phone as if he doesn't expect anyone to be in his path.

Storm skates up to him. "Excuse me," she begins, high-pitched and fancy. Blythe almost laughs at her code switch as she asks if the stranger recognizes the Guardian's name.

The stranger looks bored. "No, but the last name is familiar," he says. "Are you looking for a *Caspian* Compton? He's the only one left. Didn't have any siblings, either."

"Uh, sorry sir, I don't think—" Storm is cut off by Blythe and Cordelia's frantic voices.

"Wait, wait, *wait*," Blythe interrupts.

"Is Caspian about our age? Maybe, perhaps, gets on with some strange, unexplainable happenings?" Cordelia asks.

The man seems slightly taken aback. "...surprisingly, yes. Are you looking for him?"

Cordelia freezes the polite smile on her face. "Yes, do you happen to know where he lives? Or where we might find him?"

"The graveyard," The man stares at her as if she's asked what color the sky is. "Where he always is."

The *graveyard*? Blythe's not the only one caught off guard. Everyone seems to freeze in place. Everyone, except of course, the stranger himself.

"But I wouldn't advise it," he continues. "Things haven't been the way they used to be."

"What do you mean?" Antonio asks.

"He's...different now," says the stranger. "But feel free to give it a shot if you want. He might actually show up. Good luck."

And with that, the man returns to his phone and circles around them to continue his walk.

The Guardians face with confused silence.

"Anyone understand what the hell just happened here?" Storm finally asks. "'Cause I sure as hell don't."

That man had no reason to lie to a bunch of random kids, which means the Guardian they're looking for may very well be Caspian Compton. And Caspian probably *is* in a graveyard, as morbid and depressing as the thought is.

But the man didn't talk about Caspian like he had passed. He talked about him as if he were just some kid with weird tendencies. And there are only two Elements left—which could mean that Caspian's not dead.

"He's the *Guardian* of the Dead," Blythe realizes aloud.

She expects the words to be a relief, and they are—to Antonio and Cordelia.

Daniel goes pale.

"Oh, hell no," Storm blurts.

"What do you have against the Guardian of the Dead?" Blythe asks.

"I'll give you one goddamn guess."

Blythe is no position to judge; the Sage of Ether is the only Sage who attempted world domination, and she's the Guardian of Ether. And she turned out fine!

But Storm's not entirely wrong. The Guardian of Death is either one of two people—a complete psychopath or a plot-twistingly kind sweetheart.

Only one of those options bodes well.

———

They make a short stop when Blythe spots a small restaurant offering poutine. It's a dish she's always been curious about but never had an opportunity to try.

She grins over her shoulder at Antonio. "Hey, Ant! Poutine?"

Antonio looks over the display. "I guess. I'm not really hungry."

"Who are you?" Blythe teases.

Antonio gives her a half smile. Oh god. Not even a full one.

"No, really," Blythe says. "I'm scared."

"Are we eating or not?" At least Cordelia is the same.

Every seat in the cramped restaurant is empty, which means the Guardians are free to slide extra chairs up to the largest table and sit shoulder to shoulder in a cramped circle. None of them care.

Their conversation drifts between topics until Daniel speaks up about the suspicious death of Lavender Heights' purple flowers.

"Maybe Caspian got to them," Blythe teases, smiling when Cordelia snickers.

"Are we really gon sit here and crack jokes about someone whose magic is literally *killing people?*" Storm asks.

"I'm too determined for a little thing like death to stop me," Blythe laughs.

She places her phone on the table as their waiter—who is also, seemingly, the only person working here—approaches their table.

They are halfway through their order when a foreign feeling settles in Blythe's chest. :ike some outside force pulling at her soul.

Her phone slips past her arm. Blythe looks behind her. There is no one. But her phone has vanished—along with the pressure in her chest.

"Uh..." Blythe's voice trails off. "Guys, where's my phone?"

The Guardians look around. "Wasn't it right there?" Daniel asks, pointing.

"Yeah?" Blythe agrees. "And now it's not?"

A missing phone wouldn't be too terrible (she's got bigger things to worry about) but she doesn't even know how it disappeared.

Storm sits up bolt right. "Wasn't Cordelia's wallet right there?"

"What?" Cordelia blurts. Storm points to a blank spot on the table. Cordelia pales. Blythe takes that as a yes.

Their waiter doesn't stop scribbling on his notepad. "Yep," he says. "That's Caspian."

The Guardians gape at him. "I didn't know he could steal phones," Blythe says. "Now I'm scared."

"How...how did he do that?" Antonio asks.

The waiter clicks his ballpoint pen. "He's a ghost."

Daniel screams. "Boy, you got some *lungs*," Storm mutters.

"A G-G-GHOST?!" Daniel stammers.

"Jinkies," Antonio mutters.

Blythe chest tightens again—there's that feeling again. She barely hears their water continue. "Yep. He takes stuff all the time. We locals have just come to accept him, eh?"

"What does he do with the things he takes?" Cordelia asks.

"Not sure. But he's been moody these past couple months. Best not to approach or provoke him."

There is a presence behind them—Blythe can't see him, but she can feel him, moving in time with that odd *feeling* behind her ribs.

The others are oblivious, but Blythe can almost see his invisible movements as he hovers toward the left side of the table—toward Daniel's grimoire.

"We'll have to—"

Blythe slams her hand on the grimoire, interrupting Cordelia. "Chill OUT!"

Caspian—or whatever the invisible force is—freezes.

"Yeah!" Blythe yells. "I can *feel* you! May as well make yourself visible now—"

His form disappears—but only from Blythe's sight. The tug in her chest is barely detectable now, and if she weren't paying attention, she probably wouldn't even notice.

He has gone somewhere far, but not so far that she can't track him down.

"Uh...Blythe?" Antonio asks.

The Guardians are staring at her, their faces sliding scales of worry (Antonio) and confusion (Storm). None of them look as disturbed as their waiter. To them, she's been talking to thin air.

Blythe holds up a hand. "Okay, I know that looked weird, but contrary to popular belief, I am not crazy. I just found Caspian."

Not a single look is interchanged. They all know what that means, and so they rush out of the restaurant with Blythe in the lead. "Sorry we couldn't stay, I'm sure the poutine's great!" Blythe shouts. The waiter seems too flabbergasted to stop them.

The force in Blythe's chest feels like an invisible string: one end is tied around something inside her, and the other is tied to Caspian. She is now sure how, or why, but at the moment, she doesn't quite care.

The other Guardians are close behind her as she traces the string through Lavender Heights, all the way to the Victorian gates enclosing the town's graveyard.

It reeks of the grey and the dead. The grass is dead, the cracked headstones are various shades of grey, and the weeping willows hang grey and dying.

The gates yawn open to a trampled dirt path. It is the exact opposite of a welcoming place.

Blythe charges in. "Caspian Compton, *give me back my phone!*"

She only comes up with a plan when Cordelia asks what the hell they're supposed to do. Caspian keeps moving—disappearing and reappearing in various parts of the graveyard. He's avoiding them.

"Split up until we find him!" Blythe declares.

"H-H-How are we supposed to find a ghost?" Daniel asks.

"He can't stay a ghost forever!" Blythe snaps.

Storm sighs. "That's not how ghosts—nevermind."

Daniel doesn't move as everyone scatters. "I-I-I...don't do well in...g-g-graveyards," he stutters.

"You don't do well anywhere," Cordelia retorts.

Storm, however, outstretches a hand, and Daniel grabs hold like a drowning man to a lifejacket.

Blythe weaves between tombstones as quickly as she can, but Caspian's weird teleportation happens too quickly for human legs to keep up.

Maybe he'll want to talk if Blythe finds his grave. Morbid, yes, but it may work.

She slows her pace, scanning every name she wanders past.

Cordelia runs up, out of breath. "Do you have a destination in mind or is this just aimless, angry wandering?"

"I'm looking for his grave."

"I thought you said he wasn't dead."

"If he's invisible and stealing people's shit, he sure as fuck isn't alive."

"And what, exactly, are you going to do if you find it? Spit on it?"

"Maybe! I want my phone back and I'm not gonna let some asshole ghost bully me! Fuck him!"

"I suppose it's better than all your other plans," Cordelia sighs.

"Aren't you supposed to be nicer now?"

"This *is* me being nicer."

An orange blur rushes up to them and melts into Storm. "I just ran the entire area and I got nothing," she says. "Or maybe that's just 'cause I don't fuck with ghosts."

"Wait, where's Daniel?" Blythe asks. The poor boy is probably having a heart attack if he has to endure this place alone.

"I had to split with him to run," Storm explains. "He'll be fine."

A faint noise rises into a scream as it nears them. "......aaaaaaAAAAAAAAAAAAAAAAA!"

"Nevermind," Storm says.

Blythe whips around. "Daniel?"

He looks more terrified than Blythe has ever seen him. His whole body trembles, his eyes gone huge. "CASPIAN COMPTON'S GHOST IS REAL AND HE TRIED TO SELL ME MARIJUANA!"

The girls are silent. His lip is quivering.

"Daniel, are you tryna said a ghost tried to deal to you?" Storm asks.

"Yes!"

"Deadass?"

"I-I don't know what that means...b-but yes!"

Storm considers this for a moment. "What were his prices?"

"*Storm!*" Blythe yells. "Daniel, ignore her. Where did you see him?"

Before Daniel can answer, Antonio joins them. "I found the Compton grave," he says, hands stuffed in his pockets. "It's like a... one of those tomb thingies. He wasn't there, but it's this way..."

His voice trails off. He's looking over Blythe's shoulder.

Daniel's hysterics distracted Blythe from the sensation in her ribs. It is only now that she realizes the feeling has centered.

Caspian is right behind her.

"Antonio," Blythe says as she turns around. "I'm starting to hate when you do that..."

A body rises from the ground. It is not solid; it is the suggestion of a form, a slight coloring of the air.

First comes a pale head with coal black eyes, heavy with bags and hair as dark as night, moving without disturbing a single blade of grass.

Then comes a torso clad in a black t-shirt, spindly legs in faded, ripped black jeans, bare feet.

Caspian Compton floats before them. He holds no expression in his face nor his voice.

"Do not go anywhere near that tomb."

Daniel runs behind Storm at the speed of light. But Caspian isn't looking at him, or any of them. His eyes burn into Blythe.

She holds out her hand expectantly. "My phone."

Caspian does not blink. Wisps of smoke echo from his skin, his clothes, his hair. His aura sends chills up Blythe's spine, as if she is looking into the eyes of something human beings are not meant to see —not without it being the *last* thing they see.

"I have *a* phone," Caspian holds up what looks like a generic blue Zadis phone. Blythe's case is gone. "I can give it to you. For fifty dollars."

Jesus Christ. The Guardian of Death is not a psychopath or a sweetheart. He's a conman.

"Wh—no!" Blythe yells. "Are you trying to sell me back my own phone?!"

Caspian does not react. He simply hovers there, echoing with ethereal dark energy. "I also have this case." He holds up a Sailor Moon phone case.

Blythe nearly loses her mind. "That's mine!"

"It *can* be yours," Caspian says. "For ten additional dollars."

"I'm not giving you sixty dollars for my stuff!" Blythe snatches her case—but her fingers go straight through the plastic. Its touch feels like pure ice.

She yanks her hand back with a startled gasp. Caspian only stares.

"We can call the police for theft of property," Cordelia snaps. "You'll get *arrested*."

"Go ahead," Caspian says. His form folds in on itself, dissipating into a ball of black smoke that wisps and fades.

"Good job threatening a ghost, dumbass," Storm snorts.

But Blythe can feel his presence. "He's still here," she growls. "He just hid."

A ball of black smoke appears to her left, and, like the reverse of his appearance, folds back into his pale body in all of his smoky glory.

Two objects drop from his hand, tumbling into the grass: Blythe's phone, with its case, and Cordelia's wallet.

Blythe snatches them up before he can change his mind. "God, you're the worst," she glares up at him, but nothing she says can earn a reaction from him.

"How can you tell where I am." Even his questions are flat—it takes Blythe a moment to realize she's supposed to answer.

"I don't know." Even if she did, she wouldn't tell him. He doesn't deserve to know.

Caspian floats toward her without shifting a single muscle. The others back away, but he keeps coming, until he is inches in front of Blythe. The chill of his presence crawls up her skin.

He stares at her with genuine confusion. "Who *are* you?"

Why does this mean so much to him? Strange things like this happen in the world of magic all the time. It doesn't mean anything, not really—it may even just be because their magic is linked, or connected, or God-knows-what. It doesn't *have* to be a big deal.

Blythe clears her throat. "I don't know if dead people need personal space, but I do, so can you um..." She gestures for him to scooch back a bit. Caspian obliges, so Blythe answers his question. "I'm Blythe and these are the Guardians."

"Hey, that could be our band name," Antonio says.

Cordelia clenches her teeth. "Please, for once in your life, think before you speak."

"I do think before I speak."

"I can read minds and I *know* you don't."

Blythe rolls her eyes. "I'm Blythe and this is Cordelia, Antonio, Storm and Daniel. *We* are the Guardians. You...you know you're a Guardian too, right?"

Caspian's head bobs. A nod. At least Blythe won't have to explain *that*.

"Good. We came all the way up here to find *you*, so you should feel bad about being such a dick. This trip cost a ton of money."

Of course, Caspian does not react.

"Yeah, maybe I was asking too much," Blythe mutters. "Anyway, here's the sitch. There's a magician governmental called the Trident Republic and they're basically trying to kill us. They mind controlled me, Cordelia, and Daniel, they sent monsters after us, basically a ton of crazy shit. We were supposed to be going to Frost Glade to keep safe, but that plan got scrapped after we left Katia, who was basically our babysitter. Instead, we're going to Electric City to save my family because the Trident Republic kidnapped them." Blythe pauses. "I think that's everything."

Caspian stares at her.

"That's your cue to speak, bud," Blythe prompts.

"Oh," Caspian blurts. Blythe waits, but nothing happens. "Mm, yeah, I checked out, repeat it all over again."

Blythe groans. "Oh my *God.*" She breaks it down again, slower this time.

"Those monsters," Caspian says this time. "They were here."

"Wait, what?" Blythe asks. She thought the Trident Republic sent monsters after them because of the shard. Why would they care about Caspian? "Did they attack you?"

"Whoa, dude, is that how you died?!" Antonio asks.

Storm pinches the bridge of her nose. "Antonio, you can't just ask people how they died."

"They came looking for me," Every word out of Caspian's mouth is spoken as blankly as the last. "Wraiths. They left when they couldn't find me. Other people came looking for me too."

"Were you...are you okay?" Blythe asks.

Caspian cocks an eyebrow. He is an incorporeal being who can teleport and turn invisible.

"Nevermind, you were definitely fine," Blythe decides.

"And I'll continue to be fine," Caspian says.

His form starts to fade.

"Wait, wait!" Blythe yells. "What about my family?"

"How am *I* supposed to help."

"I don't know!" Blythe says. "You're the Guardian of Death, you could do anything! Electric City is dangerous; you could help us get through there."

"I'm flattered, truly," Caspian doesn't sound like it, but he nevertheless continues. "But there's nothing I could do."

"You're a literal ghost who can teleport and steal without detection," Blythe insists.

Caspian shakes his head, his hair swaying in its own wind. "You need to leave," he says. "And don't come back."

Just like that, he's gone. But Blythe can feel his presence lingering, even though she can no longer see him. She refuses to just give up and let him go.

"I know I'm a total stranger to you, and you have absolutely no reason to care about helping me, but family could die, Caspian. That probably means very little to you, but it means the universe to *me*. My mom and my dad and my sisters are all I have. And if I lost them...I-I just can't lose them. This wouldn't take long. As soon as I get my family back, you never have to speak to me again. You could hate me if you wanted. Just help me this one, single time."

Caspian fades back into view. But, for the first time, he is not looking at her. He stares off to some far corner of the graveyard. His fists are balled at his sides as his gaze snaps back to Blythe.

"I'm not responsible for what happens while I'm with you," he says.

"Oop, nope, I don't like that," Storm says. "Blythe, don't you agree to that shit."

Blythe ignores her. "Nobody's going to die, right?"

Caspian stares off again. This time, he shakes his head no.

Blythe should ask more questions. She *knows* she should. But she doesn't want to bite the hand that feeds her. An agreement is an agreement.

"Well, on those grounds, we'd be happy to have you," she says.

"Cool," Caspian's form starts to fold in on itself again. "Just don't expect me to be there the whole time."

He curls into a tiny ball of smoke and blinks out of sight. This time, he takes the presence in Blythe's chest with him.

He has actually gone.

A weight lifts from Blythe's shoulders. She has every Guardian now, all of them, on her side. Cordelia and Daniel and Antonio and Storm and Caspian—excluding the missing Guardian, but they don't count and hardly matter.

Blythe doesn't even *need* them. With the team she has now—a hacker, a thaumologist, a thief, a vigilante, and, uh, a chef?—Electric City won't know what hit it. Nothing can stop them—

"You dumb bitch," Storm reprimands. Her arms are crossed, jaw clenched.

"What?" Blythe asks. "I know it was shady but he said no one would die."

"Not just that," Storm snaps. "This was all too easy. He was gettin' at something and it had nothing to do with his magic. Something's up."

Before Blythe can ask her to elaborate, she skates toward the exit. Getting a warning about the future from the Guardian of Time leaves a rock in Blythe's stomach.

Daniel, Antonio and Cordelia are giving her looks. Blythe doesn't know them well enough to judge what they all mean, but she can tell Cordelia is bewildered and ready to leave.

As they go, curiosity takes over Blythe, and she looks to the far reaches of the graveyard, where Caspian was glancing.

Through the fog, she glimpses a man in a suit. Watching, as the Erasers do. Always watching.

SEVENTEEN

Cordelia falls in step beside Blythe, eyebrows raised. "Electric City?" she asks.

If Blythe had considered this back home, when all she had was a destroyed café, a yellow Volkswagen, and her own determination, she would've instantly rejected the idea that she could ever find the other Guardians, much less convince them to help her.

Now she travels with five other pairs of feet, five people with their own distinct strengths and talents. They have left their homes and their families to help Blythe reunite with her own, and they are willingly traveling into a city where unspeakable dangers await them.

"Grateful" is an obscene understatement for the powerful emotions swirling in Blythe's heart.

"Electric City," she agrees.

Storm pulls a piece of beef jerky from her bag—this girl has infinite snacks—and Antonio stares at her until she rolls her eyes and produces a second beef jerky for him.

"If we can find a car, I can hotwire it," Storm offers.

"What?" Blythe asks. "Who showed you how to do that?"

"My brother."

"How did he know? Why did you *want* to know?!"

Storm cocks her head to the side. "Do you want a car or not?"

Theft isn't Blythe's preferred route, but they don't really have a plethora of choices, so she groans and shouts for Caspian.

He materializes beside streetlamp, arms folded, legs crossed lazily in front of him. Blythe asks if he knows of any available cars.

"You can use Old Man Bill's truck," he says, and leads them to an old house with an even older car parked in front of it. Blythe recognizes the model: a Lincoln Continental.

"It runs fine, but he never uses it," Caspian explains.

"Did you really try to sell Daniel weed earlier?" Cordelia asks.

"No. I don't even have weed."

"Aww," Storm sighs.

"I have silver-root," Caspian continues. "But that's mine and not for sale."

Daniel's eyes light up. Blythe's pretty sure he told her that's the last plant he's looking for.

From what Blythe knows about it, it's a plant that magicians often smoke. It's similar to weed, but Blythe's never tried it before.

Before Daniel can speak to him, Caspian disappears in a puff of black smoke. The Lincoln unlocks with a click. All four doors swing open at once.

"Ard, you see how you just turned invisible and started throwing doors open and shit?" Storm yells. "That's what we *not* about to do."

She grumbles as she climbs into the driver's seat. "Blythe and her dumb ass letting the Grudge's emo cousin tag along with us like this is a *game...*"

"Thank you, Storm," Blythe calls sweetly.

After a few moments of listening to her complain about ghosts while Blythe anxiously glances at the house and *prays* Old Man Bill doesn't notice the group of teenagers jacking his car, the engine roars to life.

Trees are not strangers to Lavender Heights, which makes entering the Tempore a breeze. However, the town itself is not particularly caring of strangers, and it bids them no farewell when they discover a small grove and plunge through it.

"The Tempore looks worse every time we enter it," Daniel mutters when their car stills.

The Tempore has not changed seasons. In fact, it looks as if it is barely capable of existing in anything other than damp nightfall. The grass lays shriveled, the trees curl like sick, gnarled hands.

Whatever the Trident Republic is doing, it has sucked the very energy out of its air. The Temper doesn't look like it'll be able to survive for much longer. One day, they might drive into a forest and crash into a random tree.

Blythe flicks on the headlights; they don't do much against the darkness, but it's all she can do.

"It looks like it's dying," Daniel continues.

"Hey, Caspian, you got anything to do with this?" Storm teases.

There is no response, probably because their resident ghost has deserted them again.

Antonio is squished between the two of them in the backseat, his face blank. Blythe hates seeing him like this. Antonio Torres is not supposed to be without a smile.

"Hey, Antonio," she calls. "Can you talk to the compass so it'll tell us where to go?"

"Okay," he agrees. Cordelia hands it to him, and he holds it gingerly. "Hey, buddy. How are you today?"

"No, you just like, have to tell it where we're going," Blythe corrects.

Antonio brow wrinkles. "That's so rude." He looks back to the compass. "Don't listen to her. I know you have feelings, I won't just shout orders at you. Is there anything you want to vent about? I'm here to listen."

Blythe takes it back. "Alright, he's fired. Daniel, it's your job now."

With Daniel's proper, specific direction, they are guided through the dying forest. They speak to each other in hushed voices, because there is something foreboding about the Tempore's emptiness that keeps them from speaking normally.

It does not help that when they reach the seven trees, their situation takes a turn for the worst.

Blythe slows the car, her arms going rigid as she observes the people gathered in front of the exit, along with the randomly constructed one-story building off to the left.

It's only when Blythe takes in their gold and white uniforms and thick boots that she realizes—this is a temporary military base.

"Holy shit," she whispers.

They even have a checkpoint complete with a tall man eying their approaching car, waiting to speak with them.

Maybe Blythe deserves this for even daring to use the Tempore. She should have known the Black Veins would start regulating it eventually.

Daniel's face is nearly pressed into the window. "Do we *have* to stop?"

"If we don't want trouble, we do," Blythe replies.

They pull to a stop in front of the man, who smiles politely as Blythe rolls down the window.

He is mustached and blonde, with a longsword at his hip and a charming glint in his eye. "Nice car you've got here, miss. Antique."

Blythe returns his smile, but without teeth. "Thanks."

Electric City is waiting right through those trees. She'll be damned if she gets caught *this* close to the finish line.

"Sadly, the Tempore's closed for civilian travel," the man continues. "As you can see, it's not exactly in the best condition. We're going to have to ask you to leave and discontinue use of it for your safety."

Blythe nods as if this is the utmost importance to her. "We're on our way out, thanks."

"Alright. Make sure you don't..." The man glances into the backseat. Oh God. They're going to get busted for piling way too many minors into a car that looks like it barely passed inspection twenty years ago.

But the look in the man's eyes is far worse than that. It's *recognition*. "Hold on a moment—"

"Oi, Valerian!" A soldier shouts to him.

Blythe's heard that name before. Back when they'd just met Daniel and Katia got a phone call from a person she called Val.

If Katia and this man are at all connected, he could obliterate Blythe's entire mission within *seconds*.

This is more than the worst-case scenario. This *is* the Bad End.

"Gotta blast," Blythe says, and slams the gas.

They race toward the trees. Something snags them to a stop. Blythe stomps the gas into the floor. The wheels only spin in place.

In the sideview mirror, Valerian has fired some sort of harpoon; one end is embedded in their fender, and down the coiling metal rope is the other end, held tight in Valerian's grip. The longsword holster at his hip is empty. Blythe didn't expect his sword to double as a fucking *projectile*.

"Are you kidding me?!" Blythe yells.

They are so close. So close. To lose everything when she can see the exit *in front of her windshield* would be a fate too cruel.

Blythe kicks the gas pedal. The tires growl uselessly.

Valerian yanks the harpoon—the whole car drags backward.

"YOU'RE KIDDING ME!" Blythe screams.

Cordelia groans in frustration. "His mind is blocked like Katia's, I can't get into it!"

Vines leap from the ground and lasso Valerian's wrists like handcuffs. The chain goes slack as his grip loosens.

It's the opportunity Blythe needs. The needle of their speedometer climbs. But the car doesn't move.

There is a sickening shredding sound as Valerian rips the vines from the ground with enough force to send the dirt flying.

The car rears backward again. Even as more vines swarm Valerian's legs, he kicks free as if they are simply an annoyance.

He flashes them his Prince Charming smile. "Surely you don't want to waste time like this, do you, Guardians?"

"Don't worry," Storm rolls down the windows, heaving her upper body out. "We got time."

She throws an object that glints in the dim light on its way to Valerian's head. A switchblade.

Valerian dodges with such swift, instinctual grace, it looks like a dance. The sharp end lands, en point, in the grass.

Storm hesitates a moment. She returns to her seat in an orange blur.

"You're giving up?!" Blythe shrieks.

Her eyes bug. "Bitch, I only had one knife!"

Soldiers line up in front of the car, shoulder to shoulder, brows heavy, daring Blythe to drive through them. Because they know she won't. She can't.

Blythe punches the steering wheel.

The car jerks backward with every sway of Valerian's arms. Hurt and pain and anger shake through Blythe's muscles.

She was so close. She was *so goddamn close.*

"We can still get out of this," Cordelia whispers. "I'll figure out what he wants and we can—"

"Cordelia, these are Black Veins' soldiers," Blythe interrupts. "We're fucked."

The car stops. Valerian returns to the window, his charming smile gone smug and amused.

"Guardians," he says. "We've been looking for you."

————

Valerian introduces himself as General Valerian Wilde of the Black Veins Imperial Army. He has over fifteen years of formal combat training, a whole fleet of soldiers at his beck and call, and Katia Darkholme on speed dial.

"Little young to be a *general,* aren't you?" Blythe spits.

It doesn't wipe the haughty look from Valerian's face. "Top of my class, miss. I've been working hard."

He escorts them into the base, a sterile building of white hallways and barren rooms. The place is crawling with soldiers and watchful eyes, powerful bodies and magicians who seem all too ready to set the Guardians back in place should they step even *one* foot out of line.

The furniture is temporary and the floor is too squeaky, especially in the room Valerian tells them to wait in. There are only two round tables and a few heavy fold-up chairs. The window only offers a view of the Tempore's depressing, slow downfall.

Blythe can't believe this is the place where her journey will be laid to rest.

"I believe this is yours," Valerian holds Storm's switchblade out, and she eyes him distrustfully as she snatches it, something that only amuses him even more.

"I sent word to Katia," he says. "She said she'll be here soon, but in the meantime, can I get you some refreshments? Tea or coffee, perhaps?"

"No," Blythe grumbles.

Storm huffs. "Coffee."

"I'll take tea," Cordelia says.

"M-Me too," Daniel stammers.

"Do you have milk?" Antonio asks.

"Traitors," Blythe grumbles.

Blythe keeps her arms crossed and her jaw clenched even as Valerian leaves. Cordelia heaves a sigh, sitting cross legged by the window while Antonio sulks into the back of the room, plopping down on the floor. Daniel seems too nervous to stray from the doorway.

Storm makes her spot on top of a table, spinning her switchblade. "Are we actually gon' wait for Katia to get here?"

"If you're dumb enough to try your luck against trained Black Veins soldiers, I guess not," Blythe grumbles. "But none of us would even get five feet out of this room."

A woman passes the doorway and locks eyes with Blythe, as if even *conversing* escape is forbidden.

Storm remains unbothered. "I'm fast enough to."

"But what about us?" Blythe asks. "What about all our stuff? The car?"

"I'm not going with Katia. If y'all fuck up and get yourselves taken in, I'm out. This ain't got nothing to do with me."

Blythe grits her teeth. Sure, Storm made it *very* clear she was only joining them to find the Angelus, but Blythe thought—well, she thought that maybe things had changed, that maybe Storm liked them—liked *her*—enough to give a shit and stick around. But Blythe is obviously a fool.

"Don't worry," Blythe snaps. "We won't stop you."

"Y-You're leaving?" Daniel stammers.

His shaking voice cuts through the tension like a knife. Storm doesn't look at him. Or, perhaps, the more accurate word is *can't*.

"Maybe," she admits, with a forced edge.

Daniel stares down at his shoes. His social skills are not good enough to tell that Storm's rough-and-tumble, uncaring attitude is a front.

The two of them have obviously bonded these past few days, but Storm can't even be truthful with *him*, this harmless boy who simply wants to make friends.

Blythe almost *wants* Storm to go.

Valerian returns with a tray of drinks like a smiling housewife. He has to deliver the glass of milk all the way to the corner, where Antonio seems content to sit alone, quietly. Blythe almost forgot about him in the midst of her own hurricane of emotions.

She waits until Valerian leaves and then makes her way to sit down beside Antonio. "Hey," she says.

"Hi."

"If I ask you if you're okay, you'll just say you are, won't you?" Blythe asks.

He gives her a guilty smile. "I am," he insists.

"Well, shit's not gonna get any worse and we'll probably be stuck here for a while so..." she bumps her shoulder against his. "Wanna talk?"

Antonio stares at his cup. "I'm sorry I couldn't help. Y'know, when we were in the car."

"It's okay," Blythe says. "There's nothing any of us could have done."

"But at least everyone else tried," Antonio says.

Blythe is quiet. She knows that feeling of powerlessness very well.

Antonio takes a breath. "I know I act really...carefree. But I always feel like everything is going to be okay. So, I tend not to read into things, and I don't dwell on stuff, so I guess I seem stupid. Or maybe I *am* stupid."

"Antonio," Blythe almost gasps. "You are not stupid. Did we...did we make you feel like you were?"

"No, no. I mean, even with the whole Katia thing back at the hotel...the problem wasn't that you didn't tell me what was happening," his eyes grow glassy. "It's that I didn't even think to *ask*."

He slouches farther against the wall. "Storm was barely here for five minutes and she knew something was wrong. I'd been with you guys for a whole day and it never even occurred to me. I just...I trusted you. Because I'm stupid. Everyone in the world is smart enough to be skeptical, but I'm dumb enough to trust people. I could meet the worst person on the planet and *still* find something to like in them. And what idiot does that?"

The words spear into Blythe's chest and crack her heart into pieces. Were these the thoughts consuming him for the past couple days? He was sitting on *this*?

"Antonio, being trusting does *not* make you stupid. You're one of the kindest people I've ever met. And you've been right so far! We're still here! We just got busted but we...we got here. We got *so* close to Electric City," she pauses. "And Storm...Storm jumped off a

246

motorcycle after I told her I didn't know how to ride one. She isn't a good role model."

Antonio shakes his head. "But I don't even offer anything. Everyone else does something. You're our leader, Cordelia's a hacker, Storm's a superhero, Caspian's a ghost. The other night, Daniel showed me his grimoire and told me about collecting his plants and studying Learned Magic with the plants he's collecting." His brows pinch. "I don't do anything. I'm nothing."

Blythe tries to think of a title for Antonio, but he doesn't fit into one. Or at least, not a traditional one.

"You're Support," she decides.

Antonio frowns at her, his dark brown Bambi eyes worryingly devoid of hope. "What?"

"You play Overwatch and team strategy games like that, right?"

"I mean, yeah..."

"Okay, have you ever played on teams where everyone wants to play offense? The game starts and your whole time is fighting and taking damage. They're fine until they're steps away from the enemy's base and their health bar is one shot away from getting them respawned. That's the *only* time anyone ever thinks about how great it would be to have a healer on their team.

"I never told you this, but before you got here, me, Cordelia and Daniel couldn't talk to each other. We traveled in silence for hours. It was awkward and we all lowkey hated each other, and sitting in that car, knowing I may never see my family again, with two people who barely wanted to be there...it was painful.

"But everything changed as soon as we met you. You always know exactly what to say. The only reason why Daniel can stand to look us in the eye when he talks is because he had such a great time talking to *you*. And that night at the hotel when I was crying, you saved me, Antonio. I...I don't know what I would have done if you hadn't come out there. Kindness is underrated. We're all focused on being self-sufficient, on being 'strong'—but people like you? People like you are the reason the world is a place worth living in. You're not dumb. You're kind. You help each of us. Without you, we'd go down from one hit when we're inches away from the finish line. You're the one that helps us get back up again. You're Support."

Antonio's face is blank. The words sink in and he laughs; it is the high, mirthful laugh that Blythe is used to, and it brings a smile to her own face.

There are tears in his eyes. Happy tears. "You know what's so funny?" he asks. "I always play as a healer."

"See?" Blythe grins. "I know what I'm talking about!"

"You do!" Antonio agrees, and Blythe is filled with the overwhelming need to hug this soft, gentle boy, and so she does, and Antonio wraps his arms around her, tight, tight, tight, and they hold each other, smiling hard.

Blythe's plans have been crushed into dust. But things could be worse. Blythe may not have her family, not yet, but at least she has people she can call friends.

Approaching footsteps steal Blythe's attention. They grow louder and louder until they consume the entire room.

Blythe knows the sound of those heels. She pulls away from Antonio so she can face the doorway head-on, fully prepared to see the form that appears.

"If it wasn't part of my job description to keep you safe," Katia growls. "I would strangle you all myself."

Katia hasn't changed since Blythe last saw her, but frankly, Blythe could have done without seeing her again.

A twinge in Blythe's chest tells her Caspian has appeared. His transparent form sits backward in a chair, across the table from Storm.

"Nice to meet you, too," he replies. Storm snorts a laugh.

Katia's hair whips over her shoulder as she turns to them. "Do I *look* like I'm fucking around?"

The last thing Katia looks like is a person who fucks around. Her glare could crumble mountains. Caspian and Storm fall silent.

"We were supposed to be in Frost Glade two *days* ago," Katia snaps. "Not only did you steal my cloak that had *all* of my shit in it, you ran across the country by *using the Tempore* like this place isn't a battlefield and your lives aren't in danger?! Like the Trident Republic doesn't have each and every one of your fucking names on a hit list? Teenagers may be dumb but my God, you are all *braindead.*"

Her eyes land on Blythe with her final words, seething and hot. Antonio places a hand on top of Blythe's as she furrows her brow, anchoring her.

Katia throws her hands up. "I just, I can't even fathom— whatever. *Whatever.* It's done, you're here, we're fine. At least all of you are in the same place."

She looks them over, discerning. "Blythe, Cordelia, Daniel, Antonio, Storm—why the hell are you playing with a knife?"

Storm shrugs, flipping her switchblade in the air. "Because nobody's gonna stop me."

Katia watches her for a moment, as if deciding whether or not she has the energy for her. She must not, because she sighs, turning to Caspian. "And who the fuck are you?"

"Caspian," he says. "Compton."

"And you changed your name because...?"

"Because I'm a boy," Caspian says. "And I missed my afternoon nap so I'm too tired to deal with transphobia, thanks."

Katia scoffs. "I'm a bitch, not a bigot," she snaps. "Now all of you fuckers stay put and don't try any bullshit. I'm gonna see if Val can secure us a ride to Frost Glade."

Katia has barely turned to go before Cordelia rises.

"Katia, wait," she calls.

Miraculously, Katia actually does. Blythe's not sure *what* this girl has up her sleeve, but she has a feeling it's going to be good when Cordelia exhales slow.

"I think you should let us go," she says.

The whole room freezes. If Cordelia is phased, she is too confident to let it show.

"Yeah, no, definitely not," Katia says.

"It may be your job to protect us, but your job functions on the very principle that Blythe *leaves her family behind!*" Cordelia's words stop Katia in her tracks. "The Black Veins security is rather tight, so I wasn't able to investigate as thoroughly as I'd like, but from what I found, there are no reports besides a formal writeup on the Fulton family's missing status. There is *no* proof that a search party has been dispatched."

It is like the air has left Blythe. Not only has Cordelia actually checked for Blythe's own family, not only has Katia *lied* to her yet again, but even worse—the Sages, the leaders of the Black Veins themselves, even *they* don't care enough to help her?

Cordelia's not even done. "You stated earlier that Electric City would be too dangerous for Blythe if she were alone. Look around. Obviously, she isn't alone anymore. We managed to find every Guardian in this room, travelling from Montana, to California, to Pennsylvania, to Canada, *while* evading attacks from the Trident Republic. And we stand before you in one piece. Unharmed. I'm sure that's more than enough proof to convince you that we are *quite* capable of handling whatever they throw at us.

"So! Considering all of that, I repeat my earlier statement," Cordelia presses her lips into a fine, serious line. "Allow us to travel to Electric City and find Blythe's family. Otherwise, you will be asking Blythe to abandon her mother, her father, *and* her little sisters to potential death. And surely—being a moral woman whose rank and station as an advisor to the Sages would *certainly* be put in jeopardy by indirectly killing the family of one of your charges—you would not want that." Cordelia pauses. "So, Katia, will you let us go?"

Katia stares Cordelia down. The room is silent.

"Goddamn, that girl actually *does* do something other than get kidnapped," Storm says.

"That convinced me and I'm not even in charge," Caspian agrees.

Blythe's chest swells with pride. That's the magic of Cordelia, and that's magic Blythe has on *her* side.

Valerian has appeared, arms crossed as he leans against the doorway. His brows have shot up.

"Did you actually manage to break through our network's security?" he asks.

"Only barely," Cordelia says.

"Quite impressive," Valerian nods. "But I do have a team investigating the Fultons' disappearance. It is just *intensely* classified to keep from the Trident Republic's prying eyes. I'm sure a smart girl like you would understand."

Relief washes over Blythe. So, she *can* trust the Sages. But if she can trust the Sages, by extension, she should be able to trust the people employed by them. Which means Blythe should be able to trust Katia.

The logic makes Blythe squirm. Her distrust of Katia is, and always has been, nothing more than an excuse to defy her. To ignore her. To stay away from Frost Glade.

There is no reason for Blythe avoid Frost Glade other than her own stubborn will.

Valerian holds out a hand. "Now, let me make sure I've got this straight. You all ran away to save Miss Fulton's family, who she believes is in Electric City."

"*And* because Katia's allied with the Trident Republic," Antonio adds.

Valerian stares at Antonio as if he's just said there are four hours in a day. "Allied with the Trident Republic?" he repeats.

Katia's words come between clenched teeth. "Why would I be allied with *the Trident Republic?*"

"Because you know Walden Oliver," Cordelia answers.

"You're...correct, she does," Valerian agrees. "But she is not working with him. In fact, her knowledge has always been one of our biggest assets. She came to us when—"

"They don't need to know all that," Katia interrupts. Her eyes wash over every single one of them. "I'll tell you this, since you all seem to care so much. Walden and I grew up together. But we haven't spoken in over fifteen years. He chose his path and I chose mine. But I've been close enough to him to know that if he wants something, he will sacrifice *anything* to get it. And right now, we have no way of knowing *what* he wants with you. I'm not here to strike deals and make exceptions. I'm here to make sure that man doesn't get his hands on you. I'm the one thing standing between you and this man making your life a living nightmare."

Blythe's gaze shoots to Cordelia, but even she looks like her resolve is wavering. Because none of them know much about the Trident Republic, and they know absolutely *nothing* about Walden Oliver besides his name.

Valerian heaves a sigh. He taps Katia's shoulder and he gestures into the hall. Katia shoots one last look at the group—"Stay put," she orders—and follows him out.

Blythe jumps to her feet. The other Guardians crowd behind her as she crouches by the doorway, her ear to the hall.

"Let them go," Valerian's saying. "We left that city nothing besides its civilians and its buildings."

Katia sounds skeptical. "What about the militia?"

"None stationed. No use defending a ruined city. If Miss Fulton is desperate to go, you ought to let her. She's clearly powerful and driven. I imagine you'll be able to get her into Frost Glade, but you'll have a hard time *keeping* her there. Let her take the others to Electric City, see that there's nothing to be found, and then come back to you. I'll talk to her when she returns. She'll know I have my best men searching for her family. She'll be alright."

Blythe digs her teeth into her lip. Valerian can't be right—what does he know? He's only...in charge of the entire Black Veins military. And has seen Electric City himself. And caused the wreckage.

Antonio places a hand on her shoulder. Blythe cast those thoughts out of her mind. Valerian can't be right. He *can't*.

"And they're Guardians," Valerian continues. "You know they can't—"

"I know," Katia interrupts. "But they can be hurt in other ways."

Blue light explodes through the hall with a *boom*. Soldiers' voices echo through the forest, and by the time Blythe thinks to move, Valerian is already rushing outside.

A stream of soldiers flood the hall, drowning Blythe's vision as they draw their weapons and rush outside. The ground shakes and the air *bursts*. Blythe feels Caspian vanish into thin air.

Something is happening.

Katia pushes through the crowd, her eyes wide. "Kids!" she shouts. "You wanted to get to Electric City? Lucky for you, here's your chance!"

Cordelia snorts. "You really expect us to believe you—"

Katia interrupts Cordelia as she pulls her hair off her shoulders and into a bun. "Changed my mind? Yep!" She snaps the elastic hairband in place. "I'm gonna get you out to your car and you're going to drive. You might see some stuff out there, and it might be disturbing, but whatever you do—don't stop. And don't get distracted. Stay *right* behind me."

Blythe thinks she's exaggerating until she brings them outside.

Assailants in clothing as black as the forest itself have infiltrated the base. Blue explosions arc like domes across the ground, sending soldiers in golden uniforms flying like ragdolls.

From the shadows come massive Calling creatures, sharp teeth that stab into limbs and red eyes that glow like coals in the darkness.

The Trident Republic is attacking.

Katia moves on the outskirts of it all, the Guardians following in her wake, as if she is Moses parting the red sea.

There is too much to see, too much to take in. The ground has turned to mud and black Calling creature goop. The sound of thundering gunshots. The overwhelming buzz of too much magic in the air.

Daniel is screaming. Sparks of electricity bounce between trees. Weapons made of pure light materialize in people's bodies. The world shakes from a sonic boom. Blythe thinks she hears Cordelia's voice, but she is not sure. She cannot discern all of the noises.

If one bullet sails just a bit too far, if one body dodges a magical attack meant to incinerate bone, if one Calling creature aims for their small bodies, they will not make it out of this alive.

Blythe can barely catch her breath.

Follow Katia, she tells herself. *Just follow Katia. Keep following Katia.*

A familiar wind pushes through the forest. Tons of magicians can control the air, but Blythe recognizes the way it is manipulated now.

And, if her memory serves correctly, there is only one man in charge of the Trident Republic's militia.

Whiteclaw.

Katia reaches their car moments before they do. It is a contrast to the rest of the world, completely untouched besides the harpoon sticking from its fender.

Katia's mouth forms the words "get in", the sound of her voice lost behind an explosion that makes Blythe's ears ring.

Antonio throws the backseat door open, rushing to open the passenger seat as Cordelia and Daniel scramble inside.

Blythe scans the trees. Somewhere around them, somewhere in the Tempore, is the man who took her family.

Katia drops to her knees, splaying her fingers wide in front of the harpoon, summoning a wind strong enough to blow it from their car.

When she speaks, this time, her voice carries clear. "Get to Electric City! I'll find you when you're done!"

A blast of air carries her above their heads and into the battle, disappearing amongst the summoned creatures of the night.

Blythe turns back to the trees, unmoving, even as Cordelia shouts her name. If Whiteclaw is here, she can figure out whether or not Valerian is right. Whether or not there truly is anything in Electric City.

She searches between the trees for something, anything, a clue or a sign. In the distance, she glimpses something bronze.

"I'll be right back!" she yells.

The Guardians scream for her as she rips her hockey stick from her back and charges forward. The sounds of the battle fall behind as she jumps over logs and pushes through bushes. The glint of a bracelet turns into an arm, which turns into a torso, which turns into Whiteclaw.

He is facing a horde of men outfitted in dark uniforms. These soldiers are not the refined men of the Black Veins military—they come without formal training and wild, unrestrained emotion burning in their eyes.

Not unlike Whiteclaw as he looks over his shoulder, catching sight of Blythe.

He shouts something to the men. And then he starts toward her.

Blythe told herself she was going after him for answers. But she catches sight of the way his hat shades most of his face against the light. It is the same way he appeared in her café.

And every inch of her skin, every thought in her mind, every fiber of her being rages with vengeance.

"So," Whiteclaw says. "The Guardian of Ether makes an appearance for a rematch."

Blythe winds back and swings.

The wind carries Whiteclaw backward before her stick lands. It slices through open air and lands on a tree, the blow snapping clean through its trunk.

The upper half of the tree races toward the ground as Whiteclaw backs away. He is like a mirage, untouchable, always just out of reach.

Blythe stalks toward him. "*Where* is my family?"

"Where's your family?" Whiteclaw repeats. "I thought you already figured out that piece of the puzzle."

Blythe slams her hockey stick against the ground. The explosion cracks through the dirt and shakes the trees.

Whiteclaw has taken to the air again, landing father away. "I won't fight you, little girl," he calls. "Especially not now and not here."

"Why?!" she yells. "You scared?"

He chuckles. "Hardly. I'm just a bit busy at the moment, as you can see."

This is the man who terrified the twins into tears, who cracked her father's head against the wall, who cut through Jamie's body and almost killed them.

He looks at her as if she is some irrelevant child who has interrupted the adult's *real* business.

Fuck. Him.

Blythe charges toward him, arcing the hockey stick above her head. He shoots into the canopy of branches, his feet planting against a shoot yards above her head.

"Or maybe I should put it like this," he reiterates. "It isn't part of the plan."

Blythe's resolve wavers at those words. She refuses to let it show in her voice. "What *plan?*"

But Whiteclaw arches an eyebrow. "Come to Electric City and see."

He speaks too confidently. As if there actually *is* something in Electric City. As if that "something" is the Trident Republic, prepared and waiting for her.

From the very beginning, Blythe has been mixed up in a game she never asked to play. She did not ask to lose her family, to leave her only friend behind in a hospital bed. She has become closely acquainted with anxiety and pain and fear, three figures that never exit her mind.

And she is no more than a pawn.

Blythe screams, the sound crawling raw up her throat. Her muscles burn as she swings the hockey stick into Whiteclaw's tree.

It falls quickly, momentum snapping branches on its way down. When it finally crashes, like a song growing to its crescendo, Whiteclaw is gone.

EIGHTEEN

Blythe barely acknowledges the Guardians when she returns to the car. She hasn't even been gone for three minutes but they are livid with her, Cordelia most of all.

Their voices sound exactly like the battle raging feet away from their window: distant and muffled and far, far away.

Blythe sets her brow as she takes them through the trees, away from the Tempore's explosions and screams and into darkness.

The silence of the world between the seven trees should be a respite. But its nothingness in conjunction with the numb, dull ache in her chest only makes Blythe feel worse.

The exit spits them into a dark street, where the van comes to a slow and easy stop.

They are beside a highway. The wind hums as cars drift past, speeding into the night. The streetlamps are hazy and the forest behind them is dull.

There is only one problem. Past the highway are buildings, homes, storefronts, and lights. So many lights, shimmering and neon and pulsing.

Electric City is supposed to be a wasteland.

Daniel stares out of the window. "Is this Electric City?"

"No," Storm says. "Can't be." It looks like—

"Las Vegas," Cordelia stares at the GPS on her Zadis. "I'm assuming the Tempore brought us as close to Electric City as it could. There are no forests in the desert, and judging from the state it was in, I doubt we could ask much more of it."

Blythe exhales, long and slow.

After all this time, all of this pain and energy, Electric City remains *just* out of reach—but isn't that just in the fashion of her life? Could she truly expect anything to work out?

The Tempore has done its best, despite being twisted under the force of the Trident Republic's hands. It deserved a better send-off than being the setting for the first battle between the Trident Republic and the Black Veins.

But life isn't fair. Not to anyone.

Blythe closes her eyes. Valerian and Katia are still back there, fighting for their lives, along with other men and women who are simply trying to protect people like the Guardians, perhaps even fighting for their own families.

The Trident Republic may be more dangerous than Blythe imagined.

"I have to say something," Blythe blurts. The Guardians fall silent. "I ran because I realized Whiteclaw, the man who kidnapped my family, was in the Tempore. I was ready to...to hurt him, I guess, as badly as he hurt me. But he refused to fight. I asked him where my family was and he said, 'Come to Electric City and see'."

Wide eyes and worry echo across the Guardians' faces. Blythe doesn't know what they're thinking, but if they're anything like her own thoughts, they understand that they could be walking straight into a setup.

"I should have been there," Cordelia says. "I should have followed you. If I could have read his mind—"

"You already helped with Katia," Blythe interrupts. "And you didn't even have to do that."

Cordelia seems to understand that. "I said I would get us out of there and I meant it," she says

Storm drums her nails against the back of Blythe's seat. "So, the General of the Black Veins military thinks that Electric City is a deserted wasteland because that's the state he left it in, but Whiteclaw talks like they got something waiting for us that we're gonna have to prepare for?"

Daniel hangs onto her every word. "I-If it's something to do with Learned Magic, I could figure it out."

"I'll see what I can find on the current stasis of Electric City," Cordelia says.

Their plan, despite being in its infancy, sounds like it could be a good one. But Blythe is tired of plans. She is tired of running, tired of fighting, tired of this adventure. She doesn't want to play more of the Trident Republic's games. She wants her family.

"No," Blythe interrupts. "None of you are doing anything. This is *my* problem. You shouldn't have to help solve it. If I'm being used as a pawn, I don't need to drag you guys into it too."

Her words make the car feel cold. These are not the words Blythe is supposed to speak as their leader. But if the Guardians are stunned now, they're about to be floored.

"I'll make the plans. I'll decide what we do. And if we get to Electric City, and things look bad, I want you guys to run," Blythe says. "Run to Frost Glade and don't look back."

Cordelia gapes with disgust. Daniel's eyes fly open. "Blythe..." he begins.

Blythe doesn't let him finish. "I mean it. The only place you guys are *supposed* to go is Frost Glade. I messed that up for my own selfish reasons. You shouldn't endanger your lives because the Trident Republic wants to ruin me. I got you guys to help me, not to be human sacrifices."

"But we don't have to leave you behind, either," Antonio protests.

"I don't know what they want from me," Blythe argues. "But I know it's not worth dragging all of you down with me."

Daniel stares at his shoes, pressing his mouth into a confused and frustrated line. Storm clenches her jaw as she stares out of the window, while Cordelia's mind moves a mile a minute as she studies the dashboard.

Antonio is the only one who can stand to look her in the eye. He is holding back how much her words hurt him, she can read it on his face. But he does not agree to her terms. None of them do.

Blythe doesn't expect them to. She just wants them to know. This journey has always been hers, and this is a cross she must bear alone.

"We should stop for the night," she says. "Get some sleep, head out in the morning. I'll make a plan for Electric City tonight. Cordelia, you just find us a place to stay."

Blythe splays her fingers out against the wheel. The easy procession of cars drifting down the highway is almost soothing, one after the other cruising a never-ending line.

Antonio glances out of the rear windshield with an inquisitive head tilt.

"Uh," he begins. "Not to redirect the conversation, but I think there's someone collapsed behind us."

"What?" In the rearview mirror, a figure is sprawled face-down on the asphalt. "Oh my God! Did I hit them?! Jesus Christ, I killed somebody!"

Antonio is effortlessly calm. "I think we would have felt it if you hit them."

"This car is so damn old, *we* would die if we hit somebody," Storm says. "They probably came out of the Tempore."

Antonio is already shimmying forward. "Open the door," he tells her. "I'm gonna make sure they're okay."

They follow him out, lingering a couple steps behind as they study the mysterious body collapsed in the middle of the road.

"Don't touch them," Blythe calls. "We don't know where they've been."

Too late. Antonio is already kneeling at their side, gently shaking their arm. The body sways, limp.

260

"Are they..." Daniel's voice trails off. "Are they dead?"

First comes a twist in Blythe's chest, then comes black smoke, and finally there is Caspian, in all of his pale skinned, dark eye-bagged glory.

"No," he answers. "Nowhere near it."

"Oh thank God," Blythe sighs. At least she hasn't killed someone. "Wait a minute, where were you?"

Caspian speaks low, as if the words are only meant for her. "Had to leave as soon as I heard gunfire," he says. "I couldn't risk my life."

He pauses, waiting for her to get it.

"I hope I'm as chill as you when I die," Blythe replies.

Antonio's mouth pinches with worry. He rolls the person onto their back—and a collective gasp bursts from everyone.

"*Damn*," Storm whispers.

Bruises mar the boy's rich copper skin and cuts leaking blood down his arms. His jeans are sliced and brown with dirt, his shirt torn. Somehow, despite all of this, he looks as if he is merely sleeping.

Thick black lashes curl against his high cheekbones, a fountain of dreadlocks stream down to his waist like inky tendrils across the grass, lips gently parted. Even in this state, he is like a painting, a living poem, a god.

"Who is this?" Cordelia whispers.

Antonio's brow sets with determination, as if this boy is an average human being and *not* making Blythe wonder if he's even completely human.

"Someone we have to help," Antonio says.

The words snap Blythe back to reality. "Whoa, whoa, whoa. Antonio, we don't know who this is or what happened to him. Let's just call an ambulance—"

"I can't just leave him here!" Antonio interrupts. Blythe's never seen him this adamant before. "He's *hurt*, something obviously happened to him!"

"He isn't dressed like a soldier, so I doubt he's from the Black Veins," Cordelia adds.

Daniel gasps. "The Trident Republic!" he yells, backing away.

"He isn't wearing black," Cordelia points out. "And I didn't see a single teenagers in their ranks."

Antonio's head snaps up to them. "Who cares? Guys, he's *bleeding.*"

"He won't be for long," Storm says.

She sinks to the boy's level and, gently, raises his perfect arm by the wrist. It takes Blythe a moment to realize, but he has less wounds than he did a moment ago.

Two of the cuts erase before her very eyes, the flesh stitching back together and leaving flawless skin.

Antonio's dark eyes stare hard at Storm. "*Some* of us aren't okay with abandoning people."

"Some of us need to shut our mouths before we lose 'em," Storm retorts.

"Guys," Blythe interrupts. "He's probably just a normal magician who was passing through the Tempore and got caught in the crossfire. He'll wake up in a minute and everything will be fine. Let's go."

Antonio shakes his head. "How is he going to get back home? He can't use the Tempore anymore. He's probably stuck here, in the middle of some city he didn't plan on being in, alone. And we're going to *leave* him."

Blythe looks down at this nameless fairytale prince, a fallen angel dropped straight from the heavens. They don't have time to be good Samaritans. If she says so, they can get him to a hospital—though soon, he won't even need one—and never see him again.

But how did he get here? And what will the system do if they get their hands on a lost and unprotected Black boy in the middle of the night? Can they really risk this?

And so Blythe sighs. Because everything's already fucked as it is, isn't it? Why not make it worse?

"Alright," she relents. "Who's carrying him to the car?"

The answer is Storm and Antonio, together, because Storm gets the boy's arm across her shoulder, but he's heavier than he looks, so

Antonio has to help her. They sit the boy upright, though his body slumps against the door.

Antonio buckles him in. "Safety first."

"We only got *three* seatbelts back there and you wasted one on the boy who's already dying?" Storm asks.

"I could've offered it to Caspian," Antonio retorts.

"Honestly, I'm offended none of you have ever asked," Caspian mutters.

Blythe's gaze drifts to the end of the road as the conversations continues. She can see a suited man hidden in the shadows, the white plain of his face barely visible.

The Erasers' presence has been almost constant these past few days. No matter where they go, or what they do, there always seems to be a figure. Simply watching.

Blythe swallows hard, stills her shaking hands, and pretends she doesn't see them.

———

The boy doesn't wake while they drive. Every eye in the car is focused on him; even Storm, who pretends to be on her phone, keeps glancing up.

Antonio is oblivious, fussing over the boy like a worried mother, making sure he doesn't move whenever the car stops a bit abruptly.

Blythe steals occasional glances in the rearview mirror. His chest rises and falls with gentle breaths. The bloodstained rips in his clothes are the only proof that they found him injured, because the wounds beneath those holes have completely healed.

Something about the curve of his cheek, the hard line of his jaw, the soft color of his lips, is hypnotizing. And that terrifies Blythe. She needs to keep her eyes on the road, but the yearn to count the hairs on his head and never look away is mesmerizing.

This boy must carry *intensely* strong magic.

"Aren't we missing the Guardian of the Body?" Blythe asks.

Cordelia snorts. "Isn't it a tad *too* cliché for us to simply happen upon the one Guardian we couldn't find?"

But Blythe's words disrupt the haze that has fallen over the car, and one by one, they all seem to regain their senses.

Blythe even realizes Caspian is still with them, sitting on the floor of the backseat, knees against his chest, something resembling a joint in his hands. Blythe completely forgot about him.

Apparently, so did Daniel, because he quickly whispers to Storm, prompting her to say, "Yo Caspian, Daniel wants to know if he can have one of those plants you smoke."

"I didn't know Daniel did drugs," Caspian says.

Daniel makes an *eep* noise and whispers some more.

"He says it's not to smoke, it's one of his ingredients," Storm translates.

Caspian takes a long drag, releasing ghostly smoke into the air. At least the windows are rolled down.

"Daniel can ask me himself," he says.

"Daniel says he's afraid of ghosts. Oh wait. I don't think I was supposed to tell you that part."

"We can do an exchange. Give me something I want."

Storm shrugs at Daniel. "It's good bargain. What? You gotta have something. Trust me, he lives in a graveyard. Just give 'm something simple."

Daniel rummages through his bag and presses something into Storm's hand.

"Uh," she begins. "I don't think this'll get you much. These jawns like a dollar at the corner store. Where'd you even get these from?"

Daniel whispers.

"Oh, you *did* spend a dollar for them at the corner store."

She hands them to Caspian anyway: two packets of Instant Ramen Noodles. Caspian stares at them.

"I..." Caspian begins in his monotone, emotionless voice. "...love ramen."

In two puffs of smoke he has reappeared at Daniel's side. Daniel shrieks, clamping a hand over his mouth. Caspian does not care.

"You can have two roots," he says. "If you would've offered me the shrimp flavored kind, you would've gotten one."

Storm recoils. "What's wrong with shrimp?"

Caspian's black eyes focus on her with a dark intensity. "Shrimp instant ramen is the greatest mistake man has ever made." Then he's gone, dissipated into black smoke.

Storm's already laughing. "I *like* him!

Antonio pouts. "Now I'm hungry."

"I can pull over into a fast food place or something," Blythe offers.

Daniel seems to be in his own world in the backseat—but this time, it is for a good reason. Blythe smiles as she watches him. He finally has all of the things he needs to perform his ritual, this thing he has been working toward for so long.

When Blythe spots the iconic golden arches of McDonalds, she swings into the parking lot. Everyone gets out except for her; someone needs to stay here with the boy, and Antonio's love for food seems to override his love of doting over injured strangers.

"He'll be hungry when he wakes up," Antonio points out.

Blythe snorts a laugh. "Nothing like some McDonald's to bring someone back from the brink of death."

Antonio snaps at her. "*Exactly*, bro."

Blythe watches them all hurry inside, explaining fast food restaurants to Daniel as they go. Then she is alone with her thoughts, the Las Vegas crowd, and their unconscious kidnapped victim in the back.

"Can you grab my wallet out my bag?" Storm stares at her from outside the window.

Blythe startles. "*Christ!* Did you just skate out here super-fast?! What if someone saw you?"

"I still need my wallet to eat."

"Isn't Antonio paying for everyone?" Of course, Storm won't allow someone to buy things for her.

"Bitch, if you don't—"

"Alright, alright," Grumbling like a frustrated mother, Blythe grabs Storm's backpack from the backseat and pushes her way through the hoodies and Nike shorts—until her knuckles brushe a folded piece of paper.

Curiosity makes her open it. It is an old photo, worn white at the fold lines. A dark skinned woman smiles at the camera, holding a toddler on her lap; a toddler that looks a lot like Storm.

"I said my *wallet*," Storm snaps.

Suddenly, the bag is gone. So is Storm.

It happens before Blythe can process that anything has happened at all. But guilt wastes no time burning in her cheeks.

Caspian materializes in the passenger seat. Neon lights spear through his form.

"I'm gonna have to apologize for that later," Blythe mutters. She's not sure why she looked at it. Storm is a secretive person, why did she even try it?

There's a small scar in Caspian's eyebrow, one that cuts through a small slice right beside his arch, where no hair will grow.

Blythe's surprised she's just noticed it. Then again, Caspian rarely lingers around like this. "How'd you get that scar?" She asks.

"Didn't you just piss someone off by being too curious?"

"Yeah," Blythe retorts. "But yours is on your face."

"I cut myself on how edgy I am."

Blythe stares at him. He stares back.

"Tough crowd," he says.

Blythe does smile at that. "Sorry, I didn't realize you were being funny."

His expression still doesn't change—Blythe's never seen happiness on him. "I just hit my head on a tombstone when I was younger. I was a reckless kid." He pauses. "Speaking of. I'm sorry for stealing your stuff earlier."

"Were you serious when you did that or was it a joke?"

266

"I do that to tourists to get cash. I used to steal from the locals but..." He squirms a bit. "That wasn't fair."

"So now you steal from a different group of people."

Caspian shrugs. Blythe's not about to make the same mistake twice, so she leaves it alone.

"Where's the shard?" Caspian suddenly blurts.

"The Trident Republic's shard?" Blythe asks, and he nods.

She's not sure how Caspian found out about it, but one of the others probably mentioned it. "Cordelia put it in her bag when we left my van. Why?"

"It seemed important," Caspian explains.

His hand goes to his right wrist. For a moment, Blythe thinks the thin, golden chain is a bracelet, but it is wrapped around multiple times, as if it is actually a necklace.

It's a complete contrast to his baggy jeans with homemade rips, his oversized black t-shirt that has gone greyish from the wash. It looks expensive.

This time, when he dissipates, Blythe feels him leave entirely. A couple moments later, the Guardians return with greasy bags packed fat with food.

"I got you a burger, Blythe!" Antonio shouts, tossing a cardboard container into the front seat. Leave it to Antonio to make sure everyone's fed.

Storm packs fries into her mouth. She, pointedly, isn't acknowledging Blythe's presence. Yikes.

Cordelia acts as their GPS, guiding them to a hotel that is not as gaudy as the Thorne, but good enough to offer them a suite with two bedrooms and a living space in-between.

"Your mom's gonna *kill* you for spending all this money," Blythe warns her.

"Surely she'll understand if I tell her all of the *other* five-star hotels didn't offer private, heated swimming pools," Cordelia bats her eyelashes dramatically. "It's our last night at a hotel. I had to empty my bank account."

But Antonio is unamused. "This is great and all, but our new friend isn't up yet and we're not even supposed to be able to *book* a room so...how are we supposed to carry him through the lobby and into the elevator before anyone asks questions?"

"With a fuckton of luck," Blythe answers.

It ends up being a very large production, with Cordelia distracting the front desk by throwing a temper tantrum about the pillows not being soft enough, while Daniel stands in the elevator doors, keeping them open for Storm and Antonio to quickly drag the boy inside.

Blythe's job? Stand at the end of the hall, look bored on her phone and tell every passing visitor that the elevator is broken.

Despite all odds, it is a success.

Storm and Antonio lay the boy across the sofa in their suite, with his feet at one end and his hair spilling down the other.

"What are we gonna do with Rapunzel now?" Storm asks.

Antonio studies him. "Pillows," he decides. "And blankets. Also new clothes."

"You better be givin' him your own clothes."

"We don't wear the same size. He's bigger than me, Caspian's dead and Daniel's small."

"I'm five-four," Daniel pouts.

"Bro, this guy's an athlete," Antonio says. "Like, could-get-a-ten-in-Olympic-gymnastics athlete."

Storm rolls her eyes. "I have a lot of baggy shit, something will probably fit him."

They slip new clothes over the boy's destroyed ones, adorning him in a throne of pillows and blankets.

Blythe, meanwhile, drifts to the corner of the room and pulls her laptop from her backpack for the first time in quite a few days.

Her "research" tabs are still open. It's almost funny, returning to them after everything she's been through.

Blythe searches through website after website, looking for the exact coordinates of Electric City, along with any form of helpful information.

She knows it's out there in the desert, but *where?* Wandering in the searing heat until they stumble across a destroyed wasteland doesn't sound like a safe plan.

The Guardians voices fade away, and then the lights, and soon the entire hotel room is irrelevant to Blythe as she sits, curled alone in the corner, pouring over words and websites.

Someone stands in front of her. The whole room has gone dark, empty and still. Blythe hadn't realized she'd been working for so long.

Daniel stares down at her, fiddling with his fingers. "I'm about to start the ritual," he says. "I-If you'd like to come watch."

His ritual to banish the spirit must be very, very personal for him. And he is inviting Blythe to be a part of it.

She closes her laptop. "I'd love to."

In one of the two bedrooms, on the peach carpet, there is an elaborate circle of small, gleaming stones, candles dripping wax, and plants.

The whole thing looks like a giant summoning circle, every item intricately placed and handled with the utmost care.

Daniel steps into the center, folding his legs beneath him as his eyes study the setup one last time.

"Whoa," Blythe gasps. "You went *in*."

"I did," Daniel agrees. "I have to be inside the circle."

Blythe chuckles. "No, I mean like, you really worked hard on this."

"Oh, of course," he says, flushing a bit. "If a Learned Magic spell backfires in the middle of its use, it can be deadly to the user. But also..." He opens and closes his round hands against his lap. "This is my one shot. If I don't banish the spirit now, I'm finished."

There is a sigh. Storm lies across the bed, her head in her hands. Blythe hadn't even noticed her. "You're not *finished*, Dan."

Daniel sets his mouth in a tight line. "You don't know that."

"Ooh!" Storm teases. "We got Sassy Daniel tonight!"

Daniel flushes, puffing his cheeks out a bit as he regards the circle again. "Alright," he announces. "It's time to begin."

Blythe feels Caspian's form materialize over her shoulder. He doesn't say anything, not even as Daniel closes his eyes and straightens his back.

Energy hums in the air, sending goosebumps up Blythe's skin. She's never experienced Learned Magic like this, the kind that is powerful without necessarily being dark.

Daniel does not flinch, not even as the candles begin to flicker and the shadows grow larger across the room. The lights blink, the stems of the plants curl and wither, and the hum of magic grows louder and louder and louder until the air is electric and singing.

And Daniel is the eye of the storm.

Blythe watches him as if to catch a glimpse something resembling a monster, or a frightening, grotesque creature made of darkness.

There is only Daniel in his ironed, white button-up, with his curly blonde hair and rosy cheeks.

Something occurs to Blythe as she watches this small boy who has never entered the world before. This boy who has always been a little too worried, a little too afraid.

Maybe, all along, it's been only Daniel.

The magic fades into a quiet buzzing that soon becomes nothing at all. The shadows shrink. The lights go still. The plants remain withered and wax still pools around the candles' burnt wicks, but it is over.

Daniel's eyes flutter open.

Storm sits up on the bed. "Did it work?"

"I don't feel different," Disappointment weighs heavy in Daniel's voice.

Blythe feels Caspian approach from behind her. "What was this?" He asks.

"Uh," Blythe begins. "Dan, can I tell Caspian about everything?"

Daniel nods without looking at her. His leg is shaking against the carpet.

"There's this spirit been trying to kill him for as long as he can remember," Blythe explains. "And he needs to banish it."

Caspian's expression doesn't change. "You can't banish a spirit," he speaks loud enough for Daniel to hear. "That's impossible. If nothing happened, it's because nothing's was there in the first place."

All of Daniel's limbs have gone still. He kneels over, face buried in his hands, and starts to cry.

Storm slips off of the bed, cutting through the circle to come to his side. She wraps an arm around his shaking shoulders.

Caspian's blank expression does not change. His eyes don't focus and his voice stays flat. "This is why I don't speak."

"It's all terrible," Daniel whispers. *"Terrible."*

Blythe feels awkward just standing there. She wants to console him too, but Storm is closer to Daniel than she is.

"If it helps, Dan," Blythe begins. "You may have been wrong, but knowing that nothing is trying to kill you has to be a *little* comforting."

Daniel barely raises his face from his palms. His brow is creases, his skin beet red.

"It isn't," he says. "It just isn't."

Cordelia's voice booms down the hall. "STOP DOING WEIRD MAGIC, IT'S MESSING UP THE WIFI!"

The moment has been broken. Daniel and Storm speak low: he is panicked, she is reassuring, the two of them in their own, impenetrable bubble.

Caspian shifts beside Blythe. A second later, he is gone. Blythe decides to take his lead.

"I'm sorry, Daniel," she says. "You too, Storm."

She doubts they even hear her.

Blythe drifts back into the hallway. Something Daniel swore was his answer is actually useless, and that overwhelming feeling of helplessness that consumes him now, of regret and confusion and pain...

Blythe worries she may soon get to know that feeling very, very well.

Blythe returns to her laptop, alone in the darkness with the sleeping boy on the couch, that living symbol of their impulsive choices, their lack of direction. Their mistakes.

The light from her screen sears into her eyes, burning the letters of the Trident Republic's name into her retinas.

———

Blythe wakes to the smell of bacon.

It takes her a moment to realize she fell asleep while working last night. She lies only feet away from the table, where Antonio is opening white containers of smoking hot breakfast food.

Her laptop is closed at her side, her hockey stick resting against the wall at her side and a blanket draped over her body.

"Good morning," Antonio chirps.

Blythe doesn't remember getting a blanket or putting her laptop away. "Did you put this over me?"

"Yep!" Antonio says. "Figured you could be a little more comfortable."

Blythe brings it tighter across her shoulders. It's the middle of summer in Las Vegas, Nevada, so a blanket is absolutely unnecessary. But Blythe appreciates the sentiment. "Thanks."

"Sure thing! How'd your work go last night?"

"I found the coordinates."

"Awesome!" Antonio beams. He notices Blythe isn't smiling. "At least, I think it is?"

They don't need to talk about this. Blythe's already cried in front of Antonio once, she can't do it again. "It is," she lies.

The boy on the couch is still asleep. Sunlight kisses his face and his skin glows like it is made of jewels. Storm's hoodie is a bit too small for his shoulders, but he looks as if they plucked him out of a magazine instead of off the road.

"What about Sleeping Beauty over there?" Blythe asks. "Shouldn't he be awake?"

"He's...fine? We think?" Antonio says. "He's breathing, at least. Cordelia said he's not in a coma, which is good. Maybe he's just really tired?"

Hm. Blythe studies the regular fall and rise of his breath. It's almost *too* regular, like when Lena would pretend to be asleep to avoid waking up for school.

"He reminds me of Rocky from the Rocky Horror Show," she says.

"What's that?"

The Rocky Horror Show is too complex an experience to accurately explain. "Nevermind."

By the time Blythe is up, washed, and dressed, Cordelia, Storm and Daniel are eating breakfast in the center of the hotel room.

Storm and Daniel are as silent as always, but heavy, dark bags hang from Daniel's round eyes. Blythe wishes she knew how to make him feel better, but what do you say to someone who has just realized they've believed a lie their whole life?

Something moves in front of the microwave.

"Morning, Caspian," Antonio greets.

Caspian shifts his dark eyes to him. The microwave is heating something Blythe can't see. When it dings, Caspian takes out a steaming bowl of ramen, moves it to the counter to add the seasoning, and floats through the wall.

He must reserve his witty quips for one-on-one conversations.

Antonio eats faster—and significantly more—than the rest of them, then grows bored waiting for them to finish and checks on Sleeping Beauty while the rest of them stay at the table.

Cordelia sets her chin in her hands. "So," she begins. "What's the plan?"

Blythe explains her ideas so far: enter the desert and search for Electric City.

"And from there?" Cordelia asks.

"We'll just have to play it by ear," Blythe answers.

The whole table takes a moment to let these words sink in. Even Daniel, preoccupied with his own situation, squints.

"Really?" Storm asks.

"There's nothing else we *can* do," Blythe says. "The Trident Republic is waiting for us. We'll just have to see what happens when we get there."

Storm's dark eyes spear through Blythe. "Sounds like you're giving up."

Blythe resists the urge to recoil. Storm's just trying to get a reaction out of her. She's probably still mad about what happened outside of McDonald's.

"I'm not," Blythe forces her voice to sound calm.

"Sounds like Whiteclaw made a move and now you're too scared to fight back."

"This conversation sounds like you need to mind your fucking business," Blythe snaps. "Because this means *nothing* to you. You're just here to find the Angelus and leave, so don't act like you give a shit."

Blythe wants to keep going when she sees anger flash across Storm's face. She started this argument and now has the nerve to get offended when Blythe pushes back?

Orange magic pulses through Storm's left eye. "You're not the only one who's watched a loved one be taken away."

They are the most personal words Storm Crane has ever said about herself.

A foreign voice speaks before Blythe can. "You're cute."

It is rich and smooth, like the finest cello playing through the room.

"C'mere," beckons the voice. It is the perfect voice for the perfect boy.

Antonio gasps—a sound that is cut off before it finishes. Blythe whirls around. But it's already happened.

The sleeping boy has jumped to his feet. One hand twists

Antonio's arm behind his back. The other grips Antonio by the throat.

Blythe jumps to her feet. Storm is instantly at her side. A puff of black smoke unfurls into Caspian.

The boy stares them down with eyes that are not grey, but a silver that could make even the prettiest ribbon of moonlight jealous.

His voice is clear, more beautiful than any song. Angelic. "Get any closer to me," he says. "And I'll snap his goddamn neck."

NINETEEN

Storm's hands curl into fists. Antonio's gaze locks on her. "Wait, Storm, don't fight—!"

An orange blur pushes Antonio aside and punches the boy in the face. His head snaps to the side, but his body doesn't flinch.

The boy's fist balls and hits Storm's stomach with enough force to knock her back into her own body. She hits the carpet with a grunt of pain Blythe has *never* heard her make.

He actually managed to hit *Storm*.

Caspian reverberates with black smoke. "If I fight him, I'll kill him."

"Don't worry, I got him!" Blythe snatches her hockey stick and runs, the magic humming as she winds it behind her.

She arcs it forward. The boy raises his hand before she can register the movement.

He catches it mid-swing. His grip is solid. Even pulling with both of her hands, Blythe can't get it to budge.

Her heart thunders. She has never been this close to the boy before. She expects to see malice in the silver eyes that stare back at her. There is only fear and instinct.

He shoves the stick backward. Blythe goes flying with it, momentum carrying her straight into Cordelia. The other girl yelps as the two of them collapse in a heap.

"Sorry, sorry!" Blythe apologizes quickly. She pushes her weight to her elbows so she is only straddling Cordelia. "Are you okay?!"

"No!" Cordelia shouts. "I was a second away from sending him back to sleep before *you* screwed up!"

Blythe turns around just in time to see Storm leap onto the boy's back. Her arm locks around his throat. The boy barely grunts as he swings her over his head, slamming her back into the ground.

The potted plant on the countertop wobbles and tips over on its own accord as Storm screams; vines snake out from the spilled dirt.

"STOP!" Antonio's voice cuts through the air like a knife.

The vines go limp. The boy stares at Antonio, gone as still as statue in front of the couch, his long hair curtaining half of his face.

Antonio's chest heaves with heavy, angry breaths. "He woke up surrounded by strangers, of course he's freaking out!" he shouts. *"Stop attacking him!"*

No one moves. Not Storm, still splayed out on the carpet, nor Caspian, his ghostly form resigned to the corner, nor the boy himself, whose hands, Blythe now realizes, are shaking.

Antonio rises slowly, raising his palms. "We don't want to hurt you, bro," he says. "I get it. We're a bunch of strange people you've never met before. But we just wanted to help."

He smiles his perfect, sunny smile. "I promise we're usually nicer than this."

The boy's eyes dart between him and everyone in the room. "Who are you and where am I?" His voice would be gorgeous if it weren't laced with so much panic.

"I'm Antonio. That's Storm, Blythe, Daniel, Cordelia—oh, and Caspian's around here somewhere. We're at a hotel in Las Vegas."

The boy tenses. "What?"

Antonio's voice remains calm and soothing. "We found you

beside the road. You were hurt and we didn't want to leave you there."

"Beside a..." Blythe watches him barely contain his confusion. "You *found* me?"

"Uh huh. You were pretty banged up, but you started to heal. By the time we got you here, you were fine. Have you ever done that before?"

"N-No, I..." the boy's voice trails off. "No."

It's an obvious lie. Antonio lets him get away with it. Every magician has to cover their tracks like that.

"All good bro, all good," Antonio draws closer as the boy calms, his shoulders dropping and his hands going loose. "Can you tell me your name?"

The boy hesitates. "Jay."

"Jay? That's nice and short. It's nice to meet you, Jay. Do you remember how you got to that road? Because we don't know what hurt you like that."

"I...I don't..." Jay stops again. "Did you see anyone around when you found me? A group of guys, maybe?"

"No, I...don't think so," Antonio says. "Do you maybe want to take a minute and eat? You seem confused and—"

Jay's expression hardens. "I'm not *confused.*"

"Sorry, I just meant, we're all just trying to figure things out. We have food in the kitchen, maybe I could bring you a plate and we could talk about this?"

Jay pushes his locs back from his face. The sun falls on him again, lighting up the straight line of his jaw and the pinch of his brows. He sinks back down to the couch, legs tucked close. A perfect portrait of distress.

"Yeah," he says. "Thanks."

Everything Jay does is a choreographed dance, every movement pure art. The other Guardians are frozen too, like time has paused to let them fully drink in this ethereal creature.

"Do they *speak?*" Jay abruptly asks.

Okay, admittedly, it must be weird to sit in a room with six complete strangers—strangers you just assumed were trying to kidnap you—who are all silently gaping at you.

"Usually you can't get us to shut up," Blythe says. "But you just kicked our asses."

His shoulders drop. "I'm...I'm sorry about that. I get...I panic sometimes," his gaze on her is palpable. Warm.

Then it is over and his attention is back on Antonio. "And I'm sorry I tricked you into getting close enough for me to choke you, I just...I thought the situation was worse than it was."

Antonio shrugs. "S'all good, I'm the one that fell for it."

They try not to crowd Jay as he eats. Antonio, meanwhile, plops down beside him as if Jay is no different than anyone else he's ever met.

"I really can't apologize enough," Jay makes a noise like a scoff and a chuckle. "I promise I'm not usually like that."

"Knocked out on the side of road?" Storm asks.

"Well, I mean," Jay smirks. "Only on Friday nights."

Cordelia laughs, a sound born of both surprise and mirth. Blythe smiles a bit too. The mystery boy has a sense of humor.

The conversation becomes almost normal then. Jay asks why they're at a hotel, if they're just on vacation or if there's another reason.

Considering the stress they just put him trough, he deserves the truth. "Um...we're in a bit of a weird situation," Blythe stumbles. "Okay, so, um. Y-You know about magic, right? Like, that's clear to you?"

Jay doesn't stop eating. "The band?"

"Oop," Storm mutters.

He knows he can heal but he doesn't know about magic? "No, like..." Blythe's voice trails off.

"Just, the concept," Cordelia interrupts. "We're operating on a lot of that. We travel together."

Lying wasn't Blythe's *first* resort. Even Antonio makes a sour face.

Jay is none the wiser. "Oh, dope. Are you travel vloggers or...?"

Storm snorts. She sits on the carpet still, watching Jay with a mix of amusement and distrust.

Cordelia's the one that actually answers. "No it's...just for us."

"Fair, fair. Where are you five stopping next?"

There are six of them. But that's only including Caspian—can Jay not see him?—who, currently, hovers in the corner of the room, spearing Jay beneath the world's shadiest glare.

"There's this city in the desert we want to...find," Cordelia says. Oh, so they're telling the truth about *that* but nothing else?

"Sounds cute," Jay says. "I'm from Florida. I mean, I stay in California sometimes, but I'm a little far from home at the moment—"

Antonio brightens. "Hey, I'm from Cali!"

"No way. L.A?"

"Nah man, San Diego."

They're about to wander down a long conversation path, but there's something Blythe needs to clear up. "Wait, what did you mean 'sometimes'?"

"Depends on my mom's work schedule," Jay says. "Anyway, I hate to do this after, um, our *exciting* introduction, but I really need to ask you guys a favor."

Antonio pops his legs up on the sofa's armchair. "Sure, dude, what's up?"

"Look, it's just...the guys I was with aren't here. And I don't have any of my stuff, I don't even have a phone, and I've never been to Vegas before. I hate to ask you guys this, but..."

Jay tilts his head a bit. His hair is too heavy to move much, but it is like a perfectly placed shadow to emphasize the silver of his eyes. The whole room seems to center in on him.

"Could you just take me the airport or something?" The words are gentle and beautiful in his voice. "If you need to stop at your desert city first, I understand. I'm not in a rush, I just need to get home and you're my only option."

"Uh—" Blythe begins.

"Sure," Cordelia says.

"W-We have space," Daniel agrees.

"Wh—wait—" Blythe stammers.

Antonio jumps up. "Of course, bro! Welcome to the club!"

"Okay, but I never agreed—" Blythe stammers.

"We gotta get you clothes because you can't keep wearin' mine," Storm says.

Cordelia gasps, clasping her hands together as her eyes light up. "We can go shopping!"

"HOLD ON!" Blythe yells. Every face turns to her, especially Jay's.

Blythe's heart sinks. She doesn't want to be the bad guy, but *someone* has to.

"Sorry," she apologizes. "Do you mind if we talk about this?"

"Of course, take your time," he agrees. "Can I just borrow someone's phone to—"

Cordelia, Antonio, Storm and Daniel instantly hand out their phones.

Jay smiles. And Blythe thought this boy couldn't be more beautiful. "Thanks."

He takes Antonio's and leaves the hotel room, the door shutting softly behind him.

Antonio's chest puffs with pride. "He took mine."

Blythe looks over all of them. "Okay, hi, group meeting." She clears her throat. "What. The. *Fuck.*"

"He's hot and I want him *here*," Cordelia says. "There's been a painful lack of attractive men around here."

"Ouch."

"Shut up, Antonio."

"I'm tired of always havin' to be the one that does all the lifting and fighting," Storm says. "Y'all can make him do it and I can sleep."

Blythe claps her hands, bringing all attention back to her. These kids have the attention spans of goldfish. "Okay, alright, but we can't take someone who doesn't even know about magic with us! That's a major liability!"

"I wouldn't call somebody who beat the shit out of us a liability," Storm retorts.

"We're only taking him to the airport," Cordelia adds. "If we go there first, we won't have to bring him to Electric City. We can have a nice drive, I can bond with him, get his number, and then we'll all move on."

"Aw, but I wanna hang out with him," Antonio pouts. "He seems cool."

Cordelia swats a hand at him without looking away from Blythe. "It's just to the airport, Blythe. Maybe we could use that time to flesh out a better plan for Electric City."

Being a liability aside, if they don't help Jay, he will have no means of getting home. And he is a Pandora's Box that *they* opened. If they could pick him up from the street, they can drop him off at the airport.

Blythe groans, stomping her feet until the frustration dissipates from her body. "Fine. We'll take him to the stupid airport," she grumbles. "But I'm never helping another person ever again."

Cordelia beams. "I'll look up directions for the farthest one."

"*Cordelia.*"

"What? It'll give us time to chat."

Blythe makes a face, sinking further into the carpet. The Guardians disperse to pack their things and prepare to go, but Blythe simply relocates to the couch, where she crosses her arms and pouts.

Fucking Antonio and his huge, dumb heart.

The door eases open. Jay slips back in.

"We'll take you to the airport," Blythe says, catching him slightly off guard. "But we're going there first."

His eyes land on her. "Thanks," he says, and then scans the empty seats. "They clear out fast, huh?"

"We're checking out today. They're packing."

"And you don't have to?

"I'm efficient."

Jay chuckles. "What's your name again?"

Blythe feels her face heat. "Blythe."

"Blythe," Her name sounds priceless in his voice. "I know you don't have to do this. You probably have hundreds of other places to be. But I want you to know I'm grateful, and if you ever need anything, you just let me know, okay? I got you."

Blythe's not sure how to respond to this. She can't look him in the eye. "...okay," she says, trying to keep the attitude in her voice, but it's already seeming forced.

Jay smiles. "I'm gonna go give this back to Antonio."

Blythe is silent in his wake, replaying the whole exchange in her head.

She repeats it to the others when they come back out.

"Did he sound vaguely..." Blythe hesitates to say the word. "Flirty?"

Cordelia nods. "That was very flirty and I'm painfully jealous."

Blythe's curls must be holding up better than she assumed.

"He flirted with me before he put me in a chokehold," Antonio says.

Storm throws up the hood of her jacket. "Nah, that nigga gay."

"Really?" Blythe asks. "I was getting fuckboy vibes."

Storm eyes her. "Fine line between fuckboy and boy fucker."

"Actually, I'm bisexual," comes a smooth voice.

Blythe's heart stops. Because, shit, Jay is coming down the hall. "And, being me and *knowing* me, I'd have to say...I am both." His gaze settles on them. "Very, *very* much both."

He grins, bright and smoldering and perfect. "We ready to go?"

———

Jay has pulled his locs into a long ponytail at the base of his neck. He frowns as they enter the parking lot, eying the Continental sideways.

"...This is the car?" he asks.

Blythe walks past without breaking her stride. "Beggars can't be choosy."

Cordelia beams at him. "We switch vehicles."

Jay is unimpressed. Blythe couldn't care less. He makes her uncomfortable, this blindingly perfect godling who is too beautiful to stare at directly, humming with too much magic that he doesn't even *know* about. And his confidence is choking. Everything about him is overwhelming.

He must be a Leo.

"Can we all even fit?" Jay asks.

"We'll make it work," Blythe says. "Antonio, sit on the floor!"

"Aw, what?!" Antonio yells.

Daniel sighs. "Thank goodness it wasn't me."

"That's the white man's manifesto," Storm replies.

Blythe wants to get straight to the airport, but the Continental is down on gas, which means they'll have to stop at a station first. Amazing.

"So, Jay!" Antonio shouts up from his place on the floor. "Tell us about yourself!"

Jay smiles down at him. "Me?"

"Yeah dude, like, what are your hobbies, what's your family like, who do you main in Mario Kart..."

"This is a very crowded first date, Antonio, but I'll bite," Jay teases. "I dunno, I'm not that interesting. I swim, I guess. And I've always been more of a Zelda guy—"

"Dude, wait, for real? I surf and I love Zelda. If you say you can cook, we'll be the same person."

"Oh no, if I tried to cook, everyone involved would die. I'd only attempt it in a life or death situation."

"Life or death like...the end of the world?"

"*Yes*," Jay agrees, emphatic. "You're gonna think I'm high as fuck but just follow me here—say aliens invaded or some shit—"

"*I think about alien invasions ALL THE TIME!*" Antonio shrieks.

Blythe can't believe this is happening. She has to listen to them go back and forth all the way to the gas station. When she finally parks beside a pump, she is all too ready to interrupt them.

"This is going to be the first stop for a while," she says. "So get out, go pee, get some snacks—"

"I want snacks!" Antonio rockets out the car.

Cordelia, who hasn't been able to say a word to Jay the whole ride thanks to Antonio, finally turns to him.

"Don't mind him," she says. "He's constantly overexcited."

"I noticed," Jay's getting out of the car too. "I like it though. You coming?"

Cordelia flips her hair as she bounces out of her seat. "Right behind you!"

"Cordelia, right?" Jay asks as they walk.

Storm and Daniel are content to wait in the backseat, like the anti-social introverts they are, so Blythe leaves them to it while she leans against the trunk, watching the numbers rise on the pump.

She feels Caspian's presence at her side before she sees him.

"I don't like him," he says.

Blythe sighs. Those words sound *really* harsh out loud. "I mean, I'm not his biggest fan either, but we're just taking him to the airport." Even if Jay *is* the final Guardian, it's far too late for him to join them.

Caspian's unkempt dark hair blows into his face, but cannot hide the intensity of his eyes. "He's only being nice because you're doing him a favor. You saw what he was like before. He choked Antonio."

"To be fair, it *did* seem like we kidnapped him. But thanks for worrying about us. For a while, I thought you didn't really give a shit about us."

Caspian is quiet. His hand drifts to the golden chain circling his wrist before he dissipates.

Blythe wonders where he goes when he leaves. Limbo? Hades? The world between worlds?

With the tank filled and Cordelia, Jay, and Antonio back in the car, they speed off for the airport.

Cordelia wasn't kidding when she said she'd find the farthest one. They end up driving down an isolated road, nothing but desert and dried ground on either side for miles.

"We're supposed to be going to the airport, not hell," Blythe grumbles, but Antonio, Cordelia and Jay's conversation is so loud, no one hears her, and she rolls her eyes.

A black car inches up behind them. Blythe's noticed it earlier. It's been traveling with them for a few minutes.

Cordelia pulls her bag onto her lap and sifts through it. Her face goes pale.

"I don't have the shard," she whispers.

Her words send a pang of fear through Blythe so intensely that her vision spots. "What do you mean?" Blythe asks without thinking. "What happened, where'd it go?"

"I had the shard when we left the petrol station and now I *don't*."

Blythe wants to rip the steering wheel straight off. "You *lost* it?!"

Something hums outside. The black car is no longer behind them. Its dark tinted windows are right beside Blythe, growing larger as it edges close. Too close.

The car smacks into them, jerking them in their seats.

Blythe's heart leaps into her throat. "What the fuck?!" she grips the wheel as hard as she can—all of the Guardians are in this car. Antonio is on the *floor*. She can't lose control of the Continental, she *can't*.

The black car pushes harder against their doors, metal screaming as it scrapes against metal. It's trying to edge them off the road.

The Guardians are all talking at once. Blythe can't listen. She barely knows how to drive. No one ever taught her how to deal with this.

Blythe revs the gas. They pull away, the needle climbing as their engine sings. The black car gains speed behind them.

"Who the fuck is that?!" Jay yells.

"I don't *know*!" Blythe screams. Her hands are starting to go numb. Half of them aren't wearing seatbelts. The Continental is too old for airbags. "Fuck, *fuck*, FUCK—somebody grab Antonio, get him off the floor!"

Headlights spear through the back window. The black car crashes into their fender, and the Continental spins. But this time, Blythe cannot gain control.

The world moves very, very slowly. The tires squeal as they careen in a half-circle, stretched, vertically, across the road.

The black car is still coming. Blythe watches it approach from her window, its crumbled hood speeding forward.

Blythe doesn't think to shut her eyes—they simply close. And then there is pain, and she is weightless, shaking and tossing like a ragdoll, the entire world tumbling off its axis.

A lifetime passes before the car falls still.

The car is filled with sounds—crying and screaming and voices and shouting names—all of them muffled.

Blythe is hanging onto consciousness by a thin, weak thread. It is fraying by the second.

Smoke billows outside the windows. Through it, the black car faces them like an emotionless face, the headlights staring like empty eyes.

The doors swing open. A horde of suited men emerge. From the driver's seat comes a pale, blue eyed man.

A bulb of black smoke appears beside him. It blooms into a boy.

Oblivion consumes Blythe's mind, but not before she watches the ghost raise his hand and present the man with a bronze shard.

TWENTY

BLYTHE ACHES.

Her entire body is only a dull throb, pulsing with every beat of her heart. Her head hangs heavy against her chest.

But her shirt is not torn. Her jeans are untouched. She does not look like she has survived a car accident.

Her feet are bound to the legs of a metal chair, rope digging into her skin. A similar one holds her wrists behind her back.

Her hockey stick is gone.

She looks up, only to have a white, fluorescent light pierce her eyes. She squints, scoping out the room, which is made entirely of mirrors, from the floor to the ceiling. An infinite number of Blythes surround her, all with ragged curls, tied to their chairs.

The blue-eyed man sits in front of her.

He is the shadowy figure Blythe has seen since she was young enough to know something was not quite right about him, but not old enough to know what that "something" was. His was the face that terrified her in her childhood dreams. *He* was her Boogeyman.

His hands move carefully, meticulously loading bullets into a semi-automatic gun.

Blythe's blood runs cold.

The Man raises his head, meeting her gaze. Most people hold emotion in their eyes, even if not purposefully: happiness, anger, boredom. There is nothing in this man's blue eyes. Nothing at all.

He does not speak. He is waiting for her.

Blythe's mouth feels like dry cotton. "Where...where am I?"

"That is classified."

Blythe's chest heaves. "Did you...w-what happened to the car? Why am I not hurt, I was in an accident—*you* crashed into us—"

"It was necessary for you to stop. It was not necessary for you to remain injured."

The words are hauntingly ominous, his soulless dedication to an unknown strict code. Was *else* was necessary, then? What did they do after she blacked out?

Why is Blythe *alone*?

Blythe tries to catch her breath. She can't stop looking at the gun. "Where are the Guardians?"

"They are not relevant to our business," The Man says.

No. No, no, *no*. They are fine. They have to be. Nothing could have happened to them. Like Daniel, sweet Daniel. Or Cordelia, who has, somehow, become Blythe's closest ally. Or Antonio or Storm or Caspian—or even Jay, *God*, he doesn't even know what's going on right now.

Pain and rage and fear boil hot in Blythe's chest. "Where. Are. The Guardians."

"The Guardians are not dead," The Man says. It is the closest she will get to an answer.

Blythe tries to move, but the ropes twist and burn. A choked cry bursts out of her. She is not going anywhere. The Man's gaze is just another restraint pinning her in place.

Blythe almost does not want to ask her next question. But it is the final, most frightening question she has.

"Please," she says. "*Please* tell me you aren't the Erasers."

The Man has not blinked once. "We have many names," he begins. "That is one of them."

Blythe's body curls in on itself. A single word drifts from her lips in a pained, weak whisper. "*Fuck.*"

Tears burn in her eyes. So, here she is. At the end of her adventure. About to be erased. It's been a long time coming, hasn't it? They've been trying to erase her since she was young.

Isn't it ironic? She would say to her parents if she could speak to them again. *After everything I went through, after all the things I accomplished and the places I've been, I got ghosted by the most familiar threat of them all.*

"The other Guardians are not dead and will not die, Blythe Fulton," says The Man. "And neither will you."

Blythe studies him. She can't decipher anything on his blank face.

"You do not understand why you are here, do you, Blythe Fulton?"

"Y-You took the shard," she stutters. "That's what you wanted."

"Untrue," The Man cocks the gun. Every muscle in Blythe's body goes rigid.

She is a teenage girl, a magician without magic, without a family or anyone to realize she's gone, strapped to a chair in a place she does not recognize.

Blythe chokes down the horrified sounds that claw at her throat. She could very well die here.

"Let's recount the events that brought you here," says The Man. "Multiple inappropriate entrances and exits of the Black Veins' Tempore. Summoning a ghost in Lavender Heights, Quebec. A motorcycle race through the streets of Philadelphia, Pennsylvania, ending it yet another inappropriate entrance of the Black Veins' Tempore. A car accident in a mall parking lot, followed by a hurricane on private residential property in San Diego, California. A short, morning tousle with us on the streets of Broughton, Montana. A magic-based hurricane attacking your family's magic-based coffee café in Washington. And finally, an altercation with a magician gang in Washington that led to you carrying a stolen magical item across multiple state lines and into one foreign country.

"And now, we are here," The Man finishes. "Because you have done more in the past seventy-two hours than most of the general magician population does in *five years*. Of course, you have little idea, because we have handled all of these events in an efficient, timely manner, as we do with all of our cases, cleaning up all evidence and witnesses, so the world does not see any hint of magician existence. But allowing this to continue would be inefficient. Once we undo one of your fiascos, you head two more."

His cold eyes stare her down. Like a machine. "There are some constant offenders we can excuse," The gun clicks. "You are not one of them."

Blythe screams. The sound is raw and sharp and terrible. "You said I wouldn't die! You *said I wouldn't die!* Half of those things aren't our fault—you *saw* what happened! We were just trying to survive! I was just trying to find my family!"

"It is not our job to care about the how or the why," says The Man. "It is our job is to keep the Underground separate from the Overground. And we do whatever we must to complete this job to the best of our ability. *You* decided to embark on this adventure instead of heeding our warnings. Therefore, *you* will pay the price. There is nothing you need to tell me, Blythe Fulton. In less than ten minutes, you will not exist."

Blythe's heart stops. Her tears burn down her cheeks, almost as much as her voice burns in her throat. "Y-You said I wouldn't die."

"And I told the truth. You will not be killed. Being erased—being *unmade*—is a different creature than death. When you are unmade, no one remembers you. Your body, your soul, your essence, and your thoughts will disintegrate into nothing. Everything you have ever owned or created will disappear. The world will believe there have always been six Guardians, not seven. Your parents will only remember having two daughters. The only sister Lily and Lena

Fulton will know are one another. Death is the end of an existence. To be erased is to have never existed at all."

Blythe trembles against her restraints. "No," the word slips out as her mind enters a blind panic.

"Repeat offenders must be handled in this manner. It is the only way."

"No! NO!"

Did he do this to the other Guardians? He can't have. He *can't*. She remembers all of them. Cordelia and Daniel and Antonio and Storm and Caspian and Jay. Cordelia and Daniel and Antonio and Storm and Caspian and Jay.

"You can't do this! You can't erase me! I haven't, I won't—"

The Man rises and aims the barrel of the gun between her eyes. Blythe's words clog in her throat. If he pulls the trigger...if he pulls the trigger...

"We have followed you since you were initiated as a Guardian. And it was out of necessity," The Man says. "There may be seven Guardians, but only one of you is the Guardian of Ether. Only one of you has the power to potentially rewrite the fabric of the world itself —and that is you. We try not to take direct action, but in the instance of your life, it was necessary for the safety of the people around you. We are grateful that your parents did not attempt to interfere and report us to the Sages. I assume it was out of fear of losing you."

Blythe shuts her eyes, but it does not help. The Erasers didn't follow the Fultons because of something her parents had done, or because of the café, or because they were just terrible people.

It was because of her. Because *she* was the Guardians of Ether. And they were waiting for her to screw up. To cause mass destruction, as the Sage of Ether before her had.

If her parents would've told the Sages about the Erasers, the Sages would have whisked Blythe away to Frost Glade before she could even start school.

Her parents didn't move from state to state to protect themselves. They moved to protect her. And she couldn't even protect *them*.

"Do you know what you could do, Blythe Fulton?" The Man continues. "You could transform this gun into sand. You could transport this entire room to a river in Italy. With nothing more than a blink of your eye, you could unmake *me*. So, make your move, Guardian of Ether. If you do not wish to be unmade, if you do not wish to be erased, then free yourself."

Blythe's whole body has gone cold and numb. She cannot die here. She wants to see her family again, to hug her mother, to listen to her father's voice, to apologize to the twins for everything. But she won't. Because she does not know how to use her magic. She has never known how.

She does the only thing she is good for, the same thing she did back at the café.

She ducks her head, pulling her body into a ball, and she cries. She cries so hard her ribs ache. Because after all of this, after how far she's come, after everything she has accomplished, after learning what the Guardian of Ether can do, *should* do...she is still incapable of anything more than crying.

She is powerless.

The Man steps back. "I assumed as much," he says. "But it was only an assumption and therefore required testing. A change of plan, then."

Through the haze of her hiccups and tears, The Man places the gun in the holster at his hip, walks to the front of the room, and taps on the glass.

A piece of the wall slides backward like a sliding door, revealing a stark white hallway. A second suited man walks in, expression equally unreadable.

He removes Blythe's restraints as The Man watches. Blythe stumbles free, massaging the red marks circling her wrists.

"I will reunite you with the other Guardians," says The Man.

The words bring her, just barely, the smallest bit of relief. Because The Man mentioned a change of plans, but that could mean anything at all.

He leads Blythe down the hallway as if the entire situation is normal. The sound of their footsteps echo off of the walls until they reach a wide, open space resembling an open warehouse—or some sort of futuristic lab, with long white tables and holographic diagrams floating in front of suited men typing on tablets.

Identical blank faces rush this way and that, unblinking. Everyone is hard at work, but Blythe cannot discern what it is they are doing. Maybe because her tears keep obscuring her vision.

They pass a white stand beneath a pillar of light. Blythe's breath hitches. Hovering above it is the bronze shard, glinting like a museum item on display. The Man does not even glance at it as they pass.

They come to a grey door. The Man swings it open—and there the Guardians are. They are crowded together, Daniel on the ground beside Antonio, Cordelia hovering over them, Storm slouched against the wall, Jay pacing. They are spotless and untouched and alive.

Daniel jumps up. "Blythe!"

Blythe rushes in and they meet her halfway. She runs into Antonio's arms, hiding her face against his shoulder. Her tears sink into his t-shirt. Someone touches her arm gently.

"It's okay," Antonio whispers, holding her tight. "It's okay."

What's happened? Cordelia's voice echoes in her head. God, where would Blythe even begin?

"Yo bitch," Storm shouts to The Man in the doorway. "You better get to fucking talking."

"What the *fuck* did you do?" Jay growls.

The Man is not intimidated. Nor does he answer. "Follow me toward the exit," he says.

"We aren't moving until you answer us," Cordelia's voice rings clear and defiant.

"You are welcome to stay," says The Man. "But you will not be offered a second opportunity to leave."

Blythe pulls away from Antonio, sniffling. She has to stop this. "I'm okay," she insists. "I just...let's just go."

The Man ushers them back into the bustling lab. Except this time, floating in the center of the room, is Caspian.

He is not looking at them. Blythe boils with anger at the very sight of his stupid face. The Man goes up to him, even as Caspian's ghostly form drifts, just slightly away.

"We had a deal," says The Man. "And for substantially fulfilling your end of our agreement, I shall fulfill ours."

"Don't," Caspian whispers to the floor. "Leave me alone."

"I cannot break the agreement. Opportunities in exchange for information," He points to the golden chain wound twice round Caspian's wrist. "That is from your family."

Caspian's eyes flare. "That's it?" he asks.

The Man stares at him.

Caspian raises his wrist. "This was my mom's. I *know* that. You broke into my graveyard, set me up with an ultimatum, and *told me something I already knew?!*"

"You will interpret the information as you wish," The Man says blankly. "What I have told you is an immense truth."

The Man walks on without him. The Guardians have no choice but to follow him. Even Caspian must, though he keeps his distance, either out of necessity or fear, Blythe is not sure.

The Man brings them to a raised platform that looks like something out of a sci-fi movie. He gestures for them to stand atop it and they do, standing crowded together as if being closer will keep them safe.

Caspian lingers behind. The Man stares at him until, slowly and carefully, Caspian enters as well.

"Wait here," The Man instructs, and leaves them.

Blythe whirls to Caspian. "What. Happened," she growls.

Caspian begins to fade. "No, don't you *dare* disappear, what the fuck happened?!" Blythe screams.

"He's letting us go," Caspian's voice wavers. "So, it's fine."

"It's not fine! Fuck you, it'll *never* be fine!"

Caspian's face fights between neutral uncaring and visible hurt. He won't look her in the eye. "I told you I didn't want to come."

As if that explains everything. As if it is *her* fault.

"Blythe," Jay says, smooth and beautiful, as he lays a hand on her shoulder.

She shoves it off. Her gaze spears through Caspian. "You told him you'd bring us to him?! For what?"

"They came to the graveyard and told me that you would be on your way and to bring him the shard," Caspian explains. "They promised to tell me what I needed to know."

"About what?! Your family?" Blythe screams. "You don't screw people over just for your own family!"

Her voice lingers in the silence. And Blythe hears her own words.

Caspian is a boy they found alone in a graveyard. His family, assuming from the tomb he did not let them see, is dead. The Guardians have never seen Caspian alive. He may very well be dead as well.

He has lost everything. All he has are memories. Maybe this is why she can't truly hate Caspian. Because when she looks into his eyes, she sees a bit of herself staring back.

This time, when Jay turns her around, she lets him, even though his words travel past her. "...says he's gonna let us go. We'll be alright. Just sit tight with us, okay?"

Blythe doesn't look at him. At the end of the warehouse, the shard hovers glimmering. Through the wall above it comes two hovering Krubim.

A young woman with a scarred face follows them. She is the one from the Tempore, still wearing her billowing sleeves—and her bronze trident pin.

She looks back and forth, as if she isn't supposed to be here. Her eyes catch on Blythe. Her lips curl into a smile as she presses a finger against them.

Swift as a breeze, she slips a bag over the shard, carries it through the wall with the Krubim on either side, and is gone.

Fuck.

Without the shard, the Angelus will have no reason to track them down, which means Storm has no reason to stay. And what if Cordelia isn't powerful enough to protect them from being mind controlled anymore?

It's too much. It's all too much.

"Blythe?" Antonio asks.

"Nothing," Blythe insists. "Just...nothing."

The platform vibrates with magical energy. The Man returns, holding Blythe's hockey stick in his upturned palms.

"This encounter will be erased to ensure confidentially," The Man says. "The seven of you and our organization will be the only ones aware of what transpired. Through no means—magical or scientific—can your memories of this event be accessed or transmitted, because they will not exist to someone who is *not* us. If you try to speak of them to someone not currently present, you will not be believed."

"...what the fuck...?" Jay whispers.

The Man continues over him. "Your previous actions cannot be overlooked, but you have recently brought into your mix a magician with a potential reach of over six million people worldwide, which means another careless magical escapade could be catastrophic."

Six *million?* Antonio frowns at their newest addition. "Is that *you?*" He asks, but Jay doesn't get a chance to answer.

"Because of this," The Man resumes. "When you leave this place, you will enter a neutral area, and all of you, excluding Caspian Compton, will be stripped of your magic upon exiting. Unless you are in a sanctioned magician-safe area, you will be unable to use magic, Outer or Inner. This brings an end to your case and, hopefully, means we have no reason to see each other ever again."

Blythe's stomach sinks. The shock echoes throughout all of the Guardians.

"You *gotta* be fucking kidding me," Storm scoffs.

"How is that fair?" Daniel asks.

"What?" Blythe yells. "*What?!*"

How are they supposed to get inside Electric City without magic? How are they supposed to *breathe* without magic?

The Man regards Blythe. "Consider yourself lucky, Blythe Fulton. If you had full control over your magic—if you *had* attempted anything in that room—we would have proceeded to erase you. However, you seem to even lack any *knowledge* of your capabilities, and therefore, are not enough of a threat to be erased."

The Man takes both ends of the hockey stick in his hands. With a quick jerk of his arms, the hockey stick *snaps*. Breaks as if it were a toothpick.

The wood shatters. A blast of magical energy escapes it.

"You do not need to be erased," says The Man. "For you are already nothing."

He drops the pieces to the floor and they clatter like the useless pieces of trash they now are.

"Go home, Blythe Fulton," says The Man.

The pile of splintered wood on the platform at her feet whispers of weak, broken magic. Without it, she has no way to fight back. Without the shard, she has no way to protect herself. Without either of these things, she has no way of finding her family.

Tears well in her eyes. "My home is wherever my family is," Blythe says. "I have no childhood *home* where I belong, no house where I grew up."

And inside of her, there comes a humming. A buzzing. An energy.

She glares up at The Man. White light bursts from her mouth as she speaks. "*You* made sure of that."

Her skin starts to glow as if the moon itself shines within her. Every inch of her is fluorescent, and just beneath her skin lies a galaxy of stars. Constellations drift up and down her arms. Ribbons of outer space have unraveled inside of her.

"You destroyed my family's lives," she hisses. "They raised me in fear, constantly running, waiting for the day they'd be able to raise me and my sisters in peace."

Her light intensifies. The whole room bleaches white, draining the world of its color.

It is all nothing to Blythe. It is all unseen. "Now they've been kidnapped," she says. "And you want me to 'go home'."

Wind whistles like a tornado has gathered. It rips at the walls, sucking its pieces into a frantic vortex around Blythe.

"You are the evil, soulless people who stop magicians from using their abilities to help the world. You are not heroes. You are empty husks."

A tear slips from Blythe's eye, but she clenches her jaw. "And *you* are the only person here who is nothing."

An explosion of pure energy bursts from her body.

As soon as it does, the platform beneath their feet opens into a gaping, open hole.

The Guardians drop. Blythe's body shifts and tumbles into a black void. Existence is quiet and dark.

And then the world reappears. It is not the place they left.

They are on a road with the night sky hanging above them. Blythe's skin has returned to a normal, un-glowing caramel brown.

It feels like someone has carved out her soul, leaving an empty, throbbing husk. Her mind is heavy. Too heavy for consciousness.

The world shifts sideways as she drops.

TWENTY-ONE

Storm's voice comes from someplace far away. "It wasn't your business, we just agreed to take you to the airport. And we didn't even have to do *that*."

"She didn't mean for that to sound so rude," Antonio's voice is closer. Clearer.

"Yes, she did," Storm snaps.

Antonio sighs in frustration. "Jay, listen. We're sorry. Really. We were just trying to help you...wait, shh, shh. Hey, Blythe."

A white streetlight illuminates the Guardians and the raindrops bouncing off of their shoulders. Antonio sits on the ground beside Blythe, letting her lean into him, her head on his shoulder.

"How do you feel?" Antonio asks.

Blythe's not sure. Drained, mostly. "I've been worse," she says.

"I haven't," Storm snorts. She leans against a streetlamp across the road. "I thought they were fucking around when they said they took our magic."

Antonio pouts. "Yeah. My wings are gone. But it's just for now! The second we're on magician territory—"

"It's bullshit is what it is," Storm interrupts.

Everyone turns away, making eye contact with anything and everything other than each other. But the absence of magic is palpable.

Now that it is gone, Blythe realizes that there was actually a constant energetic buzzing around her, inside of her, that has died.

It feels as if she's been cut off from the world.

Cordelia stares at Blythe. "At least you got to use your magic for the first time before you lost it," she says. "We didn't know you could do that."

"*I* didn't know I could do that," Blythe mutters. Her magic has never responded to her. Ever. But something must've happened back there, something that just made her snap.

Antonio shrugs. "I thought it was cool. Except for the part where you passed out."

"Yeah, sure," Jay's voice pierces the conversation like a blade, sharp and sardonic. His dreadlocks have fallen long and loose, just as black as the sky behind him. "Still doesn't explain why the *fuck* no one told me anything."

"We thought—"

"I don't care about what the fuck you *thought*," Jay interrupts Cordelia. Antonio tries to speak, but Jay won't allow it. "You're all bullshitting me right now. You mean to tell me you just *happened* to find me beside a road, noticed I could heal, and then you were going to...what? Just let me go home? When you had like, forty crazy ass...*magicians* after you? That doesn't make any sense. None of this makes any goddamn sense."

Apparently, Jay knows about magic now. Blythe's glad she was unconscious for that conversation. Doesn't seem like it went well.

"*I* was the one who wanted to take you with us," Antonio says. "It was my idea. I saw that you were hurt, and when you started to heal I thought...I thought that made you one of us. And that you should come with us."

"And what would you get out of helping me?" Jay snaps.

Antonio recoils like Jay has just asked him to murder someone. "I

301

didn't do it to get anything out of it. I just didn't want to *leave* you there. So, if anyone deserves to be yelled at for all this, it's me. It's my fault you're here. And I'm sorry."

Jay seems like might just yell at him. But he only scoffs, shaking his head.

Blythe may as well make it worse. "The Trident Republic took the shard," she says. "I saw one of their members sneak into the Erasers' base and leave with it."

Storm, the one who this affects the most, only folds her arms tighter, staring off at some unseen point.

"I can protect us," Cordelia promises. "I'm sure we'll be fine."

Blythe's not sure if she believes that. But she's not really sure *what* she believes anymore. Between Jay's self-obsessed anger, the Erasers and their self-righteous justice, and the Guardians' eyes all looking to her for leadership, who is *Blythe* supposed to look to?

The pieces of her hockey stick are beneath the streetlight, both ends fragmented and ragged. But the Continental is nowhere to be seen. And they are on a street with grass and towering palm trees. This does not look like Nevada.

"Where..." Blythe's voice trails off. "Where are we?"

The Guardians don't answer right away. That scares Blythe the most. "We figured out not long after you fainted," Cordelia finally says. "We're in Miami."

"Florida?" Blythe's voice is a broken, shrill whisper. "Do we... have our things?"

"Most of our stuff was in the trunk," Daniel answers. "And we have a few backpacks but..."

Blythe's heart thumps in her chest. "Do we have money? Cordelia, you could—"

"Remember when I said I...emptied my bank account for the hotel?" she asks. "In hindsight, it wasn't the smartest idea."

Miami is so far from Nevada. It is on the complete opposite side of the country. "Though, we could still use the Tempore," Cordelia says, then glances to Jay. "It's a time bending forest. Takes no time to travel through and can get you across the world in seconds. We could possibly also use it to get you home."

"The Trident Republic has either made that place into a death trap, or there's Black Veins soldiers everywhere," Storm says. "It's not an option anymore."

"W-Would we even be able to use it without magic?" Daniel asks. "I think we'll just have to...travel like normal people."

Whatever hope Jay held in his face is gone. "So," he begins. "You're miles from where you needed to be, you're all stranded, and I'm stranded with you."

Blythe studies them. They are tired. Everyone is soaking wet from the rain, hair stuck to their skin, clothes drenched dark. They have been traveling across state and country lines for almost a week nonstop, until heavy bags became permanent under their eyes.

They are tired. They have battled monsters and escaped the Erasers and now they have even lost their magic. They have no money and are comically far from where they need to be, with no feasible way of getting there.

And they are *tired*.

Blythe's eyes burn as she stares at her hockey stick. She doesn't know what to do. She *doesn't know what to do*.

"I just wanted to find them," she whispers. "I didn't want to ruin anything. I wasn't trying to be difficult. I just...I just wanted my mom and my dad and my sisters back."

She bites her lip to hold back the tears. "I was terrible to you, I lied, I kept things from you, I was a *bitch*. Now you're stuck in the rain, stranded in fucking Florida, for something that has nothing to do with you. Because of *me*. And there's nothing I can do to fix any of it! Because I've barely known what I was doing from the start! Everything that went wrong, everything you all went through, it's all my fault. And I can't even make it better. You probably hate me, and you *deserve* to hate me, but please just know that I'm sorry, I'm *so* sorry, I'm so fucking sorry..."

Tears spill from her eyes, hot on her cheeks. They are

indistinguishable from the rain that soaks through her clothes, but her body shakes as her mind replays the guilt, over and over again.

This is not the Erasers' fault. It's not even Caspian's fault. It is hers. Only hers.

Rollerblades scuff against the ground, coming toward her. When Storm speaks, her voice is gentle with supportive strength. "Pick your head up, sis."

Blythe looks up.

"I'm gonna be honest, you have pulled some shit," Storm says. "Like when you forgot to tell Antonio y'all weren't going to Frost Glade. Or when you agreed to let a damn ghost come with us and he screwed us over like I knew he would. And I swear to God, you are the nosiest bitch alive. But we put up with it. Because you've done a lot of good too, and you have a cause worth fighting for. We want your family back too, Blythe. We travelled with you through getting arrested, getting thrown to hell and back inside a rusty old 1950's car, facing the goddamn magician boogeymen...and last time I checked, ain't none of us said we was leaving."

Daniel, Cordelia and Antonio stare down at her, raindrops shining in their lashes. But they are not looking at her with anger, or malice, or hate. There is nothing like that in any of their eyes. Cordelia looks at her with sympathy, Daniel with concern, and Antonio with hope.

They just want her to be okay.

"You admitted it yourself, you got us into some shit," Storm says. "So now it's our turn to get us all out. You're not alone, Blythe. You got a whole group of people who agreed to be here. I said I wouldn't leave until one of us got what we wanted. Even if it takes another three, four weeks, even if we have to live off of cheap fast foot and hitchhike for hours, we are getting into Electric City. And you best *believe* we walkin' out with your family."

Antonio squeezes Blythe tight as she wipes the rain and tears from her face.

"You just have to trust us," Storm says.

Cordelia, whose life she indirectly saved back in Philadelphia. Daniel, who she has always supported and who has supported her in turn. Antonio, with his huge, overflowing heart, who probably loves Blythe as much as her own blood relatives. And Storm, this mysterious vigilante, who could have left as soon as Blythe told her they no longer had the shard, but is kneeling in front of her as if she could will strength and power straight into Blythe's bones.

Somehow, through some weird twist of fate, these people have not deserted her. She has shown them the worst sides of herself, and yet here they stand, refusing to abandon her.

Blythe's words come out through choked sobs. "I trust you," she whispers. "I trust you."

Storm nods. Daniel gives his awkward half-smile. They're here for her. They're here. Blythe's going to get her family back.

And they're going to keep going. They're always going to keep going.

"We just need a car," Cordelia says. "And money, preferably."

A loud sigh directs everyone's attention to Jay.

He stands like a god in the rain, strands of baby hair curling along his face. "If you tell me what the fuck is going on, I'll help you. We could catch an Uber to my house from here, it's not too far."

Blythe sits up a bit straighter. "I thought you lived in L.A."

"I said I lived in a couple places," Jay corrects. "The L.A house was just closer at the time. I can get you guys a rental and tickets back to Vegas, but you'll be on your own after that."

"As soon as we're set up with WiFi, I can get to work on our infiltration of Electric City," Cordelia says. "I can have a full layout of the city by tomorrow morning."

But Storm is still looking at Jay. "Nigga, are you rich?" she asks.

Jay, pointedly, does not answer.

Their Uber saves them from the rain, a huge Ford truck that rolls to a stop in the road behind them. Antonio helps Blythe up, but as they walk, something pricks in Blythe's chest. A tug that tightens and settles. She stops in the doorway.

"Caspian," she calls into the night.

She can see him down the street, a formless cloud of dark mist. Blythe wants to leave him there, to return back to his sad graveyard in Lavender Heights, a town with dying tourism and dying plants. But what Caspian did was not done out of spite, but out of stumbling yearn to survive. And, technically, Blythe has done no better.

"You should..." Blythe's voice trails off. "You should come with us."

He does not answer. He disappears, taking the tug in her ribs with him. Which means he has genuinely, completely, gone.

"Caspian's still here?" Antonio asks.

Blythe feels a chill in the air, but it is simply the rain. "Not anymore," she says.

The Ford is dark, but at least it is warm and dry. Blythe settles in the third row of seats between Cordelia and Daniel. All of them are dripping onto the leather seats.

"Was there really a person there or is this just a Blythe thing?" Jay asks.

"No, Caspian's real," Storm says. "He must've died when emo bands were still a thing." Her braids shake as she turns to Blythe. "I can't believe he did us like that. I *liked* him."

"I think it was more complicated than that," Blythe mutters.

Between the rhythm of the windshield wipers and the rain tapping against the glass, their ride is almost soothing. The farther they drive, the more the weather lightens, until the only remnants of a storm are the puddles of water on the sidewalks.

They find themselves pulling into an affluent area where new houses stand like modern castles. Palm trees sway outside of their picaresque porches. These are the homes of young millionaires and beautiful heiresses.

"Right here's fine," Jay says to the driver. "Thanks."

They hop out in front of a white house with pillars towering above its front door and a massive, sprawling driveway.

"Whoa, dude!" Antonio exclaims. "This looks like a house from a movie! Your room must be huge—wait, where are you going?"

Jay is walking in the complete opposite direction of the door. "I don't live there," he says over his shoulder. "I'm just not allowed to get dropped off in front of my house. C'mon."

The Guardians exchange quizzical looks, but follow him nonetheless. He travels down quite a few quiet streets, bathed in golden lights, until they reach a steep hill.

And, cresting over said hill, is a mansion.

It is white, modern and boxy, with windows that span almost every inch of its exterior. A glass bridge links the furthest right wing to furthest east, and beneath it spans an azure pool the size of a basketball court. The shadow its form casts along the grass is the shadow of a titan.

"Wait a minute..." Blythe begins. She's seen this place on YouTube videos, like the one she watched with Jamie on her parents' anniversary. "This is Hoffman Manor."

She looks Jay in his face. And as he stands silhouetted by this monolith of a home, she *finally*, truly, sees him.

He is a perfect blend of his parents: his father's commanding height and toned muscles, his mother's deep copper skin and dark hair that is so thick and beautiful, it sings of secrets it will never tell. His eyes are like the grey of his mother's, but better, multiplied by a thousand, until their beauty is almost unfathomable.

"You're JOSHUA HOFFMAN?!" Blythe screams, gaining a gasp from everyone—except Daniel.

Jay's lips are set in a line. "Yeah."

"W-Who is Joshua Hoffman?" Daniel stammers.

Cordelia spins around to him. "Did you just ask *who Joshua Hoffman was?*"

"I-I think so," Daniel agrees.

Jay is already starting toward his house; the Guardians scuttle after him like a bunch of ducklings. Who would have thought their biggest distraction would turn into their greatest ally?

"Do you really not know who the Hoffmans are?" Cordelia asks. Daniel shakes his head.

Cordelia scoffs. "You fool," she says, and Daniel makes a face. "Charles Hoffman is the creator and CEO of Zadis Industries. He is the most innovative mind of the century. He develops technology fifty years more advanced than anyone alive—he invented *my phone*. And Elizabeth Hoffman has won three Oscars, two for Best Actress. She is the most gorgeous woman alive and does active worldwide charity work. And *they* got together and made *him*." Cordelia swoons. "A god among men."

"Oh! I know Charles Hoffman," Daniel says. "My parents used to speak of his work with thaumol—"

"Time to go in," Jay interrupts.

Their shoes click against the spotless tile leading to the back door. The scent of the pool's chlorine has taken over the air.

"We could've gone in through the front but we've got this extra ass security system. It's annoying," Jay says. "This is easier." He places his hand on a scanner beside the door. With a beep, the lock clicks.

If his parents are home, they could be meeting *celebrities* tonight. "Is anyone home?" Blythe asks. It's the least invasive phrasing of her question.

But Jay's brow still furrows. "No."

He leads them up a narrow staircase, where their voices bounce off the walls. "Joshua was in a lot of iconic movies as a kid," Antonio says to Daniel. "But he stopped when we were all around like, nine."

"People say he's heading to the Olympics soon," Storm adds. "I mean, I'on know much about swimming, but he's a *bullet* in the water. Doesn't even need to come up for air. Like a goddamn fish."

Alright, now Blythe wants to join in. "He always runs from the paparazzi. And he won't take pictures. Ever. Like a celebrity cryptid."

Daniel seems bewildered with all this new information, his gaze hopping from one person to the next.

"I bet he's as smart as his father," Cordelia muses. "Can you imagine being that talented? That creative? And that *attractive*."

"I-I-I've never been any of those things," Daniel admits.

Antonio laughs before turning to their host. "Hey, Joshua, have you ever—"

Jay stops. It is so sudden, Blythe almost runs into him. The look he sends over his shoulder could cut diamonds. It is the same look Blythe saw in his eyes back in the hotel.

"Don't call me that," he says. "Ever."

Gone is the charming, flirty boy from the gas station. This is someone else entirely. Even Antonio seems slightly off-put. "Sorry," he apologizes. "I didn't know."

But because he is Antonio, he bounces back easily. Jay does not. His muscles stay tense and his jaw stays locked, even when he brings them into the kitchen.

The conversation has been killed. When they see the kitchen's massive countertop and fridge setup, with a bird's eye view of Miami, no one even voices their awe.

"You guys can do whatever you want," Jay says. "Treat it like it's your own place. Just don't get lost."

"We could get lost...?" Daniel whispers.

Jay doesn't answer that. "Cordelia, you said you needed WiFi? I have a laptop for you."

Antonio opens the fridge, revealing an interior that stands even taller than him. Storm and Daniel quietly split to explore, but Blythe follows Cordelia and Jay.

Jay brings them to a sitting room with an enormous flat screen imbedded in the wall, above a holographic fireplace. He pulls out a laptop from a bookcase; leave it to the creator of Zadis himself to leave computers lying around his home.

"Do you code as well?" Cordelia asks, crossing her legs on a cream sofa that looks like its hovering in midair.

"No," Jay says. "I don't know anything about it."

Cordelia looks slightly disappointed. "Oh. Well, you could always learn. I could teach you if—"

"I'm not interested," Jay interrupts, passing her the laptop. Then his gaze turns to Blythe. "Could you come with me?"

Blythe doesn't know what he could possibly want to talk to *her* about, but she's too curious to refuse.

"Yeah, sure," she agrees.

Jay guides her a few rooms back, finally stopping in front of a staircase that leads to more unknown wonders.

"Just tell me what's going on," Jay says. "Point blank. No bullshit."

"You're the one that brought me out here," Blythe says.

"No," Jay sighs, shutting his eyes.

"Oh, you meant with...magic and everything," Blythe realizes. "Sorry."

She lays out everything she can about their whole adventure. From start to finish. At first, it is for Jay's sake. Then it is for hers; recounting everything that has happened to her these past few days is almost therapeutic. But Jay's silver eyes haven't strayed from her once.

"I have one question," he says when she is done.

"Of course."

"Why did you let Antonio bring me with you, if you were so pressed for time?"

Blythe hesitates. "At first it was just because he refused to leave without you. Then...look, I don't think you'll like this part," she admits, but Jay is willing to hear anything now. "But we think—*I* think—you may be the last Guardian."

He doesn't react. "Is that it?" he asks.

That went a lot smoother than Blythe anticipated. "...yeah," Blythe says, cautious. He has to say *something*.

Jay leans back a bit. And he chuckles, smiles out the window with a relieved, "Holy shit."

"What?" Blythe stammers.

"I was thinking like..." he rolls his eyes, throwing up a hand. "I don't know, that you guys were trying to kidnap me? But in a really elaborate way? Then I thought I was being paranoid again, and obviously I *was*, because y'all are cool. You're just *wrong*."

"Oh, no! We weren't—no," Blythe blurts. She can't disagree emphatically enough. "We never wanted to hurt you. But...you know that even if you're not a Guardian, you're probably a magician—"

"No, it's nothing like that. I've been doing that weird healing thing my whole life. People just aren't supposed to see it."

The two of them tend to speak over each other, Blythe and Jay, as if both of them want to be the one to say their piece and to say it first.

"But...it's literally magic," Blythe protests. "No normal human being can heal like that."

Those words twist Jay's expression into hard, cold stone. "Let's not do this, Blythe. If I say I'm not one of you, I'm not one of you."

A part of her wants to apologize for upsetting him. But that part is small and stupid. "What do you have against magicians? You just learned we existed an hour ago."

"Nothing. I think you're all adorable. But *I* am not one of you. Don't say that I am."

His locs whip behind him as he starts up the stairs. "I'll be in my room. We can leave tomorrow morning."

Blythe wants to tell him off for being immature; she juts out her hip, ready to lay into him.

On the wall, above his head, hang photos in golden frames. Family photos. They look like they are all from photoshoots, where paid professionals organized their every pose to be displayed on magazine covers. But the Hoffmans still look like a family.

There's Charles, stoic and suited; Elizabeth, perfect makeup with a movie star's smile; Jay—perfect, indescribable Jay...and a small boy who shares the family's gorgeous dark skin, but with his father's dark eyes and his mother's loose curls.

In every picture, the boy is always at Jay's side.

Jay has opened his house to them. And the Guardians have

spoken about him and his parents as if they were idols at a museum, while he walked *right* beside them.

Blythe stood here, insisting he categorize himself as something he clearly does not wish to be labelled as.

Even if she is right, she is being ungrateful.

"Jay?" she calls.

He stops at the top of the stairs. "What?"

"I'm sorry, okay? I don't know why I'm trying to...convince you about the whole magician thing. It's...it's stupid."

Jay hesitates. His voice is still hard. "Sure."

Right. That had to have seemed anything but genuine. "I was looking at the pictures and is, um," Blythe hesitates, pointing. "Is that your brother?"

Jay glances up at the photos. "Yeah," he says. "That's Theo. Too smart for his own damn good. He's always building stuff, messing with Dad's prototypes." He smiles. "We had to send him off to a boarding school for little geniuses like him. Couldn't keep up with him. Especially not me."

"You're smart."

"Nah, I know what my strengths are and *thinking* has never been one of them. Nobody's smart like Theo anyway."

Blythe's not sure of what to say, but Jay doesn't speak either. Blythe can't stand the silence.

"Your house is beautiful, by the way," she adds, just to break it. "You didn't even have to let us stay here but I'm grateful you did."

"Of course I did," Jay says. "I hate seeing a pretty girl cry."

Blythe must be wearing her shock, because he smirks. "What? You don't think you're pretty?"

This conversation has taken a turn. Blythe knows she's pretty—she's got a cute body too—but she didn't expect it to factor into her "my entire family got kidnapped and I have to rescue them" experience. "No, I just...I've had to prepare for a *lot* of unexpected things these past few days, but nothing quite like that."

Jay laughs, a sound like chiming bells. "You'll get used to it the longer you're around me," he says. "How about this: let's just chill. We can head upstairs, talk about stuff that isn't freaky-magic-bullshit, actually get to know each other. Don't be nervous, I don't bite." His bedroom eyes are *sinfully* tempting. "Unless you want me to."

Part of Blythe wants to let him guide her by the hand up that movie star staircase, to a room that is probably going to take her breath away.

But that part of her remains small and stupid.

"I should really help Cordelia," Blythe says. "She's working on saving my family, and I can't just leave her to handle all that alone."

"I get it," Jay nods. "But that just means you'll have to come back and visit me again sometime."

Blythe bites back a smile as she starts off. "After we kick the Trident Republic's ass I'll...let you know."

"I'm looking forward to it," Jay starts up the stairs and then turns back around. "Goodnight, Blythe."

Blythe, however, does not stop. "Goodnight, Jay."

———

Cordelia is exactly where Blythe left her, and Blythe catapults onto the sofa beside her. "Jay either asked me out or is trying to hook up. Or maybe both."

Cordelia doesn't look up from the laptop screen. "Did he mention his bedroom at all?"

"Sort of?"

"Hook up. To be fair, he did warn us that he was a fuckboy. But I called dibs first."

Blythe snorts. "You can have him."

"Have him, visit this gaudy house, marry into a famous family and raise beautiful, biracial children who are both beautiful *and* intelligent? Thank you, Blythe, I don't mind if I do."

Blythe laughs. When she's like this, Cordelia's actually enjoyable company.

"Back to business," Cordelia says. "This whole 'no magic' thing is annoying, but Electric City *is* a magician city, isn't it?"

"Yeah."

"So, once we're inside, we'll be fine. It's just a matter of getting there. Now, we already know where Electric City is, but we'll want to make sure we have a plan for actually navigating *inside*. You know, what buildings we'd like to check out, any locations that have had suspicious activity as of lately."

"I trust you," Blythe says. "You'll figure something out. But we also don't know what the Trident Republic has waiting for us, I mean, it could literally be anything. Maybe we should have some sort of escape plan or..." Blythe's head is devoid of ideas. Of thoughts. It's like her mind has tired of making them.

Cordelia glances up at her. "Get some sleep," she says. When Blythe only stares at her, she elaborates. "You've been driving going nonstop for days, always fighting, always leading us, always *thinking*, and I..." Cordelia takes in a breath, as if she can't find the words. Then she starts anew.

"I was the first Guardian that Katia found," she says. "I didn't have the...best attitude. I didn't know about magic and, prior to the roof incident, I had my whole life planned out. I knew who I was. Cordelia Deleon, the girl who got the highest marks and made friends with the popular kids in the elite cliques. The girl who had the best clothes, the perfect makeup, and invitations to every important party. But most of all, I was the girl who always knew what to expect."

She pauses. "But when this happened, I no longer knew anything. Not...how I fit into the world, or who I was. I was a Guardian, but one of seven. I was the Guardian of the Mind, which is noteworthy, but not the most powerful Element." She purses her lips. "When Katia found me, she told me not to be rude to you. Because you were the Guardian of Ether, which made you important. And it made *you* the girl I wanted to be.

"I was so jealous. And angry. I hated you before we even met. And when I saw you were pretty, smart, determined and capable...I was livid. Because I've had to use my intelligence for everything I've ever wanted. But for you? Things just...fell into your lap. When you went after something, the stars aligned perfectly, and everything fell into place. You were brave. Fearless. And the universe loved you for it.

"I pretended hacking the Trident Republic was *my* thing, because I wanted to embark on a journey too. I spent most of my time amassing critical information on the Trident Republic, but sometimes I'd sit beside you in the car and stare at a blank screen on my phone. Pretending to have a mission as meaningful as yours."

She looks Blythe in the eye. "But I don't have one. My mission was selfish. Yours is selfless. You're sacrificing everything to save your family, and at first I thought it was ridiculous but now I...I want to help you."

Blythe can only stare at her. Because the girl she is speaking to now is completely different from the girl Katia introduced her to. And this Cordelia—this warm, empathetic, passionate person—is a thousand times better.

Cordelia places a hand on top of hers. "Go to sleep. I'll handle everything with the same amount of fierce vigor that you conjure every single day." Cordelia smiles. "I'll help save your family."

Tears blur warm in Blythe's eyes. She holds tight to Cordelia's hand. "Thanks, Cords."

Cordelia holds up a perfectly manicured finger. "But if anyone asks," she adds. "We never had this conversation."

———

Blythe's not sure where the bedrooms are. When she goes upstairs, there is only echoing silence, like Jay has been swallowed into a void. In fact, the more Blythe walks through long hallways overseeing the pool, past a romantic balcony, the more the silence grates on her.

She can't even hear the wildlife outside. The silence permeates everything, as if the other Guardians aren't even here.

Hoffman Manor no longer feels like a home. It feels like a cold, unwelcoming museum where no one is meant to reside...but Jay does.

Does he live with this?

The thought of being constantly, painfully alone makes her think of Caspian. Is he back at the graveyard now, sulking in the thick fog and the emptiness?

Blythe doesn't hate him for what he's done. She wonders if he knows that.

Finally, she stumbles upon a bedroom with an untouched, made bed and a dresser devoid of personal items. It must be a guest bedroom, because it feels like a hotel room.

She drops her things inside, shutting the door behind her. This is the first night she's been able to twist and style her hair before bed, and also the first night she's actually had a good night's rest.

When she wakes, still inside this cloud-like bed, it takes her a moment to remember that she and the other Guardians just happened to find Joshua *fucking* Hoffman collapsed on the side of the road—and are now in his house.

Wild.

She jumps out of bed, pulls out her twist-out (and is *very* happy with how her curls fall once she teases them a bit), gets dressed, and is repacking her backpack when a familiar tingle settles in her chest.

Blythe straightens as soon as she feels it, focusing her attention on the corner of the room.

"Hey Caspian," she says.

Ghosts aren't supposed to appear during the day and Caspian looks odd with morning light filtering through him.

Still, Blythe is happy he is here, slouching against a wall and staring at Blythe from the corner of his dark eyes.

"Why are you still bothering me?" he asks.

"Uh," Blythe scoffs. "Dude, *you* came in here." *Dude.* God, Antonio's rubbing off on her.

Caspian's face pinches. "I only came because you were...thinking about me. Or worried about me. Or something."

"The Guardian of Death isn't supposed to read minds," Blythe retorts.

"I don't," Caspian says without missing a beat. "You know where I am, I know how you feel."

Oh. Blythe almost drops her hair conditioner. Her bond with him stretches both ways? Caspian's been reading her emotions this entire time? Without saying anything? But honestly, Cordelia is a mind reader, so it's not like Blythe's not used to people picking around in her brain.

Instead, she asks, "What's that like?"

"What's being a living Caspian-tracker like?" he counters.

Blythe chuckles. She's missed Caspian's humor. Even though he doesn't laugh and watches her in silence, Blythe really, truly hopes she can convince him to stay.

"Not that bad actually," she answers. "But if you can feel what I feel, then you know I'm not upset."

"I do. And I don't understand it." He is unmoving and his gaze is unwavering. He really, truly means that.

Blythe sighs. "They...promised to tell you something about your family, didn't they?" Caspian nods, but only barely. "And your family's not...around anymore, are they?"

He hesitates. This is possibly more than he wants to tell her. "Yes."

"Did they tell you they would give you some information if you helped?"

"I didn't even know what they were talking about," he admits. "They said if I turned in the group of kids that came for me and gave them the shard, they would tell me..." he stops. "I didn't have a choice. I tried to get you to leave. Then I heard about your family and I just thought...I thought I could help. But obviously I made a mistake, and I'm sorry, and I think I should be on my way now."

Blythe doesn't even let him take a breath after the end of his sentence. "No," she says.

His face finally shifts, eyes narrowing into a glare. "Why can't you just hate me and let me leave so this can be over?"

"Because I think you're a good person who made a mistake," Blythe says. "And I've made plenty of mistakes myself. Plus, what're you gonna do? Go back to Lavender Heights? Where you'll sit in a graveyard and be lonely?"

"I'm sorry if I don't feel like I *deserve* to be here anymore," Caspian spits.

Blythe can't change his emotions. No amount of talk can erase his own guilt. But she could try to help, at the very least. "You can't change what you did. But you can change what you *will* do. Going forward."

Caspian stares at her as if the words have stumped him.

"Sometimes I read my mom's self-help books," Blythe explains.

"Sounds like it."

There he goes again. Blythe can't even hold back her smile. "If you actually want to go back to Canada, I won't force you," she says. "But I'd miss you if you left."

Caspian fidgets with the chain on his wrist. He doesn't speak or react, probably because he is allergic to emotion and would *never* express anything he couldn't help. But he doesn't disappear either. It is as close to a "yes" as Blythe will get.

"Everyone's downstairs in the kitchen," he says instead.

Blythe doesn't push her luck. If he wants to keep this casual, she has to let him. "Sounds like we're gonna have breakfast."

"I don't think I can go down there," Caspian says as worry creases his forehead.

So, Blythe holds out her hand. "Then we'll go together."

Caspian stares down at her, his black eyes vacant. Blythe expects him to reach out and intertwine his fingers with hers, so they can walk through this labyrinthine of a house together—

"I appreciate the kindness of this gesture, but hands tend to get sweaty," he says.

Blythe drops her hand. "Alright, that's fair."

Static crinkles, like an intercom system clicking on. Jay's voice bursts into the room. "Hey, if your names are Blythe, Antonio, Cordelia, Storm, Daniel, and-slash-or Caspian, could you kindly tell me where you are because I do not feel like walking around to find you."

"What the fuck?" Blythe shouts.

"That is *not* a valid indicator of your location, try again," Jay replies.

"How are you talking?"

"This is an intercom system, but you're really not helping me here."

Cordelia's voice appears. "We're in the kitchen!"

"Thanks, Cords," Jay says, and it shuts off.

Caspian glares up at the ceiling. "He's moody," he says. "That's annoying."

Blythe sighs. If she had the time and energy to get into it, she would. But she needs to save this positive energy for Electric City. Lord knows she's going to need it. "You just don't like him," she says plainly.

Caspian simply stares straight ahead, as if ignoring her statement will make it less true.

They find the kitchen alight with both sunlight and noise. A tray of food sits on the marble island countertop, courtesy of Antonio: fluffy pancakes, golden French toast, an array of sausages and bacon, bowls of fruit.

The Guardians are seated around it, Antonio talking a mile a minute, Storm falling asleep with her chin in her hand, Cordelia cross legged, and Daniel studying them all avidly.

"Morning!" Blythe shouts.

Storm's eyes pop open. "Damn, girl!" she says. "Look at all that hair!"

Blythe flips her curls, voguing. "Finally got to do a good twist-out last night."

319

Caspian's form fades into the room, gradually, slowly. All of the Guardians' eyes lock on him. Silence falls.

Caspian instantly disappears.

"*Get back here,*" Blythe whispers, and Caspian melts back into view.

"Guys," Blythe announces. "Caspian and I talked this morning and we decided he's going to be staying with us."

"Judas is what!?" Storm screams.

Daniel's eyes pop open, dancing excitedly. "That's from the Bible! That's the first reference anyone's made that I've understood!"

Suddenly everyone's congratulating him as if they've completely forgotten the point of the conversation—which, knowing the Guardians, they totally have.

Blythe has to steer them back. "Daniel, that's amazing and I'm so proud of your Biblical knowledge, but we gotta talk about what happened last night."

Everyone falls quiet, giving Caspian their attention—most of which is skeptical and reluctant. "Um," he begins. "I'm sorry. I made a mistake—"

"A damn big one," Storm interrupts.

"Let him speak!" Blythe snaps.

Caspian waits for them to settle, then starts again. "I made a mistake. I didn't want to do it, but I take full responsibility for... turning you guys in. And indirectly being the reason you ended up here. It's my fault things got ruined, and I'd like to help make them right again. And I swear on my life, it won't happen again."

"But you're already dead," Antonio points out.

"I—well," Caspian hesitates. "You got me there."

"Seriously?" Blythe interrupts. "Look, if you guys can forgive me for being an asshole for my family, you can forgive him for being an asshole for *his* family."

"Oh, is that what this is about?" Antonio asks. "Sorry, all the words got me confused. I'm cool with you, Casp! That guy seemed mean, I'd be scared of him too."

Cordelia squints at Antonio with annoyance and confusion. "Do you even know where you are right now? Do you know where *we* are?"

"Yeah, we're at Jay's house. We're all here eating breakfast and Jay's taking a shower."

Storm throws up her hands. "Pause. How do you know *exactly* where he is?"

"I spent the night in his room!"

Blythe could interrupt them, but she's more interested in watching this play out. Storm cocks her chin in her hand while Cordelia glares at Antonio, and Daniel just tries, desperately, to keep up with the conversation.

"And what did *y'all* get up to?" Storm asks.

Antonio takes a swig of orange juice. The poor boy is completely oblivious. "Oh, we didn't sleep until like three AM. I don't even think I've even *seen* three AM on a clock before."

Cordelia clenches her jaw. Storm nearly falls out of her chair. "*Antonio!* I didn't know you got down like—"

"I mean once you start watching Vine compilations you can't stop, y'know?" Antonio continues.

Storm deflates. Cordelia moans in relief, turning her face to the heavens. Daniel whispers, "You were watching foliage for hours...? How did you even find footage like that...?"

Blythe turns to Caspian, who watches the Guardians with a vacant sort of apathy.

"I'm pretty sure they're fine with you," Blythe says.

An echoing voice makes the whole room go still. "Let me tell you, there is nothing like being in your own damn house and changing into your own damn clothes."

The most beautiful boy in the world, a living portrait of human perfection, descends the staircase with a hypnotizing, effortless grace.

In clothes that actually fit, and with his eyes brighter than ever, Joshua Hoffman is a *vision*.

"Don't you guys look cute," Jay smiles. "Anyway, I feel like we should start over. I mean, I met you guys by, uh, threatening to kill Antonio. That sucks on multiple levels besides the obvious 'murder' part—one of which being that Antonio is God's gift to this earth."

"Bro!" Antonio yells. "You look *great*!"

"I can't brag but—" Jay does a dramatic spin that makes his hair whip. "—I know a little about cleaning up. Anyway, I was saying something, but I forgot what it was. Are those blueberry pancakes?"

He breezes over to the table and rips off a piece before anyone can even answer. "Oh—also, I booked your plane tickets, your flight's in a couple hours. Cords, does your plan accommodate for that?"

"I-It's not time based," Cordelia stammers.

"God, if I hadn't gotten banned from the jet, we could have used that," Jay says. "Aw man these are just normal pancakes. Disappointing. I love fruit."

"You got banned from your *jet*?" Antonio asks.

"Oh, it's a great story. Starts on the upper east side of New York City. Anyway, I'm ready to go whenever you are."

Jay's eyes land on Blythe—but she is, momentarily, too stunned to reply. This boy has donned three separate personalities within the one day they have known him, and this one is almost too rapid to keep up with.

"We're...ready now?" Blythe looks to Cordelia, who nods pointedly. "Yes, okay. We're ready now."

"Then all we need is a car," Jay flashes his red-carpet smile. "I'll pick something with some *speed*."

TWENTY-TWO

Hoffman Manor has no shortage of modern wonders. It shines as marvelously in the day as it gleams in the night. Off to the back, preceded by a long gravel driveway, is a two-story garage with a door that dwarfs Jay as he approaches it.

Jay places his hand on the scanner attached to the wall. But the screen turns red.

"*Access restricted,*" it chirps. "*Please contact administrator.*"

"Dude," Antonio says. "I think you got banned from more than your jet."

Jay's back is to them, but judging from the way he snatches out his phone, he is not pleased.

"Do you want to tell me why I can't get into the garage?" he snaps once the ringing stops.

A pause. "*Yes,* I'm home."

Another pause. "That's not my goddamn problem. I'm busy."

The Guardians shuffle awkwardly, hands in their pockets or arms folded as they stare at the horizon, at the house, at anything other than Jay.

Blythe can't relate. She watches Jay like a hawk, listening to the other line. His silence stretches for so long, Blythe almost forgets he was talking.

"I'm not 'being like' anything," he says, but his voice has lost its edge. "I didn't know *what* happened that night. I still don't. I just sort of passed out and...I don't know..."

His every emotion looks as if a painter has drawn the curves of his face with the finest brush. Even his frustration is a form of art. "Just get me into the garage," he whispers. "I don't—I don't want to talk about this anymore."

He hangs up. But his energy has already extinguished, leaving behind a quiet boy who clenches his jaw.

"I'm sorry you had to hear that," Jay apologizes.

"Was that your dad?" Antonio asks.

Jay kicks at the tile with the toe of his red bottoms. "Nah," he says. "Just a...friend."

"I knew it," Storm says. "The Hoffmans look like they whoop ass."

But Blythe squints. "Your friends have more access to your own house than you do?"

"It's complicated," Jay places his hand on the scanner. This time, it lights up green.

"Fucking finally," he mutters as the garage door glides into the ceiling.

Displayed in front of them is a whole showroom's worth of sleek cars, lines upon lines or Porches, Teslas, Bugattis, and models Blythe can't even identify.

"Jesus *Christ*," Cordelia gasps.

Jay regards them with the same amount of dull disinterest he's given to the rest of his house. "My dad collects them."

"HOLY SHIT!" Storm screams. She bolts into the garage so quickly her skates scream against the ground, dark eyes wide as she drinks up every spoked rim and touch-activated dashboard she can find.

The rest of the Guardians trail after her, buoyed by her excitement, and Blythe watches them with a smile.

It's nice to see them so happy over something as small as a bunch of nice cars.

Jay lingers beside her, but only physically. His gaze is empty, mind a hundred miles from here.

"...Would you guys care if I joined you?" he asks.

"Joined us how?" Blythe asks. "To Electric City?"

She doesn't want to reject him—at least, not *all* of her wants to reject him. But this sudden change of heart is...suspicious.

Her words do little to bring Jay out of his trance. "Yeah."

"Of course you can!" Cordelia yells.

"Dude, heck *yeah*," Antonio says. "You could be our sponsor or something!"

Jay musters up a smile. If Blythe hadn't seen him laughing earlier, she wouldn't be able to tell it was fake.

She lowers her voice as Daniel, Storm, Antonio and Cordelia talk amongst themselves, moving toward a Tahoe in the back of the garage.

"You can come," she says to him. "But only if you tell me what changed your mind."

Jay's jawline draws straighter as he clenches his teeth. "Can I talk to you on the plane?" he asks.

"The whole reason why we got into that accident with the Erasers was because one of our friends fucked us over," Blythe says. "I'd like to keep that from happening again."

Jay's silver eyes spear into her. "I'm not going to get you into trouble. I know fuck all about magic," he pauses. "That's the whole problem."

Ah. So, it's a self-discovery mission. Blythe chews her lip as she watches Cordelia roll her eyes at something Daniel says, Antonio leaning an arm on Storm's shoulder as she points out something on the truck's tires.

Jay could end up being a liability—*especially* in Electric City. But the others will never leave him behind. They're already too attached to him...and, as much as Blythe hates to admit it, so is she.

"Fine," she says. "We'll talk on the plane."

They pile into the Tahoe that Storm has picked out—but Jay takes the driver's seat.

"I always drive," he says when Blythe outstretches her hand for the keys. "And didn't Cords yell at you about chilling out or something?"

Blythe always drives, that's how this works. But honestly? It'd be nice to sit and scroll through her phone while someone else does the work.

So she gets in the passenger seat, chin in her hand as she watches Hoffman Manor sink in the rearview mirror.

Antonio pokes his head in from the back seat. "Shouldn't you be wearing shades?" He asks. Blythe almost answers, but he's talking to Jay. "Or some other celebrity disguise? You gotta stay safe, dude. I don't want you getting ambushed or something."

"Nah, I'm good," Jay answers. "Nobody even knows what I look like."

"Is that why you don't take photos?" Cordelia asks. "That's genius."

"No, I...just don't like them," Jay says, and then, with the experience of someone who is used to diverting attention, easily changes the subject.

The Guardians fall for it, hook line and sinker. But Blythe doesn't. As he got in the truck, Jay angled all of the mirrors in an...odd way for a driver. He'd moved them all away from himself, so not a single one could reflect his face.

And from the moment they enter the airport, the shift in the air is palpable. The Guardians have always garnered looks from people; they're a group of mostly non-white teenagers, often found in places they shouldn't be. People tend to pay attention. But they've never paid attention like they do now.

Tourists lugging huge suitcases freeze, eyes zeroed straight on them like sniper crosshairs. Entire families stare at their every move until they drift out of sight. Or, no, not all of them. Specifically, Jay.

Conversations abruptly halt as he passes, as if his very presence is too overwhelming to be ignored. Eyes stalk him wherever he goes; endless, unblinking, dumbstruck staring.

Jay is not oblivious. His expression is too blank to be anything but forced.

Blythe casually drifts to his side. "Does this...always happen?"

Jay does not even blink. "Yeah."

———

Jay failed to mention that he brought first class tickets—apparently, to him, it wasn't worth mentioning. Antonio is overexcited and Cordelia is relieved, but Jay simply slouches into his window seat, chin in his hand.

Blythe takes the seat beside him. Behind them, Storm's earbuds blast music while Cordelia and Antonio softly argue over whether or not first class has a better movie selection.

"So," Blythe begins. "...Can we talk about what happened back at your house, or...?"

Jay stares out of the window as if the clouds could steal his attention away at any second. "Yeah. But if you don't want to listen, I get it. It's a long story. I just...I think it might have something to do with everything. And I just...it might..." He stops himself, shutting his eyes. "Sorry, sorry. I'll just...I'll start at the beginning."

"Take your time," Blythe says. "We've got a whole flight ahead of us."

Jay lets out a long, slow breath. "It's about the night you guys found me."

Blythe sits up straighter at those words. She'd always wondered what, exactly, happened to him.

"I was at a house party in Florida. And I was drinking. A lot, as in, probably-went-overboard 'a lot'. And I was being a dick, I guess, so one of my friends called...okay, remember the person I called before we went into the garage? He called a group of them to take me home. They're kind of...my friends, I guess, but also kind of in charge of me—"

"Babysitters," Blythe interrupts, blunt.

"Kind of," Jay agrees. "Anyway, I was pissed about the whole thing, but the guys came and dragged me out. We were on the way back home and we took this shortcut through the woods—" His eyes fly open. "Mother of fuck."

Blythe leans toward him. "What's wrong?"

"It's the Tempore. The shortcut through the woods we always took. It's been the Tempore this whole time. I've been using the Tempore for three years and I didn't even know."

Jay sinks in his seat, staring at the seat in front of him as if all of his truths are written there.

"You've used the Tempore?" Blythe asks, reclaiming his attention.

"Yes. No, I-I'm sorry," he stammers, running a hand through his hair. "They'd always take me through this shortcut in the woods whenever I got...trashed."

Blythe's nose wrinkles before she can stop herself. "You get drunk *that* often?"

"Not *that* often," Jay says. He gets banned from his family jet and dragged home from parties for being too drunk.

It's probably pretty often.

"Anyway," Jay powers through. "We got into the Tempore, and this is where things get blurry. I remember my friends talking like something was wrong, but I wasn't really paying attention. Then we heard explosions. To clarify, my friends...they get into some shit. They're basically in a gang. Stop making that face, let me talk. So, at the time, I assumed the noise was gunshots. I don't really remember anything else until I got knocked to the ground. People were yelling for me, but as I got up, I remember seeing, through the trees and shit, there were these...these weird lights? And...okay, you've seen Star Wars, right?"

Blythe nods. "I love Star Wars."

"Same," Jay agrees. "Imma be real with you, I *was* crossfaded. So, I might be remembering this wrong, but I swear there were orange lights, and this man...he was in this long like...coat? A black coat? And he was holding two lightsabers."

"I think that was definitely whatever laced weed you smoked," Blythe says.

Jay thinks about it for a moment. "Probably. Anyway, so, I'm looking at this Emperor Palpatine hallucination, and it looks like it's coming closer, lightsabers drawn. And I'm thinking, shit, I don't know how to use a lightsaber. I don't even have one."

"*Jay.*"

"Listen, I'm tryna tell you! So my friend screams at me to run, right? So I do, and I'm not running into Palpatine, but I can't go backward, because my friends are doing God knows what back there. But as I'm running something...grabs me. Purposefully. Not like how somebody grabs you when they're just trying to fuck up anybody and everybody. Like this person—or this thing—specifically wanted *me*. And it was...it was dragging me? And I remember seeing fire, but not feeling it, and then I was falling. I don't know how I fell. But everything got dark, like the whole world shut its lights off. And then I woke up in the hotel with you guys."

Blythe can feel Jay watching for her reaction. She makes sure her words are phrased perfectly. "Something was taking you? Are you serious about this or are you—"

"No, no, that part was real," he says. "My friend, when I called him back at the house, he was...worried. He thought something had happened to me. And it makes me wonder—about, you know, everything. Because why would these random magicians be interested in *me* if I wasn't...if I didn't play some part in this?" Blythe is quiet, letting him fill in the silence. "I remembered what you said about the Trident Republic, and the war, and what they did to you, and I think..."

Blythe waits for the words, the admittance that he *is* a Guardian.

"I think I might be a goddamn magician," he says.

Alright. Baby steps.

Blythe draws herself up straighter. She would take his hand to reassure him, but Jay is still Jay, and she is *not* convinced that he will understand the gesture platonically. So instead, she simply speaks.

"You already know I think so too. We all do. I mean, it sucks that you just got your magic taken away by the Erasers because of *me* but...at least you know. And there's nothing wrong with being a magician. Plenty of people are."

"I know that. I just didn't want another reason to not be..." his voice trails off. He stares out at the sea of sky beneath the plane's wings.

"Not to be what?" Blythe asks.

Jay hesitates, as if the word has lodged in his throat. "Normal."

Blythe can't say she understands, because she doesn't. She was always the new kid, the unknown girl who had to make herself into someone interesting enough for people to enjoy her company.

She is an artist who believes that making an impact, standing out from the crowd, can sometimes be the only thing separating a good creator from a legendary one. "Unique" is something she chose to become.

But here is a person who captivates the attention of anyone who sees him. He is a boy who effortlessly shines like the brightest star in the night sky. And all he wishes to do is fade.

"I'm sorry," Blythe apologizes. "About everything. I...I know this is all a lot to take in. Especially after what happened to you that night."

"At this point, that was just another Friday night," Jay says. When he catches the surprise on her face, he smiles. Except the happiness doesn't reach his eyes.

"When chaos is constant," he says. "It starts feeling like comfort."

Jay flashes his black card and rents a truck large enough to comfortably fit all of them.

Blythe has replaced Cordelia in the passenger seat, since Jay has replaced her in the driver's, but Cordelia is still their navigator, using the map to Electric City she has constructed on her Zadis.

Jay follows her instructions as best as he can, until they're driving through the desert with nothing but flat land for miles.

They'll be in Electric City soon. Blythe bounces her leg against her seat, over and over. Keeping still is a thing of the past.

Jay has retreated into himself, the exact opposite of the extroverted flirt he was this morning. But all it takes is a couple words from Antonio to get him crack a real smile.

Storm makes them crank the AC up to the highest point.

"I'm cold," Antonio complains.

Storm pops her gum. "And *I* don't give a shit."

"My jacket's in the back," Jay says. "You can grab that."

Antonio throws it on; it's big on him, and the sleeves swallow his arms. "Aha! Look! You can't see my hands!"

Caspian appears in the backseat beside Storm, balancing a bowl of Ramen on his lap.

Storm stares at him. He looks right back at her.

"I can share," he offers.

She makes him travel back to God-knows-where to bring back a second fork, but he does, and they quietly share the bowl while Daniel fights with Cordelia over the radio.

Their gas needle drops lower as day submits to night. It's all fine until the truck sputters to a stop.

This wouldn't be a problem, except for the fact that they have no backup containers in the trunk and there isn't another gas station for miles.

"Wayment," Storm says. "There are seven of us in this truck.

Seven. Did not a single one of us think there could be a possibility we'd need more gas?"

Shame spreads its tendrils through the silence of the car.

"Damn," Storm sucks her teeth, staring out at the desert. "We deserve to die here."

Blythe tries to think of a plan. Walking probably isn't the best idea, but she can't think of—

"I'll call my friends," Jay offers. "They could probably take us the rest of the way."

"They'd come out to the *Nevada desert*?" Blythe asks.

"For me?" Jay asks. "Most certainly."

Antonio raspberries. "My friends leave me on read."

"*I'd* never leave you on read, bro," Jay says.

Antonio grasps his heart. "*Bro.*"

Jay winks at him, snatching up his phone and hopping out of the car.

The moment the door closes behind him, Storm blurts, "He fucking his friend."

Daniel looks traumatized just from hearing that.

"*Storm!*" Blythe shrieks.

"Please don't say that," Cordelia whines. "I was already envisioning what colors our wedding reception would be."

"Girl, you barely even talked to him!" Storm shrieks.

"I'm biding my time!"

When Jay opens the door again, he tells them that his friends agreed, but it'll take them about an hour to reach their location, even *with* using the Tempore.

Which means the Guardians have to stay occupied in the middle of the desert for sixty minutes without killing each other.

"We could play twenty questions," Antonio offers—and is instantaneously shot down.

After a few moment of chit-chat and idle social media scrolling, Daniel opens his car door. "I'm going to take a walk," he announces.

"Anyone is welcome to join me." He doesn't wait for anyone to follow. He simply starts off, hands in his pockets.

Everyone stares after him in silence. "Is Daniel...doing something by himself?" Cordelia asks.

Blythe sighs wistfully. "They grow up so fast."

Storm ends up following him, telling Caspian to join them. Caspian hesitates at first, but Storm does not take no for an answer —"I wasn't asking," she says—and off they go.

Blythe makes a mental note to ask one of them what they talked about when they get back. Nosy habits die hard.

"Hey," Jay says, tapping her on the shoulder. "Let's go up to the roof."

A wry smile comes to her face. "Why?"

"Antonio told me you like the stars, how 'bout you show me some constellations?"

Blythe's smile grows as a clever idea pops into her head. "Sounds great, yeah, can't wait—*HEY ANTONIO!*"

Antonio's blonde hair flops as he snaps his head up from his phone.

"Come look at the stars with us!" Blythe beckons.

He lights up like a Christmas tree. "Oh heck yeah bro, I love a good bonding session! Cordelia, you come too!"

Blythe smiles sweetly at Jay. "You don't mind, do you?"

"Of course not," Jay counters, not missing a beat. "I get to hang out with three of my favorite people."

He reaches up to the roof and hoists himself up with annoyingly effortless agility.

Antonio hurries after him, leaving Blythe to realize her mistake and sit, quietly, under the heat of Cordelia's glare.

"Wait," Blythe says. "Let me explain."

"I'm a mind reader but go on."

"See, what had happened was, I thought...I thought I was being clever. Because I was like ooh, he's trying to flirt with me, let me just get Antonio to like, shut that shit down."

"Uh huh."

"But I forgot he was unstoppably bisexual."

"A powerful thing to be."

"And *he* thinks he's ending up with one of us."

"Mmm."

"So, really, *I'm* the idiot here because I just gave him exactly what he wanted."

"Of course."

On top of the truck, beneath the stars, Jay lays on his side, close to where Antonio sits criss-cross-apple-sauce. Cordelia crosses her legs at the ankle, while Blythe kneels to better point out the stars.

Blythe's always found the night sky comforting. Even with the blinking lights of passing airplanes and clouds that block their vision, the stars still shine brighter without the competition of city lights or smog. Those pockets of light in the darkness warm Blythe's heart. The night sky just feels like home.

"Alright," she begins. "So, that one right there is Libra—"

Antonio bounces up. "That's my Zodiac sign!"

"Oh, that explains a lot," Blythe says.

Cordelia leans forward, hair swinging over her shoulders. "Where's Gemini?"

"Ohhhhh, so does that," Blythe murmurs. "It's probably not visible right now. There's—"

"I love Libras," Jay interrupts.

"Jay, no, fuck off," Blythe picks up a piece of rock from the bed of the roof and tosses it at him. She is *not* letting him corrupt Antonio.

"Don't get jealous," Jay smirks, swatting the pebble away. "I'm sure I love your sign too."

"Plot twist, there *will* be a quiz on these once I'm done explaining them," Blythe teases. "So keep talking if you want."

Jay feigns apology, sinking backward. But he can't hide his smile. "Sorry. I'll be quiet."

Blythe points out every constellation she can name. Cordelia is curious about where their names come from, and soon Blythe is dazzling them with her knowledge of constellation lore.

Their celestial discussion lasts so long, they are still deep in conversation when Caspian, Daniel and Storm return.

Storm skates up, throwing her arms into the air. "Y'all really waited until we left to have a party?!"

"Sorry," Jay says. "This is for cool kids only."

"I exist outside of both time and space," Caspian says. "The only thing stopping me from disappearing from where I now stand and reappearing on that roof is my own will."

Blythe dramatically raises her chin, putting on her bitchiest voice. "That and your *obvious* lack of Cool Kid Energy."

Caspian stares at her, stoic and unblinking. "That one hurt."

Daniel picks with the hem of his sweater, eyes pleading. "Is this cyberbullying?"

They quickly explain that no, this is not cyberbullying, it's just regular bullying, but they're just teasing because of course the three of them are welcome to join.

Caspian appears at Blythe's side instantly, but getting Daniel onto the roof is an elaborate task. The poor boy can *not* climb, and they try to teach him how to set his hands and pull up to the roof, but he keeps slipping until Jay takes him by the hands and pulls him all the way up.

With everyone comfortably settled, Blythe continues through her lesson of the night sky, stopping at every single star she recognizes. After what feels like forever, she finally runs out.

"I think that's it..." Blythe's voice trails off as something catches her eye. Right in front of her. "Wait, no..."

"What?" Cordelia asks.

"It's...that's Calyvorra's Crown," Blythe says. "It's my favorite constellation."

The last time Blythe saw Calyvorra's Crown, she was stargazing with her family on a picnic blanket with a container of green grapes in her hand.

This is the first time a memory of her family does not burn like liquid fire in her chest. She misses them, of course, and it hurts. But she is almost...comfortable where she is now, here with the Guardians, stranded in the middle of the desert.

"That's cute, dude," Antonio smiles. "Why's it your favorite?"

"It's made up of seven stars, but...if one of the seven isn't shining, or if it's not bright enough for you to see, you'll miss the whole constellation. And I..."

Blythe's voice trails off. Why *does* she like it?

"I always loved that unity, I guess," she says. "That it's a circle, without a clear beginning or end or hierarchy. Even though they're in different positions in the sky, they are equal. And you can only see their true beauty when they are all gathered together."

She expects someone to make a joke, or for Storm to burst into laughter over the corniness of it all. But she doesn't. No one says a word.

They sit, together, all seven of them, all Guardians, staring at this constellation, existing together in harmony and silence.

It is getting late. Storm is the first to fall asleep, which makes sense. But the surprise of the century comes when Daniel Quinton himself, the boy who has been too afraid to shut his eyes for even a moment, falls asleep beside her.

One by one, each of them drift off, Cordelia beside Blythe, Jay and Antonio off to the back, still gathered on top of their truck in the middle of the desert.

The only ones awake are Blythe and Caspian, sitting shoulder to shoulder in the soft summer breeze.

Blythe smiles at him. "How was your adventure with Storm and Daniel?"

Caspian is quiet a moment. "Daniel kept to himself. He's still afraid of me but he's coming around. And I talked with Storm. She was mad but I think we're alright now."

"I think she was just hurt."

"I don't blame her."

"What about you, though? Are you happy you stayed?"

He doesn't answer. *"Yes"* is the word he doesn't want to speak.

"Can I tell you a secret?" he asks instead.

Blythe shimmies excitedly. "I *love* secrets."

She expects Caspian to show her something, perhaps. Or speak some truth she never would have guessed about him.

Instead, before Blythe's eyes, Caspian begins to solidify. His grey pallor becomes pale, living, skin. His black t-shirt becomes cotton instead of air, his messy black hair stills against his forehead.

And his eyes...they shift from ghostly black holes to dark, beautiful irises. The scar in his eyebrow becomes even more visible, a cut right through the tail that could almost be purposeful.

"I'm not dead," he says. "I just like being a ghost."

Blythe is absolutely speechless.

"What the *fuck*?!" she finally yells. "What the *FUCK*?! You're ALIVE?! And you're cute! What the fuck! Why didn't you ever tell us?!"

Caspian's face burns pink at the compliment, and he looks away, hiding a bit. "I never told you I was dead, either. My *parents* are dead. I'm still here. I just figured letting you guys assume would be funnier. And it was."

"You are so *annoying*!" Blythe shouts through her laughter.

The sound of her voice must be contagious, because Caspian chews his lip as he stares at the horizon, as if he could hold back the smile that is curling on his face.

It is the first time Blythe has ever, *ever* seen him smile. Happiness is an emotion she hopes he will wear more often.

"Don't tell the others," he adds.

"I won't. But why? Is it personal?"

"I just want to shock the shit out of them."

"Of course you do."

When Caspian falls asleep, Blythe is alone again. Except, not entirely.

Blythe could have run into any number of criminals, of heartless people. The *Guardians* could have been anyone at all; they could have been selfish, or cruel, or dangerous.

Instead, fate has gifted her with them: Cordelia and Daniel and Antonio and Storm and Caspian and Jay. These beautiful, talented, loving people who are risking everything to travel with her into a war zone. They've sacrificed so much just for her.

Blythe's eyes burn with tears. She doesn't want to cry and risk waking one of them up. But Blythe owes them so much. They have given up everything for her, and she would give up anything for them. She owes them her life.

Something sparks on the horizon. Headlights, moving at full speed. Jay's friends have arrived.

Blythe bangs her fists on the metal roof.

"Wake up!" she announces. "Wake up, get up, they're here!"

Daniel shoots up, face flushed and curls tangled, squinting. "W-Who's here?"

"Better be Jake from State Farm because this truck sucks," Storm mutters, rubbing the sleep from her eyes.

A second pair of headlights crescent the horizon. And then another. And then another. Their engines sound more like a buzzing hive. Blythe then realizes that they are not pairs, but singular, individual, *motorcycle* headlights.

"Uh, Jay...?" Blythe asks. "How many people did you call...?"

Jay blinks awake, squinting through the light that illuminates every inch of his perfect face. He smiles brighter than Blythe has ever seen, leaps off of the truck, and lands perfectly on his feet.

"ROCCO!" he yells.

Storm bolts upright. "*Who?!*"

The blood drains from Blythe's face as the Angelus pulls into sight.

TWENTY-THREE

THE ANGELUS ARRIVES IN A CRESCENT CURVE, THEIR headlights erasing all shadows along the van. Rocco has barely jumped off his bike before Jay tackles him in a hug.

"What the fuck?" Storm whispers.

These men shot at Blythe in Washington, kidnapped Cordelia in Philadelphia, and terrorized Storm, these men with their leather jackets with sharp eyes and bodies hardened by fights, let out a chorus of Jay's name as if he is their prodigal son.

Rocco holds Jay at arm's length to scan him up and down. "*Christ,* Jaybird, where've you been?!" he snaps. "We spent days lookin' for you! I was about to lose my goddamn mind—"

Jay cups Rocco's face in his hands. "Before you lose your mind, just look at me," he says. "I'm fine. I told you I was fine."

Rocco places his hands on top of Jay's. "Yeah, on the *phone* after we thought you were fucking dead—"

"Roc," says one of the men, eying the other Guardians.

Rocco looks up. And his face hardens.

"Oh, sorry, I forgot to introduce you," Jay smiles, leaning his body into Rocco's and outstretching a hand to them. "Roc, this is Antonio,

Blythe, Cordelia, Storm, Daniel, and Caspian's...somewhere." He snaps his attention to Rocco. "Apparently, anyway? I haven't seen him. They might be fucking with me—"

But Rocco is still squinting at them. "Jaybird...how long've you been hanging with these kids?"

"Just the past few days."

Blythe can't take this anymore. "He broke my arm!"

"I thought you said they dislocated it..." Daniel mutters.

"Broke your arm—*they kidnapped me!*" Cordelia yells.

Storm is ready to lunge straight through Rocco. "They've done a lot more bullshit than that," she growls.

Jay's smile slowly fades. "What are you talking about...?"

Rocco shakes his head. "Okay, look. There was an altercation back in Philly. Nothin' too serious. It's in the past. Over. And we don't need to dig into other people's business, do we..." His gaze cuts into Storm. "Napoleon?"

Storm freezes. She told Blythe she donned that name to protect her true identity. And yet here her real name is, spilled out in the open.

Rocco lifts his chin, flexing his fingers. "Got on the same skates and everything. Storm, right? Can't be too many girls with names like that—"

"No," Jay interrupts. "No, no, no. We are not doing this, we aren't." He shoves Rocco away from him. "Somebody better tell me what the *fuck* is going on."

"What's going on is these assholes telling me what I need to know," Storm jumps off the truck. Magic no longer runs on her side, but that doesn't stop her from snatching out her switchblade.

Rocco is the only Angelus member who doesn't draw their gun.

"What the fuck?!" Jay screams. "Don't shoot her!"

The men hesitate. Their grips loosen. "Uh," One of them turns to Rocco. "D-Do we listen to him or—"

Rocco's nostrils flare. The only person he seems to care about, in this moment, is Jay. "You aren't allowed to shout orders at them."

Jay's fists have clenched. In his eyes is the same defiance he showed Blythe when she tried to coerce him into admitting he was a magician. This Jay is beyond reason.

"*You* work for *my* family," he growls. "I do whatever the fuck I want."

"Jaybird," Rocco's voice strains with barely concealed rage. "There's a whole situation going on that you can't understand—"

"And whose fault is that? Nobody has ever fucking told me *anything*. And I understand perfectly that she—" He jabs a finger toward Storm. "—is with me. Which means you can't touch her."

The Angelus must understand this, because the guns go down and away, even as they raise their brows and let out low, confused breaths. "They don't even have the shard anymore, so what's the point..." someone mutters.

Rocco's gaze skirts across all of them before narrowing on Jay again. "Come here," he orders, and again when Jay doesn't move.

Blythe fears they'll fight, but they simply back away a couple paces and speak in voices too low for Blythe to hear.

The Guardians and the Angelus are left alone. Staring at each other. Because this situation can't get any weirder.

"H-Hey, isn't that my switchblade?" Twin gestures toward the knife in Storm's fist.

Storm glares at him. "I can stab it into your arm if you want it back."

Twin pales. "You can keep it."

Blythe jumps down to guide Storm back a bit, but she yanks away.

"Just relax, okay?" Blythe whispers. "We don't have magic—"

"I on't need it."

"Storm, *please*. We can't risk it."

Storm presses her lips together. She looks over her shoulder, to Caspian, Antonio, Cordelia and Daniel, crowded together atop the truck. Her muscles, finally, go loose.

Blythe glances to Jay and Rocco. Jay is like a statue, arms folded and silently unconvinced as Rocco speaks avidly with his hands.

Who, exactly, *is* Jay in the world of magic? And why does the Angelus bend to his words? Jay said something about the Angelus working for his parents—but why would the Hoffmans hire a magician gang?

More importantly, why would they hire a magician gang who works for the Trident Republic?

Rocco stills, looking angrily defeated. Jay only returns to the group, shoulders set, while Rocco ambles behind him, hands stuffed in his pockets.

"Alright kids," Rocco announces. "We'll take you to Electric City. *Including* Napoleon."

Storm eyes Jay. "Ion't need you pulling favors."

"Well, we ain't telling you shit and we ain't fighting you either," Rocco snaps. "So get on or go the hell home."

"Storm," Blythe pleads. "We have to get to Electric City somehow. And this is our only option."

Storm stays battle poised and rigid. And then she tucks the switchblade into her pocket.

It's time to go.

The Angelus mounts their bikes. "Pick a seat and hold tight!" Rocco shouts over the revving engines. "These are not amusement park rides and we are *not* responsible if one of you falls off and cracks your neck!"

The Guardians scuttle from the rooftops and onto the Angelus' bikes, including Storm, who tosses herself behind one of the men like a toddler throwing a tantrum. Blythe chooses to ride with one of the twins—they seem the least dangerous.

Jay is the only one still standing, arms crossed tight in front of Rocco's bike, eyes spearing sharp into him.

"Alright, look, Jaybird," Rocco says to him, in a voice softer than Blythe ever thought he was capable of using. "We fucked up. I was shitty to your friends, but it's all good now. You can go to this city and do...whatever it is you said you wanted to do, alright? C'mon, let's go."

Jay's Adam's apple bobs as he swallows, considering this. Finally, with a roll of his eyes, he swings himself onto Rocco's bike.

They shoot like rockets through the desert. The only voice shouting above the growing crescendo of the bikes' growls is Cordelia's as she shouts directions.

Soon, Antonio starts chatting it up with his biker. That boy can make friends with *anybody*. Then again, so can Blythe.

She leans closer against the boy in front of her. "Hey, Twin!"

He scoffs. "You too, huh?!"

"Sorry, um, I don't know your name!"

He hesitates. "It's Jerry," he says. "Lil' Jerry!"

"Yikes! I can't call you that and still take you seriously—"

"Did you have something to say? Or did you just want to bully me?!"

"Oh, yeah, no, sorry! How do you guys know Jay?"

"We work for his ol' man!"

"How'd that happen?"

"I don't know the details, not my job! All I know is, Hoffman paid us to start watching out for his kid. Gettin' into too much trouble, I think! We were just supposed to keep an eye out for him on the streets and shit until Rocco...I mean, the rest is obvious!"

It's enough for Blythe to chew on as they drive. How mischievous do you have to be for your father to get a magician gang to babysit you? And how reckless do you have to be to start hooking up with the leader of said gang?

Joshua Hoffman needs Jesus.

Blythe is still lost in thought when she sees something rising from the horizon. At first, she does not realize where those lights are coming from.

And then she feels it—that hint of magic carried on the wind that raises goosebumps on her skin, telling her that a magician city is near.

Her breath, every bit of it, escapes her. Her mind goes empty and her heart races.

Lying ahead are the remnants of a city skyline. Large, awkward spaces separate the remaining towers. The closer they draw, the more details Blythe can make out: chunks blown out of buildings, a skeleton of a structure made not of brick or concrete but steel beams. Stark white light bursts from deep within the heart of the city as if somewhere, deep inside, life still thrives.

A whole city of magicians, cloaked by the heat and dust of the Nevada desert mixed with a heartbeat of magic to shield it from Common's eyes. A whole metropolitan existence hidden from prying eyes, turned to a wasteland because of one attack.

Electric City.

Blythe blinks rapidly to keep tears from welling her eyes. Amidst the wreckage and the debris and the confusion, her mother, her father, and her little sisters are waiting.

They are here. And it is time.

The white light of the city's heartbeat grows brighter and brighter until they reach the city's edge, where fields of sudden, magic-formed grass grows amongst dilapidated, empty brick houses. The people who once called this place home have only recently evacuated, if the destroyed décor still lingering on the doors and lawns is any clue.

The bikes slow until they come to a complete stop. The white light echoes across the front of the motorcycles and makes odd shadows out of their Angelus' faces.

Blythe is on her feet immediately. It is as if the city is drawing her in. Her family is here. And they are waiting for her.

With every step she takes, she feels a humming grow louder within her, stretching and filling every vein as if a dam within her has broken.

They are back on magicians' soil. Their magic has returned.

Blythe can feel the Guardians' energy as they rush to catch up with her. "Be careful out there," Rocco says as Jay jumps off. Jay doesn't look back at him.

Antonio hurries to Blythe's side. "Thanks!" he calls over his shoulder, waving to the Angelus.

Storm skates past with her jaw clenched hard. "Don't thank them."

"Oh, sorry! I have to take that back!"

One of the Angelus bikers cups his hands in front of his mouth and shouts, "Don't forget to text me that tostones recipe!"

"Yeah, bro, of course!"

"You got his number...?" Another biker murmurs.

But Rocco stands. "Wait!"

His voice pins them in place. Blythe watches his every move as he jumps to the ground. She is very surprised to find him actually staring back at her.

"Lemme talk with the curly haired girl," he orders.

"Her name is Blythe," Jay snaps.

"Yeah," Rocco is unbothered. "Whatever."

Blythe hasn't even agreed before Rocco is walking off, somewhere where no other ears will be able to pick up on their words.

"What if I don't want to?" she shouts.

His expression is grave. "I think you do."

There is very little in the world that Rocco, leader of the Angelus, could ever offer Blythe. But her curiosity *has* been peaked, and Blythe would never pass up an opportunity to learn something she didn't know before.

"Go ahead," Storm prods her. "We can use our magic here. I'll snap his neck in half a second if he tries something."

Blythe smiles at her as she starts off, following Rocco to the driveway of a house with a sweeping white veranda—and all of its windows blown out.

Rocco takes out a cigarette. He snaps his fingers and a flame jumps from his bare skin, lighting the end, smooth and easy.

"Is this to apologize for my arm?" Blythe asks. "Because if not, I don't wanna hear shit."

Rocco sucks his teeth, snapping his head to the side. "It's more important than your damn arm. You're lucky I didn't break it."

Blythe glares right back. The Angelus can't hurt them, not now and not ever—or at least, not for as long as Jay likes them. She can stand here, silently, until the end of time, and absolutely nothing will happen to her.

"No one's afraid of your hissy fits, little girl," Rocco bares his teeth. "You aint getting' a fucking apology out of me."

Blythe doesn't budge.

Rocco groans in frustration. "I swear to—fuck this shit—*fuck*, I'm sorry about your damn arm," he growls. "Now listen. This is serious."

Nothing about Rocco's appearance reveals any new information —dark hair styled like he's an uncaring bad boy who is still ruggedly handsome, snake tattoo twisting across his neck along with more (honestly, pretty cool looking) tattoos dancing across his fingers. He's young, probably in his twenties—definitely older than Jay, who is a minor, and Blythe could *totally* send Rocco's ass to jail if she just dialed 911.

She doesn't respect him any more than she did back in Washington.

Rocco's voice drops low. "Jay likes you guys," he whispers. He actually sounds sincere for once. "And he wants to tag along on your little adventure, so we gotta let him, but I figured I'd talk to you about this since you seem like you're calling the shots."

Blythe raises her eyebrows.

"The Hoffmans are cool with the Trident Republic," Rocco continues. "Jay doesn't know it, but they won't hurt him—"

"Wait, what?" Blythe interrupts. Jay's a Guardian. Well, maybe. Probably. But still, it's one thing to hire a gang to babysit your kid. It's another to be on good terms with the *Trident Republic.*

"I said what I said," Rocco snaps. "But just because the Trident Republic won't hurt Jay, doesn't mean some other crackhead in this city won't."

"Careless use of the word 'crackhead' is really insensitive to—"

Rocco steamrolls right over her. "And Jay gets...in these moods. He'll get real quiet and just be alone for a while or just...gets freaked out by stuff. Starts to panic. So keep an eye on him."

Oh, Blythe knows. She remembers the Guardians' very dramatic introduction to him. Blythe wonders if it's just nervousness or actual, chronic anxiety—or if Jay even recognizes the difference within himself.

But Rocco definitely doesn't care about any of that.

"You really just pulled me aside to—"

"Shut up and watch out for him," Rocco snaps. "'Cause if anything happens to that boy, the next part of you that gets dislocated will be your *skull*."

Rocco breezes past her, as if that line was a mic drop worthy of a dramatic exit.

But then he walks back. "Listen, I feel real bad about that. You're like, sixteen. My sister's your age. I can't be out here threatin' sixteen year old girls, I'm not a monster. I apologize."

"It's a little late to care about that since you already fucked up my arm," Blythe says. "But it's fine. I'm not scared of you."

"A'right. Cool, cool. I will have to hurt you though, if, y'know."

"Yeah, I get that."

"Okay. We on the same page?"

"Uh...I think we're on the same *chapter*, which is as close as we're gonna get."

Rocco bobs his head in a nod. He's turned to leave, for real this time, but the twist of his brow says that there is something else he wants to add.

"And tell Napoleon..." he hesitates. "Tell her Madame Deveraux goes by a different name when she's not in the Fae Lands. And if she really wants to find her, she needs to try New Orleans. But you didn't hear it from me."

Blythe doesn't understand any of those words, but that's okay, because they aren't meant for her. The only thing that surprises her is that Rocco has actually given up the information Storm needs.

She didn't think this boy was capable of doing anything even remotely positive.

"...thanks," Blythe says.

"You kept Jaybird safe when I couldn't," Rocco shrugs. "Favor for a favor."

The Angelus leaves in a symphony of roaring bikes, sinking toward the horizon, the same way they appeared.

And the Guardians are left in front of Electric City.

TWENTY-FOUR

BLYTHE HAS NEVER SEEN A CITY THAT IS BOTH REGAL AND destroyed, like a person struggling to their feet after being shoved to the ground. Katia said this place would be crawling with monsters, that they'd be fighting for their lives the second they stepped into Electric City.

But the air is still, hot, and silent. It smells like burning gas and despair.

Cordelia's research has resulted in a list of buildings where Blythe's family may be waiting. Their first destination is an abandoned prison where people have, reportedly, spotted groups of militia-like men hurrying in and out, along with various other suspicious activity. It's not much, but it's enough reason to investigate.

Storm warns them to stay on guard because the Trident Republic is known to associate with the Fae, and the Fae are—and her brow knits at this word—unpredictable.

"We *cannot* make a commotion or draw any sort of attention," Cordelia says. "The Trident Republic is already expecting us. Our best course of action is to keep them from knowing we're here. We are sneaking into these buildings, searching for any traces of Blythe's family, and sneaking out. No large fights, no explosions of magic, *none* of that."

They are silent as they travel, stepping over rubble and fallen street-lamps strewn across the sidewalks, keeping their eyes on the darkness behind the windows of every building.

While most of Electric City has been destroyed, some spots glow like polished pearls. Blythe notices this as they travel down a road that stretches endlessly toward the horizon. On the left side, neon lights flash outside of casinos, glass windows display finely dressed mannequins, restaurants boast their decorated outdoor tabletops. But there isn't a face or person to be seen.

On the right are craters burned deep into the ground, the edges singed black as if scarred by fire. Loose metal bars dangle from buildings, dropping to the ground with a cracking sound that spills into the silence. A coat has been has been discarded on the ground, trampled by dirty footprints and covered in ash.

Electric City must have truly been electric.

"What happened here?" Jay asks.

"The Black Veins attacked," Blythe says. "To take a stone."

The Black Veins army charged into this city and desecrated it, all because the Trident Republic happened to find a magical stone while digging up a plot of land. It sounds silly as Blythe stares at the wreckage.

Blythe doesn't say it, because she can't even believe it's true, but she almost doesn't blame the Trident Republic for starting a war.

Coming up on the Guardians' right is a cluster of white tents lined with white-blanketed cots. A shelter. Instead, families huddle together, dressed in plain, uniform-like attire. They aren't wounded or injured, but each face Blythe can see is grim or lost or painfully blank. They must be the people who once called Electric City home.

Past the shelter are a row of houses. Or, perhaps they used to be houses. Now they are simply crumbled bricks and debris.

The house at the end has experienced the worse; its neighbor collapsed into it like a domino, leaving only a third of its remains intact. The only remaining proof of the structure it used to be.

"His fiancé was still inside when it happened," says a voice.

Across the street is a woman. She sits on the pavement, unkempt grey hair kept in a braid. Her large, unblinking eyes are watching Blythe.

Antonio's face goes pale, as if the images of someone being crushed alive in their own home are playing in his head. They're certainly playing in Blythe's.

"I'm so sorry they had to experience that," Jay says. The perfect, polite, neutral response. Blythe can feel his hand on her shoulder, easing her forward gently.

The woman isn't done. "I was here," she says. "I seen it happen. I was in the Quick Mart when I heard the noises. People screaming. Glass shattering. I hid behind one of the stands, too scared to come out. But I watched out the window, watched one of the soldiers toss a bolt o' lightning through the bricks so hard, every single house lit up white and fell. Like they was made of straw. I stayed there for a while. Saw General Whiteclaw come back too, screaming her name."

Blythe freezes. "Whiteclaw?" she blurts.

The woman nods emphatically. "The general," she repeats. "Whiteclaw."

Jay pushes harder this time. Blythe's feet move forward, one in front of the other. But she barely registers it. Whiteclaw's wife was in there. She died in her own home.

What must that feel like, to lose someone you planned to spend the rest of your life with? To fall in love with someone, to memorize know how they think, to enjoy what they enjoy, to intertwine your existence with theirs, only to have them snatched away in the most painfully terrible of ways?

Blythe isn't sure she wants to know the answer.

Exhaustion starts to spread its tendrils over the Guardians, and Blythe is not immune. They've been travelling non-stop for hours. Besides their short nap on top of the truck, they haven't rested once.

Electric City doesn't seem to be boasting any five star hotels, so they make do with an abandoned mattress store sporting a broken window, where people have been taking advantage of its shelter.

It's empty when they crawl in, dirty blankets lying wrinkled on the floor and smelling sharp and sour. But it's the best they can do.

They agree to rest for two hours; it'll still be nightfall when they wake, but it'll grant them a bit of time to recharge.

Antonio passes around snacks: chips (that have gotten a little crunched up) and (fluffy but crumbled) muffins. Blythe crosses her legs and eats her muffin piece by crumbly piece.

Cordelia comes to her side. She squats instead of sitting, because she refuses to touch this floor with any part of her that isn't the bottom of her shoes.

"You don't have to feel bad for him," she says.

Of course she knows what's lingering with Blythe. Cheating mind reader.

Blythe's not sure if "pity" is exactly what she feels. Or even how she *ought* to feel. "I know," she answers. "But I do. I mean, how can I not? He lost his fiancé. Over a stone. It's a terrible thing to...to experience. He's been hurt. But that doesn't mean I forgive him for hurting me."

Cordelia nods even though she is studying every shift in Blythe's expression. "Alright. As long as you're okay."

"Okay" is definitely the right word. She is neither troubled nor apathetic. She is simply "okay". The Black Veins soldiers took Whiteclaw's city, took his house, took his fiancé's life. And then he took Blythe's family. What a twisted, horrid cycle.

Antonio seems to be explaining something to Jay, and if his chipper voice is any indication, it's more bearable than Blythe's own thoughts.

"It's Antonio's School of Magic," he says. "Lesson one! My hair isn't dyed, you said something about that earlier and it's been bothering me ever since."

"It's not?" Jay asks.

352

"No, dude," Antonio pouts. "Mom says my dad had blonde hair."

Cordelia's jaw drops. "That's insane."

"Caspian is literally a ghost," Storm says. "And you are flabbergasted by Antonio Torres being a natural blonde."

"It happens in magician genes sometimes," Antonio explains. "It's like how Jay's eyes are more silver than grey!"

Jay's hand flies, dramatically, to his chest. "You're waxing poetic about my eyes, getting me all hot and bothered over here."

Antonio smiles at him. "They *are* very pretty."

Jay sprawls out in a faux faint that his Oscar-winning-actress-mother would be proud of. "He called me pretty," he sighs.

Daniel is the first to fall asleep, head rested on his leather bag. Everyone else follows suit until it is only Blythe, kept awake by the hum of her own thoughts.

There is more on her mind than Whiteclaw and his fiancé.

She crawls over to the spot where Storm sleeps, sprawled out on her back. "Storm," she whispers, shaking Storm's shoulder a bit.

Storm yanks her arm away. "What, *what...*?"

"Remember when Rocco talked to me? Before he left?" Blythe asks. "At the end, he...he gave me some information on Madame Deveraux."

Storm's eyes open.

"He said that she goes by Eve when she's not in the Fae Lands, and that you can find her in New Orleans. Does that make sense to you?"

Slowly, as slowly as if the weight of the world rests on her shoulders, Storm sits up. "...yeah," she says. She seems to be thinking. "Yeah," she repeats. "I know what it means."

"Is it...what you were looking for?"

"Yeah," she says. "That's exactly it."

It takes a moment for everything to click. The only reason Storm agreed to stay with them was for the information Blythe has just given her.

Even when they lost the shard, Storm still didn't have what she needed in order to leave. Now it is not the information itself that makes her hesitate—it is the fact that she now *has* it.

Storm doesn't look at Blythe as she reaches over and picks up her rollerblades. She doesn't speak. Blythe doesn't know what to say either. She knew, logically, Storm would leave after this, but a part of her naively hoped Storm, for some reason, wouldn't.

Her rollerblades slip onto her feet, quick and easy. Her hands dance through the laces.

"Long ago, I made a mistake," Storm says. "And I hurt somebody I cared about. So I tried to cover it up. And I tried to run from it. But that only made things worse. So now I have to fix it."

She stands, straightening her hoodie. Blythe doesn't want to pry, because Storm hates that, but maybe now is the best time to ask.

Blythe's voice is soft. "Is that why only one of your eyes lights up when you use your magic?"

"...yeah," Storm answers. "But that's my burden. And I gotta set it right. I made a deal with you, and I don't..." she hesitates. "I don't go back on my word."

She stuffs her bag with her switchblade, her phone, her tangled earphones. "Y'all will be fine," Storm continues. "You're here in the city, everything's way more chill than we thought...y'all will be fine. I'd stay if I could, but I gotta do this. I can't put it off anymore. She could be gone by the time I get to Louisiana, I don't..."

"I understand," Blythe forces a smile. "Deal's a deal."

Storm nods. "I'm glad you told me."

"Of course."

Storm's gaze drifts to the others. "Say goodbye to Daniel for me?" she asks. "And, y'know. All of 'em. Caspian too."

Blythe nods.

Storm starts toward the door. But something makes her stop.

"It was my mom," she whispers. "In the picture."

The one Blythe found in her backpack. The one where Storm was a small child, but still so much happier than Blythe has ever seen her now.

Blythe has a feeling happiness isn't the only thing Storm has lost.

"I'm sorry," Blythe says. The threat of losing a family member has hung over Blythe these past few days, but it has never truly dropped. Not like it must have for Storm.

"...does it get better?" Blythe asks.

Storm stares out into the night, at the ghostly corpse that is Electric City. "It gets...easier," she says. "And you adapt, because that's what you do. When they're gone, they're gone."

In a fluid motion, muscles flexing, Storm throws on her leather jacket. Her left eye is alight with magic.

"Unlike me," she says. "You still have a chance."

In a blurred, orange flash, Storm Crane disappears.

———

"Where's Storm?"

Daniel is the first to notice her absence when everyone wakes. Blythe managed to sleep after Storm left, but only until Cordelia's alarm went off. Not much has changed since they all fell asleep; Electric City is just as hauntingly quiet as it was an hour ago.

"She...had to go handle her own stuff," Blythe says. She's not sure how else to put it.

But no one reacts. They don't get it. "When's she coming back?" Daniel asks.

Blythe lets her lack of an answer be the answer.

Jay scoffs. Cordelia's brow quirks. "She just *left*?" she asks. "Now?"

Even Caspian, who sits transparent and silent on a mattress, arms resting atop his knees, wrinkles his nose.

"I never really told you guys this, and I doubt Storm did either, but...we had an agreement," Blythe explains. "Between her mission and my mission, she'd leave to chase whatever came first. And her mission came first."

"What?" Antonio asks. "Okay, so she had to leave, that tracks.

But she didn't even wait until we woke up so we could say goodbye?"

Daniel's mouth falls open. "She didn't even want to *stay?*" he whispers.

Blythe's not sure how to twist this in the best way. In a way where the others won't hate Storm.

"Storm is..." Blythe's voice trails off. "Stubborn. She said she didn't do favors. I think she just couldn't live with proving herself wrong."

Daniel looks down at his hands. His face is flushed red. He may just be trying to keep himself from crying. "We didn't even get to say goodbye."

The words hang in the air for a moment, their team of six awkwardly staring at the ground and the emptiness that now lingers around them.

"We have to keep going," Blythe finally says. "Storm...she wanted us to keep going."

Traveling feels different even though the city has not changed. Blythe no longer hears the crunch of rollerblades against gravel. When she checks over her shoulder to make sure the Guardians aren't lagging, it's odd not to see Storm checking right along with her.

They'll just have to make do.

"We're two streets away from the prison now," Cordelia updates, lashes blinking against the bright light of her phone. But Blythe draws to a stop. They're passing by a surprisingly familiar building.

It's the Gilded Wardrobe, the thrift shop they visited in Broughton. It is oddly similar to the Washington store—sad lawn, dilapidated sign and all—with only a slightly different exterior that allows it to blend smoothly into Electric City's aesthetic.

With Storm gone, they are down their most experienced fighter. Jay may be powerful, yes, but Blythe has no idea what he's capable of when he's not fueled by desperation and panic. They'll need all the protection they can buy.

And the Gilded Wardrobe sold Blythe her hockey stick. Maybe they can fix it.

"Hey guys," Blythe says. "Let's stop here first."

The bells tinkle as they enter. Blythe has to keep herself from gasping because everything about this store, from its setup to the items on its shelves—the Matryoshka dolls, the silver globe, the glass airplane—is exactly the same as the Broughton store.

The same curly haired boy even slouches over the register.

His gaze shifts up to them. "Oh. I remember you," he says. "Except there's more shady-looking teenagers with you. And that lady's missing."

"How..." Blythe's voice trails off. "How are you here?"

Register Boy sighs, rolls his eyes, and begins a monologue he appears to have delivered a thousand times. "The Gilded Wardrobe has thirty different locations across the country. These stores promise equally amazing items and prices because they are the *same* items and prices, with the same workers, in the exact same room." He stares blankly at them. "I'm literally in thirty places at once. Still getting minimum wage."

"Wow," Blythe says. "I actually feel really bad for you."

Register Boy shrugs. Sympathy has no effect on him. "Are we done with the interrogation? Are you actually gonna shop?"

The other Guardians take that as a cue to disperse, inspecting the wonders displayed on the Gilded Wardrobe's shelves. But Blythe approaches the Register Boy.

"Um, I was hoping you could help, actually," Blythe says. She places the two pieces of her hockey stick on the display case. "It broke. I mean like, snapped."

Register Boy eyes the snapped bits. "Thank you for clarifying; I never would have known that's what happened."

"Anyway," Blythe ignores him. "I wanted to know if you could, like...fix it?"

Register Boy gives a resigned sigh. "I would if I could, but I just work here. I'm not magic, I'm just me."

"But it still works!" Blythe insists. "The magic is still in it."

"Did you try clapping your hands and believing?"

When Blythe cocks her head to the side, annoyed, he sighs again. "We have some...tape. It's basically a white duct tape that never peels off. That's it. That's all it does. I could slap that on there."

"Yes! Please! Thank you!"

He rummages below the display case. "I'm just giving you tape, I don't think I deserve adamant thanks."

Blythe holds it steady as he wraps it around. The magic wakes, slowly, through the wood, rising from a spark to a steady electric flow, like a heartbeat pulsing against her skin, as if the hockey stick can sing to her again.

A smile spreads on her face. The Trident Republic won't know what hit it.

"Thank you," Blythe repeats.

"There you go again."

Antonio rushes up, all smiles and energy. "Is this a shield?!"

He holds up a dome-shaped object that isn't fashioned out of wood or metal, but layers upon layers of porcelain scales.

Register Boy taps his glasses. Rows of lens slip out and stack in front of his squinting eyes. "It's called a dragonshield," he says. "It is made from the shred scales of a breed of dragon that sleeps beneath Japan—"

"I want it," Antonio blurts.

Register Boy stammers. "—oh, um, okay."

"Great!" Antonio says, and throws it on his back like a knapsack.

"It's fifty-six dollars," says Register Boy.

Very slowly, Antonio's gaze slides to Blythe in a desperate call for help.

"Um," Blythe begins. "We don't really, uh. Have...money with us...."

Register Boy's dark brows furrow. "You expect to leave with items despite having no money?"

Blythe puts on her most convincing smile. "We'll pay you back, I swear."

"And," Antonio leans on the display case. "We can, y'know." He winks, wiggles his eyebrows. "Slip you a Washington or two later for the favor."

Register Boy looks like he's about to burst a blood vessel. "Washington is on the one-dollar bill."

"You heard him," Blythe says.

Register Boy glares at her—and then closes his eyes and sighs. "Y'know what? I don't need your horrible bribes. You can take the stuff, I'm sure no one cares."

Daniel creeps up to Register Boy. "Do you have knives?" he asks.

"Daniel!" Blythe yells.

From the back of the store, Jay yells, "Daniel *snapped!*"

Daniel jumps, clinging his hands together. "T-They're for Storm," he explains. "What if she comes back?"

Blythe doesn't have the heart to tell him that Storm won't be joining them. Not anymore.

"Okay," she says instead. "Go ahead."

Register Boy sets him up with a set of four obsidian throwing knives which look, admittedly, quite impressive.

"Does your demonic possession want anything?" Register Boy asks next.

Caspian fades into view *just* enough for Blythe to see his unamused expression.

"No, he's fine," Blythe answers.

"How did you see me?" Caspian asks.

The only voice that can rival Caspian's constant unenthusiastic monotone is Register Boy's disinterested underpaid drawl. "I see everything," he says, nonchalant. "Anyone else want to steal some valuable items from me? Better take 'em now, while I still have a job."

Cordelia and Jay approach the glass case, Cordelia acting as if she would rather be anywhere else in the world, Jay raising a hand.

"I'll take something," he says.

Mr. I'm Not A Magician wants a magic item? "You will?" Blythe blurts.

Jay shrugs. "When in Rome."

"Get him a bow," Antonio teases. "We'll turn him into Legolas."

"Mm, no, I'm better with close range combat."

Register Boy studies him, as if running through a mental list of the store items. "I got it," he says after a moment.

He slides open the display case and presents them with a long white pillow of watches. They are all intricately beautiful, but the one he takes delicately into his hands is as red as blood. Its face is pitch black, with barely readable Roman numerals.

"Give me your dominant hand," Register Boy says.

"I'm ambidextrous," Jay answers.

"Fine, show off, give me either hand."

Register Boy clasps the watch around his left wrist. It looks nice on him—then again, everything looks good on Jay.

"Now, twist your wrist and close your fist like you're grabbing something."

Jay starts to. Register Boy jumps back. "Wait! Do it over there, not in my direction."

Jay faces the wall and twists his wrist. The watch snakes into his palm like a living creature. It melts into a liquid, shifting and growing forward, forming a sharp point and a long, straight edge before it hardens into a completely new object.

Jay is holding a sword with a handle as black as onyx and a long, crimson blade. It is a sword sharp enough to kill.

Blythe gasps. "Whoa! Bro, you look so cool!" Antonio shouts.

Jay weighs it in his hand, studying it. "What's it do?"

Register Boy's jaw *literally* drops. "What's it—it's a sword!" he screams. "A Bloodsword that you can literally carry around with you because it's also a sick-ass watch! *A Bloodsword!* Is that not good enough for you!? Do you need it to cook filet mignon too—"

Jay's losing what little patience he has. "Just tell me what the fuck it does."

Register Boy pinches the bridge of his nose and groans. "Bloodswords absorb the blood and-slash-or the lifeblood of the creatures they attack. That's how they get their color."

"So, it's already been used?" Cordelia asks. Her words earn an awkward silence.

"By the way, there's no proof that our items aren't cursed," Register Boy blurts. "We literally have *no* screening for that. There are hundreds of magical artifacts, heirlooms, and weapons floating around the world and we'll take any of them, no questions asked. We don't even accept returns, which means you're stuck with everything you purchase. For life." He pauses. "Anyway, enjoy your items!"

Cordelia scoffs. "My God, do you hand out weapons of mass destruction to anyone who walks in here or just us?"

"Usually I sit here and critique the lives of strangers via my Instagram feed without paying much attention to...anyone," Register Boy answers. "But you guys give off an oddly relevant vibe, even though I have no idea why."

"We're Guardians," Blythe says. "And we're kind of a big deal."

Register Boy's eyebrows shoot up. "Could've fooled me."

Could've—? Blythe recoils. "You work at a crusty thrift shop that sells magicians' *trash*--"

"Ay, don't do it to him, Bee," Antonio interrupts, shaking his head solemnly. "He doesn't even deserve to be dragged."

If Register Boy is at all offended, he doesn't show it. "Wow," he drawls.

Antonio points at him. It is a warning. "And I'm the nice one."

The Guardians are already heading for the door, new weapons in hand—the boy asks Cordelia if she'd like anything, but she plants her hands on her hips and asks if it *looks* like she's about to ruin her manicure trying to decapitate some slimy Calling creature, which shuts Register Boy right up—but Blythe pauses in the doorway.

"What's your name?" she asks Register Boy. He acts like he loathes their existence, but to be truthful, he's done a lot for them. The least she can do is call him by his proper name.

"I don't think I'm important enough for you to remember my name," he says. "I mean, it's a little late to introduce new people, isn't it? I mean, the final act—"

Blythe glances down to his shirt, hoping to spot a nametag. Bingo. "So, Rodger?" Rodger the Register Boy.

He sighs. "Forgot I was wearing that."

Blythe smiles as she heads out. "Thanks Rodger," she says.

He doesn't smile back, but he does watch them go, his expression not quite a smile but not quite a sneer.

"Hey, Guardians," he calls as the door swings closed. "Good luck. And come back soon."

———

The abandoned prison looks exactly like Blythe imagined: barred windows, whitewashed silhouette towering against the night sky and surrounded by looming barbed wire. But they can't just walk straight in—of course not, because that would be easy and *wouldn't* give Blythe a headache.

Instead, they have to travel, on foot, through an underground tunnel that dips down into the earth and opens in front of the prison's entrance.

A chill runs up Blythe's spine as they approach the tunnel's dark mouth. Electric City has always been silent, which isn't surprising, but this is almost...too serene. Are they really about to head *straight* into their first building of interest without a single person stopping them? Are they *really* that stealthy?

Katia's words race back to her, as if her ancestors have gifted her with this reminder. *As soon as you walk in, a sniper waiting on the roof across the street has you right through the skull.*

Blythe checks behind them. On the roof of a blown-out brick building stands the scarred woman with the billowing sleeves.

"Aw," she says. "I was hoping to get you while your back was turned."

From her beckoning hands, a flock of Krubim rises like a cresting wave, cloaks blacking out the night sky as they descend onto the Guardians.

TWENTY-FIVE

Blythe slams her hockey stick into the leader of the Krubim wave. The explosion ricochets through their crowded bodies, sending them backward in a mass of fluttering black fabric.

"What the fuck are these things?!" Jay shouts.

"Don't worry about it, just get rid of them!" Blythe replies.

The Guardians hear her loud and clear. A second flock arcs downward like a mass of falling arrows. Roots burst from the ground, dripping in clumps of dirt. Their gnarled tendons twist along black capes, tugging the creatures from the sky. But most of the Krubim soar past their sluggish movements. They are too swift to catch.

A flash of white and Antonio is in the air, wings glowing against the black sky. The Krubim shoot after him. He is fast on the wind, baiting their sharp talons above the rooftops, yards away from the others. But Blythe doubts the diversion will last long.

"Why didn't we ever practice like, fighting maneuvers?" Blythe asks. "So I could be, like, I don't know, Alpha-Seven-Beyoncé or some bullshit and we could roll out Power Rangers style?"

Cordelia yells, "Because your plans suck!"

"Wait a minute, my plans don't—"

A Krubim shrieks much too close to Blythe's ear. She whirls around—too fast. Her feet twist and she hits the ground as a black cloak soars overhead.

It passes just in time to reveal the giant bird from the Tempore, the one with talons the size of school buses. It opens its black beak and caws. Blythe's very organs tremble from the noise.

Fuck. The Krubim they could probably, maybe handle. That thing? Definitely not. *Absolutely* not.

The ground shakes as the bird barrels forward, straight toward Daniel and Cordelia. Blythe calls to them, but they already see the thing. Daniel throws himself into Cordelia, both of them collapsing into the asphalt as the bird barrels past like a runaway train.

Jay's voice pierces through the cacophony of Krubim shrieks. "*Antonio!*"

The Krubim hoarse has swallowed Antonio whole. Their claws tear feathers from his wings as Antonio struggles to stay afloat, wings fighting to flap, face twisted with pain as his hand reaches, stretches, upward—before a Krubim's body thumps straight into his chest, and he plummets like a falling star.

Blythe pushes to her feet, but Jay has already crossed whole yards, running faster than Blythe has ever seen a human being run. He dives forward, catching Antonio in his arms only a moment before he hits the ground.

The woman makes a noise of distaste from the roof. "I thought it'd take longer for the Sages' Guardians to fall but I'm not exactly complaining—"

She gasps. Her hands fly to her head as her body shudders, falling to her knees.

From her position, still lying on the ground, Cordelia's gaze is steeled on the woman. "I have her!" she says. "She won't be able to summon anything else, but I need to concentrate, so if someone could watch my back, it'd be much appreciated!"

Blythe darts. "I got you!"

She's barely moved three feet before sharp claws sink into her side. Blythe screams, jabbing her elbow back as hard as she can. Her arm collides with a solid torso. The Krubim shrieks, recoiling just far enough for her to slam the hockey stick against its head. It dissipates into black goo at her feet.

Everything is happening so fast. Too fast. Roots burst from the ground, wrapping around the giant bird but it tears straight through them. Jay is pulling Antonio to his feet but Antonio's body slumps against him.

Another wave of Krubim rises in the air. The Guardians will be swarmed if they stay here.

"Run for the tunnel!" Blythe orders.

Daniel leads the charge into the darkness, roots poking through the ground at his feet. Blythe catches up to Cordelia's side.

The sound of their running feet echo off the curved brick walls. Cordelia is too preoccupied to fight the Krubim, and Daniel's vines are effective, but slow. If something comes for the three of them, Blythe just has to fucking swing.

Blythe checks over her shoulder. Antonio's arm is thrown over Jay's shoulders, and though Antonio is walking, it is only barely. His wings droop, covered in bald, pink patches where the feathers have been torn. He does not look okay.

The Krubim wave closes in from behind them, filling the tunnel opening. They have about a minute before that wave of beasts is upon them.

Fuck. Fuck. Fuck.

"Daniel, protect Cords!" Blythe yells. The Krubim wave only grows larger as she heads for Jay and Antonio, like a tumultuous cloud of tattered fabric and yellow bodies.

"I can carry him," Jay says. "But I can't fight at the same time."

Blood drips from a cut on Antonio's temple. His words are hoarse and quiet. "I'll be alright just...gimme a sec..."

They don't have a second. The first few Krubim are already coming.

"Go on ahead," Blythe orders. "I got this."

The look on Jay's face is defiant, but he doesn't question her. Maybe he knows they don't have the time, or maybe he doesn't want to leave Antonio to fend for himself. Either way, he presses on.

And Blythe is left to face the storm. She sets her feet apart, squares her shoulders, and as the first shrieks ring in her eardrums, she starts swinging.

With every arc of her hands, the hockey stick connects with a body, setting at least four more back. She's hitting them as fast and as hard as she can. But they keep coming.

"Daniel!" she yells. "Make sure nothing hits—"

The ground is already erupting, cracking, shaking. Roots coil around the Krubim's bodies, holding them in place, pinning them mid-air. Blythe's muscles burn and she gasps for breath, knocking them from the air as quickly as her body will allow.

But it's not enough. There are already too many, and more are coming.

They are not going to win like this.

Caspian appears at her side. "Question."

"*Now?!*" Blythe shrieks.

"Am I allowed to kill things?"

"Monsters? Fuck yeah! I don't care what you—"

Caspian disappears in a streak of black smoke.

"—do..." Blythe's voice fades into silence. A wall of smoke is clogging the tunnel entrance. It pours as if from the mouth of a machine, black and frothing, stretching from the ground to the bricks above without leaving a single inch uncovered.

A Krubim flies through it. The smoke slips across its skin, draining the yellow into a sickly grey. Its mouth opens and emits a strained noise, not quite a cry and not quite a shriek. But even that does not stop its body from curling, withering, and dropping.

Every cloaked form in its wake does the same, shooting through the smoke only to shrivel and crash into the ground. Their dying bodies form a waterfall of countless cloaks pivoting and crashing into heaps of lifeless bodies. They are dropping like the drooped stems of every lavender flower in Lavender Heights.

Not bad for the Guardian of Death.

Caspian's face is impassive as he returns to Blythe's side, watching his wall of death obliterate Krubim after Krubim, the resulting growing pool of black goo on the ground.

"I never got a chance to use that before," he says.

"This is the only time I'll allow it," Blythe replies. "Could you fill a room full of people with smoke like that? Hypothetically speaking, of course?"

Caspian's black eyes are completely expressionless. "Nothing's stopping me."

"Jesus, Casp."

A pointedly cleared throat claims Blythe's attention. Cordelia's nose is wrinkled, her eyes narrowed with the force of concentration. "Let's keep moving, mm? The longer this goes on, the harder it is to keep her incapacitated."

Jay sighs, shifting Antonio's weight against him. "I hate to be a killjoy, but should we really be walking *into* the place we got ambushed outside of?"

Blythe jabs a finger over her shoulder at the literal wall of death. "You wanna go that way? Into that stuff?"

"Forward is our best option," Cordelia agrees. "If they're this desperate to keep us from getting in, there's got to be a reason. We can't turn back now."

Daniel gives a determined nod of agreement.

Jay dramatically holds up a hand in surrender and they travel forward, walking to the soundtrack of the dying Krubim behind them. Their pace is brisk but, as everyone is careful to ensure, not so brisk that Antonio strains himself.

Daniel watches him with drawn brows. "A-Antonio, are you okay?"

"S'all good my dude," Antonio croaks. "Don't worry about me. I just...need a second, that's all."

Jay studies him. "Don't you pass out on me," he says, low. "I'll have to carry you bridal style if you do."

"Not gonna lie bro, that sounds great right now."

Blythe wishes he would've have said that, because Jay, of course, obliges. "Alright, brace yourself," he says.

"Oh God, Jay, please be careful," Blythe begs, but Jay is already sweeping Antonio into his arms.

"I got him, I got him," Jay insists, as Antonio lets out the smallest grunt of pain at the shifting of his limbs.

Jay instantly freezes. "Good?" He checks.

Antonio musters a smile. "Good."

"Can you carry me, too?" Cordelia asks. "I'm simply tired of walking."

"Sorry, the Jay Train only has one seat and it's booked, but if you don't mind flying coach, I can piggyback you."

Daniel pouts. "If Storm were here, she'd carry us."

Blythe scoffs. "I don't know what alternate-universe-Storm-Crane *you're* thinking about, because the one I know absolutely would *not*—"

The ground shakes. The tunnel grows dim. Blythe stills, holding her breath, because up ahead, a wall of oil black feathers blocks their only exit.

"Oh," Daniel sighs. "I hate that bird."

The bird plunges, head first, through the tunnel—but its form is too big for the structure to contain. Its feathers burst through the bricks. Debris goes flying as dust rains from the ceiling. The whole world seems to quake as the whole tunnel rips around them.

Cordelia's eyes flash to Blythe. "Please tell me you have a plan for that thing."

"Working on it," Blythe answers.

"Well, work fast, because it's running at us!"

The tunnel cracks from its every massive movement. Roots rise, but aren't fast enough to catch its limbs.

Caspian is handling the Krubim. Daniel's vines aren't working. Cordelia can't concentrate on anything other than the woman. Blythe can't take that thing alone without risking her life. Antonio is injured.

"Take Ant!" Jay drops Antonio against Blythe. Antonio's not heavy, so it's not hard to hold him upright, but Blythe still stares after Jay as he sprints forward.

"Joshua Hoffman, you'd better have a plan!" Cordelia screams.

He runs like he does, fast and sure, shoes slapping against the ground as he runs straight toward the creature that dwarfs him like an ant.

And then he stops, arms outstretched, palms first. Blythe doesn't get it. He's in the center of the bird's path. It'll run straight into him.

Oh.

The creature's body hits Jay like a speeding car hitting a wall. And Jay is impenetrable—he does not flinch, not even a single muscle, as the bird's feathers drown him.

The whole tunnel stills. The creature tries to press forward. It bends its odd, oil-formed body against Jay. Its claws rake through the asphalt. But it is moving in place. Jay does not budge.

Joshua Hoffman is holding back this fifty-foot monstrosity with his bare hands.

"Oh. My. *God!*" Blythe yells over Cordelia's wordless shrieks of excitement.

"Heck yeah bro, go beast mode!" Antonio shouts as Daniel applauds with earnest.

But they're still sandwiched between this creature and a flock of dying Krubim. There *has* to be a way to get rid of that damn bird.

The memory of Katia's fight in the Tempore hits Blythe like a bolt of lightning.

"Jay!" His locs fly as he looks over his shoulder at Blythe. "Stab it in the neck!"

His forehead wrinkles. "Wh—"

The bird charges forward, burying Jay under a mound of slick feathers.

"Oh my God," Antonio breathes. "You killed Jay."

(He must be suffering from blood loss or something because that's absolutely ridiculous.)

The bird moves about a foot before it freezes. It starts to caw, the sound sharp and alarmed and desperately shrieking. Its feathers flap, knocking through the walls. Probably because its body is being raised into the air.

And there is Jay, teeth gritted with the weight of the bird against his back, rising to his knees like Atlas himself.

The Guardians absolutely lose their *minds,* cheering at the tops of their lungs as Daniel claps even more emphatically.

Blythe shrieks, "Hercules *who?!*"

"He should be carrying the weight on his legs, not on his back," Caspian says.

"Throw it!" Antonio shouts. "*Throw it!*"

Jay screams as he pivots his weight forward. The bird catapults, its round girth crashing through the brick walls, bursting wide open into the night.

The whole tunnel shakes. As if it's going to collapse.

"Oh fuck, we gotta run!" Blythe tries to shift Antonio's weight in her arms—but he is extending his wings. "No, Antonio, don't—"

"Too late," he says, teeth gritted. "Caspian, grab Daniel!"

Antonio hooks one arm around Blythe's waist and the other around Cordelia's—and he soars.

The only time Blythe has moved with her legs off of the ground was on a particularly daring rollercoaster—and flying with Antonio feels exactly like that.

She chokes down her screams, wrapping her arms across his body —the complete opposite of Cordelia, who is openly yelling her throat raw.

They are approaching the exit at the speed of sound. "Bro, you better be behind me!" Antonio yells as they rush past Jay.

Despite just throwing a gigantic Calling creature, he is barely even out of breath. "I'm good!" He promises.

A blast of air hits them as they fly from the tunnel. Antonio is losing altitude, the ground rushing closer and closer until Blythe's body rolls across it.

Honestly, falling isn't anything new at this point.

In front of her is a small, stone staircase (good thing her head didn't land on that). She pushes up to her elbows, staring up at the entrance of the prison, foreboding and grey.

They're here.

Cordelia sits up bolt right, eyes wide. "She broke free!" she yells. The scarred woman.

Blythe would be more invested if blood wasn't trickling down Cordelia's nose.

"Cords—" There must be too much compassion in Blythe's voice, because Cordelia glares.

"I can handle this," she insists, hastily dabbing the drops away.

Caspian races out of the tunnel, a screaming Daniel in hand. Jay is right behind him. The mortar and brick collapses into the tunnel on his heels.

The bird swings its heavy body upright. "You're kidding me," Blythe groans.

It has barely bleached out a shriek before Jay runs for it. He digs his hands into its oily feathers and scales up its body like an expert, straight to its neck.

The bird twists, swinging itself to the side—but a pair of roots grab it by the wings, pulling taught.

Jay leans backward just enough for his watch to slip into his fist and grow into a Bloodsword, its dark palor indistinguishable from the night sky.

He plunges the blade into the flesh of its neck—and the bird shrieks. It flails helplessly against its prison of roots.

Jay jumps down, sword sawing through its body as gravity carries him to the ground.

The bird melts in large, thick globs of formless black puddles. It sways and caws, a moving, melting carcass, until its head slips off, and the body turns into a still, dripping mountain.

Jay steps back, chest heaving as he catches his breath. "I don't—I-I don't know how I did that," he says, his words coming out much too fast. "I didn't even—a-and there's this *ringing*—"

"Jay, breathe, it's okay," Blythe interrupts. He turns to her, eyes wide.

"That ringing?" She asks. "That humming, the feeling that every single cell in your body is supercharged with energy? That's magic. That's what it feels like. You're okay."

Jay takes a moment, assessing himself and the world around him. Blythe smirks. "Still don't think you're a Guardian though, huh?" She teases.

He smiles a bit. "I dunno, man," he says. "I drink a lot of protein shakes."

Baby steps.

"Did anyone see what *I* did?" Daniel asks. "I held that bird down. It was quite a spectacle."

"I would say I saw it, but I honestly wasn't paying attention," Caspian answers. "I can pretend like I did, if that'd make you feel better."

Daniel deflates with a sigh. "Lies just aren't the same."

Jay turns to Antonio. "You flew. Are you okay?"

Antonio musters a smile. He is still lying on the ground, barely pulling his torso up. "I kinda had to. It's ok though, I think as time goes on they'll...heal..."

His voice trails off as Jay rushes to kneel beside him and inspect the cuts along his arms.

"Ideally, we should wrap these up," Jay mutters. "They're not incredibly deep but they can still be infected..."

"Jay!" Blythe blurts as he takes grabs his shirt collar. "It is state law that you keep that shirt on, we need to walk into this prison with as little distractions as possible!"

"You were going to take your shirt off for me?" Antonio teases. "Dude. At least take me out to dinner first."

"Just thought I'd show you what was coming after the main course," Jay replies.

"Oh my Gooooooood, you're corrupting my sweet boy and turning him into *you*..." Blythe whines.

Jay pouts. "I'm not your sweet boy?"

Cordelia groans, tossing her arms at her sides like a toddler throwing a tantrum. "Are all of you forgetting we almost *died*? And that woman just broke free and could conjure more of God knows what after us?!"

The Guardians fall silent as they stare at her.

"I, personally, was celebrating the 'almost' part of 'almost died'," Jay says.

Antonio nods. "Yeah me too."

"Dying's not even that bad," Caspian adds. "Or that hard."

But Cordelia is right. It's a miracle all six of them aren't trapped beneath the tunnel's pile of collapsed bricks and debris. That could have gone infinitely worse—and just because they managed to scrape by this time doesn't mean they'll manage it next time.

And they haven't even gotten *into* the prison yet.

"No, she's right," Blythe says. "We need to head in. And we need to be on high alert when we do."

The prison doors fly open. The chill in the air sends goosebumps up Blythe's spine. In the doorway stands a tall man with a hat shielding his face.

Whiteclaw.

"By all means," he says. "C'mon in."

A blast of wind hits Blythe like a speeding truck. The air is sucked from her lungs, and her head hits the hardness of the ground so hard, everything goes black.

———

Cold restraints hold Blythe flat against a hard, stone wall. She can't move. At all.

Her vision is blurry, but she can make out a large space, the prison cafeteria most likely, except the round metal tables are bare and the only other objects present are the wall of security monitors in the back of the room.

Whiteclaw stands in front of them, surveying their screens as their light silhouettes him, his back to Blythe.

The monitors display an array of rooms inside of the prison. One of which shows a group of teenagers who look suspiciously like the other Guardians, in a cell that is too small to fit all of them. Jay is not with them, and they barely seem conscious.

"Your friend did a number on Tahira, didn't she?" Whiteclaw's words bounce off of the concrete walls. "She's laid down in her room. Probably's gonna stay there for till her head clears. God knows how long that'll be."

Metal restraints press against Blythe's wrists, her ankles, her shoulders and torso. Blythe fights against them. They do not budge.

She is tired of being tied up, tired of being separated from the Guardians, tired of being stuck in situations just like this.

"Where's my fucking *family*?!" she growls.

Whiteclaw doesn't even face her. "I figured we could go through some basics before we got straight to business," he says. "First of all, you can stop fighting for your life. We aren't gonna kill you."

"You almost made me throw myself off a *roof*."

"Still on about that roof thing?" Whiteclaw pulls out a cigar. "Here at the Trident Republic, we operate under Walden's orders. And Walden Oliver doesn't kill people. Unless, of course," he says, flicking his lighter. "He has a damn good reason."

Blythe turns up her lip at this cocky man and his arrogant nonchalance. "And what *reason* could I give him?"

"I'm not him, so I'm not gonna pretend to know, but I imagine 'not cooperating' is one of them. And let me just say, we'd hate to kill you. You'd be *much* less use to us six-feet-under."

Those words give Blythe pause. Specifically, the word "use".

"You look surprised, love. Let me clear it up," Whiteclaw pauses, billowing smoke into the air. "The roof incident? Publicity stunt. Whole world heard that song, love. Wasn't nothing but a message to the Sages. Tellin' them to get their asses in gear and take us seriously, showing we had some magic on our side that would make 'em tremble."

Blythe's heart thunders in her chest. Because she knows where this is going. Oh, does she *ever* know where this is going.

"Naturally, we couldn't *actually* let them take you to Frost Glade. That'd defeat the purpose. But the question, then, was what could make you *want* to come here? Now, don't go congratulating me on all this, I don't think of the plans, I just carry 'em through. This was all Evangeline and Walden. They figured: Ether's the strongest Element. Gotta be the strongest Guardian. So what if we took the Guardian of Ether's family right in front of her and dropped a couple clues that she'd get them back in Electric City?"

This has never been about her family. None of it. The Trident Republic wanted *her*. They strung her family along to get her to come running.

And she did. She left Washington. She left Katia, the woman sent by her allies, who was only there to protect her. To run right into the Trident Republic's arms.

Whiteclaw flashes a smile. "No hard feelings, right?"

"Fuck you," The words bubble up, hot, from deep within her. "*Fuck you.*"

"Don't be like that," Whiteclaw sucks his teeth. "I told you, cooperation is encouraged. You won't get your family back otherwise." He pauses, taking another drag. "Let me show you something."

Whiteclaw moves toward the security desk, presses some buttons.

Three of the screens spring to life. Two of them show ornate rooms decorated with plush rugs and polished furniture.

The first is a bedroom. Blythe gasps. Tears spring to her eyes, and she blinks them away, because her mother is on the bed, eyes closed against the pillows, and beside her is her father, paging through a novel.

On the second screen is a living room with a large TV and a white leather sofa. Two little girls play on their knees, dolls dancing in their hands. Lily and Lena.

Blythe has not seen their faces in a lifetime. They look so happy, so peaceful. And they're *alive.*

"Your family is in good hands," Whiteclaw's voice shatters her tranquility. "Of course, those first few days, they fought it tooth and nail, but like caged animals often do, they accepted their fate." His eyes lock on hers. "But everything could easily change."

He presses another button. Blythe's heart seizes. Nothing happens, not at first.

Large men in bulletproof vests charge into the rooms. Her parents bolt upright with a start. The men snatch them to their feet, forcing them out of the room, out of the camera's view.

The twins are seized so easily; Lena's mouth opens wide with a scream Blythe cannot hear.

Blythe breath hitches. "No! *No!*"

She glimpses another figure in the hall, not in white, but in normal clothes—more people in the house? More kidnapped prisoners?

"Why are you hurting them if you want me!?" Blythe screams. "I'm *here!* Why—"

"No one's been hurt," Whiteclaw interrupts. "Not yet. I don't want to overstep my boundaries and explain too much, but..." He pauses. "Walden wants to make a deal with you. In exchange for your cooperation, he will free your family."

Blythe's blood goes cold.

It isn't because the Trident Republic is holding her family hostage to turn her into a pawn, or a living weapon to win their stupid war, or to make her fight against the Black Veins and the Sages themselves as a twisted ploy, because to them she is simply a Guardian and not Blythe Fulton, not her own person, not someone who has her own fears and dreams and would never want to be even tangentially involved in this sick mess.

But because, more pressingly, Walden Oliver, the leader of the Trident Republic and the man Katia said she was breaking her back to protect them from, is going to be here.

Even with the Guardians at her side, Blythe cannot expect to fight him and win.

"Did I not mention that bit?" Whiteclaw asks, coy. "Walden Oliver will be here soon. And he will explain what he expects from you in order to return your family."

The third monitor displays an all-white space that looks like a mix between a cell and some sort of vehile. Her family reappears inside, shoved in by the Trident Republic militia. A door slides down from the ceiling, trapping them in that small, cramped space. Lily cries as Lena clings to Jamal.

I'm so sorry, Blythe wants to say. *You never deserved this. I'm going to fix this. I can fix it.*

Movement flashes in another screen. The Guardians are talking adamantly, trying to break through the bars.

Whiteclaw's back is to the monitors. Blythe can't let him turn around. He can't catch what they're doing. They need time.

"I saw your house on the way here," Blythe blurts. "Some lady told me about what happened."

Whiteclaw pulls the cigar from his mouth, watches the end smolder as its smoke curls into the air. Silence.

"It doesn't feel good, does it?" Blythe goads. "Losing people you love."

Whiteclaw's voice is harder than she's ever heard it before— it is the first time he is not laughing at her through his words.

"You're sixteen years old, little girl," he spits. "You don't know the half of it."

Over Whiteclaw's left shoulder, a monitor shows someone running through the halls, someone with long black dreadlocks.

Rocco said the Hoffmans were allied with the Trident Republic. Maybe they didn't put Jay in a cell because they didn't think they needed to. Maybe they expected him not to care.

"I know that everyone in the Trident Republic thinks they're an underdog," she says. "That you get a free pass to ruin as many lives as you want because *yours* got screwed over."

"Don't start talking about shit you know nothing about," Whiteclaw growls. "You may have walked through the wreckage for ten minutes, but you don't know the goddamn half of it."

Jay has reached the Guardians. The guards outside of the cell are collapsed on the ground—probably Cordelia's doing—which leaves Jay free to rip open the cell door.

The Guardians swarm out, pausing to speak silent words before running down the hall and out of every camera's view.

"Tell me," Blythe goads.

Whiteclaw falls for it, narrowing his eyes and furrowing his thick brows. "Evangeline called Walden and I down to the labs. She'd barely been there for an hour with the stone and she was starting to tell us about it when *your* soldiers came in. We hadn't been prepared for an infiltration. Not at fucking all. And they ripped the stone straight from Jellie's hands, kicked her on the ground like she was a fucking dog when she fought back. It happened so fucking fast, so goddamn fast— they were in and then they were out, leaving thousands of dollars' worth of damages. They'd stolen priceless information and data.

"We thought they'd breezed through the city and came straight for the lab. Then we looked outside. They were going through the streets like an infection, destroying anything they could touch. I watched one of our men get thrown through a hospital so hard that the entire *building* collapsed. Do you know how many patients were in there? How many pregnant women, newborn babies, people with routine fucking surgeries? Your news calls it an attack, but what happened here was a fucking *massacre.*

"I saw them in the streets near my house. And I knew Dizzy was there, I *knew* it. She probably didn't even realize what was happening, and she sure as hell was the exact opposite of a trained magician. I bolted out as fast as I could, as *fast* as I fucking could, and..." his voice trails off. "I couldn't get there in time. As you can see."

He exhales, long and slow. "Maybe that'll paint the fucking picture for you."

Blythe stares at him, steeling her voice against the horrors he has thrown at her.

"It does," she says. "And you're right. I'm a sixteen-year-old girl who doesn't know shit. And I'm restrained against a wall while you hold my family's murder above my head. Because there's nothing wrong with that at all. And that makes *you* the hero."

Whiteclaw stares off at the wall. "Wait till you grow up. You'll do a lot of things for the people you love."

"So, because someone hurt *your* family, you harm *mine.*"

Whiteclaw is silent. "Didn't expect you to understand," he mutters.

A knock interrupts the conversation. It is the first time Blythe notices the door on the left side of the room.

Whiteclaw sets down his cigar, rolling his shoulders back as he goes to open it. Jay looks up at him.

"The hell are you doing here?" Whiteclaw asks.

Jay punches Whiteclaw across the face. Blythe hears a *crack* as his body drops to the floor like a sack of flour.

Jay, meanwhile, flashes her a winning smile. "I accept all sorts of payment in return for these rescue missions, just so you know."

Blythe can't even think of a witty reply. Not after the places her mind has been—the death of so many innocent people, the knowledge of how her own family could be next on the list if she doesn't...if she doesn't do whatever Walden Oliver expects her to.

Jay hurries up. "Hey, you alright? Did he hurt you?"

"No, I'm fine," Blythe insists. She doesn't want to talk about it, anyway. "They didn't put you in a cell?"

He rips the restrain over her left wrist straight from the wall. "No. Told me to stay put until they figured out what to do with me. It just took me a minute to get away and find my way around. The others should be up here soon, I already got them out."

He snatches off the other handcuff and, for a moment, Blythe's shooting toward the ground.

Jay grabs her by the waist. He smells of warmth, honey, and something divine.

"Gotcha," he smiles.

Blythe laughs as he sets her down, but the sound is hollow. "Thanks. But, um, I don't..." She's not even sure how to say this. "I-I don't think I can leave. *Should* leave."

Jay leans back a bit, raising an eyebrow. "Explain."

"She's cooperating, Mr. Hoffman," says a voice behind him.

Jay turns around, pushing Blythe further behind him.

Whiteclaw rises to his feet. His mouth and chin are soaked in blood, all pouring from his nose.

Anger burns in his eyes. "I'm not supposed to hurt you, so you better get out of here before you make me do something I shouldn't."

Jay's muscles go taught. He outstretches his hand and the Bloodsword slips into it.

Whiteclaw barks a laugh. "You think you're gonna fight me? That I'm gonna get my ass kicked by some spoiled rich boy who left his house for the first time? You learned two things about magic and now you wanna play white knight and get the girl."

Wind kicks up around them as Whiteclaw's bronze cuffs begin to glow. "Well, let me tell you something," Whiteclaw growls. "Out here in the real world, there *are* no heroes. There are only winners...and those who drop off the face of the earth."

A wind tunnel breaks into the room, shattering the glass. The metal tables groan as they sweep across the floor.

"Blythe," Jay speaks without tearing his glare from Whiteclaw's face. "Run."

"I *can't*," Blythe insists. "The only way they'll let my family live is if I stay here."

"You better listen to her," Whiteclaw warns. "This is no place for a sheltered boy who's never felt pain before. Go ahead. Glare at me. But you don't know what suffering is."

Jay screams, a reckless, enraged scream. He charges forward, sword raised.

The wind grows into a vortex, a palpable force that forces Blythe to the ground. Her ears pop as she pulls herself into a ball, tucking her nose against her knees to hold in a pocket of oxygen.

But Jay? He is running. A table flies toward him and he slices through it with a perfect swing of his arm. The Bloodsword moves through the metal like a knife through butter.

The tip of the blade races across Whiteclaw's face next, a sound that is sharp and sudden.

When Jay raises it again, Whiteclaw screams. Not out of fear, or because of his injury, but some otherworldly, twisting pain that Blythe cannot see.

Whiteclaw grasps his head as he sinks to his knees, blood waterfalling down his nose and his cheek.

The air goes still. The winds vanish. His body goes limp against the floor.

In the doorway is Cordelia Deleon. "Oh my," she says, watching Jay. "I can't believe I ruined my chance to watch you swing that sword again."

"Cordelia!" Blythe yells.

The girl's dark eyes find her and she runs over. "Are you alright?" she asks. She holds out a hand to help Blythe up, and Blythe takes it—though considering it's Cordelia, it's more of a nice gesture than an actual physical benefit.

But who cares? Cordelia is here. If anyone can help make sense of this mess, it's her.

"I am now," Blythe says.

"Then let's go. We need to search this building—"

"Actually," Blythe's voice makes Cordelia stop in her tracks. "I'm...I can't...leave."

"Excuse me?"

A dark, echoing shadow floats into the room. Caspian. Daniel and Antonio are behind him, both wearing almost identical expressions of confusion.

"W-What do you mean you can't leave?" Daniel echoes.

With all of them focused on her, silently demanding answers, Blythe tries her best. She explains what she can, the bits she can put into words—it is a ruse, and it has been from the beginning. Her family is not in any current danger, but they could be if Blythe does not obey.

To make matters worse, Walden Oliver himself is coming. She doesn't know when, or what he is capable of, or even what he looks like, but she can't risk defying him. Even *Katia* is wary of him. So Blythe needs to stay put.

Cordelia shakes her head. "Nonsense."

She rushes up to the monitors, pointing a long, slender finger at the screens.

"You saw them here, you said?" she asks. "I'll see if I can find where these cameras are stationed. I've got a good bit of information on Electric City's major facilities; as long as this isn't a feed from some secret underground bunker—which I *doubt*, because the Trident Republic certainly doesn't have the resources or money for that—I should be able to find where they've taken your family."

Cordelia whips out her phone, scrolling through and glancing, occasionally, up at the screen.

Antonio comes to Blythe's side. "She'll get it," he assures her. "And we'll go find your family, wherever they are. The Trident

Republic's not going to make you do *anything*. I mean, we got this far, didn't we?"

Blythe is too afraid to agree. If Cordelia can't do this, Blythe will have to face Walden Oliver herself. She doesn't even know what to expect, or what he might ask of her, or—

"I found it," Cordelia interrupts. "It's the transport tower, the tall building we saw when we got here. Second floor of private miniature jets."

A long, *long* exhale leaves Blythe. If she were alone right now, she would not have stood a chance. But she is not alone. And, as long as she has the other Guardians, she will *never* be alone.

"Cordelia," Blythe says. "I really do love you."

Cordelia smiles sweetly. "I love me too," she says. "Now let's hurry, there's an exit just down this staircase."

Blythe leads the way down the stairs; the sounds of the Guardians behind her are like a chorus of reassuring blankets. She is not alone.

They push past a massive set of emergency exit doors and reappear into a world with a dark, black sky. It has to be every bit of three A.M.

The Guardians shoot past the prison's grounds, running shoulder to shoulder.

"The transport tower isn't far, but we need to hurry!" Cordelia says. "I'm almost certain they placed your family in automated flying jets with preset coordinates, which mans they can be sent out at any moment. Whiteclaw isn't out for the count just yet, and if Walden Oliver gets here before we find your family—"

"Do we always have to review every way things could go wrong?" Daniel interrupts.

Cordelia sneers at him. "Do you always have to speak?"

Something about their bickering is reassuring. Maybe the familiarity of it, unchanged even from their time in the San Diego mall.

Blythe can see the transport tower from here. It is a spire of a building, the tallest structure left in the Electric City skyline, piercing the sky like a needle.

Their final destination.

Footsteps and shouting race after them. A whole group of Trident Republic militia are hot on their trail.

Limping behind them, bloodied and injured and unstoppable, is Whiteclaw.

Well.

This'll be interesting.

TWENTY-SIX

THE GUARDIANS HAVE PERFECTED THE ART OF HOLDING A conversation while running at top speed through a neon city that may or may not be out to destroy them.

"The transport tower is basically a discombobulated mix of an airport, a hotel, and Lord knows whatever else," Cordelia explains.

"So they got private jets and planes *inside* the building?" Storm scoffs. "What, the twelfth floor got a landing strip too?"

"It'd make for an interesting visual," Caspian says. Blythe doubts he is completely present. Or sober.

Cordelia raises her phone, checking the details. "Seems to be someone's idea of an interesting invention. At the very least, it probably brings in some tourism, but it's not our job to be concerned with the building's history. We're fast approaching its parking garage entrance, so we'll enter through there and work our way up to the top floor."

Blythe rolls her eyes. Of course they need to reach the top floor. Any other floor would be *far* too relaxing and anti-climactic.

"You guys know we still have company, right?" Jay asks.

Blythe does know. With the Trident Republic militia making as much of a ruckus as they are, it's impossible not to know. The Guardians may have lost them a couple streets back, but that doesn't mean they've given up the chase. And it can't take a genius to decipher where they're going.

"Dude, there's nothing we can do," Antonio says. "There's like, fifty of them at this point."

"We can't just let them follow us into the transport tower," Jay says. "By the time we get to the doors, they'll haul us back outside."

"Well, what do you want to do?" Blythe asks. "Take on all of them? They're all magicians. They can all do the same freaky ass shit we can."

Jay gives an impatient snort. Out of all of them, he's taking this whole "talking while sprinting" thing the easiest. "Can we separate?" he asks.

"I can communicate with everyone via telepathy, so I'd assume, yes," Cordelia answers.

Jay draws his head back. "Wait, you could read minds this whole time?"

"Never without permission."

"Lie detector determined *that* was a lie," Blythe mutters.

Jay holds up a hand, stilling the conversation. "Alright. Anyway. You guys get into the transport tower. I'll hold the militia off."

"On your own?" Blythe asks. "You know Whiteclaw is with them, right?"

"Trust me, I can take them. I've got really good stamina," he says —then smiles.

"As much as I'd like to leave you to die, I don't think I should," Blythe teases. "Caspian, watch his back."

Caspian says, "No thanks."

"*Caspian.*"

Jay eyes her. "I don't need your imaginary friend. Trust me. I'll be fine."

Antonio shakes his head. "Dude, no, I'll stay with you."

"Antonio, you're limping as it is—and even if you weren't, all you do is fly. I love you, but you need to go. All of you."

"No, *nope*, I hate this—"

"Blythe," Cordelia interrupts. "We don't have time. And he can heal. He'll be fine."

Jay smiles, gesturing at himself. "Look at me. I'm eye candy, I can't *die*."

When they reach the transport tower's parking garage, everyone charges forward except for Jay. "Don't die, bro!" Antonio shouts.

"What he means is: be careful," Cordelia translates.

"Will do," Jay promises. He watches them go for a moment before he calls, "Hey, Blythe."

Blythe looks back at him. With his sword in-hand and his shoulders set, brown skin gleaming in Electric City's hard fluorescent lights, he looks all the part of a hero.

"I think I might be one of you guys," Jay says. "A Guardian, I mean."

Blythe feels herself smile. "I think so too."

As she hurries after the others, Blythe says a silent prayer to all of the forces of the universe to protect that valiant, dumb, rich boy.

The entrance gates to the parking garage have been roped off with yellow caution tape. The smeared glass of the booth reveals an empty leather chair; no one is on duty and every parking space is achingly empty, leaving only a quiet dripping and the smell of spilled oil.

"Sorry, tourists," Blythe teases as they hop the tape. "Electric City's closed."

"I assume the whole transport tower is closed," Cordelia replies. "They've got more important places to funnel their tax dollars."

"Who'd want to come to Electric City anyway?" Daniel mutters.

"*Daniel!*" Blythe gasps while Antonio chastens, "Bro, don't be rude!"

Cordelia mutters to her phone as they step into the elevator. "Diverted the security cameras...alright. I've worked it out from here.

This elevator will take us up to the first-class lobby, but we'll have to navigate the rest of the way."

Thankfully, the elevator does not attempt to serenade them with smooth jazz, and their ascent is mostly silent. Through the glass of the back wall, Electric City lies before them, half-standing and half-desecrated.

She can even see Jay. The militia outnumbers him, but he is effortless and unstoppable, like Achilles sawing through the Trojans. He'll be alright.

The elevator doors open, revealing a gaudy lobby embellished with bronze: the Trident Republic's signature metal. Large potted plants adorn the corners of the overstuffed seating area. The receptionist desk is unsurprisingly deserted.

Cordelia wasn't lying when she said this transport tower was an odd amalgamation of a hotel and an airport. Beyond the lobby is a vast space resembling an airport's check in, with rows of seating and a baggage check.

Cordelia's wedges click against the tile. "Do you remember when we first met, and I was always on my phone because I thought I'd infiltrate Electric City?" she asks Blythe.

"You said you weren't even doing anything half the time," Blythe says.

"Well, yes. But for the other half, I was working on *this*."

The whole city seems to groan. Blythe's gaze flies to the windows behind them. At the edge of the city, where the buildings meet the desert, every light dies. Signs go black and whole streets disappear. The power failure spreads as darkness sweeps toward them like a wave, blackening every source of light until even the transport tower has gone dark.

Daniel gasps. "Oh my god," Blythe says. "You just shut Electric City down."

Cordelia isn't even phased. "The power's been knocked out in almost every buildings, which leaves most of the doors unlocked and opens all of the emergency exits and staircases *without* sounding alarms which, obviously, works in our favor." she pauses. "But yes, I just shut Electric City down."

"*Dude*," Antonio breathes. "All my friends are so cool."

Cordelia sweeps her hair from her face with a dramatic, haughty grace. "Anyway," she says, pretending she isn't blushing with pride from that comment. "This is the hotel area. It'll probably be spotty with security investigating what caused the power shortage, but we can easily avoid them. The first thing we'll have to do is—"

The lights blink back on.

"Is that supposed to happen?" Blythe asks.

Cordelia is frozen, staring above. "...no."

"Shit," Daniel says.

"Daniel!" Blythe yells. "Watch your mouth!"

Cordelia rushes for the receptionist desk, the others hurrying in her wake. A touch screen is imbedded in the marble behind the counter, and her fingers fly across the screen. She inputs numbers and access screens that Blythe's never even *seen* on a computer before.

"They've connected to a power reserve," Cordelia finally says. "I didn't realize they had one of those. Damn it."

"Can you fix it?" Daniel asks.

"Yes, I just..." Cordelia's voice trails off. "I need time."

The floor shakes. Footsteps. Something is coming.

"We don't have time," Caspian says.

Blythe pushes everyone behind the desk, where they crowd together on the floor. Cordelia drops to her knees, low enough to keep the top of her head from sight, but high enough to still tap silently on the touchscreen.

Antonio peeks over the countertop. "Oh that's..." his voice trails off. "Not good."

Blythe sits up straighter, following his gaze. Coming down the hallway is a suit of heavy metal armor, clanging with every heavy footstep. The sword at its side is long enough to scrape into the tile as it moves and its body is large enough for its helmet to brush the ceiling.

Blythe can't see any signs of a living body inside of it. Judging from the two, piercing orbs of blue light spearing through its helmet like eyes, it is powered, solely, through magic.

"Please tell me that isn't the building security system," Blythe whispers.

"Oh, it definitely is," Cordelia says. "This code suggests it's... magic based? I can't find any traces of it here so it's *definitely* not technological."

Daniel, their resident thaumologist, wrinkles his nose. "It's probably Learned Magic," he says. "Which means it's powered by an external power source. If we shut down the source, we can shut down the security system. But we'd have to find it first."

"We *don't have the time*," Caspian repeats. "Not if we want to get to Blythe's family before their jet disappears—"

"Forget about the security system," Cordelia interrupts. Her eyes blaze on Blythe. "You won't even be able to reach the jets while the power is on. I have to work on shutting it off, but there's more you need to do in the meantime."

"Oh no," Blythe says.

"I'm going to stay here. You all will go on without me, but you *must* follow my instructions to the letter."

"Oh no, we're bad at that."

"First, find the security office. It should be somewhere within the airport sector. Inside, you'll find a keycard. Next, travel east to the airport gates. You'll see a glass bridge. Cross that and you'll enter the area for exclusive flyers. There you'll find a security door. When the power goes out, *get through that door.* With the power on, the door is locked unless you flash an ID badge—which we do not have. Once the power off, it unlocks, so you *need* to be through it by that time. Past the doors lie a staircase. Take it all the way to the top. Then, use the keycard to access the loading dock for the private jets. Your family will be inside one of them."

"You just said so many words and I don't know how many I understood," Blythe says.

"I'm a mind reader, you got all of them," Cordelia snaps. "You just don't want me to stay behind. But you'll be fine."

They fall silent as the knight's piercing eyes scan the lobby. It must've decided the area is clear, because it turns its back as if to return to whatever magical hell it walked out of.

The Guardians bolt, running as quickly and silently as possible past the check-in terminals.

"She said to find a security office, right?" Blythe asks as they near the metal detectors. "It should be around here, this is all of the security stuff—"

Someone grabs her arm. "Stop!" Antonio whispers. His grip is hard as he yanks her down, to the floor, behind a row of seats. It is only when Blythe stills that she hears the echoing, heavy footsteps that are not their own.

The stark white lighting makes it ridiculously easy for her to peek through the seats and see that there are *more* oversized suits of armor, stalking through the waiting area, blue eyes scanning.

"We should crawl," Antonio says.

Blythe wrinkles her nose. "You're kidding," she balks. He very much isn't.

Moving on her hands and knees, Blythe shimmies forward, angling her body through the maze of seating. Fuck this place for having a wide-open floor plan.

"I see a security door," Daniel whispers. "On our right."

Blythe spots it against the wall—an open counter with a "security" sign hanging above it and, off to the side, an inconspicuous looking door.

"Okay, breaking and entering when we're stuck on our hands and knees, no sweat," Blythe mutters.

"Not for me," says a monotone voice.

Blythe does not see Caspian move, but she feels his energy surge above the chairs and phase through the door as if it were thin air. Having a ghost thief as a friend comes with some perks.

Blythe looks over her shoulder. Daniel watches their surroundings with huge, steely eyes. Antonio leans back against the empty seats that shield them, shutting his eyes tight. He must still be in pain. Blythe feels terrible for him—especially since, because he is Antonio, he won't even complain.

Blythe can feel the knights moving from the shudders in the floor. They're getting closer.

"Caspian, can you *please* hurry..." she whispers. If he can feel her emotions, he'd better know how badly she's rushing him.

Caspian reappears at her side. Empty-handed. "I think I saw it," he says. "It's on a slot in a machine. I need to slip something else in there to replace it. I need a credit card."

Blythe doesn't have one. Antonio shakes his head. Daniel doesn't seem to know what a credit card is.

There's a sound like a sword dragging through carpet. It sounds as if it is directly right behind them.

"Could you use anything else?" Blythe begs. Caspian shakes his head.

Daniel shifts, reaching into his bag and, after a short tearing noise, produces a blank page of his grimoire. Blythe's jaw almost drops. She's never seen Daniel treat his grimoire as anything less than holy— and he's *ripped it.*

"Here," he says, holding it out. "I-It's pretty thick paper, especially if you fold it."

Caspian snatches it. "If you don't hear an alarm," he says, already disappearing. "Suppose it worked."

A flicker of movement above the seats catches Blythe's eye. A knight towers above them, its form filling Blythe's vision as its eyes flash from blue to stark, blood red.

"Oh," Antonio says. "Maybe the red means he likes us."

Blythe draws her hockey stick. If she swings, she'll attract the attention of every other knight within a twenty foot radius.

But there's one option she's never tried before.

Blythe aims the handle at the gleaming silver of the knight's chest plate. The hockey stick charges, magic filling until the wood is boiling in her hands.

A beam of white light bursts from the handle and pierces through the metal, leaving a blackened, gaping hole.

"That thing shoots laser beams?!" Antonio yells.

"Holy shit, Rodger wasn't joking," Blythe breathes. "Wait a minute, I could've been using that this whole time!"

The knight topples to the floor with a clatter so loud, the other three knights snap their attention over. Every blue light lands on them and instantly turns red.

"Okay, maybe my plans *do* suck," Blythe says.

Caspian reappears—dangling a keycard. Blythe snatches it. "Go, go, go!" She yells.

They push to their feet but the tile is smooth—too smooth for running. Blythe fights to keep her balance as she pushes her body to move faster, faster, faster. The suits of armor echo like a cacophony of jangling pots and pans behind them; very large, very powerful pots and pans, carrying very sharp swords.

"My magic's not working on them," Caspian says.

"They're Calling creatures and essentially moving statues," Daniel explains. "They aren't alive in the first place."

Caspian cocks his head to the side, curious. "I've been faced with my only weakness."

Up ahead is a balcony opening onto a glass bride. Bingo. Cordelia's next step in her instructions. "Make a hard right, follow me!" Blythe orders.

She runs onto the bridge without looking at her surroundings—and the boys follow her blindly. Blythe realizes her mistake when hundreds of tiny blue lights echo beneath her feet.

During its operation, the transport tower must have been used by hundreds of people, because stories below them is the heart of the building: an array of wide space and terminals as large as a football field. Also present below them is a slew of gigantic knights, enough to cover almost every tile on the floor.

All at once, their eyes switch to red.

"Uh, hey Blythe?!" Antonio screams.

Blythe pumps her legs faster. "Don't stop running!"

A crack spears through the glass. One of the knights has thrown its sword, which now sticks out of the glass yards ahead. A second sword crashes through the bridge.

Cracks spread like spiderwebs under Blythe's feet. "No, no, no," she stammers.

The bridge shatters, taking her body down with it. Her heart leaps into her throat as the ceiling fills her view. She is rushing toward the ground, along with a thousand glass shards, where she will probably be skewered, torso-first, onto some magical knight's sword.

Blythe is screaming before she even thinks to open her mouth.

There is a sound she has never heard before, like the entire earth is tearing open and birthing forth something moving fast and determined. She hits something rounded and soft. It is definitely not a floor—or a sword.

She tumbles over rough texture as her shirt catches on thorns and leaves. Finally, her body comes to a stop. She is in a sea of vines, but not the tiny ones she is used to Daniel creating. These are the bright green plants of fairytales, the ones that are large enough to shoot into the heavens and hold a giant's weight.

"Daniel!" Antonio screams from somewhere above. "Holy shit!"

A few yards below her, cradled in nest of leaves, Daniel lies with his palms outstretched. His face has contorted with so much concentration, he has gone red.

The vines are still growing. The reach like hands toward the other end of the bridge, breaking through the remnants of glass as they braid and twine into their own sloped path. It is not perfect, but it is climbable.

Antonio is already starting up, securing his flip-flops against the thorns. Beneath her, Daniel shifts into high gear as well, climbing with less grace but just as much determination. Blythe follows their lead, digging her fingers into the plants' flesh. Only the sound of Daniel's gasp stops her.

He drops, suddenly, body tumbling through the vines. "Daniel!" Blythe yells. Why can't that boy climb?!

He lands on his leg—hard. A scream bursts from him. He is too far behind for Blythe to reach without scaling backward, laid on the smallest vine, barely a story from the sea of knights.

Suddenly, it goes dark. Every light has shut off. The power is down.

"Oh no," Antonio says. They have to leave. *Now.*

"Get to the staircase!" Daniel's voice scratches over the words.

The knights' red eyes illuminate his curled body as he clutches his knee in his hands.

"Daniel—"

He interrupts Blythe. "I'll be fine!"

His grimoire slips from his bag. Daniel watches it fall, landing in the midst of red eyed knights that are slowly realizing they need to scale up the vines.

All of his work, all of his studying, has just been lost. But Daniel does not flinch.

"You have to get on the elevator," he says. "You can come back for me."

Blythe can't leave him. Daniel's not Jay—and there are hundreds of those knights down there and he's injured—

"It's okay, Blythe," Daniel insists. "I'm not scared this time."

Caspian appears beside her. "I can try to find the power source. It'll shut all of those things off."

"Yes, go," Blythe says. In the blink of an eye, with the smallest burst of black smoke, Caspian has disappeared. "We'll be right back, Daniel!" Blythe yells. "Caspian's going to try and shut those things off! Don't go anywhere!"

"I think I'll go running," Daniel says. "That was a joke, like you guys do. Was it funny?"

Blythe smiles down at him, this precious boy who has only ever wanted to make friends, this boy who has ventured into the world for the first time and has become so very brave in the process. "Very," Blythe lies.

Blythe climbs, leaving Daniel farther and farther behind, to orchestrate an army of vines that pick off an ever-growing number of red-eyed knights.

At the top, Antonio pulls her up to solid flooring. "This is *not* how I imagined this going," Blythe whispers. The Guardians were supposed to be *with* her, not being picked off one by one.

At least they've made it to the area with the security door. From here, they just need to climb a staircase, and then they're there.

The security door is just ahead. White pillars box this area in a square, with a huge window on their right, where the city lies hauntingly dead and dark.

Antonio's gaze is unsteady, but he covers it with his voice. "It'll be okay. We'll get up there, find your family, and everything's going to be peachy—"

The security door swings open like it *isn't* made of thick steel. A line of red-eyed knights step out.

"Yeah, no, maybe be a little worried," Antonio says.

Something shrieks outside the window. Blythe barely has time to shield her eyes before a giant creature bursts through the glass.

It is a Calling creature Blythe has not seen before; its black, oily body is like a floating snake, long and coiled, but its head has a Piranha's rows of large, sharpened teeth that are sharp enough to rip through bone without a second thought.

Blythe outstretches her hockey stick. "Antonio...if you can transform into animals...like a really huge wolf or something... and I mean *really* big wolf...I think now's a good time to do that..."

Antonio's gone pale. "I definitely can, but I have not learned how."

Blythe's hands shake so badly she can't hold the hockey stick straight. "Can you learn in the next three seconds?"

396

An orange blur speeds past them, shooting straight for the floating snake. The creature snaps its jaws against the new assailant, but the blur circles it effortlessly, tossing a rope that coils around its body before tying itself to each pillar, moving faster than Blythe can process, pulling tighter and tighter until the creature only twitches in mid-air, held as still as a museum exhibit as the blur catapults into the knights, toppling them to the floor.

The orange blur stills in the center of the room. The Harlequin mask has returned to her face, but against all odds, it is still her.

"So, I was halfway down to Louisiana, right?" Storm begins. "But travelling without magic's a bitch, so I figured, why not come back, help out a little, then get a free ride? And there was only *one* building with a whole militia tryna beat *one kid's ass*, so I figured y'all were in here."

Blythe makes a face.

"Or," Storm tries again. Her voice has lost its false bravado. "Maybe I do pull favors."

"You came back!" Antonio yells.

"Alright, don't rub it in, we all knew it was gon' happen."

Blythe purses her lips. She doesn't have time to argue or ungrateful. At least Storm's here.

"Was Jay okay?" she asks instead.

"Young boul's fine. He should probably be back in here within like, three minutes," Storm says. "And let me just say, fighting *with* him is way more fun than fighting *him*."

"Good," Blythe sighs. "Look, Daniel needs your help more than us right now. He's back there—"

"Say less," Storm says, ready to zoom off.

"But there's a bunch of knights back there," Antonio warns. "Are you sure you can handle—"

Storm sucks her teeth. Her eye blazes orange with magic, the light echoing sharp off of her features. "I'm a superhero, bitch. I can do anything."

The orange blur speeds out of their sight.

A chuckle bursts from Blythe—not one of amusement, but complete shock. The Guardian of Time has returned at the eleventh hour.

The staircase behind the security door is a concrete tower of silence. Blythe can't say she isn't thankful for the momentary peace it gives them.

Antonio moves slowly, taking each stair one at a time. Blythe keeps pace with him. Jay was right—Antonio *is* limping.

"At least Storm's back. How do you feel now?" Antonio asks, because of course he's worried about her.

Blythe takes in a long breath. "Worried. I mean, don't get me wrong, Storm's a major asset. But I still pictured this going a lot smoother and with less...incapacitations. How are your wings?"

Antonio reaches toward his back, squinting. "Honestly?" he asks. "I've never hurt them this badly before. So, I don't...I don't know."

The building shakes. At this point, it could be from anything— another set of Daniel's vines, Caspian trying to find the source of the security system, Cordelia hacking the whole transport tower or something. Blythe doesn't even bother to look.

Antonio does. "Oh cr—"

He grabs Blythe, wings already sprouting from his back, and jumps into the air. Blythe holds him as tightly as possible as he flies. What did he just see?

She looks behind them—and straight into the mouth of the snake creature's jowls, sharp teeth snapping *far* too close to their feet.

"*Antonio!*" Blythe shrieks. The thing chomps through stairs like fucking Pac-Man, flying just as fast as they are.

"I know, I know! Don't worry, I got you!" But Antonio is speaking through gritted teeth. He won't be able to fly for long.

Blythe can't even aim the hockey stick behind them—not if she doesn't want to risk Antonio dropping her. Her only aim is *up*.

Antonio flies around the spiraling corner, just a hair away from hitting the wall. The creature isn't as lucky. Its body slams a hole into the concrete.

The top floor is fast approaching, the concrete roof right above it. "Shoot through the ceiling for me!" Antonio orders.

"What? Why?"

"Please, just do it!"

Blythe aims the hockey stick's handle. A beam of light cracks through the concrete; Antonio flies right through the pieces of debris that rain down upon them. They are soaring toward the night sky.

Blythe doesn't understand. The entrance to the top floor is on their left. There's no reason to go *outside*.

Then Blythe realizes. "Antonio, don't you *dare*."

He is barely keeping afloat. "Don't worry about me." His dimple appears in his cheek as he smiles. "Just go find your family, okay?"

"*Antonio--!*"

He throws her into the doorway. Her body hits the ground before she can even fight back. Antonio shoots out of the ceiling with the creature's curved teeth on his heels. It doesn't even glance in Blythe's direction, which is, of course, exactly what Antonio planned. It only travels up and out.

The world is quiet. The only sound Blythe can hear is her own heartbeat. She used to love the sound of lonely silence. Now she is not so sure.

All around the transport tower, the Guardians are risking everything to ensure she gets to her family. The gratitude in her chest is so strong that it aches.

Blythe really does owe these kids her life.

Behind her is another double security door, this time with a card reader on its left. Blythe swipes the keycard and the doors click open.

She walks into a rounded space, the likes of which she has never seen before. It almost resembles a loading dock, but it really just looks like a room with a bunch of jet-shaped escape pods embedded in the walls.

Their doors and windows face inward, but everything else is already outside, poised to burst into the night with the flick of a switch. Blythe counts about thirty of them, a crescent shape of tiny white jets sized more like luxury cars.

Blythe heads to the nearest tiny window and peeks inside. Through the darkness, she can make out two rows of white seats, not counting the cockpit. It looks...cramped. Blythe realizes, with a hitched breath, she has seen the inside of these jets before. Her family was forced into one.

She checks the next few jets, cupping her face against the windows. They are empty. Her family is not here.

A thin staircase beckons from the back of the room. Blythe's sneakers slap against the metal as she heads up into an identical space of escape-pod-jets, still half in the walls with their other half unseen.

This space looks familiar. Blythe glimpsed it on Whiteclaw's security feed.

This is where her family is.

"Mom? Dad?" Her voice echoes off the walls. "Lily? Lena?" No one replies.

A tablet stands atop a podium. Blythe taps the screen until it sparks to life, requesting an access code. Useless.

She peeks through the window of the nearest jet. Empty. She looks at the next one; just as empty. She peeks through the third. A woman sits inside.

"Mom!" Blythe screams. She yells so loud her throat starts to ache. Her fists bang against he glass. "It's Blythe! I came—"

But the slumped, unconscious person is not Blythe's mother. And they do not react.

The lack of light makes it difficult to be sure, but Blythe soon makes out an orange sundress. Blythe has seen this woman's strong jawline and dark hair before.

It is Sofia Torres. Antonio's mother.

A sudden cold spreads through Blythe's core. She races to the next jet.

A boy, a man, and a dog are inside, all of them still and unconscious. Storm's older brother, Mikey. Her father. Her *dog*. All of them still and unconscious. Blythe bangs against the window. They do not stir.

"No, no, no," Blythe chants.

The next jet. A woman with strawberry blonde hair and a dark-haired man with a pinched face, their legs extended, heads lolled back. Daniel's parents. The Quintons.

The next jet. A Chinese couple Blythe does not recognize, but she can see Cordelia's perfect posture in their backs. Behind them sits a young woman whose makeup and classy fashion are identical to Cordelia's. The Deleons.

Blythe's trembling hands fly to her mouth. It feels like time has frozen, like all the world is closing in.

Daniel's phone calls that went unanswered. Cordelia's mother not contacting her about the money she spent. Storm's brother and her father not being home in the dead of night. Hoffman Manor being so painfully empty.

The Trident Republic did not take only *Blythe's* family. It has never been just Blythe's family. It's all of the Guardians. Blythe was just lucky enough to be there when her family was taken. She wasn't the only one this happened to—she was the only one who *knew*.

Cordelia, Blythe thinks, hoping she is heard. *Get up here. Tell* everyone *they need to be here.*

She runs to the next jet. The Hoffmans will be there, she knows it. They must've been betrayed by the Trident Republic, the people they dared to trust.

But it isn't Jay's family. It's hers.

Her mother and her father are slouched in the front, Lily and Lena hidden in back. Lena's hair is still loose, from back in the café when Blythe tried to redo her ponytail. All four of them are as still as the others, but their chests rise and fall with even breaths. They're alive, they're just unconscious.

Blythe lets out a low breath. She'll get them out. But not just her family. She'll get them *all* out. Once Cordelia gets here, she can hack into the touch screen on the podium, and from there—

"Congratulations," comes a voice. "You actually managed to see the setup."

Blythe is not surprised to find Whiteclaw when she turns around.

His shirt is dirty and covered with dried blood, just like his face. His eyes are hard and in his fist is a Bloodsword. *Jay's* Bloodsword.

He tosses it at Blythe's feet.

Blythe's breath chokes in her throat. He must've wrestled that from Jay. There is no way anything has happened to Joshua Hoffman. Storm said it herself—he was fine.

But if *Jay* couldn't hold his own...then the others...

She has mistaken the silence of the transport tower to be something normal. But she cannot hear the sounds of magic or fighting or movement. And Cordelia hasn't responded.

Whiteclaw spits a wad of blood from his red-stained mouth. "Truth be told," he says. "I'm done playing games."

Blythe stares Rue Whiteclaw down. Her heartbeat rises, a thumping, determined song in her ears. This man has endangered not only herself and her family, but each and every one of Guardians— and everyone *they* love.

Blythe is not tied to a wall this time. She is not cowering in a café either, powerless and confused and scared to death of this arrogant, callous man. Blythe grips her hockey stick. It thrums with the power of Ether pulsing through it, and through her.

This time, Blythe is ready.

TWENTY-SEVEN

WHITECLAW'S FINGERS DANCE ACROSS THE PODIUM'S illuminated screen. His voice rises, scratchy and grating, in his throat. "You weren't actually supposed to make it here. But it hardly matters. Walden's on his way."

Blythe steadies her breathing. Walden Oliver is not here. Not yet. She still has a chance.

Whiteclaw laughs at her. His blood-soaked grin glistens with hubris. "You didn't like what you found up here, huh?" He drawls. "We had to keep it a surprise. Couldn't have all of you trying to chop our heads off. We're not dumb, we know what we can't handle. We needed all of you here—we didn't need all of you *pissed.*"

Blythe does not respond.

"Do you think it's a coincidence we spread a rumor about Electric City being dangerous?" Whiteclaw continues. "So you wouldn't try to get here alone? You may be the Guardian of the most powerful Element, but you're only one of seven. And why settle for one?"

Whiteclaw draws back from the podium. A pleasant voice echoes through the speakers. *"Emergency escape activating. Level one jets evacuating for pre-planned trajectory in T-120 seconds."*

Emergency escape. Pre-planned trajectory. Whiteclaw has activated an evacuation for the Guardians' families—straight out of Electric City.

Blythe charges at him. The wind pushes against her shoulders, shoving at her legs—but she refuses to budge. She side-steps out of the gale and her whole body twists with the force of her hockey stick sweeping through the air.

Whiteclaw ducks, a jagged, slow movement. He is exhausted. And injured.

Good.

Blythe slams the stick into the floor. A crater explodes into the concrete, sending cracks beneath her sneakers and jostling the jets against the walls.

But Whiteclaw shoots into the air, untouched, hovering just out of her reach. His eyes are cold and empty, even against the blinding light shimmering from his bronze cuffs. "I suggest you stop swingin' at me," he growls. "I might have to fight back—"

"Shut up," Blythe growls. *"Shut up!"*

She swings upward, stretching her shoulder muscles until they burn. The stick collides with his calf.

Whiteclaw goes flying. His body rolls across a jet, collapsing to the floor.

He'll get up.

And he does, gritting his teeth. And in his eyes, finally, is the anger that rages through Blythe —the anger that has burned within her since the night she saw his face in her café.

"Damn kids," he growls. "These mother*fucking* kids."

Air chokes out of Blythe's body. All of the oxygen has been sapped from the air. Blythe stumbles, grasping at her neck. But she does not drop her hockey stick. She *will not drop it.*

"Walden said to keep you *busy,*" Whiteclaw scoffs. He speaks over the sound of her raspy, desperate gasps. "Shoulda known nothing he says is ever that fucking easy. The most annoying thing is that you're too valuable to kill. Ain't that ridiculous? The seven of you get to destroy this entire tower and none of us can do more than rough you up, when innocent civilians in this very city died for so, *so* much less. But I guess," he huffs. "That's just the privilege of the Black Veins."

Blythe's mind is swimming. Straining.

The dark, warm depths of unconsciousness beckon to her.

"*Security system deactivated*," announces the voice.

Caspian.

The Guardians are still down there. Still fighting. Still alive.

"It takes a total of eight seconds for someone to pass out. I'd say you have about four more," Whiteclaw continues. "Wanna give up now?"

Blythe's fingers claw desperately at her throat. The Guardians are out there protecting *her*. Making sure that she can finish what they came for. To give up would be to let them down.

Oxygen isolates her, each molecule deserting her atmosphere...as Whiteclaw's cuffs glow brighter with each passing moment.

Whiteclaw's weakness has been staring Blythe in the face since the night he walked into the Full Cup. Magical items can take all forms, even something as odd as a hockey stick. And Whiteclaw uses magical weapons, just like Blythe does. His just happen to be glittering on his wrists.

Blythe's hands won't stop shaking. She can't even feel the handle of her hockey stick against her palm as she aims it toward Whiteclaw's wrist.

The laser fires—flying too far left, past him, into the wall. But it catches him off guard.

His loss of concentration is enough for Blythe to take in a gulp of air, filling her burning lungs. She aims for his cuffs but he dodges before the stick even fires.

"Smart," he says. Blythe curses. He's not going to let her just shoot them off.

She rises, swaying but desperate, and runs for him. The hockey stick winds easily behind her, like second nature.

She's barely swung forward before Whiteclaw grabs it with both hands. Blythe pulls back. The stick doesn't move. He has her pinned.

Whiteclaw forces her backward, gripping the stick in his fists until her back slams against the freezing stone wall.

"*T-50 seconds*," the voice echoes.

His presence is hot and suffocating. He reeks of iron and blood. "If you were smart, you'd be breaking your family out," he spits. "Instead, you're trying to stop me, so you can...do what? Save all of them? By the time the countdown is over, you'll lose everyone. *Your* family included."

She should not answer him. He doesn't deserve to know her thoughts. But words come growled between her teeth anyway. "I'm not abandoning the people they love."

Blythe tries to slip to the left. Whiteclaw shoves her back harder. He is an unyielding force, like a metal crusher, and she cannot move.

But with Whiteclaw's fingers gone white around her hockey stick, he's placed his bronze cuffs right at her neck.

Maybe pushing away is the *opposite* of what she needs to do.

"You care more about a group of kids you *just* met than your own family?" Whiteclaw goads.

Blythe tightens her grip against the wood. She summons all of her will. Her energy. Her power. She remembers the warmth of her magic, how it felt when it visited her in the Erasers' lab. How it coursed through her, thrumming and chilling and strong.

She thinks of the Guardians. Cordelia and Daniel and Antonio and Storm and Caspian and Jay. How badly she wants to—*needs to*—make them proud. How she refuses to let them down.

Stars and constellations swirl along Blythe's arms. Galaxies open beneath the bronze of her skin, birthing piercing white light from her pores. Magic surges down her arms, pooling in her hands, humming and buzzing and growing, growing, *growing*.

Whiteclaw's eyes fly wide. Blythe has always been the girl

without magic, the powerless Guardian. But pure Ether, the strongest of the seven Elements, is radiating from her skin.

"Those kids are my family too," Blythe says.

Energy explodes from her hands. It is like the force of the hockey stick amplified by a thousand, turning the world stark, blinding white. It is heat, it is electricity, it is the raw power of magic itself let loose.

The sound of Whiteclaw's raw scream comes first. Blythe cannot see through the white light—it has swallowed the world—but she can feel the force of his hands disappear.

Blythe catches her breath as the world eases back into view. The broken remains of Whiteclaw's cuffs lie scattered on the ground, burnt to blackened crisps.

And then there is Whiteclaw.

Wind twists around him like his own magic has turned on him. His mouth gapes open, hands at this throat as his wide eyes lose their focus.

"Oh my God," Blythe whispers. Daniel told her about this, how dangerous Learned Magic can become when it is broken mid-use. And now the air has gone from Whiteclaw. Just like he took the air from her.

"Seven seconds until you pass out, right?" Blythe asks.

He stumbles to his knees, shoulders trembling. Blythe almost expects him to rise, to break free and rush at her in rage.

His body pitches forward and collapses. He is still. But Blythe waits, because he could get up again like a forgotten enemy in a video game.

"*T-30 seconds,*" says the voice.

Nevermind. Blythe doesn't have time to wait. He's down now, that's all that matters.

Blythe rushes to the podium. All of the numbers look like Greek. Shouldn't there just be a huge, red stop button?

Footsteps rush up the stairs. A chorus of voices echo her name. And there is Cordelia, Jay behind her and Antonio behind him, Storm carrying Daniel at the very back. Caspian melts into view at her side, always at her side. Their eyes are wide and their bodies are scuffed and cut and tired.

Blythe has never been happier to see them.

"I got your message," Cordelia says. "It just took us a second to get up here."

"Fucker stole my sword," Jay says, rushing over to snatch his Bloodsword up from the floor. "You good, Blythe?"

But the weight of their gazes makes it hard to speak. To explain. "The jets," Blythe says. "The jets, they...they have everyone."

"Girl, what?" Storm cocks her head to the side. "You sure you good?"

Jay peers into one of the windows. "Holy shit. Blythe, your parents are white?"

"Those aren't my parents, they're Daniel's," Blythe blurts. The words come out sharp and hard. "The Trident Republic took *all* of our families."

"*T-20 seconds,*" says the voice.

Blythe watches the Guardians rush to the windows, all speaking at once. Antonio checks every window until he sees his mother, but Daniel is hyperventilating, trying desperately to keep his injured knee off of the ground. Storm's face has turned to unreadable stone, even as Antonio starts screaming Spanish words Blythe cannot understand. Cordelia moves slowly, arms crossed tight, and Caspian watches all of them, resigned to sympathetic silence.

They are all coming to the same realization: the Trident Republic has used them and taken their loved ones as hostages.

"*T-15 seconds,*" says the voice.

Blythe is about to make it all so, so much worse. "That voice is counting down to an evacuation that'll send every jet on this floor off to God-knows-where."

A new level of horror blooms across their faces.

"Cordelia, there's a computer here," Blythe points to the podium. "Can you—"

Cordelia runs over.

"*T-10 seconds,*" says the voice.

Her hands shake as she types. It feels like she spends an eternity staring at that screen.

"I don't have time," she says. "I don't know how to open all of them at once, I can—I can only open one. I-I don't have time."

"*T-5 seconds,*" says the voice.

The screen shines hard against Cordelia's face. Tears well in her eyes. "This was never about me," she whispers, and presses a button.

A single door slips open. Inside, resting in the shadowy darkness, is Blythe's family.

"*Emergency evacuation initiated,*" says the voice.

All at once, the jets burst into the night. It's almost beautiful, the way their flight patterns synchronize as they sail into the darkness.

There is nothing beautiful about the Guardians' expressions as they watch their families disappear: the clench of Storm's jaw, the tears streaking Cordelia's face, the despair that has extinguished every hint of light in Antonio's eyes.

Only one jet remains.

"*Initiating full Transport Tower lockdown,*" says the voice. "*In T-60 seconds.*"

Caspian stares upward. "...What is that?"

Daniel takes in a long, shaky breath. "I-I-It sounds like we won't be able to leave," he answers.

"We can take the jets downstairs," Storm says. "If we're quick enough we might be able to tail the ones that just left."

Those words have everyone darting for the staircase, moving at the speed of light without a second look back.

"Blythe!" Calls a voice, stopping her at the very top stair.

Lily.

The twins run for her, curls bouncing and hands outstretched. She catches them in her arms, crushes them against her. They are warm and safe and *alive*. "I missed you," she whispers into their skin. She wants to be the strong big sister they know she is, but sobs are already escaping her.

"You're crying on us," Lena whines.

Blythe laughs, a choked, hoarse sound. "I'm sorry," she whispers. "I love you guys, okay? I need you to know that. I love you so, so much."

She watches her parents approach through the blurry haze of her tears. Her fathers' constantly worried brow, her mother's strong gaze. She has *ached* to see their faces again. And here they are.

Her throat is thick, almost too tight to speak. "Mom, Dad, I..."

Jamal kisses her forehead without a word. She can feel his tears drop onto her cheeks.

Her mother grabs her tight when she stands. "Blythe, how did you get here, baby?!" she asks. "Where...where are we?"

"We're in Electric City," Blythe explains. "And we're inside a transport tower that's about to go on full lockdown if we don't get out as quickly as possible.

"Where's the exit?!" Jamal asks.

"Back this way, follow me," Blythe says.

"Good girl," Jamal nods. "Lily, Lena, c'mon with me!"

It is the first time Blythe has seen her family in weeks and an alarm is going off while Whiteclaw lies collapsed on the floor—a sight that Jamal directs the twins away from—but none of it matters. She has her family back. She is whole again.

The other Guardians are too busy searching for an entrance to the jets to notice the Fultons coming down the stairs.

Here, the jets are slightly different, with two buttons built into the wall beside each jet door.

"How do these things work?!" Cordelia asks.

"Who gives a shit," Storm says. She slams one of the buttons and the jet door slides open. They pile in, helping Daniel and Antonio in first before they each follow suit. Even Caspian's ghostly form slips in after them.

Blythe's staring must be obvious, because Amber asks, "Blythe? Do you know those kids?"

"They're the other Guardians," Blythe answers. "They...they helped me."

Blythe starts toward them, but Jamal moves toward the complete other side of the room. He presses the bottom button and the jet shoots out into the sky, leaving a wide opening in the wall.

He rushes to a different jet, trying the top button this time like Amber shouts at him to do. The door swings open. Blythe watches her parents set the twins inside, asking for seatbelts, asking each other if they know how to fly a jet.

"Hurry up, Blythe!" Lena rushes. "Come on!"

Over Blythe's shoulder, the Guardians are leaving in search of their families. Blythe knows that feeling. She knows how those tears on Antonio's face feel, how fiery Storm's determination is in her chest.

They are starting the adventure she is ending.

Her family is on her right, getting the twins buckled in. The Guardians are on her left, shouting at each other and slamming whatever button they can touch.

Cordelia lingers in their doorway. Her eyes are puffy and rimmed pink. She opens her mouth, then closes it. "Go," she finally says. "What are you still standing there for?"

"I'm sorry," Blythe apologizes. She's not even sure what for.

"Don't be sorry. I made my choice. Just do one thing for me when you get home, Blythe Fulton." Cordelia smiles a real, genuine smile that makes her as radiant as the moon itself. "Take a nice, big, long nap."

She steps inside the jet, and is gone.

This could very well be the last time Blythe will ever see Cordelia Deleon. It could be the last time she sees any of them. There is no guarantee she'll be able to track them down. She could text them, yes, and follow them on social media—and they'd be the same as every other friendship Blythe has ever had.

"Blythe!" Amber has called Blythe's name like that for as long as Blythe can remember. Whenever she was little and would dawdle

ASHIA MONET

because she was distracted, or when she grew old enough to be defiant and forge her own path. The sound of her name, when called like that, is nostalgic. It feels like home.

This is all Blythe has ever wanted. To return home with her family. To see Jamie again. To sleep in her room. To forget about everything.

But Storm abandoned her own mission for Blythe. Antonio supported her even after she'd done him wrong. Daniel ventured further into a world that terrified him. Jay was willing to become a part of a world he yearned to reject. Caspian overcame his ties to his own family, to his past, just to stay with them. And Cordelia... Cordelia has put Blythe before *herself*.

Blythe's heart crumbles as she walks toward her family's jet.

The twins are in the far seats, her parents seated in the cockpit. Jamal is trying to figure out the buttons. "Get in, sit beside the twins and hold onto them."

There are two buttons on the wall just outside of the jet's doorway. The one on the top says OPEN. The one on the bottom says EJECT.

Blythe knows exactly what will happen when they land in Washington. They will fix up the Full Cup and reopen its doors. The house will fill with noise, summer vacation will resume, and life will readjust to its normal state of being.

Everything will be okay.

Blythe's lip trembles. "I love you all," she says. "And when you get back home can you...can you let Jamie know I'm okay?"

The twins stare at her, confused and unblinking. But her parents understand. "Blythe," Jamal's voice is hard. "Sit down—"

Blythe slams the eject button.

The door slides shut before anyone can move. Blythe watches the jet eject from the wall, bursting out to fly over Electric City, soaring above the darkness, soaring toward the horizon, toward Washington, toward home, toward Jamie and the Full Cup.

All she has ever wanted is for her family to be okay. Because her

412

family is her life. And the Guardians...they're her family too. And she owes them her life.

Blythe races toward their jet as the final sirens wail and the light burst violent, blinding red. She squeezes into the backseat, beside Antonio, as every voice yells her name, demanding to know why she's returned.

"You have families to save," Blythe says as she buckles up. "And I, obviously, have an *amazing* track record of saving families."

Antonio wraps his arms around her. He is quiet, face streaked with tears. Beside him, Daniel offers Blythe a weak smile. He is still holding his leg, which looks twisted and pale.

The row of seats in front of them hold Caspian, more solid that usual but still squeezed in the corner as if it will render him unseen, and Cordelia.

Storm and Jay scramble for the eject button in the cockpit. The radio springs to life. Storm shouts, "Fuck, wrong button!"

"A number of Black Veins cities across the globe have frozen in time after reporting hearing a strange song," comes Alastair French's smooth voice. *"This has been categorized as a direct attack, and the Black Veins has officially declared war against the Trident Republic. I repeat, the Black Veins has officially declared war against the Trident Republic."*

Alastair French pauses. *"God help us all."*

So, that's what they have to look forward to. The world was dangerous enough when the Trident Republic was just trying to agitate the Sages. An all out war will be...well...

"Christ," Caspian whispers. Blythe could not agree more.

"Found it!" Storm shouts as she slaps a button.

Cordelia looks over her shoulder. The light is dim, but Blythe could recognize worry on Cordelia's face even in pure darkness.

"We don't know where we're going or how long it'll take to get there," Cordelia says. She sounds like she thinks Blythe has made a mistake.

But Blythe hasn't made a mistake. She's made a choice. A sacrifice.

"Who cares," Blythe says. "We'll get there someday."

The jet sighs, shifts into place, and just like that, they are thrown into a sea of stars.

Once upon a time, a young girl lost her family and discovered a new one.

The Guardians will return in

Dead Magic Book Two

ABOUT THE AUTHOR

Ashia Monet is a speculative fiction author whose work always includes found families, queer characters of color, and the power of friendship. She loves The Adventure Zone, cosmic horror, sweet treats, and, most especially, the color pink. You can visit her at www.ashiamonet.com, or any of the social media links below.

 twitter.com/ashiamonet

 instagram.com/ashiawrites

CPSIA information can be obtained
at www.ICGtesting.com
Printed in the USA
LVHW010124190720
661061LV00001B/183